Misty Shadows Of Hope

1870

Ginny Dye

Misty Shadows of Hope

1870

Copyright © 2018 by Ginny Dye

Published by Bregdan Publishing
Bellingham, WA 98229

www.BregdanChronicles.net

www.GinnyDye.com

www.BregdanPublishing.com

ISBN# 9781790478538

Printed in the United States of America

For Beth Tielke

1931 – 2015

Thank you for keeping my hope alive during dark times that threatened to extinguish them. You are my "Mom by Choice". My world is not the same without you in it – I will always miss you!

A Note from the Author

My great hope is that Misty Shadows of Hope will both entertain, challenge you, and give you courage to face all the seasons of your life. I hope you will learn as much as I did during the months of research it took to write this book. Once again, I couldn't make it through an entire year, because there was just too much happening. As I move forward in the series, it seems there is so much going on in so many arenas, and I simply don't want to gloss over them. As a reader, you deserve to know all the things that created the world you live in now.

When I ended the Civil War in The Last, Long Night, I knew virtually nothing about Reconstruction. I have been shocked and mesmerized by all I have learned – not just about the North and the South – but now about the West.

I grew up in the South and lived for eleven years in Richmond, VA. I spent countless hours exploring the plantations that still line the banks of the James River and became fascinated by the history.

But you know, it's not the events that fascinate me so much – it's the people. That's all history is, you know. History is the story of people's lives. History reflects the consequences of their choices and actions – both good and bad. History is what has given you the world you live in today – both good and bad.

This truth is why I named this series The Bregdan Chronicles. Bregdan is a Gaelic term for weaving: Braiding. Every life that has been lived until today is a part of the woven braid of life. It takes every person's story to create history. Your life will help determine the course of history. You may think you don't have much of an impact. You do. Every action you take will reflect in someone else's life. Someone else's decisions. Someone else's future. Both good and bad. That is the **Bregdan Principle**...

Every life that has been lived until today is a
part of the woven braid of life.
It takes every person's story to create history.
Your life will help determine the course of history.
You may think you don't have much of an impact.
You do.
Every action you take will reflect in someone else's life.
Someone else's decisions.
Someone else's future.
Both good and bad.

My great hope as you read this book, and all that will follow, is that you will acknowledge the power you have, every day, to change the world around you by your decisions and actions. Then I will know the research and writing were all worthwhile.

Oh, and I hope you enjoy every moment of it and learn to love the characters as much as I do!

I'm constantly asked how many books will be in this series. I guess that depends on how long I live! My intention is to release two books a year – continuing to weave the lives of my characters into the times they lived. I hate to end a good book as much as anyone – always feeling so sad that I must leave the characters. You shouldn't have to be sad for a long time!

You are now reading the 14th book - # 15 will be released in late spring 2019.   If you like what you read, you'll want to make sure you're on my mailing list at www.BregdanChronicles.net. I'll let you know each time a new one comes out so that you can take advantage of all my fun launch events, and you can enjoy my BLOG in between books!

Many more are coming!

Sincerely,
Ginny Dye

Chapter One
March 18, 1870

Carrie could feel trouble in the air the moment she stepped from the train onto the wooden platform at Broad Street Station in Richmond, Virginia. She glanced around anxiously as she tried to identify the source of her unease, but nothing seemed unusual or out of place. The church spires of Richmond towered over a city just beginning to sport the bright green leaves of spring. Bright sunlight sparkled off the remnants of an earlier rainstorm. The western horizon was still dark with clouds being blown away by a brisk March wind.

Carrie took a deep breath as she tried to quell her sense of unease. Perhaps she was just tired due to the long train ride from Philadelphia.

"You feel it too?"

Carrie turned to gaze at her stepmother, Abby Cromwell. She was thankful she wasn't imagining it, but also alarmed that it wasn't just her imagination. "I do."

Her eyes scanned the crowded platform as travelers jostled each other to get on the next train before it departed. A screeching whistle made it impossible to say more, but a closer look at the men and women scurrying along revealed the strain on their faces. Carrie had gotten used to the constant tension during the war, but she had hoped five years would have relieved the ever-present worry and fear. Her instincts told her this was something new, however. She wanted to grab someone and demand an explanation, but she knew their driver was waiting.

"Mrs. Wallington! Mrs. Cromwell!"

Carrie turned toward the voice calling their names. She grabbed her satchel more tightly as she followed Abby to a carriage proudly sporting the name, *River City Carriages*. Anthony had only been gone a week, but Carrie had missed him terribly. Her husband didn't often have to leave Philadelphia, but when he had informed her he was needed in Richmond for business, she hadn't questioned it. Every new endeavor needed attention, but now she suspected she should have asked for more of an explanation. Had he been called to the city because of what she was feeling?

She pushed aside her concerns and smiled widely when she recognized the driver. "Marcus!"

Marcus Garrison leapt from the driver's seat. "Hello Miss Carrie. Miss Abby." His brilliant smile flashed across his ebony face. "I'm real glad you two made it all right."

Carrie reached out to grip his hand. "Things at River City Carriages must be very busy for one of the managers to be driving a carriage."

Marcus shrugged. "Anthony wanted to come get you, but he was needed at the office. The other drivers are out, but all the horses were cared for, so I was more than happy to step in. I've missed both of you."

Carrie grinned. "You have the look of a man happy to have his wife home." She and Abby hadn't seen Marcus since her father had traveled into the Virginia mountains several weeks earlier to bring home the wife Marcus hadn't seen in fifteen years.

Marcus' smile grew more blinding, even while his eyes misted with tears. "It be like a dream every single day, Miss Carrie. I have to pinch myself every time I walk in the house and find Hannah there." He cleared his throat. "Your father is a mighty fine man."

"It meant almost as much to him as it does to you, Marcus," Carrie assured him, knowing it was true. It had been a moment of redemption for Thomas Cromwell to put a family back together after so many years of destroying families through slavery.

Marcus turned his eyes to Abby. "I'll never be able to thank your husband for what he done," he said.

"You don't need to," Abby answered, her gray eyes glowing with joy and compassion. "You'll never know how much it meant to him to find Hannah and bring her home to you. It's beyond time for there to be happy endings to some of the horrible situations slavery has caused in America."

"Yes, ma'am," Marcus said firmly. "It's given some of my friends hope that someday they'll find their own families."

"And Jacob?" Carrie asked softly. Her father had told them about the son sold away from Marcus and Hannah when he was only a year old.

Marcus' face tightened with emotion. "We're lookin', Miss Carrie. Having Thomas bring Hannah back to me has given me hope that one day we'll find our boy. I don't know how, but we're gonna keep trying."

"He would be fifteen now?" Abby asked.

"Yes, ma'am," Marcus agreed. "It's takin' time, but there are a lot of things in place in the black community now to reunite lost ones. Ain't no one knew what to do right after the war, but now we got a network to find people. We ain't gonna give up," he vowed. His expression changed abruptly as his voice took on a new tone. "We just got to keep fightin' for what's right," he said firmly.

Abby spoke the words that instantly sprang to life in Carrie's mind as a different emotion suddenly filled his eyes. "What's really going on, Marcus? I can tell you're hiding something. Carrie and I can both feel that things aren't right. What's the real reason Anthony isn't here?"

Carrie's heart caught. Surely, Marcus would have told her right away if something was wrong with Anthony. "Marcus?" she asked fearfully.

He turned to her immediately. "Ain't nothing wrong with your Mr. Anthony," he said. "He just couldn't get away to come meet you."

"Then what is going on?" Carrie demanded as she released her pent-up breath. "I can tell you're hiding something."

Marcus shook his head ruefully. "You women know too much."

"We don't know *anything*," Abby said sternly. "That's the problem. I'm counting on you to change that."

Carrie bit back a smile as Abby transformed into the woman who had bravely taken over her dead husband's business years ago, fighting against the system to build incredible success. It was easy to see why she had won against daunting odds.

Another loud screech of the train whistle, combined with the roar of the engine beginning its next journey out of the station, drowned out all possibility of conversation.

"Let's get back to the stables," Marcus yelled. "I promise you'll get all your answers then."

Carrie and Abby exchanged a glance and then nodded reluctantly. If they wanted real answers, they needed to leave the cacophony of noise.

Carrie forced herself to relax as she stepped into the carriage. Anthony was alright, and her father was home on the plantation. She could face whatever else was going on.

Her hope for quick answers faded as they fought their way through congested streets that made progress painfully slow. They were forced to a standstill several times while they waited for the road to clear in front of them. Richmond grew more crowded every time she visited. By the time she finished her surgical residency in Philadelphia at the end of the year and returned to the Virginia capital to start a practice with Janie, she suspected it would be faster to walk everywhere she went.

"We'll get answers soon," Abby reassured her.

Carrie managed a smile. "You can sound as calm as you want, but I can tell by your eyes that you feel what I'm feeling." The farther they had driven, the thicker the air felt. Trouble was already in her city, or it was on the way. The fact that she could feel it, when she was usually oblivious until trouble was staring her in the face, made her more nervous.

Abby returned her smile and reached out to take her hand. "You know me too well," she said wryly. "I'm looking forward to getting some answers too," she admitted.

Angry voices from a cluster of men on the sidewalk broke through their conversation.

"A city can't have two mayors!" A portly man with a balding head and a red face pointed his finger at a slightly built man with a belligerent stance.

"Then Chahoon ought to step aside and let Ellyson claim his rightful position," the other man retorted, his narrow face as red as the first man's.

A tall, stooped man with an oversized head topped by a black hat interrupted their argument. "Neither of you two gentlemen was here during the war," he snapped, his anger laced with sadness. "Richmond has seen more than its fair share of violence and misery. We don't want more."

"Then you should keep your niggers in place," the smaller man growled. "Everyone knows Chahoon is counting on them to help him hold his position. They may be free, but Richmond belongs to the white man. The sooner they figure that out, the better things will be."

Carrie stiffened as she saw Marcus straighten in his seat. His back was ramrod straight but his face was emotionless. Years of slavery had taught him to not reveal his feelings, but she could well imagine what he was thinking. She opened her mouth to say something to the arguing men, but Abby stopped her with a tight squeeze of her hand.

"Don't," she said softly. "It won't do any good, and it will only put Marcus in a bad situation if he needs to protect us."

Carrie scowled but realized she was right. Her mind whirled with questions as the road suddenly cleared in front of them. Marcus urged the team forward, leaving the heated conversation behind them.

Minutes later they pulled to a stop in front of River City Carriages.

"Carrie!"

Carrie pushed aside her troubled thoughts as her tall, handsome husband pulled her into his arms and kissed her. "I missed you, Anthony," she said as she looked up into his green eyes surrounded by a thatch of sandy blond hair.

"I'm glad you're here," Anthony replied, before turning to hug Abby.

"Are we safe?" Abby asked immediately.

Anthony's smile faded. He waved Marcus into the stables before he took their arms and led them into his office. "You're safe here."

Carrie stared up at him. "What's happening? The city feels like a powder keg on the verge of exploding."

"I wish I could say you're wrong, but I would be lying," Anthony answered solemnly.

Carrie and Abby remained silent while they waited for him to continue.

"Mayor Chahoon is unwilling to step down," Anthony began.

"Why would he need to?" Abby asked. "I didn't know his term was up, and I wasn't aware of an election. When I left three weeks ago to visit Philadelphia, everything seemed to be running smoothly."

"It's changed," Anthony said heavily. "George Chahoon has served as mayor since 1868, but when Virginia was readmitted to the Union in January, the legislature passed some new laws. One of them was called the Enabling Act."

"I remember," Abby replied. "It allows Governor Walker to appoint councilmen in any city. There have been no city or town governments since the end of the war because the Federal Government has controlled everything."

"That's right," Anthony agreed. "That all changed three days ago when Governor Walker appointed a new council that has nothing but white conservatives."

Carrie frowned. "I thought blacks were making strides in being part of Richmond politics." She knew her absorption with her surgical work had diminished her awareness of what was happening, but she was still shocked to discover Governor Walker would appoint a city council that had no black representation.

"We had hoped," Anthony replied. "The evidence does not support that. The first thing the new city council did was appoint Henry K. Ellyson as the new mayor."

"Isn't Ellyson one of the publishers of the *Richmond Dispatch?*" Abby asked keenly. "He's quite conservative."

"Yes. He's also quite Virginian," Anthony responded. "He grew up nearby and has been heavily involved in politics and public service his whole life. He, along with most Richmonders, is eager for control of the city again."

"You mean Ellyson isn't a New Yorker chosen by the government, like Chahoon is," Carrie stated. She understood that Richmonders were chafing under the Federal guidelines and restrictions, but she feared what putting Ellyson in office would mean for the black community fighting so hard to be recognized. "Are they forgetting Chahoon grew up here in Virginia, too?"

"It doesn't matter to them," Anthony answered. "Too many people believe he's a pawn of the North because he was appointed by a military governor. When he took office two years ago, he started purging the government of former Confederates. He became even less popular when he fired ten white police officers and created a special, twenty-five-man black police force with a black chief."

"Probably the only reason Richmond has enjoyed any peace in the last two years," Abby observed.

"I agree with you," Anthony said, "but Chahoon has made a lot of people unhappy. They consider him a hated carpetbagger and they want him gone."

"There has been no election at all?" Carrie asked.

"None. Under the Enabling Act, one isn't necessary. The new city council has the power to appoint a new mayor, at least theoretically. In reality, Chahoon has no intention of giving up his position because he doesn't believe it's in the best interest of the city. As of today, Richmond has two mayors," Anthony finished.

"Two mayors," Carrie echoed. "How is that possible?" The angry conversation she had overheard was making more sense. "It's as if the war is being fought all over again between the North and the South!"

"It's a mess," Anthony said heavily. "Yesterday, right after the city council chose Ellyson as mayor, he went down to the police station to take command. He found Chahoon there, along with much of his police force. They flatly refused to turn over the building to the incoming administration."

Carrie visualized the scene in her mind. "I'm sure that didn't go over very well."

"That would be putting it mildly. Five hundred white men volunteered to take care of the situation for the newly appointed mayor," Anthony replied. "Ellyson swore in two hundred of them as special officers. Richmond not only has two mayors; now we also have two police forces."

"Oh, dear God..." Abby muttered. "When did this happen?"

"Yesterday. It's taken only twenty-four hours for the whole city to be in turmoil."

A long silence filled the office as they envisioned the possibilities that could transpire.

Carrie broke the silence. "What happens now?"

Anthony shrugged. "That remains to be seen. The council met in an emergency session last night. They promised to support Ellyson and to punish the men they view to be conspiring against their decision."

"There's going to be trouble," Carrie said grimly.

"I'm afraid so," Anthony replied. "I wish I believed this could end without violence, but I don't think it's possible." His face tightened. "If I could have stopped you two from coming, I would have. Unfortunately, it was too late to get a telegram to you when things came to a head."

"If there's going to be trouble, I want to be with you," Carrie said firmly, glad their daughter, Frances, had stayed behind on this trip because of school. She was safe with their cook, Deirdre and her daughter, Minnie. The two girls were fast friends.

Anthony met her eyes. "I'm hoping you and Abby will leave for the plantation tomorrow."

"We're not supposed to leave for three more days," Carrie protested, knowing even while she spoke that Anthony only cared about her safety. It would give him peace of mind if she was on the plantation with her father and Abby.

"Carrie..."

Carrie held up her hand. "Please don't," she implored. Surely Anthony could understand that after losing Robert to racist violence, she could never relax on the plantation while she worried about him. She watched as a resigned acceptance settled over his face.

"Will you at least stay close to the house?"

Carrie considered the question. "Where do you plan on being?"

"The house, or here at the office," Anthony assured her. "I won't do anything unwise to put myself in danger."

Carrie wished she could be confident that was true, but she had no choice except to trust him. She settled for a compromise. "I love being around the horses, my dear. I'll come with you when you need to be at the office. I'll be safest with you," she added demurely.

Anthony chuckled, laughter lighting his eyes. "Do you always get your way, wife of mine?"

"I assure you I do not," Carrie replied, fighting to shake off the memories assailing her.

The smile faded from Anthony's face. "I'm sorry," he apologized as he took her hand. "I'll be happy to have you join me every time I leave the house for as long as you're here."

"Thank you," Carrie responded, suddenly eager to be in the safety of her father's house on Church Hill. "How long before you're ready to leave?"

"Give me ten minutes," Anthony answered, obviously reading the expression on her face. "I'll drive us there in one of the carriages."

Carrie shoved aside the knowledge that he was making sure they had transportation at the house in case of trouble. Instead of having a driver take them home and pick them up in the morning, he would stable the horse in the small barn behind the house. The thought of the barn made her heart quicken with longing for her beloved Thoroughbred, Granite, but she would be back on the plantation soon enough. She wouldn't leave Anthony while there was trouble in Richmond.

When Anthony left the office to confer with Marcus and Willard Miller, his other business manager, Carrie turned to Abby. "I know Anthony will get you to the plantation if you want to go tomorrow. Father would never forgive me if my stubbornness caused you to be harmed in any way."

Abby smiled as she shook her head. "Your father knows you better than anyone in the world, Carrie. Both of us admire your stubbornness. We'll go out together when it's time." Her voice softened as she reached for Carrie's hand. "Anthony will be fine here."

Carrie took a deep breath. "You don't know that." Experience had taught her that lesson far too well. She thought she had put Robert's murder behind her, but the violence permeating the air had reawakened all her fears.

"You can't live your life in fear, Carrie," Abby said gently.

"No," Carrie agreed, willing away the memories that lurked behind her eyelids. "But I can make sure I'm with my husband if he needs me. At least this time, when I know *for sure* trouble is coming." She'd been returning from Philadelphia when Robert was shot by a vigilante. She would never be free of the haunting belief that she could have saved him if he had been treated immediately. She refused to think about her daughter, Bridget, stillborn minutes after Robert died. There was nothing that could make her leave Richmond right now.

Abby opened her mouth again, and then nodded. "I'm quite sure I would feel the same way," she admitted. "I'm staying with you until you're ready to go to the plantation."

"Thank you," Carrie said fervently. She would have understood if Abby had chosen to leave, but she was grateful for her presence.

※★人业

Carrie admired the brilliant bank of white azaleas lining the front of the house when the carriage pulled up to her father and Abby's three-story brick home. Bought in the months before the war, it had provided shelter for family and many government workers. Though Thomas and Abby lived on the plantation now, they had decided to keep the city house for times such as these. Anthony, along with many other family members and friends, stayed there whenever they were in the city.

In spite of Carrie's worry, she grinned when Micah and May stepped out onto the porch.

"Welcome home!" May called. "Ain't you two a sight for sore eyes."

Carrie leapt from the carriage and ran up the sidewalk. "Hello, May. Hello, Micah. It's wonderful to see you!" She hugged them both, glad the two continued to have a home. For that reason alone, she hoped her father and Abby would keep the house for a long time. They had started out as her father's slaves, but had become treasured members of the family, as was May's husband, Spencer. Carrie couldn't imagine coming to Richmond without them waiting for her. "What's for dinner?" she asked brightly.

"You ain't changed none, Miss Carrie," Micah said with a chuckle. "You might be some fancy doctor, but food always be the first thing you think about."

"You eat May's cooking every day," Carrie retorted. "Can you blame me?"

Micah chuckled again. "I reckon I can't."

"I'm starving too," Abby added as she walked onto the porch.

Anthony strode up amidst a new flurry of greetings. "You all carry on like you haven't seen each other in ages."

Carrie rolled her eyes. "Men are always jealous of how strongly women feel things," she said dismissively. "You're supposed to be more advanced than that, Anthony."

"Evidently I have a way to go until I'm that enlightened," Anthony teased. "As long as I'm eating May's cooking, though, I can deal with my limitations."

May shook her head, laughter lighting her eyes and crinkling the wrinkles on her face. "Y'all can stop carrying on now. Dinner will be ready in about an hour. I reckon that gives Miss Carrie and Miss Abby time to freshen up after that long train ride."

Carrie stepped into the house and sniffed appreciatively. "Fried chicken..." She rubbed her stomach in anticipation. "I was hoping I would get your famous fried chicken."

"You're weren't hoping for nothing, Miss Carrie," May scolded. "You came here knowing I couldn't give you nothin' else!"

Carrie laughed. "That might be true," she admitted as she headed upstairs. Micah was already in front of her with her bags. "A bath will make me appreciate your fried chicken even more." As soon as the words were out of her mouth, every bone in her body ached. The long jostling train ride, combined with a stressful afternoon, had finally caught up with her. Carrie could tell by the look on Abby's face that she felt the same way.

Carrie sighed when she entered her old bedroom, feeling the comfort encase her like a soft quilt. She and Anthony had already decided they would live here when she and her friend Janie started their new clinic in nine months. Frances was thrilled with the idea of living in Richmond and spending time on the plantation when Carrie needed to treat patients at the clinic she had opened after the war.

"That was an awfully heavy sigh." Anthony entered the room and walked over to wrap her in his long arms.

Carrie leaned against him, resting her forehead on his broad chest. "I'm happy to be doing my training in Philadelphia, but the last ten years have been nothing but challenges and upheaval. Is it wrong to want to settle into something that will keep me in one place for more than a few months?"

"No," Anthony replied, moving his fingers through her hair gently.

Carrie moaned in ecstasy as he loosened the pins that held her wavy black hair in a bun and began to massage her tired scalp. "How do I live without you when we're not together?" she breathed.

"That's a question I hope we won't have to find an answer to for much longer," Anthony replied. "When we moved to Philadelphia, I hoped I wouldn't have to come to Richmond so often for the carriage company."

"But the continuing chaos in our capital city means you have to be here." Carrie could feel Anthony's nod. "How can the current events impact the carriage company, though?"

"I'll tell you, but not until after you've had a hot bath."

Carrie considered arguing, but the prospect of a steaming bath was too hard to resist. "Whatever you say," she answered, batting her eyelashes as her green eyes gleamed with mischief.

Anthony grinned. "I've learned it's actually quite easy to make my wife compliant. I simply suggest what she already has every intention of doing."

"Such a wise man," Carrie murmured playfully as she allowed Anthony to unbutton the back of her dress.

A knock at the door made her slip into the dressing area while Micah brought in buckets of hot water to fill the bathtub. A few minutes later, she slipped into the clawfoot iron tub, closed her eyes, and let the bath soak away her travel aches.

*****

Relaxed and refreshed, Carrie slipped into the open chair between Anthony and Abby. She rubbed her hands together happily as May carried a heaping platter of fried chicken from the kitchen, its mouthwatering aroma reaching her before the food did. Within a few minutes, it was joined by fluffy biscuits, fresh greens picked from the garden that morning, and freshly harvested honey-glazed carrots.

"This is absolutely delicious," Abby said gratefully as she took a bite of her chicken. "Thank you so much, May."

"You're welcome, Miss Abby. You look a sight better than you did when you first got here."

"That wouldn't take much," Abby admitted. "The hot bath brought me back to life."

Carrie watched the easy affection between the two women. They had become extraordinarily close during Abby's first months in Richmond as she struggled to transition into being a Southerner. They were the best of friends, but May still insisted on calling her *Miss* Abby because she was afraid of retribution if someone were to consider her too forward in her communication with a white woman.

"You like that chicken, Miss Carrie?" May asked.

Carrie looked up, alerted by the careful nonchalance in May's voice. Closer examination revealed the older woman's eyes told a different story. "It's wonderful," Carrie said enthusiastically. She was certain she knew where this conversation was headed.

"Better than that Deirdre lady?" May asked, her voice still carefully modulated.

Carrie bit back a smile. "You know no one else can cook fried chicken like you, May."

"For sure not some white woman from Ireland," May said with a sniff.

Carrie couldn't hold back her laugh. "Do you have something against white women from Ireland?"

"Only if they be trying to take my place," May retorted.

"No one could take your place," Carrie answered honestly, glad Annie wasn't there to hear this discussion. She had never known competition as intense as the one that existed between Southern black cooks. Moses' mother, Annie, presided over the kitchen at Cromwell Plantation with an iron fist and well-deserved pride. "I can hardly wait to get back to your cooking all the time." It was true. Carrie loved Deirdre and enjoyed the food she cooked for her in Philadelphia, but nothing compared to the incredible meals May prepared.

"That's right," May said with a snort of satisfaction.

"Where is Spencer tonight?" Carrie asked. "I thought he would be here for dinner." Spencer, May's husband, had been Carrie's driver around Richmond for many years before he and May had met and fallen in love.

They lived together in a downstairs room of her father's house.

"Oh, he be out and about," May said evasively. She grabbed a platter and then disappeared through the swinging door into the kitchen.

Carrie stared after her. What had caused that look on May's face? She knew she hadn't imagined the shuttered eyes and the tightened lips as soon as she asked about Spencer. She directed her next question to Anthony. "What's wrong with May?"

Anthony hesitated, but then met her eyes. "Things are rather tense in the Black Quarters right now."

"Because of the situation with Chahoon and Ellyson?" Carrie knew the answer before she asked the question. She looked up at Micah when he walked in with a fresh plate of sliced radishes. "Where is Spencer?" she demanded. "And don't tell me he's out and about," she warned. "Is he going to be all right?"

Micah sighed and glanced toward the kitchen.

"Just tell me," Carrie ordered. "You know I'm going to find out anyway."

Micah nodded reluctantly and opened his mouth to answer, but his words were interrupted by a knock at the back door. Moments later, two burly black men entered the dining room, their faces tight with tension. Carrie couldn't identify either of them, but it was obvious they were regular visitors.

"I'm sorry to interrupt y'all," one of the men said. "This be real important."

Carrie remained silent, content to listen.

"It's okay, Ben," Anthony responded. "I know it's important if you're here tonight."

Carrie didn't have time to ponder the meaning of *tonight* before Anthony turned to her and Abby.

"I'd like to introduce you to Ben Scott and Manley Potus. Gentlemen, this is my wife, Carrie, and my mother-in-law, Abby Cromwell."

Ben's eyes sharpened, even as he dipped his head in polite acknowledgment. "It's a pleasure to meet both of you. Mrs. Wallington, your husband be a fine man."

"I happen to agree with you," Carrie said warmly. "It's nice to meet you." She was eager for the greetings to be done with so she could discover what had brought them to the house.

Ben turned to Abby next. "I worked for you and your husband before the factory burned, ma'am. Both of you be real fine folks. I got me another job, but I miss workin' for y'all."

"I'm so glad you were able to find another job," Abby said sincerely. "I know it was a hard time."

"Yes, ma'am," Ben agreed, "but being out of work for a while gave me time to work on some real important things here in the city, so I reckon it happened just like it was meant to."

Micah stepped forward. "Which is why you're here tonight?" Both his voice and his eyes revealed his impatience.

Ben hesitated as he glanced around the room.

"Speak your mind, Ben," Anthony said. "Both of these women have done more to fight for equality in this country than anyone I know. You can talk freely. What's going on?"

Ben hesitated a moment longer, obviously not sure how much he should say, and then blurted out his reason for being there. "There's going to be trouble tonight."

Chapter Two

Anthony's gut tightened, and he once again wished he could have stopped Carrie and Abby before they reached Richmond. "What kind of trouble?" he said, trying to control the strain in his voice.

May bustled through the kitchen door with a platter full of pound cake still warm from the oven. She placed it on the table wordlessly, her eyes fixed on the visitors. The chandelier over the table revealed the stress in every line of her face.

Anthony waved his hand toward the empty seats at the table. "Micah and May, have a seat. I know you'll want to hear whatever Ben and Manley have to say." He nodded his head toward the two men next. "Please, sit down. Tell us everything you know."

He knew Carrie and Abby's minds must be exploding with questions. "Before you do, though, let me fill Carrie and Abby in on some of the background story." He smiled as impatience flashed in Ben's eyes. "I promise I'll talk quickly."

Ben managed a smile. "That be fine, Mr. Anthony."

"Ben Scott is very active in fighting for equality in the black community," Anthony began. "He has built something of a reputation in the city." He wondered how much to say but knew Carrie and Abby would want nothing but the truth. "Ben is a militia captain in the Black Quarters. He's been active in leading demonstrations and activities to improve the lives of blacks in the city."

"Not that it's done much good," Ben muttered.

Anthony ignored him, as eager as everyone else to hear what Ben and Manley were doing there. "The latest battle was in regard to the city streetcars. In January, right around the same time that Virginia was admitted back into the Union, Ben went into a 'whites only' streetcar to protest the rule that keeps blacks from accessing transportation. He was immediately thrown off by the conductor. He couldn't effectively challenge the rule because he was alone. He went to the police station and swore out warrants against the driver and the conductor, but nothing happened."

Both women nodded but remained silent, aware there must be more to the story. The wind had picked up as night had fallen. Whistling sounded around the window frames as branches brushed the glass. The sound intensified the already heightened stress in the dining room.

"Ben and three of his friends tried again a short time later. Instead of being thrown off, the streetcar was driven to the stationhouse, where they were all arrested. A small crowd of protestors gathered, but they were rather easily dispersed." Anthony's voice tightened as he thought about what had happened next. "The following day, there were at least five hundred black men and women who packed the mayor's courtroom for the trial. The evidence made it abundantly obvious that black rights have deteriorated in recent years, instead of getting better. Three years ago, only two of Richmond's six streetcars refused black passengers. Now it's ten out of twelve. They try to get away with it by calling them *ladies cars,* but the truth is that there are plenty of white men who ride them. Only the blacks are refused."

"Preposterous," Abby said disdainfully.

Anthony watched Ben's eyes relax even more as he became aware he was among friends and allies. "Mayor

Chahoon ruled against Ben and his friends. They were jailed for inciting to riot, and for perjury."

"We didn't say one word that weren't true," Ben said firmly.

"No, you didn't," Anthony agreed.

"What did the black community do then?" Carrie asked.

"Nothing," Ben admitted in a frustrated voice. "We been beat down so much in the last couple years that there be a bunch of people who won't fight back."

"So you went to jail?" Carrie asked in horror.

Ben shrugged. "I'm out now."

Anthony didn't know everything that had happened to Ben while he was incarcerated, but enough to know it had been bad. He turned his attention to him. "So, what is going on now?"

Ben looked around the table. "You heard about Chahoon and Ellyson?"

"Everyone is aware," Anthony replied, impatient to hear the whole story.

"Chahoon done asked for my help. He asked me to lead a special police force of twenty-five black men from the Quarters to help support him."

"After what he did to you?" Carrie burst out. "After sending you to jail? How dare he?"

Anthony knew that if Ben was here talking about it, he must have already agreed to the request. "You're doing it."

"Yes," Ben said, his voice low but determined.

"Why?" Abby asked. "After what has already happened, why would you put your life and freedom in jeopardy again for a man who obviously doesn't support you or the black community?"

Anthony had the same question rampaging through his mind, but the stoic acceptance on Micah and May's faces said they already knew the answer.

"Ellyson done got two hundred men ready to take over control of the city. As much as I don't like Mayor Chahoon, I know what it would mean for the black community if the conservatives get the power they be on the verge of getting." Ben shook his head. "It be bad now, but I figure it will get a whole lot worse." He straightened his shoulders. "I'll do whatever I can to stop that from happening, even if it means helping Mayor Chahoon."

"It could get real bad," Micah warned.

"I know," Ben said, his eyes revealing he was fully aware of what might happen.

Anthony scowled. He knew Ben would give his life for what he believed in if that's what it would take.

"The war has ended!" Carrie protested.

"Not here it ain't," Ben said flatly. "Far as I can tell, it really ain't ended nowhere in the South, but we just happen to have a battle to fight, right *here* right now."

"We're hoping that if we can help Chahoon hang on to power," Manley added, speaking for the first time, "that he'll show his thanks by making things better for us."

Anthony wasn't so sure that would happen, but there was a more important consideration. "And if Chahoon doesn't win? What will happen to you then?"

A grim silence filled the room, the wind whistling even louder as March winds roared into the city.

"I reckon we can't let that happen," Ben said finally.

Anthony knew Ben and Manley felt like they had no choice but to take action, but he doubted their efforts would be successful. Still, if he were in their shoes, he supposed he would do the same. "What can we do to help?" he asked.

Ben smiled. "Everybody in the Black Quarters got a whole bunch of respect for you, Mr. Anthony. There be a whole lot of the militia that be driving a carriage for you right now."

"And you want to choose them for the special force you're putting together," Anthony stated. It was pretty much what he'd expected.

Ben nodded. "They be the best we got."

"What about Eddie?" Carrie asked, her eyes anxious with worry.Anthony, too, had thought of Eddie. His wife, Opal, had been a slave on Cromwell Plantation before the war, and Carrie was close to the whole family. Eddie and Opal ran a successful restaurant in the city, and they were very much involved in the fight for equality.

"He already be part of it, Mrs. Wallington," Ben said.

Carrie stiffened, but nodded in resignation. "Of course he is. Eddie has been part of the militia for a long time. He would want to be in the center of things."

"He knows how important it be," Ben replied.

""Of course," Anthony replied, although he could not stop the vivid images of what might happen to Eddie from flooding his mind. A squad of twenty-five black militia against the two hundred-strong white police force chosen by Ellyson hardly stood a chance. "Why isn't Chahoon putting together a larger force?"

Ben shrugged. "After everything he done, he probably don't figure I can get more men to go to battle for him."

"I thought things were improving for the black community here," Carrie said. "What went wrong?"

Ben shook his head heavily. "I reckon there were a lot of folks that thought we ought to be free, but they don't figure we ought to have a voice in things. I kinda figure the Republican Party thought we would just fall in line with whatever they wanted 'cause we would be so grateful. We all be real grateful to be free, but there's a whole bunch of us that got a clear idea of how things ought to be for blacks. We aim to fight for it. We done made a lot of people unhappy, I guess. Now they be pushing back and trying to keep us from going any further. Lots of black folks have gotten real discouraged and decided things ain't never really gonna change. They learned that lesson during slavery days. Why fight if you got no chance of winning?"

Anthony was sadly aware of just how right he was.

"You can't give up, Ben," Abby said firmly.

"I ain't giving up," he assured her, "but it's right hard to keep the others from giving up. I don't expect you to know what that's like."

"No?" Abby asked, her gray eyes fixed on him. "I was part of the fight for your freedom for decades. There were times I thought we would never win, and times when many abolitionists gave up and walked away. They were convinced they were fighting a losing battle."

"What kept you fighting?" Ben asked, all his attention focused on Abby.

"My grandmother," Abby replied. "She lived in a time when women had it even worse than we do now, but she used to tell me to keep all my dreams alive." Her eyes softened as she remembered. "She told me that achieving anything that matters requires faith, believing in myself, vision, hard work, and endless determination." She paused. "I translated that into the belief that I can achieve what I want as long as I never give up."

"You've done that," Ben said admiringly.

"Not quite," Abby replied

"What do you mean?" Manley asked. "You've done things most other women never even dream of. Not just black women—*any* women."

"I've never voted," Abby said quietly. "We've been fighting that battle for a long time, but I know we'll be fighting it for a longer time. Just like the government is trying to make sure blacks don't have power, they're doing the same to women."

Silence filled the room for a few minutes.

"I reckon I never thought of it that way," Ben said finally.

"Just don't give up," Abby said with deep compassion in her voice. "There are many times you'll want to, and many times you'll think you probably *should*, but you just have to keep pressing forward."

"For how long?" Ben asked, the vulnerability in his voice giving away just how raw his emotions were right then.

"As long as it takes," Abby replied. "There are many people who fought for your freedom and didn't live long enough to see it come, but without them fighting, it never would have happened at all."

Ben's face tightened as he considered her words, and then he straightened his shoulders as renewed determination filled him.

Anthony knew Ben was wondering if he would live through the fight ahead of him as Mayor Chahoon and Ellyson struggled for control of Richmond.

A knock at the back door startled all of them. Micah disappeared for a moment and then reappeared with a tall, young black man.

"Carl!" Carrie exclaimed. She jumped up to give him a quick hug. "What are you doing here? Why aren't you at the restaurant?"

Anthony watched Carl carefully. Eddie and Opal's son was also part of the Black Quarters' militia now that he had turned eighteen.

"It's good to see you, Miss Carrie," Carl replied, "but I don't have much time." He turned to Ben and Manley. "My daddy sent me. Mayor Chahoon and a big group of his supporters have barricaded themselves in the Old Market Police Station. They received a demand from the governor to give up, but they're not budging. Ellyson has cut off all food, gas and water to the building. His police force is headed that way now."

Ben took a deep breath. "That's our cue to leave." He glanced around the room. "I hope you'll pray for us."

*****

Carrie was the first to break the silence after Ben, Manley and Carl disappeared through the swinging kitchen door. "May, is that where Spencer is?" Her heart tightened at the thought of the man who had protected her so many times she had been in danger.

"Yep."

Carrie looked at May carefully. Her words spoke of calm acceptance, but her stormy eyes told another story. Carrie knew, far too well, the fear May was feeling. She wouldn't diminish the fear by saying Spencer would be fine. No one knew that. Far too many good men had already died in their country. "I'll wait up with you until there's word," she said softly.

"As will I," Abby added.

May shook her head vigorously. "You'll do no such thing. The two of you been travelling all day. You need your rest."

"So do you," Abby said, "although I doubt you'll be getting any. Would you do the same for us?"

May tried to maintain her defiance, but it crumbled as tears filled her eyes. "Thank you," she murmured.

"I'm going out to discover what's happening," Anthony announced, standing as he spoke.

Carrie tensed, pushed back her chair, and stood. "Then I'm coming with you."

"You most certainly are not," Anthony said firmly. "It's not safe for you out there."

"It's not safe for you, either," Carrie replied. "Have you forgotten your promise from this afternoon that you wouldn't do anything unwise? And the other promise that you would let me accompany you every time you left the house if it would make me feel better? Well, it will make me feel better." The idea of going out into what was certain to be violence was hardly comforting, but it was better than staying behind to see if her husband returned. She wouldn't keep Anthony from going, but she was going to make sure she was available if help was needed.

Anthony stared at her as he shook his head. "Carrie..."

Carrie waited quietly. She knew he had too much respect for her to refuse, and that he understood the basis for her fear. "I'll get my medical bag," she finally said. "I'll be right down."

Anthony held up his hand to stop her. His face tightened as he battled with his emotions. After long moments, when no one else spoke into the tension, his hand fell limply at his side. "I'm not going. There's probably nothing helpful I can do anyway. I could never live with myself if something were to happen to you."

Carrie sagged with relief but tried to keep her face expressionless. She had sent Robert off to war countless times, but this was different. At least, she hoped it was.

"It's the right thing, Mr. Anthony," Micah said. "I appreciate you wanting to help, but this here be a black man's fight. You might do nothing but make it harder."

"How?" Anthony asked sharply.

"Your being there could light a fire that might not need to be lit," Micah said. "There be lots of whites that hate us just for being black, but they hate you more 'cause you ain't standing with them. I hear about it from all over the country. More white teachers being beaten by the KKK than black teachers. The Klan figure you ought to be fighting *with* them, not against them. Those Conservative Democrats think the same way."

"But if I can help..." Anthony started to protest.

"Iffen I thought you could help, I might think you should go against Miss Carrie." Micah's expression clearly said he was glad that wasn't the case. "But you ain't gonna be no help. Neither will I. You're too white, and I'm too old. Mayor Chahoon may have only asked for twenty-five men, but I can guarantee you that when the word gets out, there's gonna be more showin' up. They may not like the mayor much, but they don't want Ellyson and his men runnin' this city. Nope," Micah said, "you stay right here." Then he glanced at Carrie. "Since you be waitin' up with May, you keep that medical bag handy. I reckon you'll be needing it before this all be over."

Anthony sank back into his chair, his face tight with frustration. "It feels wrong not to help," he muttered.

"You be helping," Micah stated. "I think you're gonna find out, come tomorrow mornin', that you won't have all the carriage drivers you need. The men are countin' on you not firin' them if they can't come into work tomorrow."

"They'll still have their jobs," Anthony assured him.

"Then you be doing the best thing you can do," Micah replied. He nodded his head toward the table. "Y'all might as well eat that pound cake. Ain't gonna help nobody by leaving it there on the table."

"He's right," Abby said as she reached for a slice. "It's going to be a long night. We just have to make the best of it."

Carrie gritted her teeth as she thought of the seemingly endless nights during the war when the entire city waited to see if the Union troops would finally win the ferocious battles fought just outside the city limits.

Ben was right. The war wasn't over yet—only now it was being fought *within* Richmond.

Her mind turned to more practical considerations as she pushed away from the table. "I'll be back in a few minutes."

"Where are you going?" Anthony asked quizzically.

"To the basement," Carrie answered. "I learned during the war to always keep a supply of medicines and herbs handy in case of emergencies. I have no idea what will happen tonight, but I want to be ready."

"Everythin' you put down there last fall is still there," May announced. "Ain't nobody been sick so we ain't touched it. I went down a few weeks ago to check that the onions, garlic and turmeric was still good. Being in the basement be a real good place for them. They be as fresh as when you put them there."

Carrie nodded with relief. "That's good." Her mind raced through what she might need. She didn't have a complete set of surgical instruments, but she always traveled with the basics. There were plenty of bandages, the onions, garlic and turmeric were excellent on open wounds, and she had a new supply of homeopathic remedies in her suitcase for the plantation clinic. She would use whatever was necessary.

"We'll all do whatever we can to help," Abby said.

Carrie smiled. "Thank you. I know you will." Her mind continued to race as she thought through all the contingencies. Even with Anthony, Abby and May able to help, if there were a lot of injuries, they would be hard-pressed to treat everyone. She tightened her lips as she envisioned what they might face if the violence was as bad as they all feared. There would be people in place to care for any of the white police force... She wasn't as confident regarding the blacks. Medical treatment and supplies were woefully scarce in the Black Quarters.

"I'll help you carry everything upstairs from the basement," Anthony offered.

"Me too, Miss Carrie," Micah added.

"I'd appreciate that," Carrie said gratefully as she pushed back from the table and stood.

A knock at the back door paused all of them in their tracks. Surely it was too soon for injured men to be arriving.

"I'll get it," Micah said. Moments later, he re-entered the dining room, followed by three black women.

A smile exploded on Carrie's face. "Jasmine! Andrea! Charlene!" She rushed over to hug the women she hadn't seen in several years. "It's so wonderful to see you. What are you doing here?" She hoped she already knew.

The largest of the women smiled through the worry etched upon her face. "We heard you be here, Miss Carrie. Eddie told us they were gonna bring anyone who got hurt here. If the injured men be too hurt to move this far, then Eddie and the others are comin' here to get you. We figured we could be of help."

"I can't tell you how glad I am to see you, Jasmine," Carrie said sincerely, and then turned to the rest to explain. "Jasmine, Andrea and Charlene worked with me in the hospital that Janie and I started in the Black Quarters during the war. By the time it was all over, they had become quite skilled nurses." She breathed a sigh of relief. "Between all of us, I believe we can handle whatever is going to happen." Five years had passed since the end of the war, but she was confident the women were just as capable. She suspected they were called upon for medical help on a regular basis.

"Helen and Celia be coming over, too," Jasmine said, her eyes snapping with purpose. "They should be here real soon."

Carrie's confidence grew. "Helen and Celia were the other two regular nurses at the hospital," she explained. Another thought entered her mind. "Did you come here by yourselves?" With so much racial tension in the city, it wasn't wise for these women to be walking around unescorted.

"Do we look like we be out of our minds?" Jasmine retorted. "We may be brave, but we ain't no crazy women. We aim to help, not be scraped out of some alley."

Carrie would have smiled if it hadn't been so true. "How did you get here?"

"Two of the men walked us over, but ain't nobody see us. We stayed in all the back alleyways, and we made sure we didn't get near no streetlamps. There be times being black be a real good thing. We don't glow in the night like some white folks I know."

Light laughter filled the room.

Carrie reached out and took Jasmine's hand. "I'm so glad you're here. Even in the worst of the war years, you were always able to keep us smiling." She sobered. "I suspect we'll need that tonight."

Jasmine squeezed her hand. "I'll do my best," she promised. She took a meaningful pause before continuing. "My two boys be part of the militia. Both of them be out there in whatever be going on."

Carrie gripped her hand harder as she thought of the two teenage boys too young to fight in the war. Both of them had helped in the hospital, carrying supplies and heating water. "Jordan and Isaiah?"

"Yes," Jasmine confirmed. "My boys be twenty and twenty-one now. They joined the militia as soon as they got old enough." Her voice was a mixture of pride and worry.

Carrie smiled. "I look forward to seeing them again, but I hope it's not tonight."

Jasmine's lips tightened. "Me and you be hoping the same thing." She shook her head. "Helen and Celia will be here soon."

Carrie realized that Jasmine was doing what countless women had done throughout history by pushing her worry behind her so she could focus on what needed doing.

"I'll go out back and watch for them," Micah announced.

Carrie could sense what he wasn't saying. He would be watching to see if they were attacked by white men who were certain to be patrolling the city that night. The realization stopped her before she reached the basement stairs. "We can't stay here," she said, her certainty growing as the words came out of her mouth.

Micah froze in his tracks just in front of the kitchen door and then swung around to stare at her. "What are you saying, Miss Carrie?"

Carrie met Anthony's eyes. "It's too dangerous for anyone who may be wounded to try to make it here tonight. There will be men patrolling the city. They'll especially be on the lookout for anyone who is black if there's violence tonight. If the men live through whatever is happening at the police station, they don't need to be put in more danger."

Anthony stood abruptly. "You're right," he said grimly. "Micah, where is the best place to take them?"

"The Black Quarters," Micah said without hesitation. He locked eyes with May, an unspoken message passing between them.

"They can get anybody who's hurt to the church," May said decisively. "It ain't that far from the police station, and them white men gonna think twice before comin' into the Quarters. They gonna know that even if there be black men who aren't down there for Mayor Chahoon, they for sure gonna protect their families." Carrie managed a slight smile, hoping May was right. "Well ladies, looks like we're going to repeat some of our war experiences." Back then, just as now, the only place for her to set up her hospital had been in a black church. Painful memories filled her mind, but she pushed them aside impatiently. There was too much to be done.

She barked orders as her mind spun ahead. "Ladies, we're going to bring the supplies upstairs from the basement. Micah, you keep watch outside. Anthony, please bring the carriage around."

Anthony shook his head. "The carriage won't work. I'll hitch up the wagon instead."

Carrie knew he was right. The wagon would be large enough to transport everyone and carry the supplies. "Perfect."

"I'm coming with you to the church," Abby said as she rose to join the women headed to the basement.

Carrie opened her mouth to protest but closed it before a word came out. She knew by the look in Abby's eyes that she wouldn't be dissuaded. Truth be told, Carrie was relieved. Abby didn't have the medical experience the other women had, but her warm wisdom and compassion would be needed. "I'm glad you're coming," she said sincerely.

"Don't even try to stop *me*, Miss Carrie," May said warningly. "My man Spencer might be one of the ones who comes in hurt."

"You're coming, May," Carrie assured her. "We'll need you tonight." Although, the breadth of May's experience was limited, she had learned a lot from helping to care for Robert, Moses, George and other patients who had passed through the house over the years.

May nodded with satisfaction. "I'm glad you're smart enough to not argue with me. Now, y'all go down and get them medicines while I load up some baskets with whatever food I can put together."

*****

Twenty minutes later, Anthony clucked gently to the large bay mare pulling the wagon. As they pulled out onto the road, each person kept their eyes fastened in the direction they'd been assigned. "Helen and Celia had arrived just as they were loading up the wagon. Their escorts had offered to accompany the wagon, but Anthony believed that more of a black presence would only create more of a problem, and so the men left, disappearing into the night as soundlessly as they had come."It would not do to be caught by surprise. They were armed, but a wagon of mostly women would be at a grave disadvantage if attacked. Carrie and Abby were good shots, but the rest of the women had never handled a gun.

"It's going to be all right," Carrie said softly. She reached over to lay a gentle hand on Anthony's arm.

Anthony locked eyes with his wife, who was seated next to him, a rifle resting across her lap and a grim determination on her face. He hated putting her in danger, but he was also glad to have her with him. At least they would be together to face whatever was going to happen.

Anthony relaxed slightly when he became aware that the whistling wind would cover the sound of their travel. Though some of the surrounding houses had lights on, he doubted the inhabitants were paying much attention to wagons or carriages on the road. Instead, they would be huddled close to the fires that were creating plumes of smoke floating from the chimneys.

His relief was short-lived as the sound of a gunshot rang out over the whistling wind. Moments later, a volley of shots confirmed that whatever they had feared would happen that night, was happening.

"Sweet Jesus!" Jasmine said with a gasp. "We gots to hurry."

Anthony urged the mare into a brisker trot. People were going to be alarmed by the sound of gunfire and would come out to see what was going on. A wagon full of mostly black women would not be a welcome sight.

No one else said a word as the mare forged forward. The wind whipped the trees into a frenzy, their branches casting ghostly shadows as they danced around the streetlamps. What had been a passably warm, early-spring day had faded into a bitingly cold evening that revealed spring had still not truly sprung.

Anthony gripped the reins tighter, grateful for the loaded rifles under the wagon seat. Even if outnumbered, he would do what he could to protect the women in his care.

*****

Carrie's shoulders slumped with relief when the wagon passed the border of the Black Quarters, but her relief was short-lived.

"Who goes there?" A sharp voice split the night as a wall of armed men stepped out into the road in front of them.

Carrie gasped and reached for her gun. It was too dark to identify whether they were being confronted by black militia or Ellyson's police force.

Anthony pulled the wagon to a stop. "It's Anthony Wallington. I own River City Carriages."

"I know just who you be!" One of the men stepped out in front of the crowd. "I be one of your drivers. Name is Conrad. What you doin' down here, Mr. Wallington? It ain't safe."

Carrie sagged against the seatback and released her hold on the gun. They were out of immediate danger...for now.

"I'm quite aware of that," Anthony responded matter-of-factly. "My wife is a doctor. Ben Scott was at our house earlier and asked for her help with any wounded men if there were to be trouble tonight. By the sound of things, there's been trouble."

"Oh, there be plenty of trouble," one of the men growled as the whole group shifted restlessly.

Carrie knew they would only be in the way if trouble spilled into the Quarters right then. "We decided it wouldn't be safe for the wounded men to try and make it to my father's house on Church Hill. We want to treat them in the Black Quarters."

Jasmine stood up, her figure imposing even in the dark night. "It's pretty simple. We gots to get a hospital set up real quick. We helped Miss Carrie—I mean, Dr. Wallington—during the war when she had her hospital down here. We aim to do the same thing tonight. We be headed for the church down on Maple Street. You gonna let us through, or slow us down so we can't help nobody?"

The urgency in her voice broke through the tension. The wall of men separated.

"Thank you for all you be doing, Dr. Wallington," Conrad said gravely. "I know exactly who you be, only back then we knew you as Carrie Cromwell. You saved my mama and my little sister when they got real sick during the war. We be real grateful for you and all the rest of you women. It means a lot."

Anthony picked up the reins, but then hesitated. "Do you know what's happening?"

"Not much," Conrad admitted. "We had someone watching from a distance away. All we know is that Ben and the militia tried to break through the barricade Ellyson's police done set up. They were just usin' rocks." His voice thickened with grief and anger. "Ellyson's men got guns. That's the sound we been hearing."

Anthony had heard enough. "Can you let them know to bring the wounded to the church?" he ground out, aware of how fast they needed to move.

"I'll go right now," Conrad promised. He turned, broke into a sprint, and disappeared into the night.

Carrie spoke hurriedly to the others. "If you can send a few men down to the church to help us rearrange things in preparation, it would be greatly appreciated."

"You'll have someone in a few minutes, Dr. Wallington," one of the men promised, his voice drifting from a dark shadow.

Anthony slapped the mare's back with the reins. "Hold on, ladies," he called over his shoulder. "I'll have you there in a minute."

Carrie stared forward into the darkness, wondering what the rest of the night would bring.

Another volley of gunshots in the distance told her it wouldn't be good.

Chapter Three

Carrie jumped from the wagon before it had pulled to a complete stop. The rest of the women piled out to join her, the inky blackness of the Quarters swallowing them. An eerie silence swirled around them, highlighting the intense feeling that the residents were waiting for trouble to find them. An occasional gunshot in the distance was a stark reminder of why they were there. Carrie shook off the deep sense of foreboding that fought to strangle her mind. "We've got to get some light in the building," she called as she began to pull boxes from the bed of the wagon. She had learned that activity was often the greatest antidote to fear.

"I help with that for Bible studies," Celia answered, turning toward the dark building. "I'll get you some light in a minute. I'll light every lantern we got." Her small, thin figure disappeared into the dark, swallowed like a bird flying off into a stormy night.

Twenty minutes later, oil lanterns hanging from the walls produced a warm glow. Every blanket in the building had been pulled out of the closets. Figures began to appear through the doors; women from the Quarters bringing more blankets and bedding. The word had spread quickly.

"You keep working on them medicines, Miss Carrie," Jasmine said. "I'll get things ready for whoever is coming."

Carrie smiled her appreciation, knowing Jasmine would do the right things to convert the church into a temporary hospital ward.

Five men had made quick work of moving rustic pews and chairs to the far walls, leaving the center for the women to create makeshift beds. Jasmine stood in the middle, directing all the action. "We need cups and water pitchers," she called out.

A woman stepping through the door with an armload of blankets passed them off and turned around. "You'll have all you need in a few minutes," she called over her shoulder.

Less than ten minutes later, a small army of women had delivered glasses and pitchers full of water for the patients.

Carrie directed her team of nurses, needing very few words because they all knew what was expected and needed. By the time the beds were ready, with a pitcher of water and a glass beside each one, Carrie had prepared several large containers full of crushed garlic, crushed turmeric and sliced onions. Her homeopathic remedies were on the same table ready for use, and the boxes of bandages were ready. Her surgical tools were laid out carefully.

Anthony appeared at her side. "We've got a big fire going outside," he informed her. "Someone brought us a huge black kettle that already has water heating. There are men waiting who will bring in hot water when you need it."

Carrie gripped his hand in appreciation. "Thank you, Mr. Wallington."

"You're quite welcome, *Dr.* Wallington," Anthony replied as he leaned over to kiss her lightly.

Carrie had turned back to her work when she heard a commotion outside.

"Here come the first ones!" someone yelled.

Carrie took a deep breath, preparing herself for the night. She heard a clock strike ten as two men walked in, carrying a third man between them.

Within moments, three more wounded men were carried in. The bright red stains on their clothing confirmed cuts and gunshot wounds.

Carrie tightened her lips and hurried toward the first patient. She knew the nurses would do the best they could for the other men until she could reach them. As horrified as she was to deal with this kind of violence in her city again, she felt an odd comfort from a familiar routine and the knowledge that she knew how to help.

She bit back a groan when she recognized the first patient. She kept her voice calm and even. "Hello, Ben. Evidently, you decided you hadn't seen enough of me tonight. I'm sorry, but I don't have any of May's pound cake with me right now."

Ben managed a slight smile from between swollen and bruised lips. "Don't reckon I could eat it right now, Dr. Wallington."

"You've been shot?" Carrie asked, beginning to probe gently for the origin of the blood seeping through his clothing.

"Reckon so. I think they got me in the shoulder."

Carrie pulled aside his shirt and located the round hole the bullet had left. His wound was serious and painful, but she was glad to know it wasn't life-threatening. Closer inspection showed the bullet had gone through his shoulder and out the back. Surgery would not be necessary. She beckoned to Helen and Andrea. "Will you please clean this bullet wound and all of Ben's cuts? Put a salve of turmeric on the wounds to stop the bleeding, and then bandage the bullet hole carefully to keep it clean."

Both Helen and Andrea nodded, their faces and eyes calm. They knew what to do.

Carrie turned back to Ben, grateful beyond words to have the women with her tonight. "You're going to be fine, Ben. I'll get you something for the pain as soon as they have you cleaned up. The bullet went right through your shoulder, so we just need to make sure it doesn't become infected. I'm going to check on the other men."

"Thank you, Dr. Wallington. I be fine. You make sure everyone else be all right," Ben said weakly.

Carrie pushed aside the questions raging in her mind as she moved from patient to patient, acutely aware of more men being carried in. She dispensed equal amounts of herbal treatments and homeopathic remedies. Only one man required the extraction of a bullet, the rest were suffering from serious cuts and broken bones.

The clock was already striking four when all the patients were finally treated and resting as comfortably as possible. Carrie took a deep breath and straightened her shoulders for the first time.

Anthony appeared at her side. "How is everything?"

"Better than I expected," Carrie said, not bothering to hide the weariness in her voice. "All the men here are going to be fine. They'll take time to heal, but no one will die, and no one will lose a limb." After all the misery she had seen during the war, that was something to rejoice over. An uncomfortable realization seeped through her fatigue. "Was anyone killed?" Images of Eddie, Manley and the other men she knew filled her mind.

"No," Anthony replied. "Eddie is fine," he added, reading her mind. "So is Spencer. They helped bring in one of the wounded. They both had cuts, but nothing that required medical attention."

Carrie smiled. "I'm so glad." Then another thought intruded. "Did *anyone* die?" Regardless of what side of the issue someone was on, she was sick of all the senseless death. She also knew that a death in the Ellyson contingency would make things even more difficult for the residents of the Black Quarters, if he were to remain mayor.

Anthony's lips tightened. "One of Ellyson's police officers was killed," he admitted. He glanced over toward the makeshift hospital beds. "How is Ben?"

"He'll be fine once his shoulder has healed," Carrie answered. "Why?" A jolt of alarm passed through her at the look on her husband's face.

Anthony hesitated and looked around to be sure no one could overhear him. "Ben is being charged with the murder," he said grimly. "I just got word a few minutes ago."

Carrie bit back a groan. "Did he do it?"

Anthony shrugged. "There was complete mayhem when the rioting broke out. I doubt anyone knows what actually happened, but Ben is an easy target because of all his activism."

"You mean they're just looking for a way to get him in jail?" Carrie asked angrily.

"I'm afraid so," Anthony replied. "They want someone to take the blame. Evidently, there were far more than twenty-five black militia who headed to the police station. I don't know an exact number, but when they arrived, they surrounded Ellyson's police force, threatened to break the barricade, and started throwing rocks. One of them must have hit the policeman in the head. Ellyson's officers were well-armed, and they opened fire." He shook his head. "It's a miracle more people weren't shot or killed. I don't know if Ellyson's men are terrible shots, or if they deliberately missed, because they knew additional killing would only make things more difficult in the future."

Carrie glanced over at Ben, who was finally sleeping. "Will they come here to get him?"

"Not tonight," Anthony assured her. "No one knows the church is being used for a hospital except residents of the Black Quarters. No one will tell where he is."

Carrie hoped that was true, but knew fear could loosen even the tightest lips. She would care for him the best she could before it was taken out of her control.

Another thought entered her fogged mind. "How many of your drivers are my patients?"

"Ten," Anthony replied. "I'll lose some money until they can drive again, but we can handle it. If they ask you, assure them their jobs are waiting for them."

Carrie's heart surged with love for her husband. "You're a good man," she said softly.

Anthony shrugged. "I wish I could do more. There are times when I wonder if America will ever accept blacks as equals."

Carrie echoed his sentiment. "All we can do is fight alongside them," she said. As she looked out over the temporary hospital, her frustration grew. "I sometimes think about how different my life would have been if I'd been born black."

"I do, too," Anthony said thoughtfully, his eyes sweeping the room as he observed the patients and the women working to care for them. "I know I can't possibly understand what they live on a daily basis. Slavery was horrible, but in many ways, they still have just as big of a fight on their hands now."

"Not true."

Carrie was delighted when Eddie emerged from the shadows. "It's wonderful to see you," she said, keeping her voice low so she wouldn't wake anyone. "I'm glad you're safe." She stepped forward to embrace him with a hug, ignoring his dirty, blood-stained clothing.

Eddie stepped back. "I'm a mess," he protested.

"An *alive* mess," Carrie retorted. "My clothes will wash."

Anthony watched them for a moment before asking, "What did you mean when you said your fight isn't as big as the one you've already fought?"

Eddie met his eyes. "Things are bad, and they might get worse, but we can't never be slaves again. Probably lots of us gonna die in this fight, but ain't no one can put us back in chains on the plantations. And besides, there are lots of things that be better. Me and Opal get to run our restaurant, and my children are going to school. I got money in the bank, and I don't have to worry about Opal being sold away from me. I figure things gonna be real bad for a long while, but I think things will be better for my children, and I have hope things will be even better for their children." He took a deep breath. "Hope. That's what keeps us going. Ain't no one who was a slave had much hope...if they had any at all." He nodded toward the door. "Now, I'm going home to my family," he said solemnly. He turned and left the church.

Carrie and Anthony stood silently, watching the lantern light flicker across the room as Eddie's words sank into their minds and hearts. Carrie hoped with all her heart that he was right, that things would be better. She was painfully aware that many would probably pay with their lives to ensure that happened. "I'm staying here a while longer." She knew the women in the community could care for the patients, but she wanted to be available if anyone spiked a fever or an infection.

"I figured you would," Anthony answered. "I'm taking Abby and May home."

"Good," Carrie said fervently. She had watched both of them work tirelessly through the long night. "They need their rest."

"Like you don't?" Abby appeared by her side. "You need rest too, young lady."

Carrie couldn't deny it, but she forced a smile. "I'm younger and stronger," she teased. "Go home and get some rest. I'll be there to join you as soon as I feel it's safe to leave."

"The work of a doctor never ceases," Abby responded, her eyes alight with love and admiration. "It was a pleasure to work with you tonight, darling daughter."

Carrie sighed, basking in the love. "I wish it hadn't been necessary, but there is no one I would rather share this night with," she said sincerely, covering a yawn with her hand. "Go home," she commanded.

"You heard the doctor," Anthony said. He turned toward May, who was sitting on a wooden chair in the corner. He lifted the exhausted woman to her feet, put his arm around her waist, and led her out.

Carrie saw the fatigue radiating from Abby and May's bodies as they walked out. She was tired, but it was also true she was younger and stronger. Taking a deep breath, she walked back down the rows of patients, checking for flushed faces or labored breathing.

Her work wasn't done yet.

Chapter Four

Rose glanced out the schoolhouse window, thrilled to see the burgeoning buds on the maple and oak trees surrounding the log building. The redbud trees were already decked with glowing purple flowers, and ferns were unfurling everywhere. She took a deep breath of the fresh spring air and then checked the road for vigilantes, more out of habit than anything else. There had been no violence since Carrie had started treating some of the veterans who returned from the war intent on revenge. The miracle of them being freed from pain had changed their outlooks on life. The men promised no more violence would happen, but Rose knew their word alone could not stop the attacks. There were too many others intent on bringing the South back under white control. Moses constantly warned her to not let her guard down, but it was hard to remember the danger on such a beautiful day.

It had been a long winter. She was thrilled to see spring return to the Virginia countryside. There was no place in the world more beautiful than Cromwell Plantation in the spring. Even though she didn't actually have much evidence of other places to support that conclusion, it didn't keep her from believing it with all her heart.

A scuffling sound at the door drew her attention. "Hello, Mrs. Samuels."

Rose smiled at the man standing in the doorway. "Hello, Alvin. Come on inside." Though it was growing warmer, the schoolhouse was still cool enough to benefit from the fire burning briskly in the woodstove.

"Thank you, ma'am."

Rose wasn't sure she would ever get used to Alvin Williams calling her "ma'am." He had returned home from the war, bitter over the Confederate defeat, and with the loss of one arm and half of a leg. Frustrated and angry, he'd led the fight to keep white children out of the school, but in the last two years, had become one of their greatest supporters. "I've got the medicine right here, Alvin."

Alvin smiled. "The men are grateful. They're all doing real well."

"I'm glad to hear they're still improving," Rose said warmly. "This is the last of the medicine, but Carrie will be here tomorrow with more. What she brings will carry us through the rest of the year."

Alvin nodded, but added, "There are more men who would surely appreciate some of that Hypericum."

Rose knew he was right. The veterans Carrie had treated with Hypericum had been given a second chance at life. Once afflicted with never-ending phantom pain from the limbs they'd lost, all but one of them had returned to a productive life. The remaining man was getting better, slowly but surely. It was just a matter of time. "You know she said she wouldn't send medicine for any of the men she hasn't seen herself," Rose reminded him.

She didn't mention that Polly could have prescribed the homeopathic remedy that was working such miracles. The usually easygoing woman would have nothing to do with the men who admitted they'd been part of the vigilante groups that had attacked the plantation. Polly would never forgive them for the attempt to kill her daughter. They had missed Amber, but killed Robert, leaving him to die as they rode off, their torches held high in the night. Polly had still not forgiven Carrie for treating the men who had been involved in Robert's murder, but that was something they would have to work out between themselves when Carrie returned.

"Do you figure she'll see them when she's back here?"

"I know she plans to," Rose said encouragingly. "I just don't want anyone to get their hopes up and be disappointed." She bit back the sentence she wanted to add: *I'm afraid if they don't get the remedy, they'll get angry and go back to vigilante activity.*

Alvin read her mind. "The men are real grateful. They ain't going to do no more violence."

"They *aren't* going to do *any* more violence," Rose corrected automatically, smiling when a red flush rose in Alvin's face. "You did ask me to correct your English," she reminded him.

"I did," Alvin relented, "but sometimes, when you feel strongly about things, you forget to say it correctly."

Rose smiled. "I know. You're doing much better. I'm proud of you."

Alvin relaxed as her praise assuaged his ego. "You say Miss Carrie is supposed to be here tomorrow?"

"That's what her last letter said."

Alvin looked uncomfortable. "The men who don't yet have medicine already have their hopes up," he admitted.

Rose's throat tightened when she saw the expression in his eyes. "And if they aren't able to get it?"

"I still don't think they'll do anything," Alvin replied quickly, "but... men in pain don't always think straight."

Rose kept her face impassive, knowing just how right he was. "Take the medicine we have. I know Carrie will do her best." Suddenly, all she wanted was to be at home with her husband and family. She reached for the satchel carrying her school supplies. "I'm ready to enjoy this beautiful afternoon."

Jeb appeared from the woods as soon as she stepped from the door, his narrow, bearded face bright with a smile. Though the violence seemed to be over, Moses still insisted on Jeb standing guard over the school every day. Jeb insisted he didn't mind, assuring her that standing watch in the woods was much easier than working the tobacco fields on the plantation. Rose suspected there were times he was bored to tears, but she also knew he used the time to read and study.

"Hello, Alvin," Jeb called.

"Hello, Jeb," Alvin replied cheerfully. "How are you?"

The two, against all odds, had become close friends. Their friendship had been cemented when Jeb had helped Alvin protect his family against vigilantes intent on destroying his home because Alvin was no longer fighting to end black independence. They saw him as nothing but a white traitor.

Watching their easy friendship, Rose was once more filled with hope for the country. Things weren't changing fast enough, but she couldn't deny there were changes.

*****

Rose relaxed as Jeb drove her home. As her head rested against the cushioned back, she admired the cardinals and blue jays flitting through the trees, their brilliant colors flashing against the fresh, green buds just starting to unfurl. They already looked different than they had this morning.

"Did you have a good day, Miss Rose?" Jeb asked.

"I did," Rose said happily. "My students are all doing well, and things have gotten so much better since they're not constantly watching for attacks on the school. Fear can play havoc with anyone, but especially with children who have known far too much fear and violence in their lives."

"They still have to be careful," Jeb said.

Rose sighed. "You sound like Moses."

"Because Moses is right," Jeb retorted. "I want to believe the violence is over as much as anybody, but the things I'm reading keep reminding me I shouldn't do that."

Jeb had become a voracious reader. After decades of not being able to read a word, he devoured everything Rose could get for him. She knew he was reading every newspaper Thomas received at the plantation. "I suppose you're right," she said reluctantly, wishing they could switch to another subject. Couldn't she pretend for one beautiful spring season that danger wasn't lurking just around the corner?

Jeb continued, unaware of her thoughts. "I *think* I believe the men Miss Carrie is helping wouldn't do harm to anyone," he mused, "but the KKK be sending people in from all over to make sure things don't get out of control in the South."

Rose was too distracted to be concerned with correcting his grammar. Unfortunately, she knew he was right. No matter how hard they worked to build relationships with the white people surrounding the plantation, they still had an entire country to worry about. The KKK would stop at nothing to promote their agenda of white supremacy. "President Grant is working to stop the Ku Klux Klan," she argued "He's not anything like President Johnson, who just turned a blind eye."

"Yep," Jeb said easily. "I know the president wants to do that, but *wanting* to do it and actually being able to do it are two different things. The South is real big. It's going to be hard to control it all."

Rose sighed, wanting to put her hands over her ears to stop the conversation. "Can we talk about this another time?" she replied, hating the pleading note in her voice. "I'm not disagreeing with you, but it would be nice to have one afternoon when I don't have to think about it."

Jeb turned to her immediately, his face creased with concern. "I'm sorry, Miss Rose. I guess I have too much time to think about things when I'm out there in the woods."

"All by yourself," Rose added. "I know you want to talk about it. I guess my heart is just tired right now."

"I understand," Jeb said. Suddenly, he pointed to the right. "Look over there," he whispered.

Rose smiled as she glimpsed three does peering at them through the undergrowth, their large eyes watchful but calm. "They're beautiful," she whispered, leaning back to let the magic of the warm spring air wrap around her once more. The reality of the world they lived in could not be ignored for long, but she would grab every moment she could.

*****

"Mama! Mama!"

Rose smiled as John started jumping up and down on the porch, calling her name as soon as he saw the carriage roll into sight.

"That's one excited little boy," Jeb said with a chuckle. "Course, he's not going to be little for long, if you can even apply that word to him now. That's the biggest six-year-old I've ever seen. He just seems to get bigger every day."

Rose grinned as she watched her son leap around. "He loves Annie's cooking. I've always known he was going to be as big as his daddy. I just thought it would take a little longer." At the rate he was growing, he would be as tall as Moses in his early teens, and then would probably surpass him. She knew such imposing size brought both benefits and trouble, but all she could do was prepare him for life as much as possible.

Her grin widened when the door opened and a miniature version of herself ran out onto the porch to join John in his wild jumping. "My daughter has no idea why she's jumping."

"She doesn't have to have a reason," Jeb observed. "That little Hope thinks the sun rises and sets on her big brother. She wants to do whatever he does."

"That's what I'm afraid of," Rose said ruefully, feeling love swell in her heart as Hope danced around the porch. Her daughter's caramel skin and dark wavy hair predicted great beauty when she was grown. She found herself wishing that her little girl would find the same kind of love she'd found with Moses. She wanted nothing less than the best for the child with such a huge, open heart.

"You ever think of what their life would be if they'd been born slaves like us?" Jeb asked as the carriage rolled closer.

"All the time," Rose said. "I thank God every day that my children will never be slaves." She knew they would face other hardships in the America they were growing up in, but at least slavery wouldn't be one of them.

John ran down the stairs as soon as the carriage pulled to a stop. "Mama! Come with me! Right now!"

Rose leaned down and hugged her son. She knew it wouldn't be long before he was taller than she was. "What are you so impatient about, son?"

Hope jumped down the steps to join them, throwing her arms around Rose as she leaned in for a hug and kiss. "John did it, Mama!"

Rose smiled. "John did what, Hope?"

"Don't you tell her," John warned as Hope opened her mouth.

Hope snapped it shut quickly, but reached up to tug Rose's hand. "You got to come see, Mama!"

Rose laughed helplessly. When both of her children were equally intent on getting her to do something, there was little use in refusing. "Where are we going?"

"To the barn!" John yelled, his eyes flashing with excitement.

"You wait right there, young man."

John sighed impatiently as he looked up at the porch, where a stout woman had emerged from the house. "I want to go to the barn, Grandma Annie."

"And you gonna do just that," Annie promised, her stern voice softened by her laughing eyes. "But your mama just got home from a long day of teachin'. Don't you reckon she deserves some tea and a few of those molasses cookies I made you and your sister?"

Rose hid her grin when John hesitated. He knew the right answer, but wasn't sure he wanted to give it. Whatever he had to show her must be very important. She could tell he was struggling with whether to acknowledge she deserved some tea and cookies. She wanted to go to the barn with him, but the allure of Annie's cooking was powerful, and it was a good opportunity to teach her son compassion.

A resigned disappointment finally fell over John's face. "She deserves tea and cookies," he said with a sigh.

"Thank you, John. I'll eat quickly," Rose promised. "I'm eager to see whatever you have to show me." She knew it must have something to do with his horse, Rascal. The two were almost inseparable.

John nodded, and a smile broke out on his face. "I'll be in the barn," he yelled as he turned and sprinted off.

Rose laughed, climbed the steps, and then settled down into one of the rocking chairs on the porch. She closed her eyes for a moment to absorb the warm sunshine making its way past the large white pillars encasing the porch of Cromwell Plantation. Moments later, she felt Hope clamber onto her lap. She opened her eyes and pulled her daughter into a warm hug. "How is my beautiful little girl?" she asked softly.

"I'm real good, Mama," Hope said earnestly. "Guess what happened today, Mama. I've been waiting all day for you to come home."

"Are you sure John wants you to tell his secret?" Rose asked. Hope had a very difficult time keeping any kind of secret, but it was obvious this one was important to her brother.

"It's *another* secret," Hope said importantly.

"Is it one you have permission to tell?"

"Yes," Hope insisted. "It's *my* secret!"

Rose suddenly remembered the previous night's conversation she'd had with Moses. "In that case, I'm very eager to hear it."

Hope grinned and opened her mouth but remained silent, her eyes flashing with impudence.

Rose controlled her laugh. Susan, the co-owner of Cromwell Stables, had been giving Hope acting lessons. Evidently, they were working on dramatic pauses. She doubted her daughter needed any help in being more dramatic, but the two had so much fun, Rose couldn't refuse.

"Well, Mama," Hope finally said, pausing again.

Rose waited, letting her eyes drift to the pasture where the first new foals of the year pranced beside their mothers. The initial batch of fillies and colts were less than two weeks old. Soon, they would be joined by dozens more.

Hope couldn't contain her news anymore. "I have my own pony, Mama!" She clapped her hands together with glee, her dark eyes dancing with joy. "My very own pony!"

"Why, that's wonderful!" Rose exclaimed. "What pony?"

Hope's eyes grew even bigger. "Patches!" She jumped down from Rose's lap, suddenly not able to keep from dancing around the porch again. "Daddy gave me Patches!"

Rose clapped her hand over her mouth to feign surprise. "Patches? You mean the pony John used to have?"

Hope nodded vigorously. "Yes! I have John's pony. Patches is all mine now. Daddy said so!" Then she hesitated. "Is it okay with you, Mama?"

Rose laughed. Even if she and Moses hadn't already agreed on his plan the night before, she never would have had the heart to destroy the joy on Hope's face. "Of course it is, honey. Do you really think you can handle Patches?" Moses had already assured her their daughter could, but she wanted to know what Hope would say.

"Oh, yes, Mama," Hope said earnestly. "Grandpa Miles and Miss Susan have taught me how to groom her and everything." Her face filled with a look of importance. "I even went riding out in the fields with Daddy and John this morning."

Rose's surprise was real this time. "You did?" She wished she could have seen her two children ride off with their father into the tobacco fields. She loved being a teacher, but she hated missing moments like this with her children. Nevertheless, it meant the world to her that both her children got to spend so much time with their father. Moses' own father had been killed during an escape attempt when Moses was just eleven, and she had never known her father, only finding out the truth of her heritage when she was eighteen.

"Yes!" Hope assured her. "When I got back, I groomed Patches all by myself and gave her food and water."

Rose leaned over to hug her daughter. "I'm so happy for you," she said, "and I'm so very proud of you."

"I knew you would be," Hope said, her voice muffled in Rose's shoulder.

The sound of an opening door said Annie was coming out with the promised tea and cookies.

Hope peeked up at Rose's face. "Mama?"

"Yes?"

"Can I have one of your cookies?"

"Do you mean *may* I have one of your cookies?" Rose asked. She was determined her children would never face unnecessary difficulties in life because they didn't speak correctly. Being almost five was no excuse.

Hope sighed. "*May* I have one of your cookies?"

Rose nodded. "I would love to share with you." Then she patted the chair next to them. "Please join us, Annie."

Annie settled her short, stout body down with a slight grunt. "Don't mind if I do."

Rose narrowed her eyes at the tired sound in Annie's voice. "Are you all right?"

"Of course I'm all right," Annie answered with a snort. "A body got a right to be tired when they cooking for as many as I am."

Rose knew she was right, but now Moses' mother had the added responsibility of caring for John and Hope while Rose was teaching. Everyone on the plantation kept an eye out for them, but Annie bore the weight of it. Hard years of slavery, and more grief than any one person should bear, had aged her beyond her years.

"Get that look off your face," Annie said sternly. "I'm right as rain. Just need to sit down for a spell. Ain't you doing the same thing? Iffen every time I take a break you gonna get all worried, then I won't be able to do it at all."

Rose smiled brightly. "The cookies are delicious," she said sincerely.

"Delicious!" Hope repeated, enunciating the words clearly around the remnants of the cookie in her mouth. She swallowed hastily, grinned at her Grandma Annie, and reached for another one.

"Hope..." Annie warned. "What did I done tell you?"

Hope's eyes flooded with disappointment as she pulled her hand back. "You told me I couldn't have any more cookies 'cause it will spoil my dinner." She paused and looked at Rose. "But... I'm sharing a moment with Mama," she said sweetly.

Rose couldn't stop the blast of laughter that escaped her mouth. "You've had one with me, Hope. Whatever your Grandma Annie says is what you need to do."

"All right, Mama." Hope relented with a heavy sigh and then turned her eyes to the barn. "Are you almost ready?"

Rose wiped her mouth and hands with the napkin Annie had placed on the tray. "Let's go find out John's surprise."

"Yes!" Hope crowed. "Mama, wait until you see. John can..."

Rose leaned down and held a finger to Hope's lips. "Don't tell your brother's secret."

Hope shook her head impatiently. "Then you have to hurry up," she insisted.

Annie shook her head, her eyes glittering with amusement. "That girl be just like her daddy when he was young." Her eyes narrowed. "And I expect just like you."

Rose chuckled. "She comes by it honestly," she admitted. She pushed aside the thought that she and Moses had never truly been free to be children, because they'd both been born a slave. It was easy to imagine the agony her mother and Annie must have experienced as they watched their children suffer. It made her shudder to think of John, Hope and Felicia enduring what she and Moses had, but their life now was what mattered. She reached down her hand. "Let's go, daughter."

Chapter Five

Rose was not as hopelessly enamored with horses as almost everyone else in her world, but she had grown to love the warm smells in the barn. Grain and hay, mixed with saddle soap and oil, along with the aroma of the horses, created its own unique perfume. She was also grateful beyond words that John and Hope loved horses as much as their father and Grandpa Miles did. It didn't matter to either of her children that Miles and Annie had been married only a short time. He had quickly become the loving grandfather they deserved but had never known. She knew Miles cherished the relationship as much as they did.

"Grandpa Miles! Mama's here!" John dashed out of Rascal's stall.

Miles appeared at the door of another stall he was cleaning. "Howdy, Rose. Your son be a mite excited."

"He certainly seems to be," Rose agreed, thrilled by the pride and love glowing in Miles' eyes as he looked at her son. She turned to John. "What do you want me to see, John?"

John answered by dashing back into Rascal's stall, leading him out moments later. "Watch this," he said proudly. He led Rascal to the cross-tie station and snapped the latches to the towering horse's halter, the black gelding lowering his head to accommodate the boy. Then John returned to the tack room, rolling out a mounting block almost as tall as he was.

As John pushed it up next to Rascal, Rose suddenly understood the mysterious sounds coming from the barn late last night after everyone had gone to bed.

"Grandpa Miles made this for me!" John announced, and then dashed back into the tack room to emerge moments later with his saddle. He carefully climbed to the top of the mounting block, designed to make him just tall enough to reach Rascal's back. He placed the saddle gently on the gelding's back and got down on his knees to grab the girth hanging down on the other side of Rascal's belly. His arms were just long enough to grab it. Focusing intently, John pulled the girth toward him and fastened it into place.

Rascal stood patiently, not moving a muscle.

John grinned, jumped off the mounting block, and then rolled it closer to Rascal's head. Once he had it where he wanted it, he disappeared back into the tack room. He reappeared with Rascal's bridle and climbed the mounting block again. Bridling his horse took only moments as Rascal lowered his head willingly and seemed to almost reach for the bit with his mouth.

Rose's heart swelled with the love these two shared.

When John had Rascal saddled and bridled, he turned toward Rose with a triumphant grin.

Rose clapped her hands. "That's wonderful, John! You saddled Rascal all by yourself."

"I told you it was something great," Hope squealed. "My brother did it all by himself!"

John nodded vigorously. "Grandpa Miles made the mounting block just for me. Now, I don't have to wait for him to put the tack on Rascal. I can do it all by myself."

Miles accurately read the sudden panic on Rose's face. "You tell your mama what else we talked about, John."

John frowned but nodded, and met Rose's eyes. "I promised Grandpa Miles that I wouldn't ever go riding by myself," he said reluctantly.

Rose was glad to hear it, but she needed to clarify something. "You also promised last fall when you got Rascal that you would never go riding on your own. Have you forgotten that?"

"No," John admitted with a spark of defiance in his eyes. "But that was before I could saddle Rascal all by myself." He took a breath. "Mama, I'll be seven years old soon. How long will it be before I can ride by myself? You know Rascal would never do anything to hurt me."

"And I'm going to be five soon," Hope chimed in. "How long for me?"

Rose fought to keep her voice and face calm. She did know that Rascal would never hurt John, but other terrifying images filled her mind—terrifying images of white men who wouldn't hesitate to hurt a little black child. "I do know that Rascal would never hurt you," she agreed, "and I know seven is a very big age, but do you know Miss Carrie couldn't ride alone until she was thirteen?"

John looked horrified as he spun around to stare at Miles. "Grandpa Miles, is that true?"

Miles nodded solemnly. "It's true, John. I know how much you want to be out there on your own, but it's our job to keep you safe, because we love you."

"Me, too?" Hope asked sadly. "Patches would never hurt me."

"You, too," Rose said firmly.

John shook his head. "Safe is dumb."

Rose fought the smile tugging at her lips.

"That may be," Miles said, "but that's the way it be." He leaned over to stare into John's face. "You and me have a deal, John. Are you going to be a man and honor it?"

John sighed dramatically as he nodded. "I'll honor it, Grandpa."

"Shake on it?" Miles asked. He seemed to realize he had to impress the importance of this issue.

John's face twisted with regret, but he stuck out his hand and shook Miles' firmly. "I won't ride by myself, Grandpa." After a moment, he grinned. "At least until I get you to change your mind."

Rose couldn't stop the laugh that escaped her lips this time.

Miles shook his head with a chuckle. "Just you be keepin' your word, boy. We'll worry about the future when it gets here."

Susan strode into the barn, her glossy blond hair pulled back into its standard long braid. "Anyone around here want to come with me to round up some of the mares still in the back field? They should start foaling soon, and I want to have them closer."

"I will!" John offered.

"Great. Let's go, John."

Rose was astonished at Susan's ready acceptance. "You're letting a six-year-old help you round up the horses?"

"He helped me last week," she informed Rose. "He may be young, but he's had so much riding experience, and Rascal is so fabulous, he can do things no normal six-year-old can do."

John nodded. "I've been trying to tell them that, Miss Susan. They still say I can't ride by myself." He appeared hopeful that a new ally might change the rules.

"And they're absolutely right," Susan said firmly, smiling when she saw John's disappointed face. "Your time will come, John. In the meantime, you have plenty of people to ride with. Your father, me, Amber, Thomas, and any of the men, will do whatever you ask as long as they have time."

"Like they'll have time now," John said in a grumpy voice. "The tobacco fields are close to being planted again. They're almost done plowing and the seedlings are almost ready. You and I both know they'll be working around the clock until harvest," he complained.

Rose was impressed by what a clear understanding her son had of tobacco farming. Of course, he did go riding with his daddy every chance he got. He would have absorbed a tremendous amount of knowledge over all that time.

Susan nodded. "That also means your daddy will be out in the fields almost every day. You know he loves it every time you ride with him."

Defeated, John led Rascal from the barn to the mounting block outside. Moments later, he was mounted and waiting impatiently.

"Thanks, Susan," Rose said.

"What about me?" Hope demanded, stepping forward so she wouldn't be overlooked. "Can I go round up the horses, too?"

Rose shook her head. "Honey, I know you ride Patches really well, but your pony isn't right for rounding up horses." She prayed she was right.

"Why not?" Hope demanded, her eyes flashing with indignation. "Patches is as good as that old Rascal." Her lips settled into a pout.

"You're right that Patches is as good as Rascal," Susan said soothingly, kneeling down to look Hope in the face. "It's just that Patches isn't quite fast enough because she's smaller. You wouldn't want her to feel bad because she can't keep up with John and I out in the field, would you?"

Rose smiled, knowing the appeal to Hope's tender heart would be much more effective than outright denying her what she wanted.

Hope hesitated but shook her head. "I don't ever want Patches to feel bad," she said sadly. "I'll stay here."

Rose hated the disappointed look on her face, but she knew that growing up behind a big brother like John was going to create many of those moments. "How about you and I go for a ride?" she offered. "I haven't seen you ride Patches since he became your very own pony."

Hope's face lit up as the pout was swallowed by a huge smile. "I would love that, Mama!"

Miles nodded. "Give me a few minutes. I'll have Patches and Maple ready for you."

Hope shook her head. "Grandpa, why can't I saddle Patches by myself? Like John does?"

Rose opened her mouth to say Hope was still too young, but Miles was looking at his granddaughter thoughtfully. "Well, I guess I don't see no reason I can't teach you how to do that. You'll have to be serious about learnin', though."

Hope pulled her tiny shoulders back as a look of importance filled her face. "I'll be very serious, Grandpa."

Miles stared at her for a few moments, considering. "You'll also have to make the same deal with me that I made with John," he said solemnly.

Suddenly, Rose saw the wisdom in what Miles was doing.

"John promised me he would never go ridin' alone. You just heard him. Will you make the same promise, Hope?"

"Of course," Hope replied instantly. "Why would I go riding alone, anyway? It's not fun when you don't have someone with you."

Rose hoped her daughter would keep feeling that way.

Miles knelt down, managing to hide most of the grimace caused by his arthritic knees. "Shake on it?"

Hope nodded, her eyes bright with focus as she shook hands with her grandpa. "I promise I'll never go riding by myself," she said solemnly. She waited almost the same amount of time John had before she added, "Until I get you to change your mind!"

Laughter rolled through the barn as Hope dashed outside to wait for Patches.

"That girl is something," Miles muttered. "She be just like you when you was that age," he told Rose.

"Before I moved into the Big House," Rose said, suddenly gripped with memories of being pulled away from her mama and made to live in the Big House as Carrie's personal slave.

Miles nodded soberly. "That changed you some, for sure, but it didn't take the fire away. You can make a folk change what they do, but you can't make 'em change their heart." He smiled. "That fire what made you start a secret school in the woods back before the war," he reminded her.

Rose nodded absently as she stared out into the barnyard, wondering what life would compel her children to do. Forcing her thoughts aside, she turned to Susan as Miles started saddling Maple and Patches. "I thought you were going to Richmond with Harold?"

"I was," Susan replied, "but then I realized the idea of getting away for a few days during foaling season was sheer lunacy. I miss my wonderful husband, but I was a part of three births yesterday. It never stops being anything but a miracle for me, and I want to make certain I can help if there are any problems."

"I understand," Rose said. "I look out into the pasture every morning to see what new lives have been released into the world." Then she changed the subject. "Why did Harold go to Richmond, anyway?"

Susan frowned. "He got a letter talking about a conflict between Mayor Chahoon and someone trying to take his place. To tell you the truth, I wasn't paying that much attention. I'm quite sure that, a few seconds after he told me, I was sound asleep. He was gone before I woke up, but he's supposed to be back tonight." She grinned. "And Carrie and Abby will be here tomorrow."

Rose returned the grin. She could hardly wait to see her best friend again. It had only been a few months since Carrie left for Philadelphia, and they exchanged letters regularly, but she was eager for some face-to-face time. "She promised to be here in the afternoon."

"Mama! Are you coming?" Hope's plaintive voice broke into their conversation.

Only then did Rose realize Miles was already outside with Maple and Patches. "I'm coming," Rose called.

*****

Rose and Hope had ridden about twenty minutes before they saw Moses coming toward them in the distance.

"It's Daddy!" Hope yelled.

Rose watched Moses approach, admiring his easy seat in Champ's saddle. Most men as large as him managed to look awkward on a horse, but Moses looked like he'd been born in the saddle.

Moses broke into a canter when he caught sight of them. "To what do I owe this pleasure?" he asked, pulling to a stop next to them.

Rose smiled and felt a familiar tingle as Moses' eyes swept over her lovingly. "I wanted to go riding with our daughter on the first day she has a pony all her own."

Hope beamed with pride as Moses smiled down at her. "Grandpa Miles is going to teach me how to saddle Patches all by myself, Daddy."

"Oh?" Moses raised a brow as he looked at Rose.

"He made a special mounting block for John," Rose explained. "Our son just saddled and bridled Rascal all by himself." She smiled back when Moses' face lit up with a grin. "Miles is going to start teaching Hope, too." Then she turned to Hope. "Do you want to tell Daddy about your deal with Grandpa Miles?"

Hope rolled her eyes but complied. "I promised Grandpa Miles I wouldn't go riding alone until you give me permission. John made the same promise," she added.

"Did you shake on it?" Moses asked seriously.

Hope nodded. "Yes. I would never break a promise to Grandpa Miles," she said earnestly.

Rose met Moses' eyes. They both knew how independent and strong-willed their children were. Their promises were important, but she knew neither of them would let their guard down.

"I believe you," Moses told Hope. Then he smiled. "You look real pretty on Patches."

Hope stared at him for a moment. "Thank you, Daddy, but I don't just want to look pretty. I want to learn to be as good a horsewoman as Amber." Her eyes glowed with intensity. "I heard Susan talking about Amber. She said Amber is the best horsewoman she's ever met." Her face puckered as she remembered. "She said she's never seen such talent in a girl her age." She nodded. "Yep, I want to be just like Amber."

"You can do anything you want to, Hope," Moses assured her. "I know Amber will help you. Just stay open to other things, my darling daughter."

Hope frowned as she thought about his words, but they were beyond her four-year-old ability to understand. "What do you mean?" she finally asked.

"I mean that you just might find something you love even more than horses." Moses held up his hand to stop Hope's protest before it tumbled from her lips. "I know you can't imagine that right now, but it might happen."

"But why would it, Daddy?" Hope asked. "I don't think I'll ever want to do anything but ride horses."

"That might be true," Moses replied, "and I would be so proud of you. But, I'll be proud of you no matter what you decide to do."

Hope cocked her head as she looked at her father. "Daddy, what did you want to be when you were my age?"

Moses took a deep breath as he stared off into the distance for a long moment.

Rose knew he was remembering. She also knew what his answer would be.

"Free," Moses said softly. "When I was your age, all I wanted was to be free."

Rose echoed his answer in her heart.

*****

Two hours later, dinner had been consumed and everyone was sitting outside on the porch. The late afternoon sun had dipped below the tree line, leaving a golden glow behind. The warm day had turned into a chilly evening, but no one was eager to go inside after a long winter. Lap quilts were keeping them warm.

"Isn't Harold supposed to be home tonight?" Thomas asked, running his hand through his silver hair as he fixed his blue eyes on the horizon.

"He is," Susan answered. She was staying in the plantation house while he was away, but their newly finished home was waiting on the land given to them by Thomas and Abby as their wedding gift.

"I saved him some of my apple pie," Annie announced. "Them apples kept in the tunnel real good over the winter."

"He'll be thrilled," Susan responded. "He asks me sometimes if I'll ever learn to cook like you do. I assure him it's an impossibility," she said with a grin. "He says he loves me anyway."

"That man be plum crazy for you," Annie retorted. "'Sides, he knows he can come get my apple pie anytime he done want to."

"That certainly helps the situation," Susan agreed cheerfully.

"I could help you learn how to cook," Annie offered after a brief silence.

Rose looked at her mother-in-law with surprise. The only other woman Annie had allowed in her kitchen was Marietta. Annie, impatient with anyone else in her domain, had been reluctant at first, but had grown to love teaching her. She talked often about wishing Jeremy and Marietta would return to the plantation with the twins she adored, but she had accepted they never would.

"I appreciate the offer," Susan replied, "but all I want to do is be in the stables. The idea of taking time away from the horses to learn to cook is just not appealing," she said honestly.

"Well, how you gonna feed that new husband of yours?" Annie demanded.

Susan shrugged, her eyes alive with laughter. "He hasn't starved yet. He knew what he was getting when he married me," she said casually. "After so many years on his own after his first wife died, he actually became quite a good cook. Between the two of us, we don't go hungry."

Rose grinned. "Harold adores you. He would probably be happy if you served him saddle leather."

Susan chuckled. "Let's hope it doesn't come to that."

Moses broke into the banter. "Thomas, is something bothering you?"

Rose looked at Thomas in surprise, suddenly noticing the worried creases around his eyes.

Thomas hesitated. "I'm fine. There's probably nothing to worry about."

"*Probably*?" Moses pressed.

"What aren't you telling us?" Rose asked, pushing down her sudden alarm as she realized her hopes of a peaceful spring might be nothing but a wild wish.

Thomas sighed. "I really don't know that anything is wrong, but I'm afraid there is potential to be," he admitted.

"You're confusing me, Mr. Thomas," Annie said. "Why don't you quit playing around it and just say what you gots to say."

Miles chuckled. "She talks to me the same way. You might as well tell us straight out. She won't give you any peace until you do."

Thomas smiled, but then grew serious again. "I'm afraid there's trouble in Richmond."

"With the Mayor Chahoon controversy?" Susan asked. "I know that's why Harold went to the city. He wanted to check out the situation, so he could write to Matthew about it."

Rose's throat constricted. "Are Carrie and Abby in danger?"

Thomas met her eyes squarely. "I don't know," he said honestly.

"Tell us what you know, please," Moses responded.

"All of it," Susan commanded, her eyes watching the empty horizon for a sign of her husband's arrival.

Rose understood the fear pounding in Susan's heart. She had felt it every day when she and Moses had been separated by the war. Silently, she reached out to take her friend's hand.

Susan smiled, but her eyes were fixed on Thomas. "What do you know?"

"Right now, I know I wish I had done a better job of hiding my concerns, because I really don't know anything. A friend came by yesterday morning who had just returned from Richmond. Ellyson has been selected by the City Council as mayor, but Mayor Chahoon has refused to relinquish his position. Each has their own police force, and they're determined to not back down."

"A recipe for a whole lot of trouble," Annie said flatly.

"I'm afraid so," Thomas agreed. "Richmond is already constantly on the edge of volatility right now. I'm afraid all this will do is intensify the problem."

Rose frowned. "Is there no reasonable person who can resolve this without violence?"

Thomas smiled ruefully, the smile doing nothing to mask the worry in his eyes. "The entire South seems to be short of reasonable people right now. The war seems to have imprinted in everyone's minds that violence is the only way to deal with problems. Action, even if it's the wrong one, seems to be much more popular than dialogue." He shook his head. "This is the same kind of hotheaded thinking and actions that got us into a war..." His voice trailed off as he looked out over the pasture.

"You're afraid Abby and Carrie are going to get caught up in it," Moses observed.

"When *hasn't* my daughter been caught up in things?" Thomas asked. "I'm proud of her for always wanting to be involved, but I also wish there were times she would just turn and run."

And bring your wife with her, Rose thought. She was all too aware that if Richmond were having trouble, Carrie would do whatever she could to help—meaning she would be in the middle of whatever was going on. The thought caused Rose's heart to constrict even tighter.

Moses reached over to take her hand. "Don't go looking for heartache," he said gently. "Abby and Carrie are remarkably competent and resourceful." He directed his comment as much to Thomas as he did to Rose.

Thomas nodded, but his expression didn't change. "I'm also thinking about Micah and Spencer," he replied. "Eddie and Opal. Marcus and Hannah. Willard and Grace." His lips tightened. "I know Anthony is in town as well..."

Susan jumped up and pointed down the drive. "Harold is back!"

Thomas stood beside her. "Hopefully he'll have some answers."

Everyone watched Harold ride the rest of the way down the drive. The easy bantering from earlier had been replaced by a tense worry.

Rose was glad that John and Hope were already in bed. She couldn't always protect them from the realities of life, but she was grateful she didn't have to tarnish the joy of what had been a perfect day for them both. She stood rigidly, fighting her resentment about the fact that her wish for a peaceful spring had already been destroyed. True, trouble hadn't made it to the plantation, but it was swirling around people she cared about.

Harold rode up to the porch and dismounted. "Do you always give people a welcoming committee?" he asked with a smile.

Susan ran down the steps and into his arms. "I'm so glad you're safe!"

Harold hugged her close and then frowned as understanding filled his eyes. "You've heard about the trouble in Richmond."

"We've heard there *could* be trouble," Susan responded. "Now we know it's true. We're counting on you to fill us in on the details."

Harold took her hand and walked up the stairs.

Annie stood up to welcome him. "I've got some apple pie for you inside. You can enjoy it with a hot cup of tea, as soon as you tell me everybody be all right, Mr. Harold."

"Everybody is fine," Harold assured her. "That's the most important thing for you to know."

"Abby? Carrie? Anthony?" Thomas pressed. "Have you seen them?"

Harold turned to face him. "They're fine, Thomas. I would tell you if they weren't."

Relief filled Thomas' eyes. "Thank God. What's going on? Has there been violence?"

"There has been violence," Harold confirmed. He told them about the riot at the police station the night before. "There were a lot of men hurt," he informed them, "on both sides, though the worst injuries were suffered by the Black Militia since Ellyson's police force used guns. The Black Militia and the other bystanders only had rocks."

Rose took a deep breath. "Eddie? Spencer? Micah? Carl?" She knew all of them were involved in the militia.

"They're fine," Harold repeated. "Eddie, Spencer and Carl were at the police station, but they didn't have anything more than a few cuts. They helped carry injured men to the hospital Carrie set up in the Black Quarters."

Thomas shook his head. "The hospital Carrie set up? Didn't she just arrive yesterday?"

Harold managed a grin. "Your daughter moves fast when it's necessary. Several of the women who served as her nurses during the war helped her convert a church into a hospital just in time. There were some men badly wounded, but no one died, and everyone will recover."

Rose managed a smile. As expected, Carrie had been right in the middle of the action. She would have been incapable of not helping once she'd found out she was needed.

"And Abby?" Thomas asked.

"She helped, too," Harold answered. "Carrie sent her home when the worst need had passed, along with May. They were looking rested when I saw them shortly before I left."

"What about Carrie?" Rose asked. "Why didn't she and Abby just come with you this afternoon?" When Harold hesitated and took a breath, Rose knew what was coming.

Harold held out a letter. "Carrie asked me to deliver this to you." Then he turned to Thomas with another envelope. "Abby asked me to make sure you received this."

Rose closed her eyes, realizing just how much she had needed Carrie to be on the plantation tomorrow.

"What does the letter say?" Susan pressed.

Rose knew Susan was counting on Carrie's arrival as much as she was. There were a lot of decisions to be made about Cromwell Stables that Susan needed the co-owner to agree with before moving forward. Rose ripped open the envelope carefully.

Dear Rose,

I already know you're worried, but I'm fine. I'm eager to be on the plantation, but I don't feel I can leave Richmond just yet. I hope there will be no more violence, but no one can count on that right now. I don't want to leave the Black Quarters without medical care. Abby and I will return to the plantation as soon as we feel they can do without us.

Love,
Carrie

The briefness of the letter told Rose how pressed Carrie was in caring for everyone.

All eyes turned to Thomas, who had just finished reading Abby's letter.

Thomas smiled slightly. "Carrie tried to talk Abby into coming to the plantation with Harold, but Abby refused. She wants to be there for Carrie, and make sure she doesn't overdo it."

"Like that could happen," Moses said with a snort. "Is she planning on shackling Carrie with chains?"

Everyone chuckled, knowing how close to the truth he was.

"Evidently, some of the men have developed an infection in their wounds. Carrie doesn't want to leave until they're all right. She promises they'll come home as soon as they're convinced they aren't needed."

"And if they're not convinced before Carrie has to return to Philadelphia in less than two weeks?" Rose asked, already knowing the answer to her question. Making her decision quickly, she turned to Moses. "I'm going to Richmond."

When Moses gave an immediate nod, she realized he already knew what her course of action would be once she received this news. She looked at Annie next.

"You go on," Annie encouraged her. "Me and Miles will look after our grandbabies. You just bring Miss Carrie back here so she can see ever'body."

"And that horse of hers," Miles added. "I swear Granite spends more time looking down the road for Carrie than he does anything else."

Rose looked at him more closely, alerted by something in his voice that made her uncomfortable. "Is Granite all right?" Even having to ask the question made her sad. The massive Thoroughbred had been a part of their lives for so long that she couldn't imagine him not being on the plantation. She also couldn't imagine Carrie having to deal with losing her beloved horse.

"He's doing fine," Miles answered, "but he ain't gettin' no younger."

Rose saw in his eyes what he wouldn't speak in words. Her determination to bring Carrie back to the plantation grew stronger than ever.

"Is the city safe for my wife?" Moses asked. "I know better than to try and change her mind, but how worried should I be?"

Harold considered his question and then answered carefully. "Richmond is a powder keg right now. General Canby sent in some troops to cool things off between Mayor Chahoon and Ellyson's police officers, but it seems everyone in the city is taking sides. When I was riding out of town, I saw several fistfights and more verbal altercations than I could count. Sentiments and tempers are running high."

Moses frowned.

Rose spoke before he could argue against her going. "I'll be careful," she said. "Jeb can take me into the city. I promise to stay close to the house."

Moses shook his head. "Don't make a promise you can't keep. You and I already know that if Carrie needs you, you'll be down in the Quarters helping her."

Rose sighed, knowing he was right. "I'll still be careful," she insisted.

"I believe she'll be safe," Harold said thoughtfully. "Things are going to be very tense until the courts resolve this, but I believe General Canby's troops will keep a lid on the worst of it. The threat of going back under Federal control will keep most of it in check."

"Would you let Susan go?" Moses asked sharply.

Harold sighed. "I wouldn't be any happier about it than you are about letting Rose go, but yes, I would."

Moses considered his answer before he replied. With a look of resignation, he said, "Thank you, Harold. I learned a long time ago not to try and stop my wife from doing what she believes she should do, but at least I'll feel a little better about it."

Thomas smiled at Rose. "You do realize that strong-willed women are the bane of loving husbands, don't you?"

"We are also your salvation, Rose retorted with a smirk. "Think how boring life would be without all your strong-willed women."

"Boring?" Thomas asked. "Perhaps. But certainly more peaceful", he teased. He turned to Moses. "I believe I can put your mind more at rest, Moses. I'm going into Richmond, too. There is no need to send Jeb. I'll drive the carriage myself. When Abby and Carrie are ready to come home, I'll bring them."

"Thank you, Thomas," Moses said. "I was trying to figure out how I could get away from the plantation myself, but leaving right at the beginning of planting season is not a good idea."

Rose grinned, happy to admit how relieved she was. Jeb would do anything to protect her, but she knew going into a racially fraught situation with Thomas would offer far more security. At least, she hoped it would...and Moses obviously believed it would.

Thomas nodded. "I'll do my best to keep all the women we love out of danger. However much of an impossible task that is, it seems to be our lot in life." His eyes glimmered with humor as he exchanged a long look with Moses, and then smiled at Rose.

Rose's only response was a glare and a haughty sniff.

She turned to watch the sun slip below the horizon, the first evening stars popping out into the darkening sky. Her mind was now centered on thinking through all the things she needed to do before she left in the morning.

Chapter Six

Carrie slowly woke as the sounds of Richmond filtered in through the open window of her bedroom - barking dogs, the rattle of carriage wheels, and the distant sound of the train whistle mingled with children laughing and playing in the gloriously warm spring air. Stretching luxuriously, she allowed the soft breeze to play over her face. For the first time since her arrival in Richmond three days earlier, she actually felt rested. Two of the militia had developed infections that required constant care. She could have left them to the care of the nurses, but with only two patients remaining, she had wanted to stay with them. One of them was Ben Scott. Although she knew that Ellyson's police force was putting out an intensive effort to find him, so far, no one had revealed his location.

His fever had finally broken early that morning.

After the nurses had assured her they could handle his care, Carrie had finally been persuaded to go home and get some rest. She and Abby had departed Philadelphia on an early train, which meant that by the time she left the hospital, she had been awake for forty-eight hours. Everything about her had felt the reality of those hours as she stumbled through the front door of her Richmond home, bleary-eyed with fatigue. May fixed her a big breakfast, of which Carrie managed to eat at least half before nearly falling asleep at the table. Abby had then led her upstairs and forced her to take a short bath in the steaming water Micah had fetched while Carrie was eating. When Abby told her to sleep for as long as she could, Carrie had not needed persuading, and was now certain she'd fallen asleep before her head even hit the pillow.

From the angle the sun was hitting her pillow, it seemed she'd been asleep for almost ten hours. As she continued to regain consciousness, Carrie wondered what had happened in the city while she'd slept. Was Ben in jail? She worried his infection would return if he didn't receive proper care. She was quite certain it wouldn't matter to Ellyson's men if he lived or died.

As her certainty of that fact grew, an idea sprang to her mind. Would it be possible to get Ben out of the city? Her thoughts turned to the time she and Robert had managed to help Matthew escape after he had broken out of Libby Prison during the war.

As she thought about the possibility, all sleep fled from her mind. She threw back the covers and hurried to the washstand to clean her face. Gazing out the window at the riotous colors of the azaleas lining every house on the block, she pulled her hair back into a long braid. Since she didn't have plans to go anywhere, it wasn't necessary to put it into the chaste bun that Richmond society deemed acceptable. If she was called out on an emergency, she could always fix it quickly.

Her mind turned longingly to the plantation. There was no need for bonnets or restraining her hair. Her breeches were waiting for her. So was her horse. Spring always awakened the yearning for wild horseback rides across the plantation, and she already knew how beautiful her secret place would be this time of year. Just thinking about it made her smile. Her secret place was hardly a *secret* anymore because she had shared it with so many people, but there were still only a few that could navigate the hidden deer trails to actually find it on their own.

The sound of laughter downstairs made her cock her head to listen more closely. The next round of mirth caused a laugh of her own to escape her lips. She would recognize her father's laugh anywhere.

Slipping into her dress quickly, Carrie made her way downstairs, sniffing appreciatively at the aroma of country ham and sweet potatoes. Fully awake now, she realized she was starving.

"Father!"

Thomas looked up from the table and smiled warmly. "Carrie!" He rose to hug her close. "I'm glad to see you're all right. I never know with the two women in my life, so I had to come find out for myself. Abby assured me you're fine, but I wanted to see you with my own eyes."

"I'm so happy to see you," Carrie said sincerely.

"Are you happy to see me, too?"

Carrie whirled around so fast she almost tripped on her dress. "Rose!" She laughed loudly and wrapped her arms around her best friend for a long moment. "What are you doing here?" she asked when she finally released her.

"When Harold told us you weren't willing to leave Richmond until you knew everyone would recover, I decided to come to you," Rose replied. "I've missed you terribly. The idea of not spending time with you on the plantation before you have to go back to Philadelphia was unbearable, so here I am!"

Carrie looked at her friend closely. Rose's voice was cheerful, but her eyes spoke another story. No one else might see what she was trying to hide, but Carrie knew her too well. She was glad they would have time to talk later. "I'm so glad you're here," she said enthusiastically.

Then she turned to her father, eager for news. Even though he'd probably only been in town for a few hours, she was sure he would know what was happening in the city. "What have you learned since you've been here?"

Thomas didn't disappoint her.

"Neither man is going to budge. I've spoken to a few of my friends while we were waiting for you to wake up." Thomas shook his head. "The situation is tense. In addition to choosing Ellyson to be the new mayor, the City Council has chosen John Poe to be the chief of police."

Micah entered the room in time to hear Thomas' last words. "That won't be no good for the black folk around here. That Mr. Poe don't care much for blacks. He figures we need to stay in our place."

"That's true," Thomas said, his voice laced with regret. "I know both men well. They're quite conservative." He paused for a moment before continuing. "Chahoon has flatly refused to vacate City Hall and the police stations. Since Poe has been blocked from entering police headquarters, he has set up his own operation on Main Street near Shockoe Bottom. He deputized the officers who clashed with the militia two nights ago, and he's busy building the force even bigger."

Carrie's eyes widened. "Is he building a police force or an army?"

"That's a good question," her father said grimly. "Mayor Chahoon has appealed to the governor for help, but Walker is standing behind the City Council."

Carrie listened closely. "What happens now?"

Thomas shrugged. "It's going to become an issue for the courts. I suspect the decision will ultimately be made by the Virginia Court of Appeals."

Carrie frowned. "That could take quite a while."

"I suspect it will," her father agreed. "The challenge will be keeping things under control until a decision is made. At some point, one of the two men will have to admit defeat and back down."

Rose had listened quietly until now. "Ellyson and Poe are both very conservative. What *will* that mean for the blacks in Richmond?"

"Unfortunately, it's going to make things more difficult," Thomas admitted. "After five years of federal control, I suspected this would happen soon, but I hoped I was wrong.

"It's going to happen all over the South," Abby said resignedly.

"Yes," Thomas agreed.

"So, blacks aren't slaves anymore, but everything is being put back in position to keep us in submission," Rose said bitterly.

Thomas looked at her sadly. "I wish I could tell you that isn't true, but I would be lying."

"That doesn't mean you don't still have power, Rose," Abby said gently. "You've always known you would have to fight for what you wanted. Nothing has changed."

"Perhaps," Rose agreed, her voice still bitter, "but at least we could pretend we had some protection when the federal government was helping us. Now that all the Southern states are being accepted back into the Union, those protections are going to disappear."

"I don't believe that's true," Thomas protested. "President Grant is still very committed to meaningful reconstruction that will make things better not only for former slaves, but for all black people."

Rose thought about what Jeb had said just the day before on their way home from school. "Jeb said something to me yesterday." She repeated the words that had been playing over and over in her mind. *"I know the president wants to do that, but wanting to do it and actually being able to do it are two different things. The South is real big. It's going to be hard to control it all."*

Carrie watched Rose carefully. Her usually optimistic friend was struggling. She didn't know what had triggered it, but she was certainly going to find out.

Abby stood, walked over to where Rose was standing, and pulled her into an embrace. "You're not alone, Rose. There is a huge battle to fight, but there are a lot of people fighting it with you."

Rose smiled but continued to look thoughtful. "I know there are many people who care, but no one cares as much as the black people who deal with it on a daily basis. As much as all of you care," she continued, "at the end of the day, you don't deal with what we do, because you're white. Only another black person can truly understand what it feels like to be black."

A long silence met her words.

As much as Carrie wanted to refute them, she knew they were true.

Thomas was the first to break the silence. "I understand what you're saying, Rose, but I think you're underestimating the ability of people to relate to something they can't truly know. I can't possibly know what it's like to be a woman, but over the years, I've learned to truly respect and appreciate women as absolute equals. I will do whatever it takes to fight for their rights because there are so many women I care about deeply. How could I do any less?"

Carrie's heart swelled with love for her father.

"I belicve the same is true for blacks," Thomas continued. "You're right that I can't truly understand what it's like to be black, but neither can you understand what it's like to be white. Or Navajo, like Chooli. You *choose* to have compassion and empathy. You *choose* to try and understand the life that someone different from you lives. All of us have certain core values and beliefs ingrained in us from our experiences of life. We can choose to doggedly live with them, or we can choose to change them when presented with opposing evidence."

Rose's eyes softened. "Like you did."

"I hope so," Thomas replied. "I believe I'm still changing every day. I suppose I always will be. I understand that blacks face a tremendously difficult struggle to gain rights in America, but I for one, will do everything within my power to help you."

"Could that have something to do with the fact that you're my big brother?" Rose teased, her eyes losing some of their bitterness.

Carrie chuckled. She remembered the day her father had discovered that Rose was actually his half-sister, the result of their father raping Sarah. The two of them had come quite a long way.

"I suppose that could be a part of it," Thomas replied with a smile, "but my feelings now extend to the entire race. A grave injustice was done to your people when they were brought to this country as slaves. I wish it could be undone with a proclamation of emancipation, but it will take far more than that to change people's hearts and minds." He paused thoughtfully. "You're right that I will always have the privilege of being white, but you can also see that as a benefit for yourself."

Rose cocked her brow. "How?"

Abby was the one who answered the question. "Because it was an army of white people who finally won the fight for the abolition of slavery. There were certainly many black people who fought alongside us, but our voices were better heard because we weren't fighting for something just to benefit ourselves, we were fighting for the *right* thing. It took time, but finally our voices could no longer be ignored."

"The same thing is happening now," Thomas added. "It will be a long fight, but as long as we don't give up, the day will come when things are better for black Americans."

Rose took a deep breath. "Better or equal?"

Abby smiled sadly. "That's a question a lot of people are asking, Rose. Blacks, women, Indians, the Irish, and so many of the immigrants pouring into our country. All we can do is fight." Her gray eyes flashed with determination. "And we will fight," she vowed.

Rose considered Abby's words. The last of the bitterness vanished with her smile. "So, grow up and stop feeling sorry for myself?" Abby opened her mouth to protest, but Rose raised a hand to stop her. "I know you weren't saying that, but it's true. There are a lot of people fighting for justice in America. If we ever hope to have equality, we can't just fight for ourselves, we must fight for equality for everyone."

Abby smiled. "Well said, Rose. And yes, I believe you're absolutely right. If we ever want *individual* equality, we must fight for equality for everyone. That's the only way America will truly become what everyone hopes it will be."

*****

Carrie patted the bedroom window seat cushion next to her. "Come join me," she invited, enjoying the feel of the air caressing her neck. Just two nights ago, the temperatures had threatened to dip below freezing. Tonight, the breeze carried the warmth of spring, even though night had swallowed the day. Flickering light from the lampposts illuminated the new green leaves of the oak trees. Anthony knew she needed time with Rose, so he was downstairs talking to her father.

Rose, standing by the other window, smiled hesitantly. "I'm not sure I want to."

"You probably don't," Carrie responded, "but you know I'm not going to let you leave this room until you've told me what's going on."

"Nothing is going on," Rose said weakly, and then managed an even weaker chuckle. "Oh, there's no point in playing this game. We both know I'm going to tell you." She sat down next to Carrie with an air of resignation.

Carrie nodded. "Talk. What has triggered this bitterness and fear?"

Rose shook her head. "Was it that obvious?" Fatigue shadowed her eyes.

"Only to me and Abby," Carrie assured her. "And before you ask, no, Abby and I haven't talked about it, but I could tell she realized what you were feeling."

"Thomas?"

Carrie smiled. "I'm fairly certain he was oblivious, but not because he doesn't care. However, that's not the issue here. What's going on?"

Rose sighed dramatically and then stood to pace around the room. Finally, she turned back to Carrie. "I didn't realize how much it bothered me." She fell silent after the brief proclamation.

Carrie waited several moments before prompting, "How much *what* bothered you?"

"Alvin's visit to the school two days ago."

"Alvin?" Carrie asked with a frown. "Why would Alvin's visit bother you? I'm assuming he came to get more medicine?"

"Yes." Rose paused, gathering her thoughts. "He told me there are other men who want the Hypericum. They've heard about how well the treatment is working, and they want some for themselves."

"I'm sure they do," Carrie said calmly. "What did you tell him?" She was going to have to pull the story from her usually verbal friend.

"That you planned on seeing more men when you were at the clinic during the next two weeks, and that you would do the best you could."

"That's true," Carrie said, puzzled as to why this had upset Rose so badly. "I've brought a lot of Hypericum with me." She waited, hoping more conversation would enlighten her.

Rose turned to stare out the window, her beautiful face reflected in the glass as the curtains billowed around her softly. "There has been no more violence, Carric. Not since you helped those men. They promised they wouldn't take part in any more violence." She paused. "They have kept their promise."

"That's a good thing," Carrie said, alarmed at the naked vulnerability in Rose's voice.

"Of course it's a wonderful thing," Rose cried, "but what if it doesn't last? What if the violence starts again?"

Carrie suddenly put all the pieces together. "You're afraid of what will happen if I don't make it to the plantation and start the new men on their medicine."

Rose looked at her, not denying the truth of her words. "I know you won't send medicine back to the plantation with me."

Carrie nodded. "It's true that I want to see the men first." Even though the homeopathic remedy she was using to treat the amputee veterans was harmless, if it wasn't administered correctly it could produce no results at all. These men had lived with enough pain and disappointment—she wouldn't add to it. As she had dozens of times since first seeing the men in December, Carrie wished Polly would treat the veterans. Polly handled everything else at the clinic, but she refused to help anyone who had been even remotely involved in the attack on the plantation that had killed Robert.

Rose nodded, her eyes sparkling with fresh anxiety. "Alvin told me that the men who don't have medicine yet, already have their hopes up."

Carrie continued to fit the pieces together. "You believe the violence could start again as a way to force us to give them the medicine." Unfortunately, she could easily see that scenario playing out.

Rose nodded again. "Alvin told me he didn't think they would do anything, but I could tell he didn't really believe it. He said that men in pain don't always think straight."

Carrie was alarmed at the panic shining in her friend's eyes again. "Rose, what aren't you telling me?"

Rose stared at her. "Nothing. I'm telling you the truth." She jumped up and began to pace the room.

Carrie shook her head. "It's not like you for something like this to create so much fear and anxiety. Are you sure something else didn't happen?"

"No, but that's the whole point," Rose blurted out. "Nothing has happened for three whole months. *Nothing.*" She took a deep breath. "Do you know how long it's been since *nothing* has happened in three months?"

Carrie understood. "Since we were children," she said softly.

Tears filled Rose's eyes as she sat back down on the window seat. "I know I should be grateful that three months have passed without something traumatic happening, but I find myself constantly waiting for the next thing, for the next attack. The day Alvin came by, I was standing in the school thinking about what a beautiful, *peaceful* spring it was. I yearned to have a whole spring that was simply peaceful." She shook her head ruefully. "Alvin's words were the first blow to the peace I had imagined. Harold's arrival with the news about Richmond shredded any remaining hope." She turned away from Carrie to stare wildly out the window.

"Your heart is tired," Carrie said gently.

"Isn't yours?" Rose demanded, swiping angrily at the tears rolling down her cheeks.

"Not as tired as yours," Carrie assured her. "I've been in Philadelphia where things aren't as volatile. And, as you so accurately pointed out earlier, I don't carry the burden of being black. I have the struggle of being a woman doctor, but I'm dealing with the consequences of decisions I made for myself. If I want to blend in without standing out, I can choose to do that." She reached out and took Rose's hand. "You never have that choice, and you live with the reality that there are many people who wish you harm simply because of your color."

Rose slumped with defeat. "I suppose that's the hardest thing. Moses and I can never relax. Two days ago, I wanted to pretend we could. We can't." Her voice shook as she continued. "I have to live with knowing my children are always in danger, just because of their color. It doesn't really matter how well they speak, or how educated they are. Too many people look at them and simply see the color of their skin. How do they fight that? How do *I* fight that?"

"One action at a time," Carrie answered. She longed to wrap Rose in her arms, but right now, her friend needed courage more than she needed comforting. That would come later. Her mind searched for a way to break through Rose's darkness. "What would your mama say, Rose?"

Rose shook her head. "That won't work this time, Carrie. Mama could never have guessed a time like this would happen."

"You know that's not true," Carrie chided. "Your mama dreamed of freedom. She wanted it for you and Moses more than anything. She watched friends escape to freedom through the Underground Railroad. If your mama had been younger, she would have been with them."

Rose sighed. "I know you're right," she muttered, "but would Mama have realized that freedom might not truly mean freedom?"

"Your mama endured more than any woman should ever have to," Carrie said sadly. "She spent her life seeing the worst in people." She paused, remembering Old Sarah's glowing eyes. "But she also saw the best. I don't believe anything happening now would surprise her."

"I suppose not," Rose admitted reluctantly.

"So, what would your mama have said?" Carrie persisted. When Rose remained silent, she waited.

The silence stretched out for several minutes.

"How long are you going to wait?" Rose demanded.

Carrie smiled. "As long as it takes."

"There are times when having a best friend who knows you better than you know yourself is a hardship," Rose complained.

"Trust me," Carrie replied wryly, "you're not telling me anything I don't already know. You have been that to me more times than I can count."

"I'd rather be on that side of the conversation."

"I'm sure," Carrie conceded, certain that now was not the time to relent. "I'm still waiting, however, to hear what your mama would say."

Rose grunted but maintained her silence. Carrie could tell she was thinking deeply.

Rose finally cleared her throat. "I remember a day not too long after I realized I was in love with Moses. I was telling my mama that I was afraid to love him because I didn't want to ever endure the pain of being separated from him by the auction block." She took a deep breath. "Mama told me that Moses' deep love would give me strength. She told me that loving Moses so much would give me courage." Her voice wavered. "I believed that for a long time, but I seem to have lost my courage. I love Moses and our children so much, my heart hurts. I couldn't possibly love them more deeply. Why isn't it giving me courage?"

Carrie remained quiet, knowing Rose had to answer the question for herself. She could almost feel the battle going on in her friend's heart.

Rose finally looked up. "I remember something else Mama said."

Carrie cocked a brow.

"Mama told me *dat strength don't come from winnin.*" Rose slipped easily into Old Sarah's voice. "*Dat our struggles be what make us strong. Dat when you goes through somethin' real bad and decide to not never give up, dat be strength.*"

Carrie smiled. "Your mama never gave up."

"No, she didn't," Rose agreed. "Even though she knew she would die a slave on the plantation, she believed *my* life would be very different. She prepared me for a different life the best she could."

"Like you're doing for *your* children?" Carrie asked.

Rose gazed at her for a long moment. *"When you goes through somethin' real bad and decide to not never give up, that be strength,"* she murmured. Her eyes finally cleared. "How long will it take me to truly grasp that? Why do I keep wallowing in fear?" Disgust dripped from her voice.

"Probably as long as it will take me," Carrie replied. "But as long as we have each other to remind us what is true, we'll keep choosing courage over fear. However, I would like to add that you most certainly don't wallow in fear. You're the most courageous person I know, Rose. But you're also human. It's all right to be tired occasionally."

Her words settled into the night air, seeming to dance with the shadows cast by the flickering lantern oil. Another long silence passed, but this one was far more peaceful.

"Am I ready to choose courage over fear?" Rose wondered out loud.

"You're the only one who can decide that," Carrie answered, but the light she saw shining in Rose's eyes again had already given her the answer. Her friend had reached deep inside to find hope again. "Biddy told me something once that I've never forgotten. She told me hope is like the sun. If we keep on traveling toward it, the sun casts the shadow of our burdens behind us."

Rose considered those words for a few moments. "Hope casts the shadow of our burdens behind us," she murmured. "I like that. Mama lived that way every day."

"I doubt it," Carrie replied. "I can pretty much guarantee your mama had days when she felt no hope at all. Days when she wondered if she could possibly live through what was happening to her. Days she wondered if she wanted to."

Rose looked startled, and then thoughtful. "You're right, Carrie. Of course, my mama felt all the things I'm feeling now. She just kept choosing hope."

Carrie nodded with relief. "Abby told me something recently. We were talking about hope for our country. She told me there will be times when we can see only misty shadows of hope, but we have to keep moving forward."

Rose smiled. "Misty shadows of hope. That's wonderful. I'm going to hang onto that when I tremble with fear over what might be coming." Her face suddenly looked very determined. "I'm also going to create some hope on my own."

Carrie was overjoyed to see the life return to her friend's eyes. "What do you mean?"

"You're returning to the plantation with your father and me," Rose said firmly. "I may not be able to change the entire country, but I can help make our small part of it safer. There may be people here who need you, but there are also people around the plantation who need you, including everyone *on* the plantation."

Carrie smiled. "We leave in the morning."

"Really?" Rose asked with a gasp of delight.

Carrie nodded. "I told Father and Abby right before I came up. Jasmine came by with a report. Ben and the other man are going to be fine, and the hospital is already set up. If there is more violence, the women can take care of most things. I believe it's safe to leave the city."

Rose smiled happily, but then her eyes narrowed. "What aren't you telling me?"

"Excuse me?" Carrie sputtered. She had been sure Rose was too entrenched in her own problems to notice anything else.

Rose sat back, examining her closely. "You heard me."

Carrie struggled to look nonchalant but finally chuckled. "I truly don't know why either of us even attempts to hide something from the other. It's useless."

"True," Rose acknowledged. "What are you hiding?"

Carrie lowered her voice to make absolutely certain anyone passing by the house couldn't hear her through the open window. "We're taking Ben Scott with us," she admitted in a voice close to a whisper.

"Ben Scott?" Rose's eyes widened. "The man who was shot?" *she* hissed. "The one wanted by Ellyson's police force for murdering one of their men during the riot?"

"He didn't do it," Carrie said quickly. "I talked to him, but then I also talked to Spencer and some of the other militia. Ben wasn't even close to the policeman who was killed by a rock that struck his head. There was too much chaos for anyone to know who threw that rock. They're simply blaming him because he's already been in trouble for trying to fight for black equality."

"It's an easy way to get rid of him," Rose said bluntly.

Carrie nodded. "It's just a matter of time before they find him. I doubt he'll get a fair trial, and I fear what will happen to him if he's taken to jail."

"He'd never get out alive."

Carrie didn't bother to argue the truth. "I talked to Father about it. He knows about the time Robert and I snuck Matthew out of the city during the war. It won't really be too difficult."

Rose narrowed her eyes. "Your father agreed to this?" she asked skeptically.

"He did."

Rose stared at her for a long moment, absorbing the news. "Just where do you plan to hide him in the carriage? He'll hardly fit into the few inches under the floorboard, and it's too warm to bury him under the blankets and attempt to pass him off as one of your hired servants."

"We're taking the wagon," Carrie explained. "Father is going to buy a large quantity of supplies for the plantation. Ben is still at the church, but Eddie is going to bring him to an alley that's well-hidden early tomorrow morning. We'll hide Ben beneath the supplies until we're well out of town."

Rose nodded thoughtfully. "And once we get to the plantation?"

Carrie shrugged. "It will take time for him to recover from his bullet wound. He'll have the opportunity to decide what he wants to do. I suspect he'll choose to go somewhere else, but that will be up to him. We're just going to make sure he's not imprisoned and unfairly tried."

Rose's eyes lit with appreciation. "I hope it works. Ben deserves a chance for freedom."

Carrie waited for her to ask the next obvious question, but Rose remained silent. She didn't need to ask what would happen if they were caught - they already knew the answer. Thomas' standing in the community wouldn't protect them from aiding and abetting a wanted killer, especially in the current political climate. Most likely, all of them would end up in jail with Ben Scott.

Carrie refused to worry about the possible consequences. It was the right thing to do.

*****

When Carrie heard the rattle of wagon wheels outside on the cobblestones the next morning, a quick glance at the grandfather clock in the corner told her it could only be her father. The sun wasn't up yet, but the hardware store and lumber supply store would be opening soon.

Leaping out of bed, she quickly dressed and went down to the kitchen. May was busy flipping hotcakes in a huge, cast iron skillet. Leftover slices of country ham from last night's dinner sizzled in another skillet. The combined smell was heavenly, but there was only one thing Carrie was interested in right now.

"Would you like some coffee?" Abby asked with a smile.

Carrie eagerly reached for the cup Abby was holding out. "Thank you! I never really understood the appeal of coffee until I worked at Chimborazo Hospital during the war. Of course, we only had the real thing for six months. Once the blockades made it impossible to get any coffee, chicory and ground acorns just didn't suffice." She held the steaming cup and inhaled gratefully. "Now *this* is coffee."

"You're spoiled rotten," May said affectionately.

"Perhaps," Carrie agreed, "but it was your coffee that kept me going for the two nights I was caring for the black militia. You should be proud of yourself."

"We all have our role to play," May said matter-of-factly. "I do my small part."

Carrie and Abby exchanged an amused look. May had been invaluable as a nurse when the church hospital had filled up so rapidly.

"False modesty is wasted effort," Abby retorted. "You know none of us could make it around here without you."

May smiled. "Yep, I know that for sure. It just be a sight better to hear when it comes from someone other than myself."

Carrie and Abby were laughing when Rose strolled into the kitchen. Abby poured another cup of coffee and handed it to her.

"Umm..."

Carrie knew Rose wouldn't speak real words until she had consumed her first cup, so she turned to Abby. "Am I right that Father just left for the hardware store?"

"Yes. He's hoping to be the first customer," Abby answered. "Micah was able to get word to Eddie last night. The city is swarming with police looking for Ben, but so far they've been able to keep him hidden."

"Is he still at the church?" Carrie asked May.

"No," May answered. "Last night he was in the basement of one of the black militia, but I ain't got no idea where he ended up. They keep moving him every few hours. Eddie knows where to have him this morning, though." She smiled through sudden tears.

"Y'all are doing a fine thing. Ben Scott is a good man. He don't belong in prison, and he certainly don't deserve to die." Then she frowned. "You know y'all could get in real trouble, don't you?"

Carrie shrugged, determined not to show how worried she was. "It won't be the first time we did something that could get us in real trouble."

"You be careful," May answered sternly. "I don't have any idea how I would get all of you out of jail."

"No one is going to jail," Abby soothed.

Rose finished the last swallow of her coffee. "It's going to be all right, May," she said confidently.

Carrie hoped Rose was right.

Chapter Seven

Lillian Richardson hummed lightly as she finished stirring the banked coals in the schoolhouse woodstove. She watched as the live coals sparked the kindling she had carefully piled. As the small pieces of wood burst into flame, she slowly added larger pieces until the fire was roaring. Only then did she close the cast iron door and step back. The fire wouldn't be needed soon, but the children appreciated the warmth when they arrived at school. The days were warm, but the mornings still started out chilly.

She made sure all the supplies were ready for the day ahead, and then turned to gaze out the window at the exploding wildflowers. Just two days of warm, sunny weather had coaxed them from their winter hiding places. Trillium created vivid splashes of white in the undergrowth, while a carpet of bluebells covered the woods to the right of the schoolhouse. White dogwoods arched their graceful branches over the forest floor. Skunk cabbage grew along the soggy creek bank, its beautiful yellow blooms making up for its namesake odor.

Lillian had learned to love spring in Virginia since her arrival from the North two years earlier. Knowing that her family outside Detroit, Michigan were probably still encased in snow, made the weather all the more pleasant. Lillian had even learned to endure the hot, humid summers with minimum complaints.

The sound of hoof beats pulled her away from the window. She was always the first to arrive at school, but had made certain to arrive earlier since Rose was away in Richmond. She wasn't expecting anyone, but she had no cause for alarm. As she walked toward the door, she pushed aside Moses' warning to not let her guard down. She was tired of always being prepared for danger.

Lillian stepped out onto the porch as three horsemen pulled to a stop at the foot of the steps. "Hello, gentlemen," she said pleasantly.

The tallest man, obviously a veteran who had lost his right arm in the war, frowned. "You ain't Mrs. Samuels."

"No," she agreed. "My name is Lillian Richardson. Mrs. Samuels and I are the teachers here at the school."

Another man with a narrow face and squinty eyes glared at her with something close to disgust. "You always teach school in pants, Mrs. Richardson?"

"I do," Lillian returned evenly, feeling the first stirrings of alarm. She wished she had taken Jeb up on his offer to accompany her that morning. It would be another thirty minutes until he arrived for the start of school. She had known from the beginning of her arrival in Virginia that her insistence on wearing clothes she was comfortable in would make her a target for some people, but she wasn't interested in changing. Her choice of clothing had absolutely nothing to do with the fact that she was homosexual. It was a matter of comfort.

"You ain't no Southern lady," the third man snapped. He was short and barrel-chested, with beady, brown eyes.

Lillian watched him carefully, relieved she had at least tucked her revolver in her pants before leaving the plantation that morning. "As a matter of fact, I'm not," she said amicably, hoping she could still diffuse the situation. "I'm from Michigan." They didn't need to know anything else about her.

"A Yankee," the short man spat out with a snort of disdain.

Lillian remained silent for several moments, holding his eyes fearlessly before speaking again. "What can I do for you gentlemen?" she asked in a firm voice, to show she wasn't afraid of them.

"Where's Mrs. Samuels?" the first man asked.

"In Richmond," Lillian replied. "She had to make an unanticipated trip into the city. Was she expecting you?"

"No," he admitted. "But it don't really matter. We were told to ask for her, but she ain't who we're here to see. We're here to see Dr. Wallington."

Lillian smiled, determined to remain pleasant. "I'm sorry, but she's not here either. She was delayed in Richmond."

"When is she going to be here?" the second man snapped. "We need to see her."

"I'm not certain," Lillian answered carefully, knowing it wasn't the answer they were looking for. "I do know she'll be here as soon as possible." She decided not to mention the violence and riot in Richmond. She suspected it would do nothing but rile these men up.

The first man scowled. "We were told she was coming."

Lillian, watching him closely, saw what he was trying to hide. "You're in pain," she said sympathetically.

He shrugged and continued to scowl, but didn't look quite as threatening. He seemed surprised that she'd seen past his menacing façade.

The beady-eyed man was not as accommodating. "There are a whole lot of us in pain," he snapped. "Thanks to you Yankees."

Lillian knew better than to argue the facts of the war, so she kept her voice calm. "I know Dr. Wallington wants to help everyone she can, gentlemen."

"We aren't gentlemen!" the beady-eyed man snapped. "And we aim to get what we need."

"Is that right?" Lillian asked, allowing some of the anger she was feeling to seep into her voice. "I believe you'll find Dr. Wallington prefers to help men who are civil. You might want to look elsewhere for help if that's too difficult." She knew she was treading on thin ice, but enough was enough.

The man flushed, but the anger didn't fade from his eyes.

Lillian was surprised when a spark of compassion flared in her. It was obvious the tall man was missing an arm, but she couldn't tell with the other two horsemen.   "Why do you need Dr. Wallington?" she asked

The narrow-faced man was the one to answer. "Me and Carson lost part of our legs in the war, Miss Richardson." His earlier antagonism seemed to have been swallowed by her willingness to confront them. He pulled up his pant leg just far enough to reveal a wooden stump.

Lillian was surprised. "You both ride so well. I never would have guessed."

"You do what you have to do," Carson muttered. Now that his secret was out, he seemed a little more talkative. "I lost my leg at Cold Harbor. Bob lost his leg in Petersburg. Larry lost his arm to a bullet in Vicksburg."

"And you've been hurting ever since," Lillian responded.

"That's right," Larry said. "We heard Dr. Wallington has helped other amputees. We're hoping she can help us."

"I know she'll want to," Lillian said. Suddenly, the men didn't seem so threatening. They were simply human beings in intense pain who were desperate for relief. Once they'd realized their intimidating approach wasn't going to be effective, they had quickly backed down.

"You got any idea when she'll be here?" Larry asked. "We can keep coming every day."

Lillian thought quickly. They might be calmer now, but she didn't want them to think she was putting them off. "That's a good idea," she agreed. "I know Dr. Wallington is going to come as soon as she can, but I honestly don't know when that will be." She pushed aside the thought that events in Richmond might keep Carrie from making it to the plantation at all. If she treated the men courteously every time they arrived, perhaps she could stave off any trouble.

The sound of laughter drifted to her from down the road. "I'm sorry, but you'll have to excuse me now. My students are about to arrive."

The three men nodded and turned their horses away as the first group of children rounded the curve closest to the schoolhouse.

Beady-eyed Carson—as she had decided to call him—whipped around to glare at her. "I heard you got white children learning with niggers at this school. I didn't believe it, but now I'm seeing it with my own eyes. That ain't right!"

"I'm sorry you feel that way," Lillian replied. "Thankfully, not everyone does. The parents of our white children are quite grateful for their education. They had no school at all until Mrs. Samuels welcomed them to join her black students." She was having to work harder to keep her voice civil. "And now, if you'll excuse me..." Lillian turned away, glad to have the distraction of the children running into the schoolyard.

Carson muttered something under his breath, but wheeled his horse around and trotted off. The other men didn't look any happier, but they remained silent as they followed him.

Lillian knew they were being kept under control by the hope that Carrie could help them. She breathed a silent prayer that Carrie would arrive home soon with a large quantity of Hypericum.

"Miss Lillian! Look at what I found on the way to school!"

Lillian turned to greet nine-year-old Silas Williams. "Good morning, Silas. What did you find?" She pushed thoughts of the men out of her mind. It was time to be a teacher.

*****

Thomas was grateful for his coat as he navigated the wagon through the crowded streets. He wouldn't need it for long, but the early spring morning was still chilly. It was a sign of the times that Broad Street was already crowded, even before the sun was fully up. Businesses were still closed, but the factories and manufacturing plants were already in full operation. Working men thronged the sidewalks, calling to each other in the still morning air. The shriek of the train whistle spoke of early morning passengers coming and going.

He stiffened when he saw a contingent of police officers round the corner closest to Ellyson's police station on Main Street. As he watched, they split into teams of two, and then walked slowly down the street, staring carefully at every black man they passed.

Thomas knew they were looking for Ben Scott, as well as trying to intimidate as many blacks as they could. He pushed aside his nervous feeling. There was nothing about a white man in an empty wagon to arouse their curiosity.

"Good morning, Mr. Cromwell!"

Thomas smiled at the man who waved to him from the loading platform as he pulled up to the hardware store. "Hello, Oliver! When did you start working here?"

"Not long after the factory burned, Mr. Cromwell," Oliver replied. "That recommendation you gave me got me a job real quick. I'm real grateful."

"You're a good worker, Oliver," Thomas answered, relieved to know that another of the factory employees had gotten a job. He was sure Oliver was paid less than the white workers, but at least he had employment.

"How's Mrs. Cromwell?" Oliver asked. "She sure be a fine lady."

"I couldn't agree with you more," Thomas said cheerfully, determined to treat this trip to the hardware store like any other. "She's doing very well. She'll be happy to know you're working here."

"You send my greetings," Oliver answered, and then reached for the sheet of paper Thomas held out to him. "This be a whole lot of supplies," he said with a whistle.

"There's a lot of work being done on the plantation," Thomas answered easily. He was sure Moses would be surprised when he saw the loaded wagon rolling down the drive, but he would understand as soon as they explained the situation. Everything would be used eventually, even if it wasn't needed now. "Do you think I can get these supplies quickly? I'm rather eager to get back home."

"Yes'sir," Oliver answered. "I'll get right on it. Shouldn't take me too long." He turned away and disappeared into the store.

"In a hurry, Mr. Cromwell?"

Thomas turned to see two of Ellyson's police force approaching his wagon. Keeping his voice and face calm, he shrugged. "It's planting season. There's always a lot of work to be done on the plantation. My men are waiting for these supplies."

"Your daughter going back home with you?"

Thomas fought to keep his face impassive. What did they know about Carrie? Why were they asking? How did they know she was in town? The questions spun through his mind. "As a matter of fact, she is. My daughter is in town for a visit. You might know she is doing her surgical internship up in Philadelphia."

"Yes," one of the men replied. "We heard about that." He paused, watching Thomas carefully. "Does that explain why she was down in the Black Quarters the night of the riot when Ben Scott killed one of the police force?"

Thomas shook his head. "I'm sorry you lost one of your men, but I just arrived in town yesterday afternoon. I don't know anything about that."

"That right?" the second officer asked skeptically.

"That's right," Thomas replied, determined not to antagonize the men. As much as he resented their knowledge and their questions, newly minted police officers were usually eager to display their recently bestowed power. He didn't mind going up against them, but there were other things more important to attend to right now.

"I heard you changed," the first officer said sharply.

"Changed?" Thomas asked with a smile. "And, what is your name?"

"Austin Dowswell."

Thomas eyed the stout young man with red hair and a wispy beard. "Harry Dowswell's son?" He decided not to mention that there was no love lost between him and the officer's father, but by the look on Austin's face, he already knew that.

"That's right." Austin's eyes were like flint. "My father told me you were a staunch Confederate during the war."

"That's true," Thomas agreed, hoping Oliver was moving quickly so that he would have an excuse to leave.

"Now we hear you got niggers working for you out at Cromwell Plantation."

"A lot of plantation owners are smart enough to have experienced tobacco field hands working for them," Thomas said evasively.

"What'd be smart is if you weren't paying more than everyone else in Virginia," Austin retorted.

Thomas bit back his sigh. Austin's father owned a plantation a little north of Richmond. Thomas and Moses' business practices on the plantation were cause for a lot of consternation and anger among other plantation owners who didn't seem to realize the profitability of treating the freed slaves like valued employees. Besides the fact that it was the right thing to do, it also made good business sense. Men blinded by prejudice and Southern aristocratic thinking weren't able to see it that way, however.

"Well?" Austin demanded angrily.

Thomas met his eyes, tiring of the exchange. "Your father is free to run his plantation the way he wishes.

As am I." He was relieved to see Oliver appear on the loading dock, pulling a large wagon behind him.

"This here be the first of it," Oliver called, oblivious to what was being played out. "We'll start getting it loaded while the rest is collected."

"Perfect," Thomas called. He glanced back at the officers. "Will that be all, gentlemen? I have quite a busy morning."

Austin scowled but didn't stop him when he stepped down from the wagon seat. "We're watching you, Mr. Cromwell. Both you and your daughter."

Thomas forced a smile. "I'm glad to hear it. The protection will be welcome." He bit back a laugh at the look of trapped disgust on Austin's face, and then turned to Oliver. "I'll open the back of the wagon so you can start loading. I'll be inside for a few minutes."

"Yes'sir," Oliver said eagerly, as he studiously avoided the officer's perusal, keeping his eyes to the ground. He leapt down from the loading platform, and then turned back to start pulling supplies off the loading dock into the wagon.

*****

Carrie, Abby and Rose were waiting on the porch when Thomas pulled up to the house. Everything they were taking to the plantation was already beside them. Silently, so as not to draw unnecessary attention, May and Micah helped them carry everything to the wagon.

Micah eyed the wagon dubiously. "You reckon there be room under all that stuff?"

Thomas held a finger to his lips and continued to load their baggage.

Carrie felt a twinge of alarm. Her father was always cautious, but the look in his eyes revealed more than caution. A glance at Abby and Rose told her they'd noticed the same thing. Instead of asking questions they knew would go unanswered, though, they helped Thomas load the huge baskets of food May had prepared for them. There was enough food to feed ten more people, but May was incapable of not sending more food than was needed. You would have thought it took days to reach the plantation, not three to four hours.

Thomas managed a chuckle when he lifted one of the baskets. "Are we taking the entire population of Richmond with us?" he asked as he hefted it in his hand playfully.

"You can't ever have too much food," May retorted. "You never know what might happen."

Thomas eyed the sky. "It's a little too warm for a blizzard, but if one comes, we'll have enough to sustain us."

"Get on with you," May scolded. "I got work to do inside. I can't stand outside with the likes of you."

Carrie was aware their banter was part of her father's plan to not give any hint of abnormality, but she longed for him to finish the loading and depart. The sooner they were far outside of Richmond city limits, the better she would feel. She shared Micah's concern, however. The wagon seemed to be brimming with supplies. Where were they going to put Ben?

Knowing better than to ask, she settled down next to Rose in the small area that had been reserved for them at the front of the wagon. Abby climbed onto the seat next to Thomas and gave him a bright smile.

"Get 'up!" Thomas called.

It was still early enough in the morning that the streets were mostly empty, at least the residential streets on Church Hill. Carrie knew the roads in downtown Richmond would already be bustling, but first they had to locate the alley where Eddie was waiting with Ben. She prayed they would find a way to safely hide Ben without attracting attention to themselves.

*****

"Hello again, Mr. Cromwell!"

Thomas stiffened as he pulled back on the reins and brought the wagon to a halt. "Hello, officers," he said calmly. He was glad all the women in the wagon were adept at hiding their fears and feelings...from strangers at least. "What can I do for you?"

Austin Dowswell smirked at him from atop his bay gelding. "Aren't you going to introduce me to your wife and daughter?" His eyes passed over Rose as if she was of no importance.

Thomas was glad Anthony was riding out to join them tomorrow because he'd had some things to handle at River City Carriages. He doubted his son-in-law would have been able to keep his temper in check. Anthony was an easy-going man, but Austin Dowswell could irritate a corpse.

"Certainly," Thomas replied. He quickly made introductions, including Rose, though he thought it wise to leave out the fact that she was his half-sister. Mulattoes were looked down on just as much as blacks. He wouldn't put her in added danger.

"Nice to meet you, ladies," Austin said snidely, and then inclined his head. "This is my partner, Wilbur Blockson."

"It's a pleasure to meet both of you," Abby said warmly. "Thank you for all you're doing for Richmond."

Carrie and Rose added their greetings.

Thomas hid his grin when both officers looked discomfited. It was hard to be obnoxious in the face of such grace. "What can I do for you gentlemen?"

The question seemed to arouse their initial animosity. "Did you hear we haven't caught Ben Scott yet?" Austin snapped.

"I have not," Thomas replied. "Should I have?"

Austin ignored him, drilling his eyes into Carrie. "I understand you might know something about that."

"Me?" Carrie was the picture of innocence. "Whatever gave you that idea?"

"We happen to know you were down in the Black Quarters the night of the riot," Austin said sternly. "What were you doing there?"

Thomas stifled his groan. He wished he had taken the time to inform the women of his earlier meeting with the officers at the hardware store. He'd been so eager to leave town, he had left them unprepared.

Carrie smiled brightly. "I was, indeed. I didn't hear about the riot until later. I'm so sorry about the man you lost."

"What were you doing there?" Austin replied in a hard voice.

"I had gone to visit one of our old slaves," Carrie answered. "Are you aware I'm a doctor?"

Austin raised a brow. "I've heard that you have degraded the image of a Southern woman by becoming a doctor up north."

Carrie merely smiled. "My friend was gravely ill and wished to see me. I went to the Black Quarters to treat her."

"You didn't leave," Austin growled.

Thomas wondered how long they had watched for her.

"Of course I didn't," Carrie answered, as if she had not a care in the world. "She was quite ill. I stayed with her until she was better. I left early the next morning. The streets were quite empty. I don't believe I saw anyone when I was escorted home."

Thomas wanted to cheer. Austin Dowswell was mistaken if he thought he could fluster his brilliant daughter. Thomas knew he was merely fishing for information based on his suspicions. He also hoped the sweat rolling down his back wasn't obvious.

"May we go now?" Thomas asked. "We have a rather long trip ahead of us."

Austin nodded, his eyes still drilling into Carrie. "We're escorting you out of town, Mr. Cromwell."

Thomas was impressed that none of the women gasped their horror. As it was, he could hardly restrain the disgust he felt from showing on his face. "To what do we owe this extraordinary consideration?"

"We don't trust you, Cromwell," Austin drawled, eyeing the back of the wagon. "Your wagon is quite full. What would you say if I asked you to unload it?"

Thomas shrugged. "Go ahead. It might take you a while, however, and I hope you're prepared to load it back in. I'm quite sure the new Richmond police force doesn't want the reputation of harassing innocent citizens." He stood as if he was preparing to step down and open the back of the wagon.

"Forget it," Austin said brusquely as he waved his hand through the air. "We're going to escort you out of town, but I don't have time for that."

"As you wish," Thomas said, hoping he was covering the rage boiling inside. If he'd been alone, he would have vented his fury on them. As it was, while he might be willing to go to jail, he wasn't going to put the women in that situation. When all of this was over, he would make sure the men were reprimanded and removed from their positions. For now, he had to play along.

Chapter Eight

The outskirts of Richmond were behind them before the two officers curtly nodded their heads and turned their horses to gallop off without a word.

All the women spoke at once.

"Father!"

"Thomas!"

"Thomas!"

Abby reached over and took his hand. "Poor Ben Scott. I know we had no choice other than to leave, but I can't stand the idea of leaving him behind."

"We have to go back," Carrie cried. "We have to wait until it's dark and return for Ben. Eddie will have no idea what happened to us, but surely he'll keep hiding Ben until we can get him out of the city."

"Thomas, we have to do something," Rose added. "We can't leave Ben. You know it's just a matter of time until they find him."

Thomas chuckled, sagging with relief against the back of the wagon seat as he tried to ignore his sweat-soaked clothes. "Oh, I don't think they'll find him."

Carrie was the first to break the shocked silence that followed his glib statement. "Father? How can you say that? The police are scouring the entire city for him."

"Yes," Thomas agreed. "They're scouring the entire city, but we're not in the city anymore, are we?"

Abby spoke carefully. "Are you all right, dear?"

Thomas threw his head back with a laugh, reached into his pocket to pull out a slip of paper, and handed it to his wife. "I was given this at the hardware store this morning, just before I left with the wagonful of supplies."

Abby took the paper from him, her eyes flashing with concern. Quickly, she opened it and began to read.

Dear Mr. Cromwell,

There was a change in plans. We wasn't sure you could get Ben out if you had to meet me in the alley. Too

many prying eyes. Ben be in the back of your wagon in the long crate. He knows not to say nothing until you tell him it be all right, but I reckon he'll be real glad to know he's safe. He's been in that crate a right long time.
Sincerely,
Eddie

"What?!" Carrie gasped. She turned and began to scour the wagon with her eyes. "Ben is in the wagon?"

"Let's ask him," Thomas suggested, a quick look around assuring him no one was in sight. "I'm hoping the letter is telling the truth." He raised his voice. "Ben, are you there?"

"Yes, Mr. Cromwell. I be back here."

The voice that lifted on the air was weak but steady.

Carrie's eyes widened with delight and relief, and then she groaned at the idea of her patient trapped in a wooden box since last night. "Are you all right, Ben?"

"I reckon I'm better than I would be if them police had searched the wagon and found me, Miss Carrie."

Carrie whirled to stare at her father. "You told those officers they could search the wagon! What were you thinking?"

"I was thinking that I hoped they couldn't see my nervous sweat," Thomas admitted. "I knew if I refused they would be suspicious and search the wagon. I decided it was better to take a calculated risk."

Abby shook her head in admiration. "My husband is a brilliant man."

"I quite agree," Carrie added, "but we have to get Ben out of that crate. He needs fresh air and food."

Thomas shook his head. "We can't do that yet. We're still much too close to Richmond. We have to get further out of the city and closer to the plantation before we let him out. I'm sorry, Ben," he called.

"That be fine, Mr. Cromwell," Ben answered. "They put me in here with some blankets and a right good supply of food and water. It's a mite cramped, but I'll be just fine until you decide I can get out. Now that I know I'm safe, I might try and sleep a little. I was scared to sleep before 'cause I didn't know if I would snore." There was a long pause. The next words were delivered in a choked voice. "I sure 'nuff appreciate what you done for me."

"I can't believe he's been in the wagon all this time," Rose murmured. She looked at Thomas. "You must have been terrified when you read that note."

"I haven't taken an easy breath since Oliver handed it to me," Thomas admitted.

"No one would have guessed," Abby said softly. She took Thomas' hand. "I'm so proud of you, dear."

Thomas shrugged. "It was the right thing to do."

Carrie smiled. After years of destroying the lives of black people through slavery, her father was busy providing redemption to as many as he could. Marcus had Hannah back. Ben Scott was on his way to becoming a free man. "I'm proud of you, too, Father."

"As am I," Rose chimed in. "Now, can we get out of here?"

Easy laughter, including a muffled chuckle from the middle of the wagon, lifted into the air as Thomas urged the horse forward.

*****

They were an hour outside Richmond before Thomas pulled the wagon into a thick clump of cedar trees that would conceal them from the road. It took all four of them to pull enough things out of the wagon to make it possible to pry loose the lid on the long wooden crate nestled almost in the center of the bed. They were only 2 hours or so from the plantation, but Ben had been confined for over fourteen hours. He needed fresh air and chance to stretch his limbs.

Thomas shook his head. "I can't believe Oliver and his friends pulled this off. This crate had to have been in Oliver's first load. Dowswell and his buddy were right there talking to me when Oliver brought it out." He released a long whistle. "What we did was nothing. The courage they showed was astronomical." He reached for the hammer he had pulled from under the wagon seat and quickly pried the lid off, the final nail coming out with a squeal of metal.

Ben emerged from the crate and took several deep breaths of fresh air. "Hello, everyone," he said. "Y'all be a sight for sore eyes." He swayed slightly. "I been lying down in that crate since last night. I reckon it's gonna take me a few minutes to get my legs back."

Carrie eyed the crate. It wasn't long enough for Ben's height, so every muscle in his body must be cramping. She thought through what she had in her medical bag. "Some blackstrap molasses will help with the cramps you're feeling, Ben." She looked at Rose. "Will you get a cup out of the picnic basket, please?"

Carrie poured some water into the metal cup and then carefully mixed in a tablespoon of molasses. "Drink this," she ordered, handing him the cup, along with the entire canteen. "Finish all of this. I know they gave you water, but you must be dehydrated after more than twelve hours in that wooden box."

Ben drank eagerly. "I reckon I didn't touch a drop of that food and water," he admitted. "I was too scared I might make noise when someone was there that I couldn't see."

"I suspected as much," Carrie replied. "Drinking that will make you feel better."

Ben finished off the canteen. "Mr. Cromwell, your daughter is a real special woman, and a mighty fine doctor."

"I couldn't agree more," Thomas said proudly.

"How is your shoulder?" Carrie asked. "Has the infection come back?"

"I don't reckon so," Ben replied. "It hurts some still, but it's better."

"I'd like to take a look myself," Carrie answered.

Ben removed his shirt so Carrie could examine the wound. Convinced it was healing well, despite all he'd been through in the last two days, she directed him to put his shirt back on. "When you get to the plantation, I want you to take it easy," she said. "You're to do no work and do no horseback riding until I tell you otherwise."

Ben gazed at her for a moment and then turned to Thomas. "Has she always been so bossy?"

"Since she came out of her mother," Thomas informed him. "You get used to it."

Ben chuckled along with everyone else, Carrie included.

Abby gazed around. "This is a beautiful spot. I know we only have a couple more hours to go, but what if we have a quick picnic here? Ben must be hungry since he hasn't eaten."

Thomas looked thoughtful. "I think we'll be safe here. If we hear anyone coming, though," he told Ben sternly, "I want you to go up into the woods and hide."

"Yes, sir," Ben answered as he eyed the basket. "That be May's cookin'? I reckon I can always eat that." He shook his head. "That woman be a real fine cook. Spencer be a lucky man."

"He would agree with you," Abby replied. She pulled out a blanket and spread it on the ground.

Within minutes, the picnic basket had been unloaded to reveal mounds of ham biscuits, fried chicken, fresh vegetables that must have been picked early that morning from the garden, and a folded napkin full of Irish oatmeal cookies.

"I reckon I would like to bless this fine meal," Ben offered.

"Please," Thomas replied.

"God, I got a lot to be grateful for," Ben began. "Thank you for keepin' me alive and for giving me another chance at life. Thank you for these fine people who risked so much to give that to me. I won't never forget it." He took a deep breath as tears clogged his words. "And thank you for this mighty fine food that May fixed. I'm always real grateful for *that*. Amen."

Carrie blinked back tears. "Amen," she said softly. Echoes rose around her before silence consumed them. Carrie ate quietly, exhausted from the stress of the morning.

*****

Carrie knew she would never tire of the feeling she experienced when she rounded the last curve of the drive and viewed her childhood home. She'd been gone less than three months, but it felt much longer.

Ben was seated next to her in the wagon. "That be your home? It's right beautiful."

The three-story, white plantation house gleamed in the sunlight. Tall, white porch pillars gave it a regal air. The two huge oak trees flanking either end finished off the splendor.

Carrie nodded. "Cromwell Plantation is my favorite place on earth," she said.

"You grew up here, too?" Ben asked Rose.

"I did. Now, my husband, who used to be a slave here, is co-owner with Thomas, and I run the school."

Ben's eyes widened. "It's good to know things are changin' in *some* places." His voice hardened. "There's still too many folks, though, who be sufferin' through real bad times. It ain't right."

"No, it's not right," Abby said as they drew closer to the plantation. "But we'll all keep fighting."

Ben nodded before his eyes shot open even wider. "Now I know why you said what you did about not riding horses, Doc." He leaned forward in the wagon and fixed his gaze on the green pastures. "All them horses yours?" he asked breathlessly.

Carrie understood his reaction. The verdant fields were dotted with glistening bay, sorrel, chestnut, black, and gray horses. As she had expected, a large number of the mares had their newborn foals close by their sides, while another group of slightly older colts and fillies cavorted within close proximity of their watchful mothers. "I'm co-owner of the stables," she replied. "My first husband started the stables shortly after the war was over."

Ben turned to look at her. "Your *first* husband? I didn't know you been married before."

Carrie nodded, grateful that the pain of remembering was just a twinge now. "My first husband, Robert, was murdered here on the plantation three years ago. It was a vigilante attack."

Ben sucked in his breath. "I be real sorry, Miss Carrie."

"Thank you," she replied. "He would be so proud of what has come from his creation." She waved her hand to encompass the fields. "This was his dream."

A shrill whinny cut through their conversation as the sound of thundering hooves rose above the clatter of the wagon wheels.

Ben stood in the wagon, his hands gripping the sides tightly to maintain his balance. "Will you look at that," he breathed. "I ain't never seen nothing so magnificent."

Carrie smiled as she watched the gray Thoroughbred race toward them. "I couldn't agree with you more. That's my horse, Granite." She leaned forward. "Father, will you please stop the wagon and let me out here? I'll join everyone in a few minutes."

Thomas brought the wagon to a stop and then winked at Ben. "You are about to witness the greatest love affair in the world."

Carrie grinned, climbed down from the wagon, and ran lightly across the road to the pasture fence. Mindless of her dress, she scaled the wooden rails and dropped down next to her horse. She laughed when Granite whinnied his joy, and then threw her arms around his neck and breathed in his smell. "Hello, boy," she murmured. "Did you miss me as much as I missed you?"

Granite snorted and bobbed his head before he relaxed into her, his head resting on her shoulder. Carrie stroked his neck, completely oblivious to the wagon pulling off. She was with her horse once more. When she returned from her internship at the end of the year, she hoped they would never be separated for a long period of time again. It seemed like she was always telling her beloved horse good-bye.

"Good boy," she whispered. "I missed you."

Granite stood quietly, his body quivering with joy.

"That's a real happy horse."

Carrie looked up as Miles appeared. "It's so hard to leave him," she murmured. Then she smiled. "I still remember the day you and Father gave him to me, when I was thirteen. It was the happiest day of my life."

Miles chuckled. "You two fell in love right from the start."

"He was meant to be mine," Carrie agreed, pulling away from Granite to give her old friend a hug. Suddenly, she stiffened, alerted by Miles' odd expression. "Is something wrong?" She searched his weathered face. "I know you too well not to see trouble in your eyes. What did you come out here to tell me?" For a moment, she wondered if another attack was imminent on the plantation, but she knew if that was the case, her father would be the one alerting her.

Miles shook his head as he looked away. "Just came to tell you how glad I be to see you, Carrie girl."

"You're lying," Carrie said flatly as her alarm increased. "You've never lied to me before, Miles. Why are you starting now?"

"I've lied to you plenty of times," Miles protested. "You forgettin' that you went ridin' the day I ran off from the plantation? We talked about making sure Granite would be ready for you the next day. I lied when I told you I'd keep doing what I always done—have your horse ready for you. I disappeared with the Underground Railroad that night." He paused. "I lied when I told you I couldn't read. Rose had been teaching me for months. I could read real well."

Carrie stared at him, her mind racing. "You lied to protect me. I couldn't get in trouble for knowing something if I didn't know it." She took a deep breath. "Why are you lying to me now?"

"I didn't say I was lying," Miles sputtered, but there was a trapped look in his eyes.

Carrie held his gaze, every muscle in her body tense as she waited.

Miles finally let out a loud sigh. "You know how old Granite be, Carrie girl?"

Carrie shook her head in confusion, but she thought back. "I got him when I was thirteen. I'm twenty-nine now."

"He wasn't a young'un when I got him for you," Miles said gently. "He was already ten. That was how I knew he would be perfect for you. He was old enough to have some sense and young enough to have all the energy and speed you wanted."

"Granite is twenty-six," Carrie said slowly, and then narrowed her eyes. She'd never really thought about the age of a horse. What was old? "What are you telling me, Miles? Is something wrong with Granite?" She forced the words out, not certain she wanted an answer.

"I don't know," Miles said in a strained voice.

Carrie knew he was telling the truth. "But you suspect there is," she said, looking up into Granite's brown eyes. She turned back to face Miles. "I don't understand. He raced up to the fence to meet me like he always does. How can there be something wrong?"

Miles held her eyes with his. "It's the first time I've seen him run in almost a month," he said, the words measured and even. "All he does is stand at the fence and watch the road."

Tears clogged Carrie's throat. "Because he's waiting for me," she whispered.

"He's been waiting for you," Miles agreed. "I ain't tryin' to scare you, Carrie girl." His voice was tender. "Granite is an old man. He's lived a long life. The war took a lot out of him."

Carrie tried to block out his words, but they reverberated through her head. She longed to cover her ears and refuse to hear him, but she couldn't unhear what had already been said. "What should I do?"

"Just love him," Miles said instantly. "He's going to want to go on the rides you've always been on, but you wants to take it easier. He'll give you all he got, if you ask him."

Carrie heard what he wasn't saying. Asking Granite for more would take him from her sooner. "Can't he just live as an old man here on the plantation for many more years?" she pleaded.

"Maybe," Miles responded quickly. "We had a horse up in Canada that lived past thirty, but…" He hesitated for a long moment. "But that ain't normal."

Carrie wanted to scream. Instead, she turned and buried her face in Granite's mane. She felt Miles' hand on her shoulder, but all she could do was take deep breaths to keep from shattering into a million pieces.

"He ain't gone yet, Carrie girl," Miles said quietly. "You still got time with him. I just thought it best you know."

Carrie nodded wordlessly, but a realization seeped through her sorrow. As hard as it was to know her beloved horse wouldn't live forever, she was grateful she could at least make sure he took it easier. "It had to have been so hard to tell me. Thank you."

"It was hard," Miles said, his voice gruff with emotion. "You done had enough loss, Carrie girl. I ain't wantin' to add to it."

Carrie pulled away from her old friend and gazed up at him. "Is life nothing but loss, Miles?" The sorrow screaming through her soul demanded an answer.

Miles looked into her eyes. "There sure be plenty of loss, Carrie girl, but you know that ain't all it is. You lost your mama, but you got Miss Abby. You lost Robert and Bridget, but now you got Anthony and Frances, along with all those memories from before. It ain't that one can ever replace the other, but I believe there always be joy waiting on the other side of pain. We just got to be able to hold on long enough until we find it."

Carrie absorbed his words, recognizing the truth in them, but shook her head. "There will never be another horse like Granite."

"No, I don't reckon there will be. Granite is mighty special, and y'all share a bond not many get to share. The best thing you can do now is make the most of all the time you got." Miles gently tipped her head up with his hand, so he could stare into her eyes. "But ain't it always like that? You already learned that you can't never know how much time you got with someone. The best thing to do with that knowledge is to make sure ever'body in your life knows how much you love them. People *and* animals."

"I know you're right." Carrie turned to stare north, her heart swirling with turmoil. "How can I go back to Philadelphia now? How can I leave Granite?" A bitter taste filled her mouth. "I would never forgive myself if something happened while I was gone." She couldn't bring herself to say *what if he dies*. The very thought stole all her breath from her. She locked her eyes on Miles. "Can you promise me he'll make it through the end of the year?"

Even before she asked the question, she knew the answer didn't matter. It wasn't whether she would be here when he died, it was whether she would be here with him while he still lived. "It's been ten years, Miles. Ten years..."

"I know," Miles acknowledged. "That war stole a lot of things from a lot of people."

Carrie thought back through the past decade. She and Granite had been inseparable since the moment he arrived on the plantation when she was thirteen. Her mother didn't think Carrie needed her own horse, but her father had understood and given Miles free rein to buy the perfect horse for his daughter. For five years, every free minute was spent with Granite.

Until the war...

Nothing had ever been the same. Granite had gone to war with Robert... He had gone missing with Robert... Her father had needed him during the long conflict... She had spent endless hours at the hospital, and then left Granite behind to go to medical school, and then again to New Mexico as she fought to overcome her grief over Robert's death... And now she was gone again.

"I wish I'd known," she whispered.

"Known what?"

"Known when our last wild run around the plantation happened," Carrie admitted. "I always loved them, but I would have loved it even more if I'd known it was the last time. I would have savored it more."

"I understand just how you feel," Miles replied. "There be a whole bunch of things I wish I had known would be the last."

Carrie couldn't miss the deep sadness in his voice. She knew, at his age, that he had suffered far more loss than she had.

"You got to savor things, Carrie girl. You can't never know when somethin' gonna end, so you got to cherish it." He gave her a small smile. "You're lucky, you know."

"How do you figure that?"

"You know it's coming," Miles said bluntly. "Death always be right around the corner for all of us. We ain't got no way of knowing when our time be, but Granite be tellin' us he ain't gonna be here forever. You got time to make every moment count. You ride him every single day you can. That will give both of you more joy than anything else. That horse lives for you. You ain't gonna be caught by surprise. I figure that makes you lucky."

Carrie held back her tears. "You're right, she said softly. "I've got time to savor him." She kissed Granite's velvety nose. "I'll be back soon, boy. We'll go to our secret place this evening. I just have to go say hello to everyone." She dreaded going onto the porch, where she knew everyone was waiting. How would she hide her pain?

Miles read her thoughts. "I 'magine Annie told them what I be doing out here."

Carrie was relieved. "You told Annie?"

"I figured it would make it easier if you didn't have to say it out loud to everyone."

"Thank you," Carrie replied. She took a deep breath, walked to the gate, and then crossed the yard to the porch.

*****

Carrie and Rose rode in silence, both instinctively knowing that was what the other needed. Granite had pranced away from the barn, nickering his joy before settling into an easy trot. Not once had he asked permission to gallop. The knowledge filled Carrie with sadness, but her sorrow was offset by the sheer joy of being with him again, riding through another spring day on the plantation. She rode with a hand on his neck, so she could feel connected. She could feel the happiness vibrating through him.

When she had left Philadelphia several days earlier, there were still gray clumps of snow on the sidewalk and a cold wind was still whistling in from the harbor. There were signs of spring in the few brave crocuses that had poked their purple and white heads from the ground, but the city was far behind the South. Richmond had been bursting with spring, but too much of the beauty was marred by soot-filled air and constant noise.

Carrie took deep breaths of the pure air on the plantation. Brown tobacco fields stretched as far as the eye could see. Last fall, the men had cleared even more land for a larger crop. Four years of clearing since the end of the war had increased the yield to almost double. Tiny green shoots revealed that planting had just taken place. The fledgling plants had been taking root under cover for the last several months; now they were free to stretch toward the sun. Soon, rich green plants would swallow the brown landscape.

She never tired of the cycle of the seasons. Now, just as she had her entire life, she loved riding through the fields, watching the tobacco grow from tiny seedlings to towering plants. The harvest would take place, the fields would lie fallow beneath the green of a cover crop to replenish the soil, and then it would start all over again.

Rose broke the silence. "There are times it's hard to believe the plantation was worked by slaves," she said. "I think about Ike Adams sometimes."

Carrie shuddered at the reminder of the brutal overseer who had tried so hard to harm Rose and Moses, and who had sent Union soldiers after her at the plantation. She would always carry the scar from the bullet she had taken in her shoulder during her escape, and would never be sorry he had been killed during the war during another attempt to end Moses' life. "I try hard to *not* think about him," she muttered.

"It's such a stark contrast to the way things are now," Rose responded. "The men are all happy. Their families are happy. The children are all in school. Everyone is making a living." Her voice filled with something like awe. "If you had told me ten years ago that this would happen, I would have accused you of being crazy."

"Holding onto hope?" Carrie guessed as she thought of their conversation just the night before.

"Yes," Rose agreed. "Things are still hard, and they may be hard for a long time, but there is at least one place in the South where things are truly better."

Carrie nodded. "Matthew tells me there are more," she offered. "His new book is telling some of the stories. There are pockets all over the South where change is being made."

"I'm glad that's true. All any of us can do is make a difference where we are." Rose changed the subject. "I haven't even asked you about Janie and Matthew. I get letters on a regular basis from Jeremy and Marietta, so I know they and the twins are doing well, but how are Matthew and Janie doing?"

"They're great!" Carrie said. "Janie adores being a mom, and Matthew is beyond thrilled to be a father. Robert is a lucky little man." She answered the question she saw shining from Rose's eyes. "It's not hard to hear Robert's name constantly. I was afraid it might be, but it's actually comforting. It's a tribute to the man I love, and to Matthew's best friend. Both of us will focus on all the amazing times we had with him before he was taken away."

Their conversation ceased as the road faded away into thick woods.

Carrie gave Granite his head, knowing he would follow the narrow deer trails that led to her secret place, just as he had for sixteen years. She took deep breaths as the rich, earthy aroma of the woods filled her nostrils. Scuppernong vines were leafing out with the promise of luscious fruit in the fall. Ferns burst forth with wavy green fronds. Purple violets wove together with white anemone. A red-headed woodpecker clung to a nearby tree, mindless of their presence as he hammered into the wood in search of bugs.

Carrie was content to absorb the beauty. The length of the shadows told her they would have to head back to the plantation within the hour in order to get home before dark, but she'd been determined to spend her first afternoon by the river with Granite.

She gasped with delight when they broke into the clearing. No matter how many times she came here, the beauty never ceased to thrill her. Sunshine danced off the ripples of the James River as it flowed to the Atlantic Ocean. The entire clearing was ringed with dogwood trees. It was too early for the wisteria to bloom, but she could tell by the bulging buds that it wouldn't be too much longer. Columbine danced in the breeze, while a carpet of violets seemed to wrap everything with a soft purple haze.

Granite snorted and pawed the ground.

Carrie laughed with delight and slipped from the saddle, loosening his saddle girth and removing his bridle so he could eat his fill of the lush grass.

Rose followed suit with her mare, Maple.

Carrie settled down on the rock to stare out over the river, but after a few minutes, she spun around so she could watch Granite.

Rose reached out to take her hand.

"I don't think I can leave him," Carrie said. "How can I go back to Philadelphia, knowing he may not be here when I come home?"

Rose didn't argue with her. Neither did she try to answer the question. She just squeezed her hand harder.

"I know I need to finish my surgical internship," Carrie mused. "There have been so many things to slow me down, but..." She shook her head as her voice trailed away.

"What about Anthony and Frances?" Rose asked.

Carrie thought through the question, not wanting to make a rash decision. "Anthony is only in Philadelphia for me. Living here would make his life much easier. Frances is happy in Philadelphia, but she misses the plantation and Amber terribly. She would be overjoyed to return home." She knew what she was saying was true. Not a day passed when Frances didn't talk about the plantation and her own beloved horse, Peaches. She had only been convinced to stay behind in Philadelphia this time because she'd been given the promise of a longer visit in the summer.

"And what about running the new medical practice you and Janie are going to start?" Rose asked.

Carrie sighed. "I know you should ask these questions, but trying to find the answers is hard."

"Yep."

Carrie chuckled around the pain squeezing her heart. "You sound like your mama when you say that. She used to ask me endless questions. When I would tell her that finding the answers was hard, she would just say *'Yep.'*"

"Yep," Rose repeated, a smile tugging at her lips.

Carrie chuckled again, but then thought about the question. "I could still start the practice with Janie. I don't have to be a certified surgeon to practice as a doctor. I'm already a doctor. And I'll still be running the plantation clinic even when I'm seeing patients in Richmond."

Rose sat quietly for a moment. "And if Granite dies when you're in Richmond seeing patients?" she asked gently.

Carrie felt a flare of resentment that quickly subsided. The only way she could make a decision was to know the answers to these questions. "I don't know," she finally admitted.

"Leaving for Philadelphia was a hard decision before you recognized Granite is old. What made you decide to go?"

"I realized I couldn't help people the way I want and need to if I'm not certified as a surgeon."

"Has that changed?"

Carrie shook her head and whirled around to look at Rose. "Are you telling me I should leave Granite and go back to Philadelphia?"

"I'm not telling you anything," Rose said calmly. "All I'm doing is asking you questions."

"But you think I should finish my internship?"

"All I think is that I'm glad I'm not the one having to make this decision," Rose said. "Carrie, I don't know what you should do. I don't know what *I* would do in the same situation, so how can I know what *you* should do. There is no one who can make this decision but you."

Carrie knew Rose was right, but knowing it didn't make her decision any easier. "I would feel like a horribly selfish person if I were to leave Granite," she whispered. "It would break my heart to not be with him when he dies. All he's ever done is put me first." She sighed as she confronted the other thought in her mind. "I also wonder how many people might suffer unnecessarily if I don't become a surgeon."

"Perhaps the most important question, Carrie, is what do *you* want?"

Carrie stared out over the river for several minutes as she pondered the question. "I don't know," she acknowledged, feeling horrible guilt and sorrow even as she spoke the words. Tears filled her eyes as she watched Granite graze.

"I know this is probably a ridiculous question because Granite is an animal, not a human, but..." Rose hesitated.

"What would Granite want me to do?"

"Yes." Rose looked relieved to not have to ask the question herself.

Carrie sighed. "I thought about that while I was riding out here." She fell silent again.

Rose allowed the silence to sit between them for a while before she asked her next question. "Can you trust God to keep Granite alive until you're finished with your internship and come home?"

Carrie felt the spark of the anger she had felt for so long. "I don't know. I never dreamed Robert and Bridget would die. How can I possibly trust that Granite will be here when I get home?" Tears flooded her eyes as the truth burst out.

Rose released her hand and pulled Carrie close into her arms.

Carrie sobbed for several long minutes before she could control her tears.

When she raised her head from Rose's shoulder, she realized Granite had quit grazing and was staring at her. She took a deep breath, looking deeply into his beautiful eyes. Time seemed to stand still as an unspoken message passed between them. Carrie caught her breath in wonder as a sure knowing filled every crevice of her soul.

When Granite finally dropped his head to begin grazing again, Carrie had her answer.

"I'm going back to Philadelphia," she said softly, relieved when guilt and sorrow didn't swallow her. In its place, was a comforting feeling of *knowing*.

"Granite will wait for you," Rose said.

Carrie turned to stare into her best friend's face.

"I heard it, too," Rose whispered as she regarded Granite with an awed look. "I'm sure I will never truly understand the bond you and Granite share, but I understand it a little better now. When I see an animal, I just see an animal." She took a breath. "Granite is more than that." She shook her head with a chuckle. "I never thought I would see an animal as an angel, but I think I'm looking at one right now."

Carrie rose and threw her arms around Granite's neck. The wind blew harder, kicking up whitecaps on the river as they stood and looked out over the water. She would miss him every day they were apart, but she had the peace to finish what she had started before the war ripped her world apart. She would go back to Philadelphia, finish her internship, and then she would come home for good.

Chapter Nine

The sun was resting on the treetops when everyone walked out onto the porch with cups of hot tea. Abby carried out a huge platter of molasses cookies, warm from the oven. All of them were stuffed from a huge dinner of beef stew and cornbread, but no one could resist the allure of the cookies once the aroma had floated into the dining room.

"Pretty soon there ain't gonna be room for all the rocking chairs on this porch," Annie declared. She gazed around, her eyes filled with love.

The porch was crowded with Thomas, Abby, Moses, Rose, Miles and Annie, Harold and Susan, Lillian, Carrie and Anthony, and Ben.

Carrie wouldn't want it any other way. "We can always arrange to fit a few more in," she teased. "As long as you keep the cookies coming, I believe we can make it work."

Conversation had centered around activity on the plantation during the meal, but now everyone was eager to hear any news from Richmond. Though it had only been two days since they'd left the city, Carrie knew any number of things could have happened.

"Now that our stomachs are full, why don't you fill us in on everything going on?" Thomas invited Anthony, who had arrived earlier that afternoon.

"Well," Anthony started with a grin, "the manhunt for Ben Scott continues."

"At least they don't know I done left the city," Ben said cheerfully. Just two days on the plantation had worked miracles for him. His eyes were bright, and he claimed he had eaten more in two days than he had in two months. Then he sobered. "What are they doin' to my friends, Mr. Anthony?"

"You can just call me Anthony here on the plantation."

Ben shook his head firmly. "No, sir. I ain't figured out what I gonna do yet, but I know I ain't gonna stay hidin' out on this fine plantation. My people need me. Calling white men by their first name, without putting Mister in front of it, is a sure way to get yourself in a heap of trouble. Black folk might be free now, but there still be an awful lot of rules we got to follow. I be willin' to break a lot of them rules, but havin' to remember whether I be on the plantation or the streets of some city talking to a white man, ain't a wise place to be in."

Anthony frowned as he nodded. "I hate that you have to think that way, but I understand."

"You accept it," Ben corrected him matter-of-factly, "but you ain't got no way of understanding. Have you ever once in your life had to think about what you were gonna call someone? Have you ever had to wonder if calling someone by their first name could end you up in jail, or hanging from some tree?"

"No," Anthony admitted. "Thank you for reminding me of that." He paused. "Can I say that I'm *trying* to understand?"

"Yep. That be a good way to put it, Mr. Anthony," Ben said with a smile. "Now, how are my friends?"

"So far, there has been no more violence," Anthony reported. "At least, not on a city-wide level. There have been a lot of fights, but very few of them have involved anyone in the Black Quarters. All the black citizens of Richmond seem to have decided to stay close to home, except for those who must go to work. The fights are between white Republican men and white Democratic men. Almost everyone seems to have chosen sides in this issue. Their sides tend to be communicated through a large number of fights and yelling matches, but there have been no more guns, and most men walk away with nothing more than a black eye."

"They gone after anybody else, seeing as how they can't find me?" Ben asked. "Since I didn't do it anyway, I figure they might pick a different target. They's looking for someone to blame," he said bluntly.

"Not to my knowledge," Anthony answered. "They're still making raids in the Black Quarters to look for you, but no one has been harmed and, obviously, they haven't found you."

Ben nodded, looking somewhat appeased. "That's good," he muttered. "They gonna decide at some point that I ain't in the city no more. They'll leave everyone alone at that point."

"I believe you're right. Eddie sends his greetings. He's quite proud of himself for smuggling you out right under the noses of the policemen," Anthony said with a grin. "Of course, Oliver almost had a heart attack when he walked out and saw Thomas with those police officers, but he's recovered."

Thomas laughed. "I never would have guessed Oliver was even nervous. I just kept being glad no one could see the sweat pouring down *my* back. It wasn't hot enough to use heat as an excuse for why I was like a cat on hot bricks."

Ben smiled, but his eyes were serious. "All of us have learned to keep things hidden. It be the only way to survive."

Abby regarded him sympathetically. "I know it's been difficult, Ben. I talked to May and Micah enough while I was there to know how hard you've fought for equal rights for the blacks in Richmond. I know you've only had a few days since the riot, but do you have any idea what you're going to do next?"

Ben sighed. "Well, I for sure can't go back to Richmond. I reckon I'll be a wanted man pretty much anywhere I go in the South. I might be able to hide in a lot of places, but I don't figure on hidin'. There just be too much to do."

Thomas eyed him keenly. "So, you're headed to the North?"

"I figure it be my only option," Ben acknowledged. "I thought about heading West 'cause I figure I'd be safe, but I'll be too far from things out there. I can still do things to fight for black rights in the North, and I got a much better chance of staying alive."

Moses, who had returned from the fields just in time to eat, looked thoughtful. "What are you going to do in the North, Ben?"

"Look for other people to join in the fight with," Ben said. He looked at Abby. "I hear the Abolitionist Society broke up a few weeks ago."

"You're well informed," Abby said with surprise. "You're also right."

Ben smiled. "I know I don't talk so good, but I can read anything you put in front of me. I make sure I read every newspaper I can get my hands on in Richmond. I can't help change things if I don't know what's going on."

"The Abolitionist Society dissolved at the beginning of March," Abby informed him. "Their work was done."

Carrie was struck by the expression on Ben's face. "You don't think their work is done, Ben?"

Ben shrugged, but met her eyes evenly. "Bringin' an end to slavery was a real good thing, Miss Carrie, but..."

"But..." Carrie prompted.

"Making folks not be slaves don't mean they be free."

"Will you explain what you mean?" Thomas asked, his silver hair catching the final rays of the sun before it dipped below the tree line. A chorus of tree frogs accompanied his question.

Ben considered his answer carefully and then began to speak. "There was a State Republican meeting held in Richmond a week ago. In spite of all that the black folk have been doing, there weren't one black man at that meeting. Them folks got together so they could plan a convention to change the party again, but they didn't ask no blacks to be part of it." He paused, his lips twisted with bitterness. "They didn't want us at their meetin', but Mayor Chahoon sure came looking for me when he figured I could do him some good."

"Do you regret taking place in the riot?" Rose asked.

Ben shook his head. "No. I didn't do it to protect the mayor. I did it to protect all the things the black community has accomplished since the end of the war." His voice grew grim. "If Ellyson turns out to be our mayor, then every political position in Virginia is gonna be held by men who don't care about black rights." His voice was fraught with frustration.

"It must be terribly hard to leave Richmond," Rose said sympathetically.

"It be hard," Ben agreed. "I gotta hope this whole thing gonna wake up the black folks again. Too many of them have given up hope 'cause they can see that the Republican Party don't really care that much about their rights."

"Why do you believe that?" Anthony asked. "The Republicans fought for the Emancipation Proclamation and the new amendments. I thought things were getting better?"

Ben snorted. "We sure *thought* things were gettin' better, but as far as I can tell, the government already gettin' tired of what they be calling the *Black Problem*. There are a lot of places in the South where the North be turning their back and lettin' things happen the way the Democrats want 'em to happen." He stared out over the trees in the distance with flashing eyes. "My people starting to give up hope, but they gotta keep fighting."

"Do you believe they'll fight?" Moses asked.

Carrie wondered if Moses was regretting his decision to not run for political office.

Ben hesitated. "Some of them will fight." His eyes filled with sadness. "Too many of them got all the fight beat out of them when they were slaves. They want things to be better, but it's hard for them to push back against the same men who kept them slaves." Resolve hardened his face again. "There be people who done already gave up. They see that Virginia is back under control of mostly the rebels. They got that control back 'cause they scared too many black folk from standing up to them. Too many of my people are afraid." He scowled. "They got a right to be."

Ben jumped up and walked to the edge of the porch and then wheeled around to face them again. "Do you know there are about six hundred thousand black folks in Virginia? They be free now, but if things don't really change, they gonna live lives not that much better than when they were slaves."

A long silence followed his words.

"Which is why you don't think the Abolitionist Society should have disbanded," Abby observed.

"I can't really say for sure. What I do know is that if white people don't keep helping us, there ain't no real hope for black folks." His voice was impassioned. "Black folk gonna fight as hard as we can, but we ain't gonna win in the long run if the people who helped make us free don't make sure we *live* free."

"Ben is absolutely right," Rose chimed in. "Black people are doing all they can, but most of us are illiterate and uneducated. They're learning as fast as they can, if they have access to education, but it takes time. Jobs are hard to come by, and their pay is less. Too many whites don't mind if we're free, but they sure don't believe we should be equal to them. They're afraid it will somehow make them less."

"The fear is making a lot of white people angry," Moses added. "They're trying to make the blacks more afraid than they are."

Ben, encouraged by their comments, continued. "Like down in Georgia. It be bad up here, but it ain't as bad as Georgia."

Thomas shook his head. "I'm embarrassed to say I don't know what's going on down there. I'm afraid being here on the plantation has made me a little lazy about staying abreast of things."

Abby laughed. "Hardly, my dear. If anything, you have *more* time to be informed because you don't have to worry about running a business. I'm afraid it's just too hard to stay knowledgeable about every single thing in this country. It's too big and there are too many crazy things going on." She laid a hand on Thomas' arm. "Please tell us about Georgia, Ben."

"It's bad down there," Ben said grimly. "Real bad. And, it's not just black folks who be having trouble. There is so much violence going on that there ain't a single Republican who can campaign in that state, white or black. I promise you when it comes election time down there, ain't gonna be hardly no Republican voting 'cause they be too afraid."

"Is all of this because of the KKK?" Carrie asked with disgust.

"The KKK be real bad down there," Ben said angrily. "There be a lot of folks who have been beaten or killed outright."

"They have to be stopped!" Abby cried.

Carrie nodded. "Matthew and I talked about that not long before I left Philadelphia. President Grant and the Congress are trying to put some laws in place to stop the violence and voter intimidation."

"They might oughta start with the Fifteenth Amendment," Ben said sourly.

Abby looked surprised. "You're not happy with the Fifteenth Amendment? It gives black men the right to vote."

"Does it?" Ben asked.

Thomas took a deep breath. "Please explain what you mean, Ben. I've read that Democrats believe the Fifteenth Amendment is the most revolutionary measure ever to receive Congressional sanction. They believe it's the crowning act of a Radical Republican conspiracy to promote black equality and transform America from a confederation of states into a centralized nation."

Ben didn't try to hide his disdain. "I've talked to a lot of the black leaders about this. The amendment says the black man can vote, but it don't say nothin' about holding office. It also don't make the requirements to vote the same everywhere in the country."

"I realize it might not be perfect, but isn't it a starting place?" Abby asked.

Ben regarded her steadily. "Is it really a starting place if women don't get the right to vote too, Mrs. Cromwell?"

Abby caught her breath. "You have a point," she conceded.

Ben smiled slightly and then continued. "It ain't so much what it says; it's what it don't say. It don't say nothing about makin' sure there aren't tests that folks have to pass before they can vote."

"He's right," Harold said, chiming in for the first time. "There is nothing in the amendment to forbid literacy, property and educational tests. While there isn't anything that says only blacks must pass these tests, it's well known that most ex-slaves don't know how to read."

Rose looked thoughtful. "Not just the freed slaves," she interjected. "Many of my white students' fathers don't know how to read or write either. They're trying to learn, but they didn't have the benefit of education when they were growing up, especially in the South. They won't be able to pass the tests either."

Carrie frowned. "That's also true for most of the immigrants pouring into the country right now. They haven't been here long enough to know the language, or they just don't have access to education. They're being used to fuel the Industrial Revolution and to make men wealthy, but they aren't being given a voice if there are requirements put on the right to vote."

"White, rich men figure they be the only ones who should have a say in this country," Ben stated matter-of-factly. Then he looked at Thomas, Anthony and Harold apologetically. "I know you three ain't like that, but you not be normal."

"I know we're not," Thomas said sadly.

Carrie had been listening closely to everything being said. "Matthew is quite discouraged. He believes the country is going back to the way it was before the war." She hated that her surgical internship kept her so busy, but Matthew and Janie kept her informed on the most important issues. She and Anthony had them over for meals at least twice a week when they were all in Philadelphia.

"Enough men didn't die the first time?" Annie snapped. "What them men using for brains? It sure ain't what's in their heads."

A chuckle sounded but died away quickly at the thought of all the men who had been slaughtered during the four-year conflict. The idea of their country once again reaching that point was beyond horrifying.

"The country is tired of Reconstruction," Anthony said. "Now that the war is over, they just want their lives to go back to normal. They're tired of talking about equal rights and making things better for the freed slaves. They want to make things better for themselves, so they're eager to focus on the economy and jobs, especially here in the South. People in the North are eager to end all the discussion and fighting, as well."

"They done had five years of Reconstruction. Black folks were slaves in this country for more than two hundred years," Ben stated. "Ain't gonna solve all the problems for freed slaves in five years," he said flatly.

"I agree with you," Anthony responded. "The question is how to keep the government focused on making things right. If they give up the fight too quickly..."

Ben finished when Anthony's voice trailed off. "If they give up the fight too quickly, then things gonna be just as bad for the blacks as they were during slavery."

His proclamation caused a long silence to fall on the porch as everyone thought through all that had been said.

"Mama!"

Rose pushed herself up from her rocking chair. "Hope was down for the night, but evidently she needs me." She paused and looked around. "Her name is helping me get through these uncertain times." She turned to Ben, her heart shining in her eyes. "We all have to keep fighting, Ben. We'll fight in different ways, but we have to fight." She took a deep breath. "And we have to fight harder to make up for those people who don't have it in them to fight anymore."

*****

Rose's departure broke the serious mood. There was much to be done in the country, but there was nothing they could do that night.

Anthony leaned over and put his hand on Carrie's leg. "Can I talk my beautiful wife into a ride?"

Carrie caught her breath. "Really?" She looked longingly at the almost-full moon climbing steadily in the night sky. "I thought you would be too tired after your long trip out here."

"Does that mean I can talk you into it?" Anthony teased.

"Oh, yes," Carrie said excitedly. She hadn't changed out of her breeches. The night was still warm, so she wouldn't need anything more. She jumped up and reached for his hand. "Let's go before you change your mind."

Anthony chuckled and stood. "If you fine folks will excuse us, we have some riding to do."

Hand in hand, the two walked to the barn, breathing in the smell of spring and horses.

"Granite!"

Carrie was rewarded with a delighted nicker when Granite heard her voice. She had planned on letting him out for the night when she returned for a final check of the barn, so he was still in his stall. "We're going for a moonlight ride, boy," she said quietly. Granite nickered again and stomped his foot as he bobbed his head over the stall door. She laughed as she entered the tack room.

Carrie and Anthony exchanged smiles in the flicker of the lantern light as they silently saddled their horses and led them out into the barnyard.

Once in the saddle, Anthony turned to her. "Feel up to a race? I know I don't stand a chance, but it's always fun to try."

Carrie couldn't help the tears that welled up in her eyes as she shook her head. She blinked them away, but not before Anthony saw them glimmering in the moonlight.

"Carrie? What's wrong?"

Carrie took a deep breath and told him what Miles had revealed to her the day before.

Anthony shook his head with disbelief. "Twenty-six? I never would have guessed Granite is that old."

Carrie had met Anthony when he came to the plantation after Robert's death in search of horses to buy. His knowledge was vast. "Is Miles right that he won't live that much longer?" She was desperate to have Anthony refute his belief.

Anthony shook his head slowly. "Miles knows horses better than any man I've ever known. He's with Granite every day. Certainly, I've known horses that have lived into their thirties, but they're rare." He continued in a regretful voice. "I'm sorry, Carrie." He reached over and tipped her face up to meet his. "I know how much you love him."

Sobs caught in Carrie's throat again. "You don't think I'm odd to love a horse so much?"

Anthony smiled gently. "Would it matter?"

"No," Carrie said honestly. "Granite is special." She reached down to pat his shiny neck. "We've already been for a ride today, so I think we'll just walk tonight."

"Perfect. All I really care about is spending time with you on a beautiful night." He paused for a moment. "And being with Granite."

Carrie smiled. "Thank you."

They rode in silence for a few minutes before Anthony spoke. "Did I ever tell you about Lightning Boy?"

"Lightning Boy? No."

Anthony looked into the distance for a long moment before he began. "Lightning Boy was my first horse. My father got him for me when I was ten. He was the horse I'd dreamed of since I was put on a pony when I was three. Lightning Boy was a dark bay. He had a white star on his forehead and one white stocking on his right front leg. He was big and fast, but he was also gentle as a lamb."

Carrie was struck by the tenderness in her husband's voice.

"I had to be forced to eat and sleep, and threatened to study. All I wanted to do was be with my horse. When it was nice outside, I would study under a big tree in the pasture. Lightning Boy would lie on the grass beside me, reaching over to nibble at my book when he got impatient."

Carrie laughed at the picture his words painted. "What a special horse."

"Yes," Anthony agreed. "We were inseparable until I went away to college. I told him everything. I didn't want to leave him, but my father said he wouldn't allow me to throw away a university education. I explained to him that I wouldn't need one, because I was going to spend my whole life working with horses, but he wasn't impressed."

"I can imagine," Carrie murmured.

"I came home every chance I got," Anthony continued, "just so I could see Lightning Boy. My parents wanted to believe I came home to visit them, but they both knew the truth." He took a long breath.

Carrie stiffened, prepared for what she was certain was coming.

"When I was a senior, I came home during the spring for a short visit. Lightning Boy didn't meet me at the front entrance the way he always did." He shook his head. "I don't know how he did it, but he always knew when I was coming home." His voice became thick. "He had died the week before. My parents didn't write me because they knew I was in the middle of exams. They knew it would destroy me."

Carrie pulled Granite to a stop, reached over and took Anthony's hand. "I'm so sorry," she said.

Anthony nodded. "I've had other fine horses, but there will never be another horse like Lightning Boy. I figure you only get a horse like that once in your life."

"So you understand what I'm feeling," Carrie whispered around the tears in her throat. "Thank you."

Anthony nodded. "I do. Most folks just see animals as animals. They love them, but they can't understand the depth some of us feel. Lightning Boy was a gift from God to me. He helped make me a man. A part of me died when he died," he admitted. "I still think about him often. I'll always miss him."

The two sat in silence for several minutes, watching the glow of the moon on the open fields. Leaves from the nearby woods reflected silver as an owl hooted a warning. The night air was full of the perfume of spring.

"What do you want to do?" Anthony finally asked.

Carrie was already totally in love with her husband, but her love expanded to a greater breadth with that simple question. She knew he understood her reluctance to leave Granite. Haltingly, she told him about her experience in the clearing the day before. "I believe I'm supposed to be in Philadelphia," she finished. "But," she added, "I plan on coming back to the plantation every chance I get. I may be here more than I'm in Philadelphia, but I'll make sure I fulfill all the requirements for my surgical internship."

"Coming home more often will make both Frances and I very happy," Anthony assured her. He squeezed her hand. "I support your decision. If you change your mind at some point, I'll support that decision, too."

Carrie threw her leg over the saddle and slid down to the ground. She beckoned to Anthony. As soon as he landed next to her, she threw her arms around him. "I'm the luckiest woman in the world to have you," she murmured. "I love you." Gazing up into his face, she pulled his head down low enough to claim his lips in a warm kiss.

Chapter Ten

Carrie was at the clinic early the next morning. Since she wasn't going to be home long, she wanted to make the most of every minute. She had slipped into the barn before she left, given Granite a carrot fresh from the garden, and promised him they would go for a ride that afternoon.

Striding into the medical clinic attached to the schoolhouse, she was pleased to see how clean and orderly it was. She wasn't surprised—Polly was completely competent to handle most medical issues when Carrie was gone—she was just pleased. Cleanliness and order were important to her, and had become increasingly important during her surgical internship. Dr. Wild had told her enough horrific stories of deaths caused by unsanitary conditions to keep her scared and alert for the rest of her career.

Carrie was putting away the new supply of Hypericum when she heard the door open. She looked up with a smile, hopeful that Polly had moved beyond her anger. One look at the tiny black woman's face told her that wasn't true. "Hello, Polly," she said evenly. "The clinic looks wonderful."

"Hello, Carrie," Polly responded in a formal voice that was so unlike the warm, friendly woman she knew. "I'm glad you made it out of Richmond safely. Clint told me what happened with Ben Scott."

Carrie took her response as a positive sign, but the good feeling dissolved when Polly stared at what she was doing with hard eyes.

"Is that more medicine for those men who tried to kill Amber?"

"It is," Carrie acknowledged, and then turned to face her friend. "I've tried for the last three months to think of something to say that will make things right with us, Polly."

"You might want to try *I'm sorry for being stupid, Polly. I've decided not to help those men who killed my husband and tried to kill your daughter.*" Polly's voice was twisted with anger and bitterness.

Carrie stared at her in shock. She knew Polly was against what she was doing, but she had hoped that time would diminish the anger. It seemed to have done nothing but exacerbate it. The sound of footsteps on the stairs told Carrie she wouldn't have to think of a response right away.

Lillian smiled brightly when she stepped through the door. "Hello, you two. It's good to see you both in the clinic. You're going to be extra busy today. The word has spread through my students to their parents that you're back, Carrie. They'll probably be lined up outside."

Polly sniffed. "I guess just about everyone will come see a doctor who is willing to give *anyone* life-saving medicine."

Lillian frowned. "I thought you told me you were going to stuff away the anger while Carrie was here, Polly. I don't see how it's helping."

It bothered Carrie that Lillian had felt it was necessary to mediate between her and Polly, but she couldn't deny it was sorely needed.

Polly scowled and looked at Carrie defiantly. "I'm trying, but it ain't so easy. Carrie, I'm here to see patients, but as soon as I see them men coming toward the clinic, I'm done. I'm going home for the day, and I won't be back."

Carrie thought through her response. She would never regret helping Hank, Newton and the other men they had brought to the clinic to get relief from the phantom pain of their amputated limbs. Polly had supported her choice in the beginning, but Hank's revelation that he had been with the vigilantes had ended it. Hank hadn't pulled the trigger, and he claimed he didn't know any violence would occur, but that didn't change the fact that when they rode off, Robert lay in a pool of blood, with Amber's body trapped beneath him. Robert had saved the little girl's life but lost his own.

Carrie had found a way to walk away from the past and choose forgiveness. Polly hadn't done that. Her hatred had grown and was eating her alive.

"How did you do it?" Lillian asked abruptly.

"Forgive them?" Carrie asked, slightly startled by the intensity shining from Lillian's dark eyes. That kind of intensity was usually the result of something personal. When Lillian nodded, Carrie thought back to that day. Hatred had blazed through her when Hank first made his confession, but seeing his pain, and then seeing the hatred that consumed Polly, convinced her she didn't want to live that way.

"I was getting ready to start a new life with Anthony," she said quietly. "I didn't want to carry all that hate into my new life. Hating Hank wasn't going to change the past, but choosing to *not* hate him was going to make life better for me, Anthony and Frances. I didn't forgive Hank because he deserved it." She relived that day in her mind, just as she had so many times. "I forgave him for me."

"It's not always that easy," Lillian said heatedly.

Carrie gazed at her, wondering what burden she carried. "I don't remember saying it was easy. I can assure you it was not. It took everything I had to let go of the anger and hatred."

"How did you do it?"

"I chose grace and compassion," Carrie said softly, remembering the freedom that had flowed through her entire being when she'd made that choice. Staring into Hank's haunted eyes had made her realize she wasn'tthe only one that had been almost destroyed by that night. "There is enough hate in this country. I didn't want to be part of the cycle. The only thing that will change it is for some of us to choose *not* to hate. I knew it was what I had to do."

Lillian was listening intently, every muscle in her body tensed as if she wanted to flee. "But *how* did you do it? *How* did you choose grace and compassion?"

Carrie searched for the right words. How *had* she done it? How had she moved beyond the pain and hatred that had almost consumed her? "I made a choice," she said. "Lillian, I believed my life was over when Robert was killed and Bridget died. I wanted to die with them. When I didn't die, I was furious to have to live a life I no longer wanted to live. It took me two years to decide life was worth living. Two years to decide I still had a reason for being alive. That day, here in the clinic, when Hank confessed to having been on the plantation during the attack, I suddenly had a target for all that anger and hatred that was still in me, lurking beneath the surface. I wanted to hang onto it and hate him with the same measure of pain he had helped give me."

"But you didn't," Lillian murmured.

"No," Carrie agreed. "Somehow, I realized I had the power to choose. To choose grace and compassion over hatred. Hank benefitted from my choice, but I benefitted far more. When I looked in his eyes and told him I forgave him, it set something free in me. I hate what he did, and I always will." She took another deep breath. "But I won't hate *him*."

Lillian stared at her. "And, just like that, all the anger was gone?"

"No," Carrie said honestly. "Sarah told me once that forgiveness is like peeling an onion. You can peel away a layer, but there is another one hiding right beneath it. It takes a long time to peel away all the layers until you get to the core." She struggled to put her thoughts into words that would make sense. "There have been many times in the past months when thoughts of what Hank did caused the anger to rear its ugly head. I had to make the same choice several times before I truly felt I forgave him."

"And you have now?"

"I believe I have," Carrie responded, "but the thing I know for sure is that I will keep choosing to forgive him if I discover more layers. It's the way I want to live my life."

Lillian shook her head, obviously struggling with what she was hearing. "You're helping Hank *and* the others. You know some of them are vigilantes, don't you? Hank wasn't the only one."

Carrie chose her words carefully. "I know some of them *were* vigilantes. They have all given me their word that they will commit no more violence. I believe them. You might think I'm foolish, but no more violence has happened. That gives me hope." She paused, thinking through what she would say next. "I know there are times when violence must be met with strong force. I'm not naïve. However, I believe when we have the choice to confront anger and violence with caring and compassion, we oftentimes have much better results. At the end of the day, all I'm really concerned about is that my family and the people I love stay safe."

"You really feel better?" Lillian asked sharply.

Once again, Carrie longed to know what Lillian was fighting to forgive, but it was up to Lillian whether she wanted to tell her. "I'm free," she said firmly. "I'll do everything I can to help any person in this community. It actually helps me make some sense of Robert and Bridget's deaths."

"And Anthony don't think you're crazy?" Polly snapped, although her voice had lost some of its earlier edge.

"He doesn't think I'm crazy," Carrie assured her gently. "He acknowledges that he doesn't know if he could do the same thing, but I disagree with him. None of us know what we're capable of doing until we're put in the position of doing it."

Silence filled the clinic, her words seeming to echo in thc stillness.

"Gabe tells me the hate is eating me up," Polly whispered, blinking hard to hold the tears at bay.

Carrie's heart swelled with sympathy. "I know it was eating *me* up. Going to see Hank that day was one of the hardest things I've ever done, but I'll always be grateful I did it." She yearned to wrap Polly in her arms, but the tension vibrating through the smaller woman's slender frame told her it wasn't the right time.

When neither Lillian nor Polly spoke again, Carrie was content to let the quiet wrap around them. The soft breeze blowing through the windows carried the sound of chirping birds, evidence of burgeoning new life after a brutal winter.

"Is it like today?" Lillian asked.

Carrie raised a brow, not certain she understood.

"Is forgiveness like spring melting away all the hard cold of winter?"

Carrie smiled. "I think that's an amazingly accurate description."

Polly turned and stalked to the window, her spine stiff as a board as she stared outside.

Carrie knew her friend was fighting a battle. She longed to fight it for her, but that wasn't possible. A quick glance at the clock told her that patients would start to arrive in a short while, but after her conversation with Lillian the day before, she suspected the three men who had come every day since their initial visit with Lillian would almost certainly be the first.

"Polly, if you want to leave, I can handle things here," Carrie offered gently.

Several moments passed before Polly slowly shook her head. When she turned around, rivers of tears were streaming down her face, but there was also the beginning of peace.

Carrie rushed forward to take her friend in her arms. Polly sagged against her, letting the torrent of tears flow. Carrie stood silently, knowing Polly had to fight this battle on her own.

When the tears finally abated, Polly took a deep, shuddering breath. "Well..." she muttered, "I ain't had a storm like that in a long time." She shook her head. "Not since that man killed Robert while he was trying to kill Amber." The words were sorrowful, but not uttered with the previous degree of hatred.

Carrie stepped back when she heard the sound of hoof beats. "Polly, the first patients are arriving. If you want to go home, you can go out the back door."

Polly took another deep breath and then shook her head. "No, I'll stay."

Carrie hesitated. "I suspect our first patients are Hank's three friends who want Hypericum." A glance at Lillian, who was watching out the window, confirmed her suspicions.

"I know," Polly replied. "If I'm going to choose grace and compassion, I reckon it's not too early to start."

Carrie smiled with relief, glad beyond words to have her friend back. The clomp of heavy feet on the stairs told her they would have to talk more later. The same with Lillian...

*****

"Hello, gentlemen," Carrie said when the door swung open and three men entered. "You must be Larry, Carson and Bob." Lillian had filled her in on everything she knew.

"That's right," the first man said. "I'm Larry. Are you Dr. Wallington?" The hope in his voice was almost pathetic.

"Yes, I'm Dr. Wallington. It's nice to meet you, Larry," Carrie said, struck by the simmering pain in his eyes. His tanned face would have been attractive if it weren't twisted with lines that made him look far older than she was certain he actually was.

"Thank you, doc," Larry replied.

Carrie didn't see the abrasive man Lillian had described, but the fact that she was in the clinic evidently absolved the need for a rough attitude.

"This is Carson and Bob," Larry added.

Carrie smiled at both of the other men and waved at the chairs against the wall. "Have a seat, please. I have everything ready for you."

All three of the men's eyes lit up.

"We're going to get some of that Hypericum?" Larry said hopefully.

"Of course," Carrie said gently. "I don't want you to be in pain even one more moment than necessary. I'm sorry you've had to wait for me to return before you could get it."

Carson raised a brow. "Are you really a surgeon?"

"That's what they tell me," Carrie said cheerfully. As she spoke, something about Bob's face triggered a memory. She stared at him hard, remembering... "You were at Chimborazo during the war, weren't you, Bob?"

Bob gaped at her. "That's right. How did you know that?"

Carrie continued to sort the memories in her mind. "Did you lose your leg at Petersburg?"

Bob shook his head in disbelief. "Yes." Suddenly his eyes grew wide with disbelief. "Were you the angel that talked that surgeon into not taking off my other leg?"

Carrie remembered the case well now that the memories were flowing. She was surprised she could sort Bob out from the thousands of men she had seen during the war years, but some cases had stood out for her. "You were barely out of your teens. I didn't want you to live your life without both legs."

"I was only seventeen," Bob admitted. "I'm real grateful I got to keep at least one of them."

Carrie did the math in her head quickly. "You're only twenty-three?" she asked with astonishment.

"I know I look older," Bob said ruefully. "I reckon the years have been right hard on me."

Carrie smiled. "You're still alive. That's what counts." She wasn't going to tell him he looked twenty years older than he was. Extreme pain could age anyone.

She quickly became all business. "I assume all of you are suffering from phantom pain from your injuries. Is that correct?" When all of them nodded, she continued. "I'm a homeopathic physician," Carrie explained. "Homeopathic physicians treat patients differently. Instead of giving you drugs to deaden the pain, we have discovered ways to actually heal you."

"That's what we've heard," Larry said, hope pulsing in his voice. "Do you think you can help us, too?"

"I do." Carrie smiled and moved over to her medicine cabinet. "There is a remedy called Hypericum," she replied, pulling a bottle from the cabinet. All three men were familiar with the name of the treatment, but she knew giving them additional information would build their confidence in her ability to help them. "Hypericum is made from a plant called St. John's wort, but the preparation of it is what makes it work so well on pain like yours." She paused to make sure the men were paying attention. "Hypericum is prepared by taking the complete St. John's wort plant and chopping it into fine pieces. Those pieces are soaked in alcohol for a long time, and then the solution is filtered, so that it's as pure as possible." She held up the bottle in her hand.

"Does it help everybody?" Bob demanded.

"*Almost* everybody," Carrie said honestly. "There is a small percentage of people that the Hypericum is not effective for, but almost all the men I've treated report a complete elimination of pain." She lifted the bottle again. "I want you to mix five drops with a glass of water, four times a day. Every six hours will be best."

"Is there something else we can do to make sure it works?" Larry asked, his eyes fastened on the bottle. "Is there something about the men who it doesn't work for that we can change?"

Carrie smiled. "What if I said only men who don't commit vigilante violence can be helped? Would that make a difference?" She kept her voice light, but she was certain these three men had heard about her agreement with the other veterans. She would never make it a condition of care because that would break the Hippocratic Oath she had taken, but perhaps they didn't need to know that.

Larry flushed. "Hank told us that if we do anything dumb, he'll make sure we never get another drop of this treatment because we'll mess up things for everyone." He looked at the other men and then met her eyes evenly. "You have our word, Dr. Wallington. What you are doing is more than anyone has ever done for us."

"Thank you," Carrie said. "Now, to answer your question, I really don't know why it doesn't help some men. I've had only one man it didn't help. I don't know the reason for certain, but I suspect it could have something to do with the amount of alcohol he drank.

Alcohol is not your friend," she said firmly. "If you want your body to heal, I would encourage you to stay away from it."

"I reckon we can do that," Larry said. "I didn't think I would ever see Hank anything other than dead drunk. He hasn't had a sip since you started helping him. He's become a different man, for certain. I don't drink much, but I ain't got a problem giving it up for good."

The other two men nodded their heads eagerly. Carrie didn't know if they truly meant it—she suspected they would agree to anything to get the medicine—but at least she had informed them.

Each man accepted the bottle Carrie held out as if it were liquid gold. Carrie knew that being out of pain meant far more to them than any amount of money ever could.

Suddenly, Bob frowned. "What happens when we run out?"

Carrie opened her mouth to explain that Alvin would deliver it to them as he had been doing for all the others.

"You come right back to the clinic and I'll take care of you," Polly said firmly.

The three men looked startled to discover they would be receiving the medicine from a black woman, but they nodded gratefully after a brief hesitation.

"Thank you," Larry said. "We appreciate it."

Carrie's heart soared with joy. As important as it was for Polly to be willing to treat these men, it was far more wonderful to know she had released the hate. She didn't miss the thoughtful look on Lillian's face. Lillian was expected at the school, but Carrie knew she had wanted to see how Polly would handle this situation.

Lillian gave her a slight smile and nod, and then slipped out the door.

Larry turned back to Carrie. "There are more of us."

"I figured there would be," Carrie responded. "How many?"

"Ten more," Larry replied hesitantly. "Is that too many? Do you have enough medicine?"

"I do," Carrie assured him, glad she had anticipated a large number of veterans in need of treatment. It would have been impossible for the word not to spread about men who had suffered for years, suddenly free of pain. Polly's change of heart was a God-sent gift. It was certainly going to make Alvin's life easier when he didn't have to deliver the Hypericum to each of the men. "Can you have all of them here tomorrow? I want to start them immediately. I'm not here for very long, and I want to make sure I can check everyone's progress before I have to go back to Philadelphia."

"I'll have them here," Larry promised.

The three men stood to leave, obviously eager to get started on their bottles of Hypericum.

*****

As soon as the men left, Carrie turned to Polly and gave her a big hug. "I know how hard that was," she said softly.

"Not as hard as I thought it would be," Polly replied with a shake of her head. "Once I got that poison out of me, everything looked different. Gabe told me it would be that way. *You* told me," she added, "but I couldn't hear it. I couldn't believe it."

"I understand completely," Carrie murmured. "The whole time I was riding to Hank's house last December, I couldn't believe I would actually be able to do what I did. Forgiving him was much more of a gift to me than it was to him."

"I've been so angry at you," Polly admitted. "I thought you were crazy, and I thought you were dishonoring Robert, and Bridget, and Amber..." Her voice caught. "I'm so sorry for how I've treated you."

"Shh..." Carrie held her close. "You loved me through all my pain and anger when Robert was killed. Besides, mine lasted much longer," she reminded her friend with a smile.

Polly chuckled and then sobered. "Hate is a powerful thing, Carrie. It's a poison that eats away at your soul. I didn't realize how much hatred I had in me from the attack until all of a sudden I had a target for that hatred." She turned to stare out the window for a long moment and then swung back around to face her. "How do you fight against all the wrong going on in this country and not let hate eat you up? There are so many people being hurt. So many wrong things being done..." Her voice trailed away before she repeated her question. "How *do* you fight against all the wrong going on in this country and not let the hate eat you up?"

"I wish I knew the answer to that question. It's so easy to let anger create anger. So easy to let hatred create more hatred."

"I don't believe that love alone can undo all the wrong things done to people," Polly stated. "I don't think it's that simple."

"I agree," Carrie replied. "It's something I struggle with all the time."

"So, what do you do?" Polly demanded.

Carrie searched for words. "Sarah told me once that *dere be times you got to do the hard kind of lovin', Carrie girl.*"

"What does *that* mean?"

"I wasn't sure at the time," Carrie admitted. "I'm not certain I know now, but I think it means that you do the right thing with compassion and grace." Her thoughts became clearer as she talked. "I think it means that you stand up to the wrong being done, without hating the people who are doing it. I think it means you fight the wrong things being done, but you choose to have grace and compassion for the people who are doing it."

Polly rolled her eyes. "How? I just see a bunch of stupid people doing stupid things."

"Perhaps by recognizing that their actions come from fear," Carrie said thoughtfully. "I don't pretend to have the answers, Polly. I'm trying to figure it out, too. I don't understand why so many people do what they do, but Sarah used to tell me that *most of the bad things in the world be done 'cause folks be afraid.*"

"I certainly wish I could have met Sarah," Polly said wistfully.

"I miss her," Carrie replied. "She was the wisest woman I ever knew." The sound of voices in the distance told her they were soon to have more patients. "I hope I never lose the memory of the things she told me. The older I get, the wiser I know she was."

*****

Moses and Anthony cantered side-by-side down the road nestled between the tobacco fields. They waved to the men hard at work, their bare backs glistening in the warm sunshine.

"The last of the tobacco seedlings are going in today," Moses said.

"How many extra men have you hired for this season?" Anthony asked, the soft dirt and crumbled oyster shells of the road absorbing the sound of the horse hooves enough to allow conversation.

"Fifty," Moses answered. "I wish I could hire more, but that's all we need."

"How many men have you had to turn away?"

Moses frowned. "Far more than I hired." He shook his head. "Cromwell Plantation and Blackwell Plantation are the only ones who pay what the work is worth. Other plantation workers are hardly doing better than they did in slavery. I've talked to Perry about this. He's turned away many men at Blackwell, too."

Anthony snorted. "Cromwell and Blackwell are also the only ones that treat their workers with dignity and don't make life miserable for them. Of course they're trying to get jobs here."

Moses' frown deepened to a scowl. "I keep hoping the healthy profits we've brought in since the war ended will convince the other plantation owners to change how they do things."

Anthony shook his head. "I wish it were just about profits. If it were, things might change more quickly.

Unfortunately, their fear and hatred are even bigger than their desire for money."

"It doesn't make sense," Moses replied, frustration filling his face. "The plantation owners are complaining that they can't make the same profits as before the war because they lost their slaves. We're proving they can make far more money if they treat their workers fairly and let them take part in the profits, but they don't seem to care." He looked at Anthony. "I don't see any change. Are things getting any better in Richmond?"

"No," Anthony answered honestly. "And I'm afraid they're going to get worse with all the political chaos between Mayor Chahoon and Ellyson. All anybody can focus on is that the freed slaves are taking jobs away from white men. Too many believe that if they can change the political reality, it will make things better for them."

"Don't they realize the business owners are a huge part of the problem? They hire blacks because they can pay them less," Moses said angrily. "They're doing the same work but getting less than half. It also makes for unfair competition. If everyone would pay the same, at least men could compete on an equal basis. As it is, blacks continue in poverty, and white men get angrier."

"Not all of us are like that," Anthony said, astutely aware of how right Moses was.

Moses waved his hand in the air. "Of course *you're* not. I know you pay the carriage drivers fairly and give them the option to make more money than they could anywhere else. That's wonderful, but is there any other white man in the entire city doing that?"

Anthony answered honestly. "Since Cromwell Factory burned? No."

"Exactly." Moses' eyes searched the field stretching out before them.

Anthony watched him. "What are you looking for?"

Moses smiled. "I'm not looking for anything. I'm planning the next expansion."

"More tobacco fields?" Anthony asked. "Aren't you working hard enough already? The plantation is making more money than it ever has. Thomas was telling me what a magnificent job you're doing."

"If we plant more tobacco, we can hire more men," Moses answered. "I can't change everything in the country right now, but I can at least give more men a chance to provide for themselves and their families."

Anthony heard an edge to his friend's voice that wasn't often there. "The situation in Richmond is really bothering you, isn't it?"

Moses gritted his teeth. "The fact that Ben Scott is having to hide for his life and move north is bothering me. It's wrong. It reminds me of what Rose and I had to go through to get to Philadelphia through the Underground Railroad. Things have always been bad, but I thought freedom would mean more to more people. There are too many blacks suffering as badly now in freedom as they were in slavery. Something has to be done." His dark eyes blazed with intensity.

Anthony continued to study him. "Do you regret not running for political office, Moses?"

Moses swung around to stare at Anthony for a long moment and then shrugged. "I made my decision."

"Do you regret it?" Anthony pressed.

Moses sighed. "I don't know." His voice was thick with frustration. "I love being here on the plantation, and I know what it means to the workers. It's enough for me, but I wonder if I'm being selfish. There are men out there like Ben who are risking everything to fight for equality for our race. What am I doing?"

"What you're *meant* to do?"

"Am I?" Moses' voice sounded tortured.

"Moses, you went to school. Both you and Rose believed you should come back to the plantation. The two of you are fighting for your people right here. You're giving jobs to a large number of freed slaves, but you're also providing proof of what is possible if people move beyond their prejudice. You're expanding the plantation to provide for more men, which means you're providing for more families. Not to mention, by doing the right thing, you're also expanding your profits."

Anthony searched his mind for the right words to relieve the agony in his friend's eyes. "I think a lot about Carric's belief in the Bregdan Principle. I read it almost every day before I leave the house. I think it's right."

Moses looked thoughtful. "The belief that every action we take will reflect in someone else's life?"

"Yes. You have about seventy-five men working on the plantation right now, both full-time and seasonal. They're feeding their families. Their kids are getting an education. They're learning how to read and write before they leave here. Moses, you have no idea what the repercussions will be throughout history. You're not just helping seventy-five men; you're helping hundreds. Right now. In the future, as their families grow, it will be thousands whose lives were changed because you followed your heart and did the right thing."

Moses remained silent, but Anthony could tell he was thinking hard. "I don't know what you're meant to do in the future. Perhaps you'll run for political office, perhaps not. All I know is that you're changing a lot of lives right now."

Moses looked up to meet his eyes. "Like you are with the carriage company in Richmond."

Anthony took a deep breath. "I hope so. Taking the risk to start River City Carriages was more than worth it when I think about all the generations of lives it can change. Carrie has helped me understand that."

Moses smiled suddenly. "Thank you, Anthony." His eyes, now free from their haunted glaze, looked to the woods again. "If we clear fifty more acres this fall, we can hire twenty more men in the spring."

"And I'll keep expanding the carriage company," Anthony responded. "I added eight more carriages recently. We'll do what we can with what we're given. If enough people do the right thing, change will happen." He chuckled. "Perhaps I should think about preaching. I sure do sound like a preacher right now. Sorry. I'll be quiet."

"No need," Moses said firmly. "Thank you. For more than just what you said, though. When Robert died, it almost killed Carrie, too. There were times I thought she would never come back to life. When she finally did, I didn't believe she could find anyone as perfect for her as Robert was." His eyes met Anthony's. "She did. I'll always be grateful for that."

"Thank you," Anthony replied, a lump lodging in his throat. "Carrie is the most special woman in the world. I'll do my best to be worthy of her."

Moses chuckled. "Trust me, I know how much of a struggle that is. I don't figure I'll ever be worthy of a woman like Rose, but I'm going to keep trying."

*****

Carrie took a deep breath when the last patient left the office with a smile and wave. She was exhausted, but happy.

"Miss this?" Polly asked.

"I do," Carrie admitted. "I'm enjoying the surgical internship, but I really just want to come back to the plantation and help with the clinic in Richmond. This is where I belong."

"We'll all be real glad when you're back here for good," Polly said, and then hesitated.

Carrie looked at her, alerted by the hesitation. "What is it, Polly?"

"Do you have to go right home?"

"Not necessarily," Carrie replied, knowing she could delay her ride a little longer. "What do you want to do?" She suspected she already knew, but she wasn't going to be the one to speak it.

Polly met her gaze. "Will you go with me to see Hank?"

Carrie grinned and nodded. "Absolutely."

<u>Chapter Eleven</u>

Carrie swung into the saddle just as the full moon rose over the horizon. Huge and golden, it called to her heart. "It's beautiful," she said softly, grateful the early afternoon rain had cleared out in time for the clouds to blow farther west.

Anthony smiled and urged his mount forward. "Did you have a good day?"

Carrie smiled at him happily. "The best. It was wonderful to see my old patients, along with many new ones. And..." She had saved the best news for last. "Polly and I are on good terms again." She knew her face was glowing.

Anthony grinned. "How did that happen? I know you were concerned about how she would respond when she discovered you were treating even more men with Hypericum."

Carrie filled him in on the morning events. "The best part of the day was going to see Hank," she said, remembering the magic of the time spent there. "Polly asked me to go with her."

Anthony whistled. "I want every detail."

"I think Hank was terrified when we got there. He was so happy to see me, but when he realized Polly was with me, he pretty much froze in place." She paused, remembering. "Polly walked right up to him, took his hand, told him she forgave him, and that she was sorry she'd hated him." Tears filled her eyes. "It was beautiful."

"What did Hank do?" Anthony asked.

"He broke down crying," Carrie replied. "I really think it helped him as much as it helped Polly. A lot of people were hurt that night on the plantation. It means so much to me that there's healing for everyone."

Anthony's interest morphed into concern. "How does Amber feel about all this?"

"She's happy," Carrie said. "She never hated the men who tried to shoot her, she just grieved Robert. There is more love and wisdom in that little girl than most adults will ever hope to have. She and I talked back in December when I forgave Hank, and Amber was so happy for me. She tried to talk to her mama, but it didn't do any good."

"People need time to do things in their own way," Anthony said. "I'm glad Polly has found some peace. I talked to Gabe about it this morning. He's been very concerned about her, but hadn't been able to get through to her."

Carrie lifted her face to the glow of the moon. "The vigilante attack was horrible in so many ways. My hope is that we can all move on now."

They rode quietly for a while before Anthony broached a new subject. "What's Lillian's story?"

Carrie looked at him quizzically. "Why are you asking?"

Anthony shrugged. "I'm not trying to be nosy, but it seems there's a lot of pain in her. It's obvious she's very intelligent, but she always seems to be holding back somehow."

"I agree," Carrie replied, once again impressed with her husband's sensitivity. "I wish I knew more about her, but I don't. I've been gone so much of the time since she moved down here from Ohio."

"Have you asked Rose?"

"No. If Lillian wants me to know more about her, she'll tell me herself."

Anthony shook his head, a teasing light in his eyes. "You're giving women a bad name, you know."

"How is that?" Carrie demanded with mock indignation.

"Aren't all women supposed to be gossip-mongers? Why should you wait for Lillian to tell you herself when you can get Rose to tell you?" Anthony asked playfully. "That's certainly what *my* mother would have done."

Carrie smiled, but quickly grew serious. "One of the things I learned in medical school is how important it is for women to support each other. I learned that from Abby initially, but being in an all-female school certainly drove it home for me."

"How?" Anthony asked.

Carrie thought through her response. "It's so easy to get caught up in competing with each other. When I first started school, I wanted to be better than everyone else. I worked hard to prove I was. Then it changed."

"What changed it?"

Carrie searched for the right words. "It was exhausting. I finally realized that I could try to be better than everyone else, or I could just be the best I could be for myself. No one is really going to care in the future, except my patients." She searched her memory. "But there was more..."

Anthony waited patiently.

"I saw women fighting each other. They put other students down to make themselves look better because it was so important to be the best. All that really did was hurt *everyone*." She shook her head. "It didn't make sense to me. Abby and I have talked about it a lot. So have Janie and I. The most important thing I can do is respect other women." She paused. "Part of that is not talking about them or talking behind their backs. If I really want to know what's going on with Lillian, I'll ask her, but I don't think it's something she talks about easily." Carrie paused. "I'll wait."

Anthony took her hand and looked at her admiringly. "I'm proud of you. That's a philosophy everyone should take. Humans would get along far better."

Carrie nodded and then changed the subject. "Are you coming back to Philadelphia with me when I leave?"

Anthony looked at her curiously. "That's what we've planned from the beginning. Why are you asking?"

"Because if things are really bad in Richmond, won't you be needed there? I saw you talking to Father. Both of you were very serious." She had wanted to talk to Anthony about it ever since she had arrived home that afternoon and seen them deep in conversation on the porch.

"Your father and I are serious about a lot of things," Anthony said evasively. "We happen to be business partners."

"Something I'm well aware of," Carrie retorted. "Anthony, were you being serious about the trouble you suspect is coming to Richmond? You don't need to be careful of me, and I would prefer you not play games."

She raised her hand quickly. "And I want to apologize right now that the words that just came out of my mouth sounded far harsher than I meant them. I'm concerned, and I'm tired."

Anthony looked contrite. "I'm sorry I was evasive. The truth is that we don't know what's happening. News is trickling in from some of your father's friends who have been in Richmond, but we don't really know how legitimate the source is."

"The news is bad?"

"It's about what we expected. Neither side is budging, so the tension keeps growing."

"Any more riots?"

"Not that I'm aware of."

"Have you heard from Willard or Marcus?" When Anthony didn't respond immediately, Carrie tensed. "What is it?"

"Once again, I just don't know." Anthony spread his hands in frustration. "I would like to say no news is good news, but it could also mean things are so crazy right now that neither of them can get word to me."

"You're worried that the violence could be directed to the carriage drivers because they work for you, and because they're black." It wasn't really a question. Anthony's expression told Carrie everything she needed to know.

Anthony sighed. "Yes," he admitted. "Ellyson is being pushed to the mayor position because he has the same ultra-conservative beliefs as the Democratic Party. They're trying to regain power now that Virginia has been readmitted to the Union. This new political push seems to be giving business owners the belief that they're free to fight for what they think is right." He paused, as if he wasn't sure he should continue, but finally did. "Too many of them resent the way we're running the company."

"Just like they resent the way Father and Moses run the plantation," Carrie said thoughtfully.

"Yes."

Carrie took a deep breath. "If things don't resolve themselves before we leave, it might be dangerous for you to come home with me." She hated putting words to her fears, but it was best to get it out in the open.

"Not dangerous for me, but it could be dangerous for the others," he admitted.

Carrie's heart squeezed with pain. Despite what he'd said, she knew how dangerous it could be for Anthony if people got riled up enough about the fair treatment of his employees. The vigilantes had not come to attack Amber, they had come to punish Robert and her father for allowing blacks too much power on Cromwell Plantation. She had simply gotten in the way of their emotion. "It could be dangerous for everyone," she said flatly, holding up her hand to stop his protest. "We both know it's true, Anthony."

Anthony closed his mouth. "It's true."

Carrie fought to keep her breathing even. "What are you going to do?"

Anthony stared at her for a long moment before he shook his head. "I don't know," he said slowly, his words laced with regret. "I'm sorry. I know that's not what you want to hear."

Carrie took a deep breath. Letting fear control her was not what either of them needed. All she really wanted to do was beg him to come home with her, to get as far away from the danger in Richmond as possible. A long silence passed before she finally found words to respond. "We don't know what's going to happen yet. Let's cross that bridge when we come to it."

*****

Carrie was surprised to see Rose standing on the porch when she and Anthony left the barn after putting the horses away for the night.

"Do you mind if I steal your wife away for a little while?" Rose asked Anthony.

"Of course not." Anthony gave Carrie a quick kiss and then opened the front door. "I'm trusting Annie will have left some cookies in the kitchen."

Carrie chuckled at the sound of his boyish hope. "Since when would there not be cookies?"

"I smelled a rhubarb pie baking after dinner," Rose said helpfully.

"You two have fun," Anthony said with a quick grin. "There may or may not be pie left in the morning."

Carrie laughed and then turned to Rose when the door closed behind her husband. "Is everything all right?" She was sure Anthony hadn't noticed the tension in Rose's deceptively light tone.

"Yes," Rose assured her. "Lillian wanted to talk to you."

"Lillian?" Carrie looked around but didn't see the other woman. "Where is she?"

"I'm right here," Lillian said quietly, appearing on the porch from the shadows that had concealed her.

Carrie was immediately struck by the look shining in Lillian's eyes. It wasn't exactly fear, but she could tell Lillian was struggling to not bolt and run. What was going on? She turned to gaze at Rose, but her friend's eyes were locked on the other woman.

"How about if we go for a walk?" Rose suggested.

Lillian looked relieved.

Mystified, Carrie followed them down from the porch, accepting the light coat Rose handed to her. There was just enough of a chill in the spring air to make it welcome.

The three women walked quietly for several minutes before Lillian broke the silence. "Thank you for doing this."

"What exactly am I doing?" Carrie asked lightly, hoping to alleviate the tension she felt radiating from Lillian's entire body.

Lillian managed a smile. "I have something to ask you, but first I need to tell you a story."

"I'm listening," Carrie said, wondering if she was about to find out what Lillian kept so closely concealed.

"I'm a homosexual," Lillian said flatly.

Carrie absorbed the blunt statement. "I see," she finally replied. "Should that bother me?"

"Doesn't it?"

Carrie thought about the question for a moment. "I don't know enough about it to know if it should bother me or not," she said honestly. "I like what I do know about you. We haven't spent much time together, but Rose and Susan love you, and Frances and Amber adore you. In my world, those are the best recommendations you could receive."

Lillian stared at her. "Do you know what a homosexual is?"

Carrie smiled, thankful she at least knew enough to answer the question. "You love women instead of men."

"It doesn't bother you?" Lillian demanded again.

Carrie gazed into her glittering eyes. "Evidently you think it's going to," she said. "It doesn't," she said firmly. "Does it bother you that I'm a doctor?"

"Why should it?" Lillian asked in astonishment.

"Because we're two women going against societal expectations," Carrie replied. "There are plenty of women who look down on me because I make them uncomfortable. I've learned to live with it, but it's never pleasant to experience." She thought about the pain in Lillian's voice earlier that day when they had talked about forgiveness with Polly. Obviously, something very painful had happened to her. "Who hurt you, Lillian?"

Lillian sighed. "It wasn't me. It was the woman I love."

Carrie waited, knowing Lillian needed to tell the story in her own way.

"Her name is Roberta. We met each other in Cincinnati when I finished school." Her eyes softened. "We lived together for two years...just as friends, of course. At least that's what everyone thought. We were careful, but there were people who figured it out." Lillian's voice choked. "There was a group of men who pulled Roberta into an alley when she was on her way home from work one evening." Tears flowed down the woman's cheeks. "They beat her with a bat." She paused, trying to steady her voice. "When she made her way home, I barely recognized her. I took care of her, but when she was better, she left town to go back to Minnesota. She said she would feel safer there."

Carrie stopped and reached out to take one of Lillian's hands, turning her so they faced each other. She knew Lillian needed to get it all out.

"I wanted to go with her, but she wouldn't let me. They scared her so badly that she said she wanted to spend the rest of her life alone." Lillian paused, fear glimmering in her eyes. "I was afraid they would come after me next, so I took the job offer to come here the day after she left."

Carrie squeezed Lillian's hand tightly. "I'm so sorry," she said. "I understand what it's like to lose someone you love."

"If she was dead, that would be one thing," Lillian replied. "But she's alive somewhere, refusing to be with me because of what could happen."

Carrie tried to imagine that. At least she had been able to grieve Robert. To have been separated from him because of the fear of what others might do would have been equally as unbearable. In some ways it would have been worse, because she would never have been able to let go of the hope that something might change. She thought of their conversation earlier that morning. "You hate the men who hurt her."

Lillian gave her a tight smile. "Wouldn't you?"

"Probably," Carrie admitted. "I certainly hated the men who killed Robert."

"But you let it go," Lillian reminded her.

"Yes." Carrie didn't need to say anything else. It had already been said that morning.

"I started peeling my onion today," Lillian whispered, tears shining in her eyes as she lifted her head to stare at the moon. "I know I can't ever be free as long as I hate the men who hurt Roberta. It's hard, though."

"Yes," Carrie agreed again. "I can promise you it's worth it, though."

"I hope so," Lillian answered. "One minute I feel better, and the next minute I want to scream my fury again."

"That sounds right," Carrie said calmly. "It takes time."

Lillian managed a chuckle as she looked at Rose. "You told me Carrie would be all right with my story. I should have believed you."

Rose reached out to touch her arm. "Everyone has the right to tell their story in their own time and way."

Carrie looked between the two women. "Why are you telling me now?"

Lillian took a deep breath as if to gather courage. "Because now that I'm starting the process of forgiving what has happened, I want to go back to the North."

Carrie was surprised. "I thought you've been happy on the plantation, Lillian."

"I have been," Lillian replied, "but I feel like I've only been living half a life. I love teaching, I love the plantation, and I love being able to ride as much as I want to, but..." Her voice trailed off for a moment. "I'm also lonely."

Carrie suddenly understood. "And you can never be open about who you are in the South."

"It's dangerous enough in the North," Lillian said slowly. "But it's akin to suicide in the South. I stand out enough in my breeches and short hair. I suspect I would have already had trouble if I weren't at Cromwell."

"I'm glad Jeb keeps watch over the schoolhouse," Carrie said, realizing Lillian was right. "How can I help you? You said you were telling me your story because you want to go back to the North, and because you have something to ask me. I'm listening."

Lillian exchanged a long look with Rose.

Carrie watched, sensing the close friendship that had developed between the two. She was glad Lillian had been able to confide in Rose.

"Go ahead," Rose urged.

Lillian took another deep breath. "I would like to move to Philadelphia. I haven't made much money teaching down here, so I'll need a place to live for a little while." She looked nervous. "It wouldn't be for long. Rose assures me I should be able to get a good job there...at least one that pays better than here."

"I would love that," Carrie said warmly.

Lillian, opening her mouth to say more, suddenly snapped it shut. "What?"

Carrie smiled. "I said I would love that."

Lillian stared at her, obviously not able to believe what she was hearing. "I promise I won't be there long."

"Stay as long as you need to," Carrie assured her. "Lillian, I firmly believe women should help each other. I lived in Abby's house when I first started medical school. Abby financed Cromwell Stables so that Robert's dream could come true. Biddy donated the funds to start the medical clinic in Moyamensing. If I can help you get a fresh start by providing a home to live in for a while, I'm more than thrilled to do it."

Lillian grinned, and then hesitated. "What about Anthony?"

"He'll be fine," Carrie said. She hoped she was right. It was one thing for her to accept a homosexual into their life. It wasn't anything she'd ever had reason to discuss with her husband.

"And Frances?" Lillian asked.

"You can't be serious," Carrie replied with a laugh, confident she was on firm footing with this one. "Frances already adores you. She talks about missing you as her teacher all the time. She'll be beyond excited to know you'll be living with us."

"I told you," Rose said smugly.

Lillian laughed, and then hugged Carrie tightly. "Thank you," she whispered. "It means the world to me."

"It will be a joy to have you," Carrie assured her. "There will be times you'll be there on your own," she hastened to add. "We're going to come back to the plantation as much as we can during the next eight months."

"So you can be with Granite," Lillian said softly. "I'm glad."

"We'll be moving back to the plantation for good at the end of the year," Carrie added, thankful Lillian understood her reason for needing to come home more often.

Lillian nodded. "I know. I'm sure I'll be in the position to make my next plans before that happens," she said confidently, before hesitating. "Only Rose and Chooli know that I'm homosexual, Carrie. I know you have to tell Anthony, but..."

"No one will hear it from me," Carrie assured her, confident Chooli had responded well because of her Navajo traditions. "Your story is yours to tell."

Lillian breathed a sigh of relief. "Thank you."

*****

Carrie snuggled in next to Anthony, relishing the warm comfort of their bed.

"You seem rather wide awake for someone who has been going all day," Anthony observed.

Carrie sat up against the headboard. "Are you awake enough for a conversation?"

"Certainly." Anthony scooted up to join her.

Carrie shared what had happened with Lillian, including her request to live with them. Anthony listened quietly until she was done, but she couldn't read his expression in the dark.

"What did you tell her?"

Carrie hesitated, still not certain how he was receiving the news. "I told her she could."

Anthony sighed. "Do you realize most of society is not as accepting as you are, Carrie?"

Carrie gazed at him. "The rest of society doesn't really concern me. You do. I can't tell how you're responding to this."

Anthony sighed again. "It could make trouble for us in Philadelphia if she's open about who she is. You said she wanted to move there because she's lonely, but what does that mean?"

"I don't know," Carrie said honestly. "After everything Lillian has been through, though, I'm quite certain she'll be careful. I'm confident she wouldn't do anything to put us in danger."

"I agree that she wouldn't do anything on purpose," Anthony replied.

Carrie heard what he wasn't saying; Lillian could create danger for them by accident. "I really don't know much about homosexuality," she said thoughtfully. "I do know it's a new term. I read about it in one of the books I found in the library. The word *homosexuality* was coined by a writer named Benkert. He had a close friend who was homosexual, who killed himself after being blackmailed. Benkert never forgot it."

"Does Benkert believe it's wrong?" Anthony asked.

"Not from what I read," Carrie replied.

"Not many share his opinion," Anthony said flatly.

Carrie searched her mind for a way forward. "Do *you* think it's wrong?"

Anthony took a deep breath. "I had a great-aunt who was what you call homosexual," he said slowly.

Carrie gasped. "I had no idea."

"It's not something the family talks about," Anthony said wryly. "I found some family pictures that made me ask questions when I was at the university. Her name was Adelle."

"What happened to her?"

Anthony hesitated. "There was no such word as homosexuality back then, Carrie. It was called sodomy. It still is in most places. The punishment in all American colonies was death."

"What?" Carrie was horrified. "Your aunt was killed?"

"No," Anthony answered. "The death penalty was reserved for males, but she was severely beaten and imprisoned." His voice was grim. "She died during one particularly cold winter."

"When?" Carrie demanded, horrified by what she was hearing. Considering the asylum where Alice had been imprisoned, Carrie shuddered at the idea of what prisons would have been like during the early part of the century, especially for women.

"It was in 1815. Pennsylvania was the first state to repeal the death penalty for sodomy in 1786. The other states eventually followed their lead, but laws mandating prison sentences of five to sixty years are still in effect." He held up a hand. "It's more unusual for women to be punished, but it happens. My great-aunt was proof."

"That's terrible," Carrie breathed.

"It's the law," Anthony said. "Having Lillian live with us could put all of us in danger. People won't be pleased if they discover there's a homosexual living with us."

"There are people who aren't pleased your wife is a doctor," she reminded him.

"Being a doctor isn't illegal," Anthony replied evenly.

Carrie studied her husband, his features clearer now that the moon had risen far enough to pour light into their bedroom. He wasn't angry, but he certainly looked troubled. "I'm sorry I told her yes without talking to you first," she said. "I didn't think it would be a problem."

"Who else knows about Lillian?" Anthony asked after several moments of silence.

"Only Rose. Lillian has asked me to not tell anyone else but you."

"She's afraid," Anthony said thoughtfully.

"After what happened with Roberta, who can blame her?" Carrie asked heatedly, and then forced herself to relax. Anthony's experience with his aunt would certainly have made him afraid, as well. "I'm sorry. I know your concern is for me and Frances."

The silence stretched out for several long minutes. The sound of owls hooting floated through the window, followed closely by the mournful howl of a coyote singing to the moon. A gentle breeze made the curtains flutter around their heads, carrying with it the sweet aroma of lilacs.

Anthony finally turned to her. "I won't pretend I'm not worried, but I believe Lillian should live with us. Frances loves her dearly. Everything I know about her says she's a fine woman. I also won't pretend that I understand homosexuality, but I would never want Lillian to be in danger. Living with us won't totally protect her, but it will help."

"Thank you," Carrie said fervently, and then grew thoughtful. "I wonder if we have to *understand* homosexuality."

Anthony cocked his head. "What do you mean?"

Carrie sat silently for a moment, giving her thoughts time to come together. "Neither of us knows what it is to love someone of the same sex. Until now, at least for me, I've never had to think about it. For you, your only knowledge is what happened to your great-aunt." Her brain worked furiously. "I suppose *understanding,* at least to most people, means they've gained enough information and knowledge to agree with whatever the issue is. But what if you learn everything you can about the issue and still don't agree? Does that mean you don't understand?"

"No," Anthony replied, his brow knit in deep thought. "It just means that you don't agree. I see where you're going..." He stared out the window before he continued. "I think you're right. We may or may not ever completely understand homosexuality, but it doesn't really matter. We can accept Lillian because of who we know her to be as a person."

Carrie nodded but knew her heart was telling her more. "Perhaps that's not enough," she said. "Perhaps we can accept *all* homosexuals until they give us a reason to not like them as people. That way, we're not rejecting the idea of who they love..." She paused to find the right words. "We're not rejecting the idea of who they love...we've just decided we don't like that person for other reasons."

"That rationale is true for blacks, as well," Anthony mused. "We choose to not reject them because of their color, but there are certainly people of every race that I don't necessarily like."

"Yes," Carrie agreed. "It's true for the Indians, and the Irish. People turn their backs on them because they say they don't understand, or because they don't want to. Really, all they have to do is accept them and get to know them as people."

Anthony smiled at her. "You're a wise woman, Carrie Wallington."

Carrie shook her head. "Many people would disagree with you," she said with a grin. "Although, I hope I'm getting a *little* smarter and wiser as I get older."

"I'm counting on it," Anthony said solemnly, his eyes twinkling with fun.

Carrie laughed as she punched his arm.

"My wife is abusing her husband?" Anthony asked in a shocked voice. "What would people say?"

"That your wife doesn't care what they think?" Carrie suggested.

"I think the better solution is to make amends by showing your husband how much you love him," Anthony said slyly.

Carrie pursed her lips and pretended to consider his proposition. "I suppose I could be convinced to see the value in that."

"Enough talk," Anthony retorted. "Come to me."

Carrie chuckled and threw herself into his arms. "There is no place I would rather be."

Chapter Twelve

Carrie was whistling as she walked into the barn the next morning to give Granite his treat. "Hello, boy!" she called cheerfully, her smile spreading when Granite nickered a greeting and poked his head over the stall door. Free to roam the pastures at night, Miles brought Granite in each morning, so she could have time with him before she left for the clinic.

"Carrie!"

Carrie grinned when Amber dashed through the door, All My Heart hot on her heels. "Good morning, Amber. What are you and that filly of yours doing?"

Amber reached up and stroked All My Heart's beautiful face. "She's helping me train the new foals."

"Is that right?" Carrie asked with amusement. "By racing around behind you without a halter or lead rope?"

Amber shrugged. "She doesn't need one. She always does what I say."

Carrie knew that was true, so there was no reason to argue the point. "How is she helping you?"

Amber's eyes glowed with excitement. "The foals are all learning to come to me by voice command. First, I call All My Heart, who of course comes right to me. Then, I call whichever foal I'm working with. They follow All My Heart's example. It used to take me days to train them, but now it only takes an hour or so."

Carrie laughed with delight. "You have the best assistant in the world," she said admiringly.

"I quite agree."

"Nothing modest about our girl." Susan was smiling when she emerged from the tack room holding a freshly oiled saddle. Her blond hair was pulled back in a braid, and her long legs wcre encased in breeches.

Amber shrugged. "Clint told me to not worry about modesty because there's nothing wrong with knowing you're good at something. I figure there's even less wrong with knowing you have the best horse in the world."

"I have to agree with your brother," Carrie replied. Granite snorted and stomped his foot. "However, I think Granite has a different opinion about who the best horse in the world is."

"Everyone is entitled to have an opinion," Amber said airily. "See you later, Carrie. I want to ride Rhythm before I have to leave for school."

Carrie watched her run from the barn and turned to Susan. "Rhythm?"

"Rhythm is one of the three-year-old mares she's training. Amber handpicked five of them this spring."

"Just like she proposed," Carrie said with admiration. "Do you think her approach is going to work?"

"*Think*?" Susan shook her head with disbelief. "There was a buyer who came by a week ago to check out the foals."

"Why?" Carrie asked. "All of them were spoken for and sold last fall."

"True, but the buyer wanted to see what all the fuss was about. His name is Tyler Prentice. He told me he's heard a lot of talk about the quality of Cromwell stock."

"What did he think?" Carrie asked, yearning for the time when she would be back on the plantation and able to spend much more time in the barn.

"He's already paid for top pick of thirty of the foals next spring," Susan said with a triumphant grin. She held up her hand before Carrie could say anything. "But that's not all. He saw Amber working with Rhythm last week when you were at the clinic, and he watched her ride March Delight before he left."

"March Delight?" Carrie ran all the horses through her mind. "The three-year-old out of Eclipse and Pudding Girl?"

"That's her. She's really something, and she's becoming even more something with Amber's training."

"What did Mr. Prentice think?"

Susan's grin widened, her eyes following suit. "He didn't say much when he left, but I got a letter from him yesterday." She paused for dramatic effect. "He has buyers for every one of the mares Amber is training, Carrie. When she deems them ready, they have homes waiting for them."

Carrie raised a brow, waiting for the rest of the information she was certain was coming.

"At *four times* the price of a two-year old who has gone through basic training," Susan finished triumphantly.

Carrie gasped. "Four times the amount? That's amazing." She glanced out the barn to watch Amber ground-training Rhythm in the large round pen. "Does Amber know?"

Susan shook her head. "I wanted us to tell her together, as partners. Can you leave the clinic early this afternoon?"

Carrie thought quickly. "Four o'clock?" When Susan nodded, she checked her watch. "If I'm leaving early, I have to get out of here. I have a lot of patients today." She walked over to kiss Granite on his velvety nose and then hurried out the door.

*****

Abby watched Carrie pull away in the carriage, her thoughts in turmoil. She rocked slowly, enjoying the beauty of a new day coming to life on the plantation.

"What's bothering you, my love?" Thomas asked.

"Who says anything is bothering me?" Abby responded. "It's far too lovely a day to be disturbed by anything."

"That may be true," Thomas said blandly, "but it doesn't change the fact that something is bothering you."

Abby turned her eyes away from the horses in the pasture and looked into her handsome husband's eyes. There was no point in denying his observation. "I'm not sure I'm cut out for retirement," she admitted. Just hearing the words out loud made her cringe.

Thomas raised a brow. "Please tell me what you mean. Are you saying you want to open another factory?"

"No," Abby said quickly. "I have no desire to do that again." The problem was, she didn't know *what* she wanted.

"But you're unhappy?" Thomas pressed.

Abby shook her head. "I'm not unhappy at all, my dear. I love you, and I love the plantation..." Her voice faded away as she wondered what was causing the unrest in her heart.

Thomas gazed at her for a long moment. "I'm confused."

Abby laughed helplessly. "How could you not be? I'm not making a shred of sense."

"What is it about retirement that you don't like?" Thomas asked.

Abby sorted through her chaotic thoughts, knowing she needed to make sense of them. "I don't miss working," she said slowly. "At least not everything I did up until the factory burned. I enjoy helping at the factories when I go to Philadelphia, but I wouldn't want to do it on a daily basis anymore."

Thomas nodded but remained quiet.

Abby knew he was giving her time to understand her own feelings. Grateful, she continued to pick through her thoughts. "I don't want to do *anything* on a daily basis anymore," she murmured, suddenly very sure that was true.

"But...?" Thomas prompted after a long silence.

Abby met his eyes, thankful for the love and support she saw there, but looked away to stare out at the pasture again. She smiled when she identified two new foals that had clearly been born the night before. She could hear Susan and Miles calling to each other over the nickers and whinnies of the horses. Clint was working in the round pen with one of the yearlings who would be picked up by a buyer next week. The joy of watching Cromwell Stables become nationally known was fulfilling and exciting, but... Abby's eyes widened when she finally identified the source of her unrest. "I don't have a purpose," she said quietly.

"A purpose?"

"Yes." Saying the words aloud filled Abby with a certainty that she had identified the problem. "I've always had a purpose. It was either to run the factory, fight for the abolition of the slaves, or fight for equal rights for women. I don't have that anymore."

"Women hardly have equal rights," Thomas observed. "And even though the slaves are free, we both know there is so much to be done."

"Exactly!" Abby said excitedly. "Women hardly have equal rights, and even though the slaves are free, there's still so much to be done." She caught her breath. "I'm not doing anything but watching from afar."

"That's not true," Thomas protested. "You made sure that Cromwell factories don't employ children."

"One small thing," Abby said dismissively. "I know it made a difference, but for a woman who is used to being involved in important causes all the time, I find myself floundering because I don't have a strong purpose."

"The plantation doesn't provide you with one?"

Abby ached at the sadness she heard in Thomas' voice. She grabbed his hand and held it tightly. "The plantation provides me with many purposes," she insisted. As she thought about it, she knew it was true. She was never without something to do—helping in the greenhouse, working at the clinic when Carrie or Polly needed help, visiting the workers' families so she could assist with any needs.

"But it's not enough," Thomas said quietly.

Abby searched Thomas' eyes. There was no judgment, just confusion. She struggled for a way to explain what she was feeling. "Perhaps Ralph Waldo Emerson expressed it best," she finally said, and then quoted one of his sayings that she knew by heart. *"The purpose of life is not to be happy. It is to be useful, to be honorable, to be compassionate, to have it make some difference that you have lived and lived well."*

Thomas gazed at her. "That makes sense, of course, but from my perspective you've always lived that way. It's one of the reasons I fell in love with you."

"I have more to do," Abby said softly. "I love what I do on the plantation, but I need to do more." She took a deep breath. "I *have* to do more." The knowing gave her a sense of peace she hadn't felt in days.

"What are you going to do?" Thomas asked.

Abby appreciated that he didn't question her need for more or try to tell her she should be satisfied with what she had now. Of course, he'd had plenty of experience with his independent daughter. "I don't know," she answered honestly. "But at least I understand now why I've been so uneasy and on edge."

Thomas took her hand and squeezed it tightly. "What can I do to help?"

Abby loved her husband more at that moment than perhaps she ever had. "Thank you," she said fervently. When Thomas raised a brow, she continued. "I appreciate, more than you can know, that you want to help. I'm quite certain your first wife would have never had a thought about this."

Thomas smiled. "You can be sure of that," he mused. "I, too, was a different man then. If I had been like I am now, perhaps Abigail would have had the same thoughts."

Abby looked at him in astonishment, realizing how right he was. Abigail had been Carrie's mother, after all. Certainly, Carrie had gotten some of her spirit from her. Abigail had been raised in a different time in the South. She had chosen to follow the dictates of her culture, but if Thomas had been open to her being more than what society deemed proper, might she have been different? "You're an amazing man," she said tenderly.

"Thank you," Thomas answered. "You still haven't answered my question, though. What can I do to help?"

"I don't know," Abby said. "Now that I've identified what's bothering me, it's going to take me some time to figure out what to do about it."

*****

Amber looked up with surprise when Carrie walked into the barn. "You're here early."

"I am," Carrie agreed. "Where is Susan?"

Amber tensed. "Is something wrong, Carrie?"

"I can't ask where my business partner is without causing alarm?" she teased.

"You're causing alarm?" Susan strode into the barn, leading a limping mare.

"What happened?" Carrie knelt to gently probe the mare's right foreleg.

"Just a strain," Susan said. "Belladonna was fine this morning when I checked on all the horses. My guess is that she stepped in a hole."

Carrie continued to probe, running her hand up and down the leg while she watched the mare's eyes for signs of pain and anxiety. "Belladonna?" she asked with amusement.

"Mama suggested the name," Amber answered. "She said it was in honor of some of the herbs you use to help people."

"It's very fitting," Carrie said with a chuckle. "It's also exactly what I'm going to use to help this young lady." She stood up, stroking the mare's neck. "I have what I need in the tack room." Minutes later, she reappeared with two bottles in her hand.

Susan and Amber watched her closely.

"What's in those bottles?" Amber asked, her eyes shining with bright curiosity.

"Belladonna and aconite," Carrie responded. "This mare's leg has a lot of heat in it and her eyes are shiny with pain. Horses can be very stoic when it comes to pain, but they'll reveal the truth if you know what signs to look for." She worked as she instructed. "Both of these are treatments I brought back with me. I was fortunate enough to meet a veterinarian in Philadelphia a few months ago who uses homeopathic treatments."

"I thought you would use arnica," Susan said, stroking the mare's neck while Carrie prepared the treatment.

"You're learning," Carrie said with a smile. "Arnica would be good for her, if that's all you had, but these will be most effective. Once the worst of the pain is gone, arnica will help Belladonna heal faster." She stopped talking so she could focus on the task at hand. She shook a small amount of granules into a glass beaker and stirred it well. When she was convinced the granules had dissolved, she stepped up to Belladonna's head and spoke gently.

"Good girl," she murmured. Carrie put her finger in the corner of the mare's mouth to encourage her to open it. Then, acting quickly, she poured the fluid into Belladonna's mouth. "Don't let her raise her head," she told Susan as she put both hands around the horse's mouth to keep it closed.

"What are you doing?" Amber demanded. "She'll have a hard time swallowing if she can't lift her head."

"You're absolutely right, Amber. I'm making sure as much of the treatment is absorbed in her mouth as possible. She doesn't really need to swallow it, though it won't hurt her. It'll absorb into her body better through contact with her gums, tongue and inner lips.

Susan is keeping her head down so more of it will stay in her mouth."

"How often do we have to treat her?" Susan asked.

"Do it twice more today," Carrie responded, "and then three times a day until she's stopped limping. It should only take two to three days. Stop the treatment as soon as she's better."

"Aren't we going to wrap her leg?" Amber asked.

Carrie nodded approvingly. "We are. Would you like to do it?" Amber was working hard to learn how to take care of everything that went wrong with her charges. "Your mama tells me you pester her to death about treatments for the horses."

Amber grinned. "She doesn't know as much as you do, but she knows a lot."

"She also tells me you're great with the horses, but couldn't care less about treating people who are sick," Carrie said, knowing Amber would read the teasing twinkle in her eyes.

Amber studied her face and then shrugged. "That's yours and Mama's job. I can't do everything, you know."

Carrie and Susan chuckled as Amber skillfully wrapped Belladonna's leg, making sure the bandage was secure enough to offer the leg support, but not so tight it would cut off circulation or increase the swelling.

"Good job," Carrie said. She patted Belladonna's neck and led her to an empty stall. "No running around in the pasture for you, girl. You're going to stay in the barn and get treated like royalty."

"Can I get back to work?" Amber asked. "I promised All My Heart we would ride down to the river this afternoon."

"With?" Susan asked alertly.

Amber wasn't allowed to ride on her own. She was more than capable of handling her horse, but Moses wasn't willing for anyone to let their guard down. It had been months since there'd been a problem, but he wasn't going to take any chances.

Amber grinned. "Abby is coming with me."

"May Granite and I join you?" Carrie asked. "Once we finish celebrating?"

Amber nodded and then cocked her head. "Celebrating? What are we celebrating?"

Susan pulled out the letter she had received from her pocket. "Do you remember the gentleman who was here last week to check out the foals?"

"Mr. Prentice? Clint and I showed him some of the new colts and fillies, but we didn't really talk. I had other work to do."

"Which he watched you do," Susan said. "He was quite impressed."

Amber's eyes were on the paper in Susan's hand. "What does that say?"

"It's a letter from Mr. Prentice. He's put a claim on thirty of the foals for next year."

"That's great!" Amber whooped. "Is that what we're celebrating?"

"It's worthy of celebration," Carrie answered, "but that's not what we're celebrating today."

Amber looked at Susan impatiently. "Could you go ahead and read that letter, Susan?"

Susan grinned and began to read.

Dear Mrs. Justin,

I'm quite impressed with the work being done at Cromwell Stables. The quality of your horses is beyond compare. I trust you have received my earlier letter in regard to the sale of thirty of next year's foals, but this letter pertains to a different matter.

I have spoken with four influential gentlemen about the three-year-olds being trained by your assistant. After describing their advanced training, I'm prepared to purchase all five of them as soon as they're ready. I believe you'll be pleased with the purchase price of $1000 each.

I look forward to hearing from you with assurance my offer will be received.

Sincerely,

Tyler Prentice

Carrie watched Amber's face go from quizzical, to blank, to disbelieving awe.

"Onc thousand dollars *each?*" Amber whispered. "*All* of them?"

"Yes, and yes," Susan responded happily. "You've done it, Amber. You came up with the idea, you proposed it to us, and you are successfully training the horses you chose. A good saddlehorse normally goes for two hundred dollars; we're getting five times that amount for the horses you're training. Congratulations!"

Amber grinned but still had a dazed look on her face. "*All* of them?" she repeated.

Carrie hugged Amber. "I'm so proud of you. That's not all we have to tell you, however."

Amber shook her head. "How could there be more?"

"Well," Carrie replied, answering her with another question. "Are you aware that the men who first started working on the plantation after the war get paid, not just their wages, but also a percentage of the profits each year?"

Amber looked confused. "I've heard my daddy and Clint talking about it. What's that got to do with me?"

"Susan and I think it's a good way to do business with the stables, as well," Carrie explained. "We already pay you for what you do, but now we're going to give you a percentage of what we make from the sale of the five horses you're training, Amber."

"I'm twelve," Amber reminded them.

Carrie laughed heartily. "Trust me, you are not a normal twelve-year-old when it comes to horses. You're a gifted professional who is a valuable part of the Cromwell Stables staff."

Amber stared at her wide-eyed, her expression saying she was trying to absorb what she was hearing. "How much?" she finally managed.

"Ten percent of the sale price," Susan informed her.

Amber swung her gaze toward Susan. "Ten percent? For each horse?" Her voice had gone from awestruck to disbelieving.

"For each horse," Carrie confirmed. "Congratulations!"

Amber shook her head and held up a hand. "Wait.'

Mystified, Carrie and Susan exchanged a glance, wondering what was going on in Amber's head.

The silence stretched out for almost a minute as Amber twisted her face in deep thought. "I don't want the money," she finally said.

"What?" Susan asked. "What do you mean?"

"I don't want the five hundred dollars," Amber said, her eyes shining with confidence. "How much are the foals being sold for this year?"

Carrie was suddenly sure what the intelligent little girl had in mind. "Three hundred dollars."

Amber nodded. "Since I'm the one training them to get that price, I would like to have first pick of two of this year's foals, at two hundred and fifty dollars each." Her eyes bored into Carrie and Susan. "That means they'll be mine, right? That when I sell them, I'll keep all the money from it?"

Carrie chuckled. Besides being an amazing horsewoman, Amber was also becoming an astute businesswoman. "They'll be yours," she agreed. "And, yes, all the money you make when you sell them will be yours."

Amber smiled but remained serious. "We can keep doing this? I can have two of the foals from each year for every five horses I train?"

"Yes," Susan answered, a proud smile playing on her lips. "I want to make clear, however, that you can train only five a year for the stables. That doesn't count your two, of course. School is still your most important job. I won't allow you to jeopardize that."

Amber waved a hand. "I know." She fell silent for a moment and grinned happily. "My business projections have just gotten far better."

Carrie laughed. "Your business projections?"

"Abby has been teaching me about business. She knows I want Cromwell Stables to be the most successful stables in America, but she also knows I have plans of my own," Amber said seriously.

"Plans of your own?" Susan asked, a stunned look on her face.

Carrie understood. She had to constantly remind herself they were dealing with a twelve-year-old girl.

"Of course," Amber said quickly. "You and Carrie pay very well, but the return on my investment is better if I own the horses myself."

Abby walked into the barn just then. "Is anyone here ready to go riding?"

Carrie burst out laughing. "I don't know. Amber might be too busy with her *business projections* to go riding."

Abby stared at her. "What are you talking about?"

Amber started jumping up and down, looking once more like a twelve-year-old little girl who had just been given wonderful news. "Abby, you won't believe it!" She explained quickly, her face glowing with excitement.

Abby laughed with delight and pulled Amber into a tight hug. "That's my girl!"

Amber grew serious. "Did I make the right decision to ask for two of the foals instead of money?"

"It was the perfect decision," Abby assured her. "Especially since you also negotiated the price down. I'm so proud of you, I can hardly stand it."

Granite chose that moment to stomp his foot and snort loudly.

"I do believe someone heard us talk about going for a ride," Carrie observed. "It's time. Will you join us, Susan?"

"Definitely," Susan agreed. "How could I turn down an opportunity to go riding with the Cromwell Stables' women and our brilliant business advisor!"

Laughing and talking, they quickly prepared their mounts.

*****

Two hours later, the four of them sat quietly as the sun began to dip toward the horizon. The sun was still up and shining brightly, but it had begun to tinge the clouds a faint pink that glowed against the blue sky.

A flock of wood ducks skimmed low over the water, their whistling sound giving an odd background effect to the gaggle of geese honking overhead. Wisteria, just starting to bloom, contributed a purple haze to the trees lining the bank of the James River. Fish jumped in search of bugs called forth by the beginning of dusk, while swallows dipped low to claim their share.

"This is the most beautiful place in the world," Amber whispered. "I never want to be anywhere else."

The other women, not wanting to disturb the peace, nodded their agreement without speaking.

Abby was the first to break the silence. "When do you leave for Canada, Susan?"

"Harold and I leave in two weeks," Susan replied. "I can hardly believe I'm going up to buy more of the Cleveland Bays. It's seemed more like a dream than reality, until now." She grinned happily. "Miles has told me so much about the stables he worked for after escaping the plantation. To be able to visit Carson Stables myself is so exciting."

"Mr. Carson is expecting you?" Carrie asked.

"I heard from him last week," Susan replied. "He's expecting our visit and is also expecting me to have a lot of money."

Carrie chuckled. The two partners, counseled by Abby, had agreed on the amount they were comfortable spending to expand their Cleveland Bay breeding stock. If all went well, they would add more each year, but they were beginning on a conservative basis.

"Felicity should have her foal any day now," Amber said.

Abby smiled. "It's been such a joy to watch Miles with Felicity's first filly, Dancer."

Carrie agreed. She'd been stunned by the beauty of the Cleveland Bay mare that Miles had returned with from Canada. When he'd approached her about breeding Felicity to Eclipse two years earlier, she had agreed they would alternate who kept ownership of the resulting foal, with him claiming the first baby. Dancer had been the result. She lived up to every one of their hopes for the crossbreeding. It had been Susan's idea to expand the breeding program, creating a unique carriage horse that would be in high demand. Her trip to Canada would be the first step in that plan.

"How many mares do you think you'll return with?" Amber asked.

Susan shrugged. "I'll negotiate the best I can and see how it turns out."

Amber looked thoughtful. "Perhaps you should take Abby with you, Susan. She's quite good at negotiating."

Abby chuckled. "Susan will do just fine." Then she pauscd. "That does bring me to something I want to talk to you about, Susan."

Susan raised a brow. "What is it?"

"I'd like to accompany you and Harold as far as New York City. If I'm correct, you'll change trains there to go into Canada?"

"We would love to have you join us!" Susan said enthusiastically. "What's the cause for this trip?"

"It's been far too long since I've visited my friends Wally and Nancy Stratford," Abby answered. "I miss them both very much. Now seems like a good time to go, especially since I won't have to travel on my own."

Susan hesitated. "I'm not certain how long I'll be in Canada."

"That's fine," Abby replied. "You can telegram me when you know your return date. I'll be ready."

"It's a deal," Susan answered. "It will be wonderful to spend more time with you. It will also give me more time to hone my negotiating skills before I reach Carson Stables."

"That will be wise," Amber murmured with a sly grin, joining in as the other women burst out laughing.

Chapter Thirteen

Carrie hurried through the tunnel with the bulging picnic basket Annie had prepared. She was determined to reach the riverbank before the sun dipped below the horizon. Sweat was starting to trickle down her back when she burst through the door to the outside.

"Is someone after you?" Rose called with amusement. "You seem a little winded."

"It isn't you carrying a hundred-pound picnic basket through the tunnel," Carrie retorted. "Annie sent enough food for ten people."

"I'm sure we'll eat a healthy share of it," Abby called. "Come sit down and catch your breath."

Carrie was more than happy to drop the basket on the bank and settle down onto the fallen tree that had gradually become "their log." She lifted her face to the final rays of the sun, grateful for the soft breeze cooling her heated body. "I can't believe my time is already up," she said softly. "It will be so hard to return to Philadelphia."

Abby reached over to take her hand. "I'll miss you, Carrie. It's been wonderful to have you here the last two weeks."

"It wasn't long enough," Carrie sighed. The idea of returning to the clogged, dirty city was almost more than she could bear. Being with her family and friends, riding Granite every day, treating her patients...Each day had been a gift. The only thing missing from it was Frances. She missed her daughter dearly, but she was looking forward to seeing Frances' face light up when she told her they would be coming down to visit a lot more often in the coming months. She couldn't wait to move back for good and always have Frances with her.

"How are the new men doing who are receiving the Hypericum?" Rose asked. "Didn't they come in to report and get more of the treatment today?"

Carrie smiled brightly, grateful to take her mind off going back to Philadelphia. "They're all doing well. Some of them have only had a reduction of their pain, but I assured them it takes a little longer with some patients. They're encouraged by their progress. A few of them have experienced complete relief in less than ten days."

"Larry? Carson? Bob?" Abby asked. "I've thought about them since you told us their stories. How are they doing?"

"Larry is without pain," Carrie reported. "Bob's is almost gone, and Carson has seen a lot of improvement." She watched a huge fish jump, landing with a splash that created a series of ripples that danced across the calm surface of the water. "They're grateful, and have assured me there will be no more trouble." She swallowed the words she didn't want to say out loud as she turned back to them.

"What aren't you telling us?" Abby demanded.

Carrie sighed, not sure why she even bothered to try to hide anything from her stepmother. Or from Rose, for that matter.

"Abby is right," Rose stated. "Your words are saying one thing, but your eyes are telling another story."

"Larry stayed at the clinic after everyone else left. He assured me he could stop any violence from the men he knew, but he'd heard rumors that trouble could come from outside this area."

"From where?" Rose demanded, her eyes flashing angrily.

Carrie was relieved to see anger instead of fear. "Now that Virginia has been readmitted to the Union, Democrats are eager to regain power. They've watched other parts of the country where the KKK and other vigilantes have spread so much fear that blacks are completely terrified."

Abby shook her head. "Why out here? I can see the reason for instilling fear in the city, where blacks are most likely to cast their vote, but we're far from Richmond."

Rose supplied the answer. "It's because of how we treat the workers. It's a threat to the old way of life that white aristocrats are eager to restore. They can't make the freed slaves bow down to them again when they see others being treated fairly. They're furious."

Abby tightened her lips. "And here I sit doing nothing."

Carrie looked at her with surprise. "Abby? What do you mean?"

"I've wanted to talk to you and Rose before you leave," Abby replied. "I'm glad we're out here this evening." She relayed her conversation with Thomas, along with the realization she had reached. "I need to do more," she finished in a troubled voice. "The two of you know your purpose. You're living it every day when you practice medicine or teach." Her voice caught. "I feel like I've lost that."

Carrie spoke carefully. "Abby, you've changed thousands of lives with the factories you started. You and Father have changed life for the residents of Moyamensing, and the lives of so many in Richmond when you started the factory there. More importantly, for me at least, it was you that helped me define my purpose when I was eighteen. You gave me the courage to pursue my dreams, and then helped make them happen."

"You did the same thing for Moses and me," Rose said. "You gave us a home when we escaped the plantation, and you helped us create a life." She paused. "You've done that for countless people."

"Perhaps, but I want to do it for more," Abby said. "I don't know how long I have left to live, but I'm still healthy and my mind still works. I love being on the plantation," she said quickly, "but I still need more."

"Is that why you're going to New York City?" Carrie asked.

"I suppose," Abby replied. "It's true that I haven't seen Wally and Nancy Stratford in too long, but I also recognize I'm looking for something."

"In New York City?" Rose took Abby's hand, her eyes troubled. "Are you and Thomas thinking about moving to New York City?"

"Oh my goodness," Abby laughed. "Certainly not. The plantation is our home."

Rose shook her head. "Then I'm afraid I don't understand."

"That makes two of us," Abby admitted. "I don't know why I'm going to New York, but I'm going. I suppose I hope something will happen that will give me some direction." She turned to gaze at Carrie. "What are you thinking? I can almost hear the wheels turning."

Carrie shrugged. "The wheels are turning, but I'm not certain I know where they're taking me yet."

"Then let's sit in silence while you find out," Abby suggested.

Carrie was happy to lose herself in the thoughts whirling through her mind. She took deep breaths of the fresh air, knowing her return to Philadelphia would spell the end of that. As she gazed out over the river, the sun dipped below the horizon. There were no clouds to reflect brilliant colors, but the glowing blue took on the shine of a golden tapestry as the sun kissed the day good-bye.

The three women sat silently, content to be together as they watched darkness envelop their surroundings.

Stars were twinkling in the sky before Carrie was ready to express herself. "I've been thinking about New Year's Day," she began, "when we proclaimed ourselves Bregdan Women."

"We formed a group because there is power in women coming together for a purpose," Rose added. "We promised to help other's become Bregdan Women." Her eyes filled with sadness. "I haven't done that."

"Marietta suggested we do more that day," Carrie continued. "We talked about forming a group of Bregdan Women in Philadelphia. We planned to invite strong women to speak about what they're doing with their lives, to inspire others to take action and remind them of their impact." She looked at Rose. "I haven't done it either."

"And I said I would start a group right here on the plantation," Rose remembered.

"All we've done so far is talk. It's time to *do* something," Carrie said firmly. "I'm committing to having my first Bregdan Women meeting in Philadelphia in June." She turned to Abby and Rose. "I want both of you to be there." Her thoughts came together even more as she talked, the pieces falling together like a puzzle. "All of us will share what we're doing with our lives. I'll invite other women to join us. Some will be there only to listen, but I'm sure I can find an important woman who will speak during the first meeting."

Rose nodded excitedly. "I'll be there, even if I have to close the school for a few days. Now that Lillian is leaving, it will take me a little time to find a suitable replacement." Her face settled in determined lines. "When I come back, I'll start a Bregdan Women's meeting of my own. I'll invite the mothers of all my students, as well as other women I know."

Abby smiled. "That sounds wonderful! It will be fun to be back in Philadelphia to start something new. I'll help Rose here on the plantation."

Carrie recognized the look on Abby's face. "Your own mind is spinning," she prompted.

Abby nodded. "It is. Like you, I'm not sure where it's taking me yet, but I'm confident I'm about to begin a new adventure." She squeezed Carrie's hand. "I'm proud of you for taking action."

"It's more than that," Carrie said slowly. Abby and Rose both cocked their heads but remained silent, letting her sort through her thoughts. "There's been a question rolling through my head for days. *Now what?*"

"Now what?" Rose echoed. "What do you mean?"

"I remember when President Grant was elected. We were so certain he would solve all the problems caused by President Johnson's years in office after Lincoln was assassinated. When America passed the Fourteenth and Fifteenth Amendments, we were sure they would make life much better for all the blacks who had been freed."

"Things *are* better," Abby said gently.

"Better," Carrie agreed. "But, now what? *Better* is not what Americans need. *Better* is not what blacks need. The Abolition Society disbanded, but Ben is right that the battle for equality is far from over. Freedom does not mean equality." She took a deep breath. "Things are better for women, but *better* isn't what's needed. It's wonderful that I can become a doctor. It's wonderful that women have more opportunities now that the war has ended, but none of us believes things are *good* for women. We still can't vote. We're still controlled by men. We're still blocked by our government almost everywhere we turn." She paused. "The question then becomes..."

"Now what?" Rose finished.

"Yes. *Now what?*" Carrie answered. "It's so easy to think someone else is going to fix this country for us. It's easy to believe if we put the right people into government, that things will become what they need to be, but..." She shook her head.

"We've been waiting a long time for things to be right," Abby replied.

"Exactly!" Carrie said. "Slavery didn't end because of our government. They were far too busy trying to appease the wealthy people in the North and South, because they didn't want to rock the boat the American economy was founded on. It took people who cared enough about the slaves to form the Abolition Society and spend thirty years fighting for the slaves' freedom. They fought the government. They fought people who wanted to destroy the movement. They were beaten. They were ostracized. And then they had to fight a war." She paused to take a deep breath. "It was their efforts that compelled President Lincoln to create the Emancipation Proclamation. It was *everyday* people who forced change to happen."

Abby's face was glowing with pride. "You've thought about this a great deal, Carrie."

"I have," Carrie agreed. "Blacks are free. *Now what*? What can I do to help them win equality? Things are better for women, but *now what*? What can I do to fight for equality for women, and for the right to vote? And that's just the beginning," she cried, her passion threatening to overwhelm her. "Women are being stuffed away into insane asylums. Children are being made to work in horrendous factory conditions. Indians are being slaughtered for wanting to live on their own land."

She stopped again, trying to corral her feelings. Forcing herself to take even breaths, she stared out over the glimmering water, knowing the final pieces were falling together in her mind. "*Now what?*" she whispered. "It's the responsibility of every person to help make America better. Yes, I want to have the right to vote, but that doesn't stop me from making a difference right now. It doesn't keep me from taking action." She turned to Abby and Rose. "I believe we can mobilize women all over the country to make things better for everyone. Everybody will do something different, but I believe all of it is equally important. No one should sit back and wait for others to take action. We have to support each other and encourage each other to take our *own* action."

"You're right," Rose said slowly, "but there are a lot of women who don't think they can really make a difference."

"I know," Carrie agreed. "That's because they believe what they have to offer isn't valuable. If they're not a doctor or a teacher or a wealthy business owner, they think what they have to give isn't needed. We must convince them it is." She turned to Abby. "Look at Amber. Certainly, she's already a natural with the horses, but you're teaching her to be a businesswoman. Who knows what impact that will have in time. What if you were to teach about that in the school? Not just to the children, but also to parents? What kind of impact could that have if some of them took what they learned and really changed their lives? How many generations would that impact?"

She turned to Rose next. "You have many parents who've learned to read and write. What if they offer to tutor children who are having a hard time learning? What if they teach women who can't make it to school? They would go to their homes and share what you've taught them. Think of what a difference that would make."

"You're absolutely right," Abby said excitedly. "Every single person has something they can contribute."

"There are people who don't care about that," Rose observed cautiously. "They just want to live their lives and not worry about anyone or anything else. What about them?"

Carrie shrugged. "Hopefully, we'll change their minds, but I already know a lot of women won't be bothered, or they'll feel differently about something I'm passionate about. I expect that."

"Like women who don't believe women should have the right to vote?" Abby asked.

"Exactly." Carrie shook her head with disbelief. "I have yet to figure that one out."

"There is nothing about their position I agree with, but I'm trying to understand it," Abby replied. "There are those who feel that women fighting for the vote are behaving unnaturally. They see it as an attack on womanhood or on those who embrace our traditional roles as wives and mothers. They believe those who tell them that having the right to vote will make it impossible to have the domestic life they want."

"But that's crazy," Carrie sputtered.

"Perhaps, but they believe it," Abby said calmly. "I remember when I first joined the suffrage movement. I fully expected every female to join me in the battle to have a say in the running of America." She shook her head. "Unfortunately, men have been quite successful in shaping how some women view what we're doing. Suffragists have been depicted in advertisements as domineering, abusive, and so physically ugly that the only way they can get a husband is to try and overthrow society."

"What?" Carrie was aghast.

"Suffragists are portrayed as genderless creatures whose beliefs and appearance set them outside the general order," Abby continued.

Rose stood and paced along the bank. "How is it possible that anyone would believe that? I've been to one of your meetings. Nothing could be further from the truth."

Abby sighed. "There are people who will believe most of what you tell them, as long as the person telling them has authority," she said. "They've used religion to try to squelch the suffragists, as well. Men have convinced many women that God is certainly not for something that goes so against the societal structure ordained by the church. As a result, many women believe you can't serve God and vote at the same time."

Carrie shook her head. "I'm quite certain God gets tired of being blamed for stupid decisions that people make. The Southern church also believed slavery was sanctioned by God," she said angrily.

"Many of them still do," Abby reminded her. "It's not just the men, though. There are many wealthy women who are used to wielding their social status to create change they believe is necessary. In all fairness, they've been able to accomplish some important things, but they're appalled at the idea that just *any* woman could create change in America simply by voting. They believe women getting the right to vote would abolish their rightful standing in society, so they're working hard to block it."

"Is that why Susan B. Anthony believes blacks shouldn't vote?" Rose asked bluntly.

Abby took a deep breath. "Susan is a good friend, but I'm afraid we disagree on this issue. She fought hard for the abolition of slaves, but she feels rather adamantly that women should have the right to vote before black men. It's not that she thinks blacks shouldn't have the vote, but she does believe it shouldn't happen before women have the vote."

"I read some things she's recently written," Rose said. "They are rather virulent against blacks."

"They are," Abby said regretfully. "I don't agree with some of the things she's said, neither do I condone them. Susan has fought a hard battle for a long time. One year, she traveled thirteen thousand miles and gave one hundred seventy-one lectures. She's been heckled. She's had rotten eggs thrown at her. She's also been accused of undermining the home, the family and the purity of American womanhood. There were many nights she had to sleep in railroad stations. She did it, and continues to do it, because she believes with all her heart that women should have a say in this country." She gazed at Rose. "She fought just as hard for the freedom of slaves, Rose. She wouldn't rest until the slaves had been emancipated. I think she's being unwise with some of the things she's saying now, but I hope it won't taint all the massive amount of good she's accomplished. I know things have been said in the passion of the moment that don't reflect all of who she is."

Rose nodded thoughtfully. "You're right. She impressed me greatly when I heard her in New York City. I know the situation in our country is going to cause a lot of hard feelings in many areas. I will remind others of how much good she's done."

"I suppose this is another chance to offer grace and compassion," Carrie added.

"True," Abby replied. "I suspect the suffrage movement is going to go through a very challenging time. My hope is that enough reason can prevail to maintain focus on the most important issue—our right to vote." She looked at Carrie. "Which brings us back to what started this whole conversation. *What now?*" She paused. "I agree that all people, but especially women, need to be reminded how influential they can be. They need to be reminded that they have the power to change lives, and they need to know that seemingly small things can make a difference."

"I believe we can do that with Bregdan Women," Carrie said fervently. "I don't know how it's going to develop and grow, but I do know I need to start it." She held up her hand. "Correction. The three of us need to start it."

"I'll be there," Abby promised.

"Me, too," Rose said solemnly. "There is nothing that would give me greater pleasure than to work together with the two of you for change." She held out her hands.

Carrie and Abby stood to grasp hands, forming a small circle.

"We are Bregdan Women!" they called to the night sky.

When they broke apart, Rose reached for the picnic basket. "I'm starving. Can we finally eat?"

*****

Anthony was waiting for the three women when they slipped through the tunnel door into Carrie's childhood bedroom. "Hello, ladies," he said cheerfully. He looked up from the book he was reading, his chair pulled close to the brightly burning lantern.

"Hello, dear," Carrie said. "I thought you would be out on the porch talking to my father and Moses."

"I was," Anthony admitted, "but I need to talk to you."

"We'll give you your privacy," Abby said quickly.

"There's no need," Anthony said with a raised hand to stop her. "I want you and Rose to know what's happening."

Carrie stiffened. "What's happening? Has there been trouble."

"No," Anthony assured her. "We plan to keep it that way. Give me a moment and I'll explain."

Carrie put her hand over her mouth to indicate compliance.

Anthony chuckled and then turned serious. "Ben is ready to leave the plantation. He wants to come back to Philadelphia with us and Lillian."

Carrie took a deep breath of relief. This was the first time that Anthony had confirmed he was coming back to Philadelphia with her. Then she frowned. "He's welcome in Philadelphia with us, of course, but how are we going to get him there? We certainly can't take him into Richmond to the train station."

"You're right," Anthony agreed. "Which is why we've come up with another plan. Instead of going into Richmond, we're going to take roads well east of the city and then swing north to Taylorsville to catch a train there. We'll be far away from where everyone is looking for him...if they're still looking. I don't believe anyone will expect him to appear there, but we'll still take measures to disguise him, and we'll make certain he's hidden in the wagon while we're traveling."

Carrie nodded thoughtfully, thinking of how she had helped Moses and Rose escape the plantation before the war. "That should work." She knew there was always a risk of someone recognizing Ben, but it was small. "It will certainly be better than him trying to do it on his own at some point."

Anthony smiled. "I was sure you would agree." He glanced at his pocket watch. "We're going to have to get up extra early because of the additional travel time."

"As well as there being less people out on the road early in the morning," Abby said.

"That's right," Anthony agreed. "I believe we'll be able to make the afternoon train, but it means we won't get into Philadelphia until extremely late tomorrow night."

"So much for May's cooking and a soft bed tomorrow. Carrie took just a moment to playfully mourn before a smile returned to her face. "It will be fun to have a new adventure, and I'm so glad we can get Ben to safety."

Abby gazed at them with a serious expression. "I know this is the right thing to do, but I want you to be very careful."

"They'll be fine," Rose said confidently. "Anthony, did you ever hear about the time Carrie took Moses and me to meet our Underground Railroad conductor? We were stopped for some food when a Confederate soldier patrolling the roads came upon us. I thought I was going to pass out from fear, but Carrie was the consummate actress. She batted her eyelashes, exaggerated her drawl, and cooed at him just as well as any of the young ladies she'd always made fun of. The poor man was so besotted that he totally forgot to insist on our travel papers. Carrie had already forged some, but it could have been difficult if he had examined them closely." Rose batted her eyelashes dramatically. "You don't have to worry, Abby. Ben is in excellent hands. I already feel sorry for anyone who tries to create a problem."

Carrie laughed along with the rest of them, but she had never forgotten the terror of that day, nor the heartbreak of watching her two dearest friends ride away from her, with no idea of when she would see them next. She shook her head to clear the image. "I'm assuming Lillian knows of the change in plans?"

"She does," Anthony assured her.

"I have one more thing to do before we leave," Carrie announced. "I'll be back in a little while."

*****

Carrie slipped into the barn, careful to not make any noise that might alert Miles and Annie upstairs. She wanted to be alone.

Granite nickered softly and thrust his head over the door. Carrie opened his stall door and joined him. She wrapped her arms around his neck and stood silently, breathing in his aroma and warmth. "I'm going to miss you," she whispered.

She stepped back and stared into his liquid eyes almost obscured by the dark. "You have to promise me you'll be here when I get back, Granite." Her voice caught. "I believe you want me to go finish my internship, but you have to be alive when I get back. I couldn't stand it if something were to happen to you while I'm gone." She threw her arms around his neck again. "Do you understand me?"

Granite nickered again, and then nudged the pocket of her breeches.

Carrie managed a soft chuckle. "My heart is breaking, and all you can think about is the carrot in my pocket?" Granite bobbed his head and nudged her again. "Fine." She pulled out the hidden treat and gave it to him. "I've made Amber promise to give you one every day until I get back."

Carrie took a deep breath and held Granite's head firmly in her hands so she could gaze into his eyes. "I'm coming back in just a month, do you hear me? I'm coming back in a month. When I do, we'll go for a ride every day that I'm here."

Granite gave a snuffling sound and buried his head into her chest.

Tears poured down Carrie's face, but she made no effort to squelch them. When her tears had run dry, she kissed Granite gently. "See you soon, big guy."

Chapter Fourteen

Armed with the two large hampers of food Annie had prepared, Anthony, Carrie, Lillian, Ben and Jeb pulled away from the house in one of the plantation wagons long before the sun was up. Jeb was coming along so he could drive the wagon back to the plantation once they had reached Taylorsville.

Anthony was thankful it wasn't raining. It might have given them more protection, since there were likely to be fewer patrols out in soggy weather, but it would also have made their life miserable during what promised to be a very long day. Even if things went perfectly, they were all going to be exhausted when they finally made it to Philadelphia that night

He glanced at the back of the wagon where Lillian and Ben rested against the large wooden crate in the center. He hoped it wouldn't be necessary, but they had all agreed they would take no chances on Ben being found and hauled back to Richmond. Reports coming in from the city revealed the tension had not diminished.

Anthony had grown close to Ben in the two weeks he'd been on the plantation. Anthony admired the man and looked forward to having him live with them for a while. He was confident they could connect Ben to the people who would help him create a new life.

"It's a beautiful morning," Carrie said quietly.

Anthony looked at his lovely wife seated next to him. "You might be the only person who would notice that right now," he said with a grin.

"Why? It truly is a beautiful morning. It's warm enough to not need a coat. The stars are twinkling, and I bet the sunrise is going to be amazing." She glanced back at Lillian. "Please tell me you think it's a beautiful morning, too."

"Is it?" Lillian asked absently, covering a huge yawn with her hand. "I don't think I had enough of Annie's coffee to wake me up enough to notice."

"I'm with Miss Lillian," Jeb said sleepily.

Carrie groaned. "Ben? Help me out here."

"I reckon it be a pretty day," Ben replied, "but I'll admit I ain't looking at the stars much. I reckon I'm going to stay on the lookout for patrols."

"Now?" Carrie asked with astonishment. "Why? We're hours away from Richmond."

"That's true," Ben answered, but he didn't stop scanning the terrain around them.

Carrie's eyes narrowed suddenly. "There's something Lillian and I aren't being told." She turned to stare at Anthony. "What is it?"

Anthony gritted his teeth, trying to figure out how to say it.

"Anthony," Carrie warned, "Lillian and I are part of this, too. It's not fair to hide things from us. Is Ben right? Are we in danger so close to the plantation?"

Anthony sighed. "There was a man who came through late last night, looking for a job. Moses didn't have one to offer him, but the man provided some valuable information that Eddie sent along with him. Evidently, the police have decided Ben isn't in Richmond anymore, but they haven't given up looking for him. It seems Ellyson's police force is eager to show they're in control. Having Ben on the run makes them look bad." He took a deep breath. "Eddie sent a warning that General Canby has authorized some of his troops to look for Ben outside the city. He heard they were going to send some out this way because Moses has hired so many workers. Seems they believe Ben might have ended up out here."

Carrie absorbed the information silently. "So, what's the plan?"

Anthony smiled in the darkness. He should have known his wife wouldn't overreact to the news. He hated that she was so used to danger, but he couldn't deny she knew how to handle it. "We're on our way to a funeral," he said solemnly.

"A funeral?" Lillian asked. "What are you talking about?"

Anthony watched Carrie glance back at the wooden box and then laugh. "It's a casket?"

"Well, it can serve as one," Anthony said. "Let's hope it's not needed."

"Brilliant," Carrie murmured, her hand reaching across the wooden seat to grip his. "I'm proud of your devious mind."

Anthony chuckled, but he was far from relaxed. All he cared about was getting his new friend safely out of the South. They had a long day ahead of them. Far too much could go wrong. Even though he was armed, he wasn't about to start a gunfight with Union soldiers. If Ben was caught, there would be nothing they could do to stop him from going to jail, and it was certain they would be hauled in with him.

*****

They were just east of Richmond when Anthony pulled the wagon into a clump of trees. The sun had been up for about an hour, but the roads were still completely empty. "Let's have something to eat," he suggested.

Carrie was more than happy to comply. Annie had given them all a ham biscuit to hold them over until they could stop, but her stomach had been growling for a long time.

The five of them climbed down and found a sheltered area where they could watch the wagon but remain unseen. By unspoken agreement, they ate in silence, listening for the sound of hoof beats. They ate quickly, packed the hamper again and returned to the wagon.

"It's time to get in, Ben," Anthony said. "I'm sorry you have to travel the rest of the way like this."

"No problem," Ben said cheerfully. "Annie said she sent enough blankets to make it like a baby's cradle, and my stomach is full. I'll be fine."

Carrie saw the nervousness in his eyes that contradicted his cheerful voice. "We'll get you to Philadelphia," she said confidently.

Ben locked eyes with her, seeming to draw strength from her confidence. "I believe you will," he murmured. "I appreciate what you're doing a whole lot."

Lillian reached out to clasp his hand. "We don't have to be quiet unless we see someone, Ben. You may be in that wooden box, but we're still going to keep working on your speech."

Ben chuckled. "I'm going to school in a casket?"

"Your English is already much better," Carrie told him. "Rose and Lillian must have been working hard with you."

Ben grimaced. "I ain't said a word that they ain't had something to say about it."

Lillian cleared her throat. "Excuse me?"

Ben shook his head, but his eyes were dancing. "You see what I mean? I haven't said a word that they haven't had something to say about," he said carefully.

"They harp on me all the time too, Ben," Jeb said with a grin. "You get used to it after a while, and I reckon I'm grateful."

Anthony laughed. "You'll be glad for it when you get to Philadelphia," he assured Ben, and then motioned to the wooden box. "Go ahead and make yourself comfortable." He and Miles had added more holes on the sides of the box to make sure there would be enough air, masking them in wood knots so they wouldn't attract unwanted attention. "Cover your ears while I hammer the lid closed."

Carrie peeked inside the makeshift casket when Anthony lifted the wooden lid. "Good grief. Annie wasn't teasing about the number of blankets. I almost wish I could change places with you."

"Yep," Ben replied. "I figure on taking a nice long nap, if I can get Lillian to take a break on all the teaching."

Everyone laughed, but as soon as Ben climbed into the box and Anthony nailed it closed, the reality of their situation sobered all of them.

"You think you got enough nails in there?" Lillian asked.

"If someone stops us and wants me to open it, I don't want it to be too easy," Anthony said soberly.

"It's so wrong," Carrie muttered. "This kind of thing shouldn't be happening anymore, Anthony."

"No, but it is," Anthony said sadly. "All we can do is get him out of here and give him a chance for a new life."

Carrie pushed back the realization of what would happen to them if they were found trying to help Ben escape. He wouldn't be the only one going to jail. She thought of Frances waiting for her at home, and then shook her head to banish the thought of not returning to her daughter. They were doing the right thing.

They were within an hour of the Taylorsville Station when they heard the sound of pounding hoof beats. They had passed other travelers now that it was later in the morning, but there was something about the sound that alerted all of them.

Lillian quit talking to Ben, knocked twice to signal that he should remain silent, and she and Jeb moved up to sit behind Anthony and Carrie.

Carrie forced herself to breathe evenly, determined to not show fear. Her heart sped up when she identified four Union soldiers cantering down the road, but her face remained calm.

Anthony raised a hand in greeting but made no movement to stop the wagon.

"Hold up there!" One of the soldiers, obviously an officer, lifted his hand in command.

Anthony complied. "Good morning," he called cheerfully. "What can we do for you, officer?"

The soldier who had commanded them to stop moved his horse closer to the wagon and peered over the side. "Where are you going?"

Carrie smiled at him slightly, her eyes sorrowful. "I'm afraid we're on a sad mission," she said. "My name is Dr. Carrie Wallington. One of my patients didn't make it, but before he died, he begged me to take him to his family's home. We're fulfilling his wishes."

The officer's suspicion didn't diminish. His dark eyes narrowed as they probed her, looking for a lie. "What did he die from?"

"A hunting accident," Carrie answered. "Evidently, his bullet lodged in the chamber when he fired. It exploded." She shook her head. "His friends brought him to me, but he was too badly hurt for me to save. It was such a shame. He had just returned from the North a few years ago to buy a small farm. He fought valiantly in the war, only to die during a hunting accident." She sighed heavily.

The soldier locked his eyes on her. "He was a *Union* soldier?" he asked sharply. "I thought you said you were taking him to his family's home?" His chiseled face had turned rock hard.

"I did," Carrie said, hoping the right amount of emotion was being revealed by her words. "His family lives just outside Chesterfield. They're Southerners, but they remained true to the Union through the war, sending their only son off to fight."

The soldier continued to watch her. "What was his name?"

"Brentley Lawrence," Carrie answered, forcing herself to maintain eye contact and not look nervous as she made up her lies. It would be impossible for the officer to know the name was fabricated. She had to hope she was convincing, and that the others in the wagon wouldn't sabotage her efforts.

"Can I see him?"

"You want to see his body?" Carrie allowed herself to look startled because it was an odd request. To respond in any other way would be suspicious.

"Yes," the soldier answered brusquely. "We're on the lookout for a murderer. We were told to not let anyone pass without checking for him."

"Oh my!" Carrie exclaimed. "That's horrible. I'm so sorry someone was killed. It is certainly your duty to look inside the casket." At the word casket, she saw the soldier flinch. She turned to Anthony. "Dear, you'll have to pry open the lid."

Anthony rose to comply, but locked eyes with the soldier. "Are you sure you want to see it?" he asked. "I'm sure you saw a lot of death during the war, but this is different."

"I'm afraid he's right, Officer. Brentley has been dead for several days, and he's already begun to decay badly. We've wrapped him tightly in blankets to lessen the smell, but it's not pleasant." Carrie waved to Anthony. "The soldier has his orders, though, dear. We wouldn't want him to get in trouble. Go ahead and open it. We'll wrap him back up once they've made their identification."

The three other soldiers pulled their horses back several steps. It was obvious they didn't want any part of disturbing the remains in the box.

Anthony reached for the hammer and pulled the first nail out, the screeching sound ripping through the quiet. "This will take me a few minutes," he said apologetically. "Brentley didn't want his family to see him like this. He made me promise to seal his casket tightly, so they would be less likely to open it. He just wants to be buried in the family plot."

The officer watched closely while he pulled out several more nails, and then waved his hand abruptly. "Stop," he ordered "I don't see the need to disturb the remains of a fellow Union soldier." He relaxed suddenly. "I appreciate you returning him to his family, Dr.

Wallington. I'm sure they'll be grateful." When he smiled, Carrie realized he was quite attractive. "I'm sorry to have bothered you."

"Not at all, officer," Carrie said sweetly. "You're simply doing your job. I appreciate what you and the others are doing to keep us safe. I hope you find the horrible murderer you're after."

"Thank you, ma'am," the officer said as he tipped his hat. "I hope the rest of your journey is smooth." He turned his horse and nudged it into a canter.

Moments later, the only evidence they had been there was a puff of dust on the horizon.

Carrie sagged into the seat. "Well..."

"Perhaps you should pursue a career on the stage," Anthony said with a chuckle. "Your talents might be wasted as a doctor." He shook his head. "When did you come up with that story?" he asked admiringly.

Carrie shrugged. "I've had all morning to think about it."

"No one would have ever guessed you were lying," Lillian said, something close to awe in her voice.

Carrie smiled. "You do what you have to do when someone you care about is in danger." She turned in her seat to look back at the casket. "Are you all right, Ben?" She knew he wouldn't speak unless they indicated it was safe.

"I'm not a dead body decaying in a shroud of blankets," Ben said, his voice muffled from the confines of the box. "I reckon I'm doing pretty well."

*****

Carrie didn't relax until the train pulled away from the Taylorsville Station, the engine belching steam as it gathered speed. As hoped, there had been no police officers at the train station, and they had seen no more soldiers. No one had looked askance at Ben, though he'd been sure to keep his hat pulled down over his face, even after settling into his seat next to Anthony.

Jeb was on his way back to the plantation. The empty casket was now hidden behind the station, left behind when they freed Ben. They'd take no chance that the soldiers would stop Jeb on the way home and become suspicious when they saw the same casket.

"We did it," Lillian said quietly, as the station disappeared behind them.

Carrie turned to her with a grin. "We did it!" Her grin disappeared when she saw the strained look in Lillian's eyes. "What's wrong?"

"I believe it's just dawned on me that I'm leaving the plantation," she admitted. "Having to protect Ben kept my mind off it for a little while, but..."

"Starting over is hard," Carrie finished, making sure she kept her voice low enough to not be overheard by other passengers.

Lillian sighed. "It's what I want, but it's hard," she agreed, her eyes full of worry. "I'm scared I'll cause trouble for you and Anthony."

Carrie didn't reveal that she and Anthony had talked about this very issue. "It's going to be fine," she said firmly. She sought for a way to distract Lillian from worrying. "Have you heard of Dr. Mary Walker?"

"No. Should I have?"

"She's quite an amazing woman," Carrie said. "She's also in complete agreement with you and me that women should be able to wear breeches."

Lillian raised a brow. "You're in a dress, Carrie."

Carrie nodded, tired of the effort it took to walk the thin line between comfort and conformity. "I know. I refuse to wear anything but breeches on the plantation or at home, but when I'm out in public, I've decided to not attract any more attention than necessary." She had thought about this long and hard. "I already deal with enough when people discover I'm a doctor. As I watched Dr. Walker, I decided I would limit what I have to endure."

"Doesn't that make you angry?" Lillian asked, looking down at her breeches tucked into boots. Her hair was loose, swinging softly to just above her shoulders.

"Yes," Carrie admitted, willing to acknowledge that she didn't have the courage Lillian did to dress the way she was most comfortable all the time. "I hope it will change in time. Dr. Walker is trying to help make that happen."

"Why is a doctor fighting for clothing reform?" Lillian asked bluntly.

Carrie smiled, glad to return to the reason she had brought up Dr. Walker's name in the first place. "Dr. Walker is not your normal physician."

"The fact that she's a woman would indicate that," Lillian said dryly.

Carrie chuckled. "True, but she has quite a story. She was raised in New York by very progressive parents. They started their own free school for children in the area because they were determined their daughters and sons would have an equal education. Her parents encouraged her to have a mind of her own and applauded her independence. She eventually earned enough money to pay her way through Syracuse Medical College, graduating with honors in 1855. She was the only female in her class."

Lillian whistled. "That had to be hard."

Carrie agreed completely. "She married a fellow medical student when she was twenty-three. She wore a short skirt with trousers beneath it, refused to include 'obey' in her vows and kept her last name after the wedding."

Lillian's eyes flared with interest. "That must have made quite a statement."

"I can assure you it did. When the war started, she volunteered for the Union. At first, she was only allowed to practice as a nurse, but ended up serving as an unpaid field surgeon near the frontlines. There was a tremendous need, but more importantly, her skills were obvious." Carrie smiled. "She also wore men's clothing during the war because it made it easier to work."

"Smart woman," Lillian said crisply.

"In April of 1864," Carrie continued, "she was captured by Confederate troops and arrested as a spy. She had just finished helping a Confederate doctor perform an amputation on a soldier who would have died without it."

"What?" Lillian asked with disbelief. "She saved the life of one of their soldiers, and they put her in jail for it? That's a fine way to say thank you."

"I quite agree," Carrie replied. "Their way of saying thank you was to throw her in Castle Thunder in Richmond."

Lillian's eyes narrowed. "I can tell by the expression on your face that it must have been a horrible place."

"It was a horrible place," Carrie said flatly. "Thankfully, Dr. Walker was only there for four months, but it was long enough to cause partial muscular atrophy in her legs and hands that makes it impossible for her to be a doctor any longer."

Lillian shook her head with sympathy. "What is she doing now?"

"She's become a writer and lecturer. She talks and writes about health care, temperance, women's rights and dress reform."

Lillian looked startled. "Dress reform?"

Carrie nodded. "She's frequently arrested for wearing men's clothing, but she insists on her right to dress the way she believes is appropriate. She is also a staunch believer that fashionable women's clothing is not good for women's health because it's so restricting." Carrie smiled. "She insists she doesn't wear men's clothes...she wears her own clothes."

"She's right." Lillian grew thoughtful. "Is it really against the law for me to wear breeches?"

"Evidently," Carrie answered. "The first law against cross-dressing was in Columbus, Ohio. More states have passed laws, but I don't know how often they're enforced. I've heard the police are more lenient with women than they are with men. My guess is that Dr. Walker is already a thorn in the side of men who perceive her as a threat to their authority, so they use it as a way to harass her."

"Yet she continues to wear them." Lillian's voice was thick with admiration.

"She is quite a woman," Carrie agreed. "I respect her as a surgeon, and I respect her for what she's doing for women."

Lillian gazed at her. "You're revolutionary in so many ways, Carrie, but you choose to conform with your clothing. Why? I know what you said earlier about your reason, but..." She shrugged. "I can't help but feel there's more."

Carrie replied with a question of her own. It was the only way she knew of to avoid having to answer a question she wasn't sure how to answer. "Don't you get tired of standing out, Lillian? Have you ever thought your life might be easier if you tried to blend in?" She had no problem with Lillian's choice of dress, but the question had been bothering her for a long time. She hadn't missed all the glares and stares Lillian had received when they were waiting on the station platform for the train.

"Of course, I get tired of standing out," Lillian said immediately. "And I suppose my life might be easier if I worked harder to blend in, but only in some ways." She paused, her eyes igniting with determination. "In the end, I believe my life would be far more difficult if I were to strive to be someone I'm not. I've tried it before. The effort exhausts me."

It was easy for Carrie to understand that. "I've gone against the grain my entire life," she said softly. "My friends despaired of me. My mother despaired of me."

"And your father?"

Carrie smiled brightly. "My father loved me. He didn't always understand me, but he loved me." Another question entered her mind. "Does any of your family know?" She wasn't going to be more specific on a crowded train. Lillian would know what she was referring to.

"I think they all suspected," Lillian said, "but it wasn't something that was appropriate to talk about. When I decided to leave our Michigan farm, my brother told me to be careful and to be happy. I haven't been back."

Carrie gazed at her. "How long since you've seen your family?"

"Six years."

"Don't you miss them?"

"It's easier for them if they don't see me," Lillian said. "If I came back to our town dressed in breeches, and with my hair cut like this, it would be hard for them. I write letters instead."

"And that's enough?" Carrie couldn't imagine not seeing her father for six years because of her own choices.

Lillian stared at her. "Carrie, would you have given up being a doctor if your father hadn't approved?"

Carrie considered the question carefully, and then slowly shook her head. "No. I had to be a doctor."

Lillian eyed her with compassion. "And I have to be who I am," she said simply.

"I understand," Carrie said slowly. "I really do understand." She realized that while she had been willing to accept Lillian's homosexuality, she hadn't been able to understand it. She thought she did now. Or at least she was much closer.

"Thank you," Lillian murmured as she lay her head against the back of the seat. "If you don't mind, I could use a little rest."

Minutes later, both of them were sound asleep, lulled by the chugging of the engine and the sound of the wheels on the track.

Chapter Fifteen

Abby hugged Susan and Harold good-bye, grabbed her satchel from the porter, and walked out of the train station into the gritty hustle and bustle of New York City. She looked around in astonishment. It had only been a few years since her last visit, but it was like walking into a completely different city.

"Things in New York City keep getting busier and crazier."

Abby whirled around when she heard the familiar voice behind her. "Michael Stratford!" She wrapped the tall, muscular young man in her arms.

"It's so good to see you, Aunt Abby," Michael replied, his sparkling brown eyes peering out from under the brown curls he so despised.

"You keep getting better looking every time I see you," Abby said. "When are you going to put the females of New York City out of their misery by choosing one of them?"

Michael grinned. "I'm happy to report that I've done just that."

Abby gasped and grabbed his hands. She wasn't his biological aunt, but she had been friends with his parents since he was a toddler. He'd always known her as Aunt Abby, and she wouldn't have had it any other way. "Who is the lucky woman?"

"Her name is Julie Malcolm. I don't believe I'm good enough for her, but I'm going to do my best." Michael's eyes softened.

Abby's heart swelled with joy at the look on his face. "How did you meet her?"

Michael reached down and picked up her satchel. "I promise to tell you the story on the way home. Traffic in New York City is even worse than it used to be, and I promised Mother I would have you to the house in time for dinner."

Abby slipped her hand through the crook of his elbow and allowed him to lead her through the hordes of people. Used to hearing different languages when she was in New York, she was still astonished at all the different cultures and dialects flowing around her. Even from the little she'd seen, the city appeared to be bursting at the seams.

As they walked, Abby thought about the last time she had corresponded with Michael's mother. She was appalled to realize it had been over eight months. "What are you doing now?" She raised her voice to be heard over the crowd. "Are you still a policeman?"

Michael shook his head. "No, I finally got my fill of the police force. I'm working with my father in real estate now."

"That's wonderful! I know you were doing an important job, but I worried about you constantly."

"You and my mother," Michael agreed. "My father has always wanted me in the business with him, and Mother has always wanted me to be safe."

"So they're both happy," Abby replied. "I'm glad. I'm also glad you followed your heart for as long as you needed."

Michael gave her a sideways glance. "You mean that, don't you?"

"I do," Abby said firmly. "Far too many people spend their life doing something they don't want to do. It makes me so sad. I'm proud of you for having the courage to go against your parents and do what you wanted."

Michael chuckled. "The reason you've always been my favorite aunt."

When they arrived at the carriage tucked away on a side street, Abby climbed onto the driver's seat while Michael stowed her bag. When he looked at her in surprise, she smiled. "I can't hear the story of you and Julie if I'm in the back."

Michael laughed. "You're right." He stepped into the carriage, his six-foot height making it an easy feat. "Julie is special," he began. "We actually met when a group of thugs went after her on her way home from work one night."

"Oh no!" Abby exclaimed.

"Thankfully, I was just rounding the corner when they grabbed her. I was outnumbered, but my billy club proved to be an equalizer. I only had to hit two of them before they all broke and ran. I walked her home that night to make sure she was safe." He smiled. "The next day was Sunday, so we went for a walk in Central Park." He spread his hands. "The rest is history."

"You're getting married?"

"I asked her two weeks ago," Michael informed her. "She said yes."

His grin made her laugh. "Of course she did," Abby told him. "You are quite a catch, young man. Congratulations!" She squeezed his arm tightly. "What does she do for work?"

Michael frowned. "When I rescued her, she was coming home from a long day in a clothing factory."

Abby couldn't miss the distress in his eyes. "The factory is not a good place to work?"

"It's more like a prison," Michael snapped. "The women who work there are paid pennies, and they're forced to slave away for fourteen to sixteen hours a day. Julie grew up on a farm outside the city. Her father and brother were killed during the war, and her mother died in the influenza epidemic. She was alone and had nothing, so she came to the city looking for work."

"She's been through such a terrible time," Abby murmured sympathetically, glad Julie's life had taken such a huge turn for the better when she met Michael. Michael's father, Wally, had taught his son to appreciate and respect women as much as he appreciated and respected his wife.

Michael nodded, his eyes grim, but they were quickly softened by a smile. "She's working for my father as a secretary now. I told her she didn't need to work anymore once we got married, but she's quite adamant that she continue." He shook his head. "I don't understand it, but I've promised to support what she wants."

Abby understood completely. "She's learned what it's like when the people you depend on are suddenly not there, Michael. She doesn't ever want to be in that position again."

"I hope she never will be," Michael said fervently. "In the meantime, I'm happy to be with her all the time at work. Now that I'm at the real estate firm, we make a great team."

"Will I get to meet her while I'm here?"

"She'll be at dinner tonight," Michael promised. "Father is bringing her home from the office. I'm sure they'll be waiting for us when we arrive."

They continued to weave their way through the congested streets, laughing and chatting all the way to the house.

*****

A long dinner full of laughter and scintillating conversation was drawing to a close. Abby sat back with a sigh of satisfaction. "This evening was just what I was looking forward to, Nancy. Thank you."

Her petite, blue-eyed hostess pushed away tendrils of graying blond hair that had loosened over the hours they'd spent around the table. "It is always such a joy to have you here, Abby."

Julie Malcolm, her green eyes shining under soft brown hair, nodded enthusiastically. "I've heard so many wonderful things about you from everyone, Aunt Abby." She had easily slipped into tradition when Abby insisted she wouldn't respond to anything else. "They were right!"

Abby laughed. "People always talk nicely about you when you haven't seen them in years, Julie."

"Not true," Julie replied. "There are many people I haven't seen in several years that I can't think of a single nice thing to say about."

Abby chuckled, but she was struck by the pained look in Julie's eyes. She could only imagine what the young girl had been through in the last five years after losing her entire family. Watching the easy affection between Julie and Michael, but also between Julie and Michael's parents, warmed Abby's heart. The rest of this lovely young woman's life was going to be so much better than the last painful interlude.

"Are you up for lunch with some of my women friends tomorrow?" Nancy asked.

"Of course," Abby replied. "Here?"

"No." Nancy's eyes twinkled with something Abby couldn't describe.

Abby cocked her head. "What are you hiding?"

"I'm not hiding anything," Nancy said quickly. "We're eating at Delmonico's Restaurant."

Abby searched her mind but couldn't come up with a reason that should be important. "I know I'm tired, but that's not ringing any bells. Somehow, I suspect it should."

"Have you heard of the Sorosis Club?" Nancy asked.

Abby shook her head. "Evidently I'm too sequestered on the plantation to know what that is." The knowledge constricted her heart. There was a time when nothing could happen with women that she didn't know about. Now, she felt like she was in the dark far too much of the time.

"It's quite the story," Julie said excitedly. "May I tell it?" When Nancy nodded, she began. "Do you remember when Charles Dickens was here in New York City during his American tour two years ago?"

"Of course," Abby responded. "I also remember it being quite controversial among women."

"As it should have been," Julie said indignantly. "Jane Cunningham Croly, an accomplished journalist here in New York City, tried to get a ticket. The evening's host, the New York Press Club, denied her one. Then, they made it worse by banning women from the dinner altogether."

"Preposterous!" Abby retorted. "I thought I knew all the country's women journalists—at least all those from New York—but I'm afraid I don't recognize that name."

"Does the name *Jennie June* ring any bells for you?" Nancy asked.

"Of course," Abby said instantly. "She's the editor of *Demorest's Magazine*. It's devoted to women's fashion."

"Jennie June is Jane Croly's pen name," Julie explained, and then returned to her story. "Jane was less than pleased when the Press Club banned all women from Charles Dickens' performance."

"As she should have been," Abby said indignantly.

"Yes." Julie's eyes glowed with passion.

Abby wanted to smile. She could see why Michael had fallen in love with the fiery girl.

"When Jane was turned away, she decided to start America's first, female-only, women's rights organization last year. She named it the Sorosis Club. Since she'd been denied access to Dickens' performance at Delmonico's Restaurant, she decided to have the first meeting there."

"I'm intrigued," Abby murmured as she thought about the conversation on the riverbank with Carrie and Rose.

"It's been a success from the very beginning," Julie told her. "Of course, most of the time I'm completely out of my league with the powerful women who attend, but Nancy insists I belong. I will admit I love every minute of it."

"Why do you love it?" Abby asked, wanting to know more about the woman Michael had chosen to be his wife.

Julie paused, considering the question. "I believe we've entered a new time when women have more opportunity. The women I meet at the luncheons make me believe I can be anything I want." She smiled shyly.

"You can be," Nancy said firmly, and then turned to Abby. "The Sorosis Club is for professional women. You may be familiar with Josephine Pollard?"

"The children's author," Abby replied. "I've purchased several of her books for Rose's school."

"Yes, and Fanny Fern is also a member."

Abby smiled. "Fanny Fern? I've read many of her newspaper columns. She's quite brilliant."

Nancy nodded. "She's also the highest paid columnist in the country, besides being a well-known author."

Abby searched her memory for something else she remembered about Fanny Fern. "Her first novel was called *Ruth Hall*. I seem to recall it was based on her life."

Nancy chuckled. "I have a copy in your bedroom. If you have time while you're here, you can read it. If not, please feel free to take it home. It's quite fascinating."

"And quite controversial," Julie added, her eyes shining with amusement. "Critics of the book decried her lack of *filial piety*," she said dramatically. "They said it was scandalous that she attacked her own relatives. They claimed there is a want of womanly gentleness in her characters." She rolled her eyes.

Abby grinned. "I look forward to reading it." She stifled a yawn. "Perhaps I can go start it now? I'm barely able to keep my eyes open."

Nancy jumped up. "Of course! I've missed you so sorely that I'm afraid I lost track of time."

"The entire evening has been lovely," Abby assured her. "I'm looking forward to the luncheon tomorrow." She looked at Julie. "Will you be joining us? Or do you have to work?"

"I insist she be allowed off from work to attend," Nancy answered. "I'm counting on the younger women coming up to carry on the fight for women's equality when we're no longer able to do so."

Abby paused at the foot of the stairs. "You're hardly thinking about stopping," she said with disbelief.

Nancy waved her hand. "Of course not, but I'm also not getting any younger. I fear we're in for a long battle." She sobered. "I don't know that you and I will see the victory, Abby. I want to assure the fight continues."

Abby nodded and then climbed the stairs, suddenly very tired. She hoped by the time she left that she would understand why she was in New York City.

*****

Susan gazed around with delight as she and Harold stepped down from the carriage that had picked them up at the train station in Quebec. The ride through the countryside had been wonderful. Verdant pastures, just coming to life with spring growth, were filled with beautiful horses. Stone houses, tucked back into the woods, still had smoke curling from their chimneys. Spring had arrived, but warm temperatures were far behind the South.

Her first glimpse of Carson Farms had stolen her breath. The lush, green pastures were populated by dozens of gorgeous Cleveland Bay horses. She had learned all she could from Miles about the breed. In order for a horse to be registered, they had to be a bay color. Any white markings, unless it was a small star on the forehead, rendered a stud inadmissible to the stud book. She knew the uniformity in color was encouraged because it made the creation of matching driving teams and pairs very easy.

"Hello!"

Susan and Harold looked up when a friendly call split the air.

"Hello!" Harold called back. He took Susan's hand and walked toward the man standing at the door of the sprawling barn, just one in a complex of five large structures.

"You must be Harold and Susan Justin. I'm so pleased you made it. I'm Paul Carson."

Susan smiled at the elderly man with a weathered face. His smile was bright, and his soft blue eyes gleamed with kindness beneath his black cap. "It's a pleasure to meet you, Mr. Carson. Miles has told us so much about you."

Mr. Carson pointed his finger at her. "You'd better be treating that man right down there in America. He was the best worker I ever had. I've never seen a more natural horseman in my life."

"He's happy," Susan assured him. She reached into her pocket and pulled out an envelope. "He sent this letter for you."

Mr. Carson reached for it with a smile and tucked it in his pocket. "I'll read it later, but I suppose I already know what it says. He wants me to give you some extra good deals on the horses you buy because the two of you have plans to expand the breed in America." He squinted his eyes. "How did I do?"

"There might be something like that in there," Susan said amicably, her lips twitching.

Mr. Carson snorted, and then grinned. "Let me show you around."

Susan had many questions that she knew Miles would have been hesitant to ask because of his position. "How did you begin breeding Cleveland Bays in Canada, Mr. Carson?"

"My father worked in the stables of the British Royal Family," he said proudly. "The Cleveland Bays pull all the carriages in the royal processions. His job was to take care of them." He gazed out over the fields and then stopped next to a fence. "When I was a boy, all I wanted was to go to the stables with him. Thankfully, I was usually allowed to. When I got older, I knew I wanted to start my own stables."

"Why Canada?" Harold asked, his interest as avid as Susan's.

"I've been in Canada since 1820," Mr. Carson answered. "There were many of my fellow countrymen who came between 1815 and 1850. The Industrial Revolution was making Europe richer, but the population was growing right along with it. There weren't enough jobs for everyone, so we came to Canada and America."

"Did your father support your decision?" Susan asked, thinking how hard it must have been for the man to watch his son leave.

"He understood." Mr. Carson's eyes glowed with the memory. "He hated to see me go, but he talked the Royal Stables into sending over ten Cleveland Bay horses with me so that the breed would continue to grow in the New World." He waved his arm. "This is the result."

"What a wonderful story!" Susan cried. She leaned back against the fence and looked around. "How many horses are here?"

"Two hundred and six," Mr. Carson answered.

"And you don't mind selling them to Americans?" Harold asked.

"Well, it makes me a little nervous to think about sending them down to the country that threw the English out so abruptly, but your money spends well." Mr. Carson's face remained impassive, but his eyes gleamed with amusement.

Susan laughed outright. "Miles was right." When Mr. Carson cocked his head, she continued. "He told me you were the funniest Englishman he ever met."

"Not that his years in slavery would have given him access to many of my countrymen," Mr. Carson said dryly. "Miles and I became friends when he was here. I hated to see him leave, but his heart was always down there in Virginia. When he finally decided it was safe to go home, he could hardly wait to get back there." He pulled out the envelope in his pocket. "Is this letter going to tell me how Felicity is doing? I have many horses, but she was special. When I agreed to allow Miles to take one of my mares, he picked the best one I had."

"Felicity is doing wonderfully," Susan assured him. "That letter will tell you about the first foal she had fourteen months ago. The filly's name is Dancer. She dropped her second foal just three weeks ago—another filly that we named Eclipse's Olivia. We're calling her Ollie."

Mr. Carson chuckled his approval and then looked thoughtful. "Eclipse? Is that her sire?"

Susan nodded. "Yes."

"Eclipse is a son of Lexington? The one who did so well on the tracks before being retired as a stud?" His eyes were bright with interest.

"Yes," Susan said again. "The crossbreeding of Eclipse with the Cleveland Bays is producing beautiful offspring."

"They would," Mr. Carson replied. "Breeding to a bay stallion will preserve the color and add to their height. You'll be breeding some mighty fine carriage horses down there in Virginia."

"That's our hope," Susan said eagerly. "I believe there will be a high demand."

Mr. Carson turned to Harold. "Do you let your wife handle everything with the horses?"

Harold smiled. "Susan is the horsewoman. I'm a journalist. I ride well enough, but horses are her passion. I've learned to simply agree with whatever her plans are."

Mr. Carson turned his eyes back to Susan. "You are the only owner of that stables?"

"No, my business partner is Carrie Wallington. Her first husband, Robert Borden, started the stables right after the war. When he was killed several years ago, Carrie took over the operation and invited me to join her."

"Killed?"

"Yes. He was murdered during a vigilante attack on the plantation."

Mr. Carson shook his head. "You Americans..." he said sternly. "Canada had her trouble with slavery for a while, but it was banned completely in 1833. I never had anything to do with it. I prefer to pay the people who work for me with money and with respect. It's better that way."

"I agree," Susan said fervently. "Carrie is so grateful you provided Miles with a home when he escaped before the war."

Mr. Carson's eyes softened. "Miles had nothing but good things to say about Carrie Cromwell."

"They're very close," Susan said. "Both of them would do anything for each other."

Mr. Carson studied her for a moment and then nodded. "Let's go look at horses. I'll make sure you're pleased with the arrangement."

Susan exchanged a look of delight with Harold and then hurried after the elderly man, who was already striding purposefully toward one of the barns.

"The best of the mares are in this barn," Mr. Carson called over his shoulder. "You'll find what you're looking for."

*****

Abby gazed around her as their carriage moved slowly through the streets of the New York City financial district. "The city is exploding," she murmured, more to herself than anyone.

"It is, indeed," Nancy replied. "Immigration is growing on what seems like a daily basis. Wally told me recently that seventy percent of all immigrants are coming into the country through our city. It has become known as the Golden Door of the world."

Abby thought about the struggles the city had already fought to overcome when the influx of immigrants created grave epidemics of flu and cholera. "How is the city handling the growth?"

"Like anywhere, there are challenges," Nancy answered. "The challenges are just bigger and more difficult here."

Abby stared at her. "You seem almost immune to it."

Nancy shrugged. "You have to be. The problems are never-ending. I've learned that I must do what I can, and then let go of the things I can't do anything about. It's either that or go quite mad from the frustration."

Abby thought about her idyllic life on the plantation. "It must be very difficult."

Nancy shook her head. "I'm not complaining. Even with all its problems, New York is the most exciting city on the planet as far as I'm concerned. We've become the leader in so many arenas." She paused and then asked, "Do you miss Philadelphia? Miss running the factories?"

Abby was glad she could answer honestly. "No, I don't miss it. I love the plantation."

Nancy continued to examine her. "Then what are you looking for here?"

Abby hesitated, but their decades-long friendship made it unnecessary to hide the truth. "I'm not sure," she admitted.

"But you *are* here looking for something?" Nancy pressed.

It was Abby's turn to shrug. "I am, but I don't know what it is. I love life on the plantation, yet there is another part of me that is discontent." She considered her words. "I'm restless. I don't want to go back to the factories, but I want something more." She spread her hands. "I just don't know what the *more* is."

"I hope you find what you're looking for," Nancy said sincerely, and then waved her hand in the direction they were driving. "There is Delmonico's Restaurant."

Abby was impressed. "It's beautiful." She examined the triangular building in the heart of the Financial District. The front door was buttressed with imposing pillars.

"It has quite the history," Nancy informed her. "Delmonico's was the first proper, sit-down restaurant in the city. Two brothers from Switzerland, Giovanni and Pietro Delmonico, opened it in 1827 as a small café serving French pastries. It took only a few years before they had grown into a full-fledged French restaurant."

"French?"

"Yes," Nancy continued. "It was quite a shift in the culture. At the time, all the best home cooks were preparing traditional British fare, and our cookbooks were British. The unique cuisine was welcomed." She paused. "Unfortunately, the restaurant burned down in 1835 in a massive fire that swept downtown Manhattan, taking over seven hundred buildings with it."

"I remember reading about the fire," Abby replied. "It was quite devastating."

Nancy nodded. "They moved to a temporary location but also began construction on this restaurant. There are three floors and a honeycomb of private dining rooms. It's the grandest restaurant New York City has ever seen."

Abby eyed the beautiful structure. "It must be quite in demand."

"If you have the money for it," Nancy agreed. "They cater to quite elite customers."

"And to the Sorosis Club."

"Yes," Nancy said with a grin. "I suspect they were horrified when the New York Press Club banned women from the Charles Dickens' performance. They've been quite accommodating of the Sorosis Club."

"How many women are members?" Abby asked.

"It started with twelve. Now there are eighty-three. It will continue to grow," Nancy said proudly. "More women come every week." She changed the subject back to the restaurant. "The food is spectacular. Wally and I seldom eat out, but we'd dined here twice with business clients." Her eyes lit with enthusiasm. "The Delmonicos bought a farm in 1834 to grow produce for the restaurant, and they offer squab, hare, quail, pheasant, grouse, venison and wild duck. As if that wasn't enough, they also have salmon and mackerel, but they're best known for their Delmonico steak. My favorite dish, which I'm told was also a favorite of President Lincoln, is Delmonico's potatoes."

"Delmonico's potatoes?" Abby asked with amusement.

"They're mashed potatoes covered in cheese and breadcrumbs. They are quite delicious!"

"Have you memorized their entire menu?" Abby teased, not willing to acknowledge she was already salivating.

"You wait," Nancy retorted. "You're not going to be able to stop talking about the food after the luncheon. I predict you'll return to the plantation and ask Annie to make Delmonico's potatoes for you." She returned to the history of the restaurant. "The Delmonico brothers have both passed away, but it's now owned by their nephew. In the last twenty years, he has expanded to four locations around the city."

Abby was impressed. "Quite the success story."

*****

Abby settled into her chair between Nancy and Julie at a table for eight. The sumptuous dining room was beautiful. Heavy damask curtains had been pushed back so the sun could flood the room with light. Fine white linen graced tables set with elegant china, silverware and crystal glasses. Vibrant conversation ebbed and flowed around her.

"You're new, aren't you?"

Abby smiled at the petite woman seated across from her. "I am. My name is Abby Cromwell. I'm here from Virginia, visiting my friend Nancy Stratford. Whom do I have the pleasure of meeting?"

"I'm Emily Schubert. I'm so glad you're here, Abby. May I ask your profession?"

Abby stiffened, surprised to realize she was embarrassed to admit she no longer had a profession, but maintained her composure. "Until recently, I was the owner of clothing factories in Philadelphia and Richmond."

"In Philadelphia?" Emily pursed her lips in thought for a moment, and then her eyes widened. "You used to be Abigail Livingston?"

Abby stared at her in surprise. "Yes, but how did you know that?"

Emily laughed. "I'm from Philadelphia," she revealed, and then leaned forward to grab Abby's hand. "I used to work for you."

"What?" Abby asked in shock. "You worked for me?"

Emily nodded eagerly. "It was a few years before the war when I began. I had a dream of going to a university, but I didn't have the funds to do it. My family could have helped me, but they were too appalled that I wanted to be a doctor."

Abby smiled with delight. "You're a doctor?"

"I am now," Emily responded, "but only because I was able to work at your factory for fair wages for three years. I saved every penny and put myself through medical school. I'm practicing medicine here in New York City now."

"At the New York Infirmary for Women and Children?" Abby asked.

Emily's eyes widened again. "How do you know about the Infirmary?"

"My daughter is also a doctor. She is doing her surgical internship in Philadelphia this year, and then she plans to return to Virginia. She started a clinic there near the plantation where she was raised, and has plans to open a separate practice in Richmond.." At that moment, she was so proud of Carrie, she could have burst.

Emily laughed. "That's wonderful!" she exclaimed, and then sobered. "I'm so grateful I finally have a chance to say thank you, Mrs. Cromwell."

"Please, call me Abby."

"I will, as long as you understand how grateful I am. Without your willingness to hire women in your factory, and your decision to pay us fairly, I could never have paid for medical school. I wouldn't be a doctor if it weren't for you, Abby."

Abby flushed with pleasure. "I am so happy to know that, Emily. Thank you."

"Your commitment to women changed my life," Emily said, her eyes glimmering with tears.

"The Bregdan Principle," Abby murmured, thinking about Biddy Flannagan.

"Excuse me?" Emily asked. "What do you mean?"

"It's a principle I learned from an amazing woman from Philadelphia. She firmly believed that every action we take will create repercussions through all of history. Hearing your story makes me realize how true that is."

"Well, I hope you keep doing it," Emily said. "Because of you, I am now helping two other women through medical school. Very few of us can do it on our own."

Abby grinned with delight. "That's wonderful! I can hardly wait to tell Carrie about you."

Emily's eyes narrowed. "What is your daughter's last name?"

"It's Wallington now, but when she was in school, it was Borden. Her first husband passed away."

Emily threw her head back with a laugh. "You tell Carrie I'll never forgive her for leaving the Medical Institute in Philadelphia."

"You know Carrie?" Abby asked with astonishment.

"Not very well," Emily admitted. "I was just finishing when she was starting her studies, but I heard wonderful things about her."

"I'll tell her," Abby promised, deciding not to mention that Carrie had chosen to become a homeopathic physician. Though it was ridiculous, she knew the American Medical Association frowned on homeopathy.

Emily turned to talk with Nancy and Julie. Abby watched them chat, wondering at the circumstances that had crossed her and Emily's path. She watched the vibrant redhead talk, her brown eyes flashing with intelligence and purpose.

The rest of the luncheon passed more quickly than she could have imagined.

Alice Cary, the president and an accomplished poet, spoke eloquently about the need to open opportunities for women in professions. She talked about plans to create scholarships for young women who wanted to attend a university and shared the vision the group had of creating many more Sorosis Clubs around the country.

Abby listened closely to everything that was said, but her head was spinning. She had her answer.

Chapter Sixteen

"You discovered why you came to New York City," Nancy observed as they made their arduous way through the city back to the house.

Abby smiled. "You know me well."

"I should, after decades of friendship," Nancy said. "We may not see each other often enough for my satisfaction, but I will always know your heart."

Abby reached for her friend's hand. "That means more to me than you'll ever know," she said softly. "I will always know your heart, too."

Nancy nodded. "Now tell me why you're here. The curiosity is killing me!"

Abby laughed, but sobered quickly. "I've been so conflicted, Nancy. I thought selling the factories and moving to the plantation had ended the impact I could have on women. I love Thomas, and I love our life there, but I couldn't shake the restlessness."

"And now you have?"

"Well, let's just say I have a plan," Abby replied. "Carrie and Rose gave me the answer weeks ago, I just didn't recognize it. All I could think was that I needed to do more." She paused to gather her thoughts. "Both of them told me that my influence and support in their lives had made what they are doing now possible."

"It's true," Nancy said. "You mean the world to both of those young ladies." She narrowed her eyes. "It was meeting Emily that gave you your answer, wasn't it?"

"Yes. I suppose the impact I've had on Carrie and Rose is so obvious that it somehow ceased to reflect that I had anything to do with it. They are both so intelligent, strong and independent. They would have become remarkable women without my help." She took a deep breath. "At least, that's what I'd started to think."

"Whereas Emily was someone you impacted without even knowing it."

"Yes," Abby agreed again. "I don't know if I ever looked out over the factory floor years ago and thought about one of those young girls becoming a doctor. Ever since talking to Emily, I can't help wondering what the rest of those workers went on to do."

"And you can't stop thinking about how much more of an impact you could have had if you'd been deliberate about helping them become all they can be."

Abby stared at Nancy with surprise. "Exactly. How did you know that?"

"I've come to the same conclusion, Abby," Nancy said with a smile. "I'm not old, but I'm getting there. There are still things I can do, but I meant it last night when I said I wanted to help make sure younger women are able to carry on the fight when I can't do it anymore. When *you* can't do it anymore." Her voice rose with passion. "It's going to be a long fight before women have equality, Abby. It's our job to feed that fire in younger women."

"I could see the passion in Julie's eyes," Abby said thoughtfully. "She has you to thank for that."

"She does," Nancy agreed. "There was a time I couldn't have acknowledged that. I believed it would be prideful to think I could have that much influence, but the truth is that I can. You can. All of us can." She leaned back to gaze at the sky for a moment before she brought her eyes back to meet Abby's. "What is your plan?"

Abby told her friend about Bregdan Women. "I'm going to be there when Carrie has her meeting in Philadelphia, but then I'm going home to help Rose start one on the plantation. I'm going to teach business skills to every female who wants to learn. More importantly, I'm going to share the stories of all the women I know who have moved beyond their circumstances to become far more than they ever dreamed." She smiled, her excitement growing as she heard the words come out of her mouth. "Then I'm going to do the same in Richmond. I believe women are the key to making our country better, but they have to believe it themselves before they'll take action. I plan on igniting the fire under as many girls and women as I can."

Nancy hesitated. "You know you'll be fighting far more resistance in Virginia than you would in the North?"

Abby waved her hand. "So be it. If Carrie and Janie are brave enough to start a medical practice in Richmond, I should have the courage to go against Southern expectations of women. I believe I'll find it rather refreshing to rock the boat down there a little more."

Nancy chuckled. "If anyone can do it, Abby, you can." Then she frowned. "Are you leaving now that you have your answer?"

"Not a chance," Abby said. "I still have to go ride that confounded subway thing that Michael was talking about last night. Besides, Susan and Harold were sure it would take them several days to finalize the purchase of the horses they want in Canada. I'm going to be here until they're ready to go home."

"Wonderful!" Nancy said, and then launched into the agenda she had planned for them while Abby was visiting.

Abby finally held up her hand while she laughed helplessly. "Did you schedule in sleep at all?"

Nancy shrugged. "Sleep is so highly overrated," she said blithely. "You can sleep on the train home." She changed the subject. "Now, tell me, weren't those Delmonico potatoes the best thing you ever ate?"

Abby grinned. "I'm already planning on having Annie duplicate the recipe," she admitted. "You're right. They were wonderful. The whole meal was sumptuous!"

"You should always believe me in the first place," Nancy said smugly. "I thought you'd learned long ago that I'm always right."

Abby rolled her eyes. "You believe what you need to believe, my friend. In the meantime, I'll give you the knowledge that I loved the potatoes."

"I suppose that will do for now," Nancy responded.

Laughing and talking, the two longtime friends passed the time quickly as their carriage driver navigated the traffic.

*****

Abby finished chewing a bite of her eggs before she turned to Michael. "Can you tell me more about the subway you mentioned the night I arrived? I'm afraid I wasn't paying close enough attention to register the information." After a good night's sleep, she was ready for a day of adventure.

Michael turned to Wally. "Father, do you still have the copy of the *Herald* newspaper that announced it?"

Wally nodded. "The top shelf of the bookcase, on the left."

Michael found it quickly. He held up the paper, so Abby could read the headline.

A FASHIONABLE RECEPTION HELD IN THE BOWELS OF THE EARTH!

Abby laughed. "That's certainly guaranteed to get attention."

Michael began to read. *"The waiting room is a large and elegantly furnished apartment, cheerful and attractive. Our new subway means the end of street dust of which uptown residents get not only their fill, but more than their fill, so that it runs over and collects on their hair, their beards, their eyebrows, and floats in their dress like the vapor on a frosty morning. Such discomforts will never be found in the tunnel!"*

"Tell me all about it," Abby demanded, fascinated by the description.

Michael shook his head. "Words could never do it justice, Aunt Abby. The Beach Pneumatic Subway is something you need to see for yourself."

"He's right," Wally agreed. "I'm not sure I believe it's the answer to the transportation problems in our city, but it's certainly intriguing."

Abby looked at Nancy. "We can go today?" When her friend nodded, she turned back to Wally. "How many people live in New York right now?"

"The last I knew it was about seven hundred thousand, but the ships pouring into our harbors are bringing thousands more every day. I often walk to work now because it is far quicker than trying to take the carriage. Are you interested in a lesson about our fair city?"

"Of course," Abby said. "I'm fascinated by what's happening here. I thought Philadelphia had gotten crazily crowded, but it's nothing compared to this."

"It's not just crazy. It's dangerous. The streets are clogged with horse-drawn vehicles. Our public transportation consists of overloaded street cars and omnibuses dragged along by ponderous six-horse teams. It's a mess. Axles break. Horses shy and create accidents. Harnesses become snarled and competing drivers get into fistfights on what seems an hourly basis."

"Philadelphia is crowded, but I don't believe it's quite so dire," Abby observed.

"That's just the beginning. Public transportation is so crowded that clothes are ruined constantly, while valuable watches and breastpins vanish into the hands of pickpockets."

Nancy shook her head. "It's terrible, Abby. Perhaps the worst thing is that the air is simply poisonous. I don't believe anyone can ride more than a dozen blocks without having a headache."

Abby knew it was bad, but she hadn't realized just how bad it actually was. "This subway will help?"

Wally sighed. "I think Alfred Beach has a good concept, but I don't believe his technology is advanced enough to accomplish his goal. I also don't believe our esteemed senator will allow it to happen."

Michael nodded. "I agree with Father, but in the meantime, the public loves it."

Abby was puzzled. "Was it built simply as a gimmick?"

"No," Wally replied. "Alfred Beach is a genius. He's a man of vision, originality, quick perception and fantastic energy. I've known him for years. I believe he's headed in the right direction, but..." His voice trailed away.

Abby frowned. "But what? You said Senator Tweed won't allow it to happen. Why?"

Michael scowled. "Because Boss Tweed, how he is known, is completely corrupt. I've known it for years, but he keeps getting away with his fraudulent schemes."

"Fraudulent?" Abby asked. "Isn't that rather harsh?"

Wally snorted. "What he's doing to the people of New York is harsh," he snapped. "He's the head of Tammany Hall, the name for the Democratic Party political machine. He's basically taken over New York City. We have a mayor, but everyone knows who runs things. Two years ago, he convinced the city that we needed a new City Hall. He assured us it would take no more than $250,000. It's still unfinished, but it's already cost over eight million dollars."

Abby gasped. "Eight million dollars?" The amount was unthinkable.

Wally nodded grimly. "Eight *million* dollars," he repeated. "The Senator has spent over $200,000 on carpets, almost three million on plastering, and another three million for furniture."

Abby tried to wrap her mind around the figures. "That's just not possible. Nothing costs that much."

"It does when you're using the money to line your own pockets," Michael said angrily. "Our Senator is doing nothing but looting our city while conditions get worse in every arena."

Abby eyed him for a long moment. "That's why you quit the police force."

Michael tightened his lips. "I couldn't work for an administration as corrupt as this one. I stayed for as long as I felt I could make a difference. I left when I knew I no longer could."

"Why does the city put up with this?" Abby asked.

"Boss Tweed has power because he's an appointed member of so many boards and commissions," Wally replied. "He has almost total control over political patronage in the city, and he ensures the loyalty of voters through jobs he can create and dispense on city related projects." He shook his head. "It's hard for me to guess how much money he's stolen. I believe the day will come when he's held accountable for what he's doing, but right now, the looting just continues."

"And he keeps being voted into office?" Abby asked. "How?"

"Because the people he represents can't vote," Michael said angrily. "Did you know, Aunt Abby, that only 6% of the population could vote when George Washington was elected president?"

Abby was startled. "I didn't know that! 6%? Why?"

"Because only white male property owners could vote," Michael informed her. "It's better now, but there are a lot of things in place to make sure the status quo is maintained. The 15th Amendment has passed, but most black men still can't vote."

"Last year," Wally continued, "the state Democratic Party decided on a strategy to win back both houses. Black males have actually had the vote in New York since 1821 but they had to own at least $250 worth of property in order to be eligible. The number who could meet that requirement was very low. The Republican party ratified the 15th Amendment last year, but Democrats put the property requirement on the ballot at the same time."

"And, wouldn't you know it," Nancy added sarcastically, "over 60 percent of New Yorkers voted to maintain the property requirement. A vast majority of black voters don't meet the requirement. Neither do most of the immigrants pouring into the country."

"Boss Tweed and his fellow Democrats won back both houses in the state legislature in large measure," Michael told her. "Their strategy worked well."

Abby listened avidly, her frustration growing. "So blacks were given the right to vote and at the exact same time, had it taken away from them. That's terrible!"

"It's happening everywhere," Nancy informed her. "We're celebrating equal voting rights, but too many white males never once considered voting when they agreed slavery should end. The slaves could be free, but they weren't meant to have a say in the country. Politicians are hard at work all over the country, making sure that doesn't happen."

Abby sighed. "It's happening all over the South, as well. I knew it was going to take a long time to make things right in our country, but I had hope that the North was leading the way."

"I wish that were true," Wally replied. "The property requirement has also silenced the vast majority of immigrants. They've come to our country with nothing, and now they have no voice because they aren't allowed to vote."

Abby gazed at him. "Do your progressive beliefs make it difficult for your business, Wally?"

Wally shrugged. "The differences between the Republican Party and the Democratic Party are nothing new. I put up with my share of ignorance and attempted intimidation, but I'm also successful enough to be able to ignore it. Boss Tweed would love to rid the city of every progressive mind, but not even he has that much power."

"Do you believe America will ever make things right with the freed slaves?" Abby asked, curious as to what he thought.

Wally considered the question for a long moment, and then shook his head. "I don't know, Abby. I want to say yes, but there is too much evidence to the contrary. The Fifteenth Amendment was just the first step in a very long journey. I'm afraid I don't have a great deal of confidence in my fellow Americans to finish what has begun."

"We'll keep fighting, though," Nancy vowed. "When women get the vote, it will be a huge step in the right direction."

Abby pursed her lips. "Only if someday, we also have the right to help govern our country. Having the vote is a necessary step, but don't you dream of women serving in Congress someday?"

"I do," Nancy agreed quickly, "but I'll admit that just getting the vote seems insurmountable at times." She turned to gaze out the window at the busy street below. "The idea of women legislators almost takes my breath away."

Abby fixed her eyes on Michael and Wally. "Would the two of you support that?"

Both men nodded immediately.

"Equal voting rights in this country will be a battle for a long time," Michael said soberly. "Not only for women and blacks, but also for poor whites, Chinese, Mexicans and Indians." His eyes filled with discouragement. "I don't know how America can claim to be a democracy when the vast majority of the people living in the country have no voice."

Abby felt a burgeoning of hope. "We keep fighting until everyone has a voice," she said firmly. "Your parents and I may not live to see it, but as long as there are young people like you to carry on the fight, there's hope that one day, our country will actually live up to the principles it is founded on."

Wally nodded. "Here's hoping you're correct, Abby. Now, in the meantime, Michael and I have to go to work. Are you and Nancy ready to go see the crazy subway running under this even crazier city?"

*****

Abby exchanged an excited look with Nancy as they wove their way through the basement of Devlin's Clothing Store. "I wonder why Alfred Beach created the entrance in such an obscure place?"

A man walking next to them provided the answer. "The passenger subway was a secret," he informed them. "He couldn't put it where anyone would see it being built, so he talked the owner of Devlin's into being part of his plan." He smiled, and then continued. "Beach first demonstrated pneumatic transit at the 1867 American Institute Fair. It impressed enough people that he received permission two years ago to build a large package-delivery tunnel under Broadway. Only..." He chuckled. "That's not what he built."

"He kept this whole thing a secret?" Nancy asked with amazement.

"Yes. While people thought he was building a large package-delivery tunnel, he actually built a demonstration passenger-transit system, complete with a luxurious station and a passenger car."

"How could he keep something like this a secret?" Abby demanded, not able to envision it. Of course, she had no idea what she was about to experience, but surely it had to be something that would have been difficult to keep clandestine.

"It was a challenge," the man admitted. "For fifty-eight successive nights, men burrowed through the earth under Broadway and Warren Street." He pointed up. "Right where we are now. They filled bags with the dirt that was dug, and then carried them out to wagons whose wheels had been muffled for silence. When those wagons pulled away, more wagons showed up with all the tools, rails and bricks they needed—their wheels muffled as well. They had to carry in the parts for the car, the wind machine...everything."

"The wind machine?" Abby asked.

The man smiled. "You'll see." He went back to his original story. "Night after night, gangs of men slipped in and out of the tunnel like thieves."

"No one heard them from above?" Nancy queried. "How is that possible?"

"No one spoke," the man confided. "During the day, nothing could be heard over the thunder of the traffic. At night, we could hear a horse clip-clop overhead." The man grinned. "No one ever knew we were down here."

"We?" Abby asked, looking at the man more closely.

"I helped build it," the man admitted. "But I was just one of hundreds of men."

"Building this took tremendous commitment," Abby observed, watching the pride on the man's face. "You must truly believe in it."

"I do," he said instantly. "This is just the beginning. Mr. Beach is going to run a line to Central Park that will be five miles long. When it's finished, it will carry twenty thousand passengers a day at speeds up to a mile a minute." His eyes glowed with passion.

Abby and Nancy gaped at him. "A mile a minute?" Abby asked. "Nothing goes that fast."

"You wait," the man said confidently. "It's coming, and when it does, it will solve New York City's transportation woes." He tipped his hat and hurried out of sight.

Abby stared at Nancy. "Is that story true?"

"It's what Michael told me as well, so I suppose it is."

Abby considered what she'd heard. "How did the city politicians respond when they discovered the existence of the tunnel?"

Nancy smiled wryly. "They're enraged because Beach defied them. This is all very new because he only revealed the tunnel a few months ago. It's been open to the public since February. Boss Tweed is even more furious because someone ignored his almighty power. They talked about throwing Beach in jail and destroying the tunnel."

"Which they obviously didn't do."

"Not yet," Nancy acknowledged. "Beach has stood steadfast in the face of their rage. He insists on going before the legislature in Albany, but I don't think there's a court date set yet."

Abby was more intrigued than ever. "Let's go see Alfred Beach's subway," she said excitedly.

*****

Abby's mouth dropped open when she stepped into the subway station. She didn't know what she had expected, but certainly not the lavish beauty surrounding her. She walked through the long room slowly, taking in the grand piano, the paintings, the fountain and the goldfish tank.

Nancy walked with her. "Mr. Beach believes the station must be beautiful. He knows people are reluctant to accept something new, even something they desperately need. However, he'll need popular support to go against Boss Tweed and Tammany Hall. In order to achieve that, he believed it would take a subway that's both practical and elegant. He paid for everything out of his own funds."

Abby gazed around to take it all in. "It's brilliant," she said quietly. "Alfred Beach is quite an unusual man. Most inventors don't realize that genius without salesmanship isn't enough. He obviously does." She smiled widely. "When are we going for a ride?"

Nancy grinned and took her arm. "Let's get our tickets!"

Abby followed her to the ticket booth, wondering how much it would cost. "Two tickets," she said.

The smartly dressed ticket seller smiled at her warmly. "Of course, ma'am. We ask for a small donation to a home for orphans of Union soldiers and sailors from the war."

Abby was even more impressed than she already had been. She opened her purse, pulled out a generous amount of money and handed it to the man. "It's an honor to support your cause."

The man's eyes widened, but all he did was nod and hand her two tickets. "Thank you, ma'am," he said formally. "I hope you enjoy your ride."

Abby and Nancy took their place in the long line.

"How does this contraption work?" a middle-aged woman with a feathered bonnet asked the man standing behind her.

"Pneumatics," the man answered. "There is a ten-foot diameter fan at the beginning of the tunnel that's powered by a steam engine. When all the passengers are in the car, they turn the fan on, and a strong blast of air pushes it through the tunnel."

Abby listened with fascination. "Like the wind pushing a sailboat?"

"Exactly like that," the man agreed.

"But how does the car return?" Abby probed.

The man grinned. "They reverse the fans and suck it back to its starting position."

Abby laughed. She could hardly wait to tell Thomas about the experience. She was sorry he was missing it; he would have loved it.

Moments later, they stepped into the cylindrical car. There was only room for twenty-two people, but the inside was elegantly done, with two long upholstered benches and lantern lights glowing on tables.

When they climbed out of the passenger car after their short, one-block trip, Abby was glowing with delight. The conductor had told them it was the first step in a much grander scheme, but she was completely impressed. It was wonderful to travel below the surface of the city, free from the crowded, gritty and grimy roads. It was easy to imagine how different the city would be if all travel happened below ground.

"I hope Mr. Alfred Beach's dream comes true," she said, taking Nancy's arm as they merged once again into the streets thronged with congestion.

*****

Susan and Harold carefully loaded the last of the horses they had purchased onto the freight car that would carry them south to Virginia.

"Can you believe we're returning with twenty horses?" Susan asked, more than a touch of disbelief in her voice as she gazed at the gleaming coats of the Cleveland Bay mares she'd chosen. "I thought we would be doing wonderfully if we returned with ten."

Harold nodded. "Mr. Carson said he would give you a good price, but I'll admit, I'm surprised too." He paused. "Actually, I suppose I'm not."

Susan looked at him curiously. "Why not?"

Harold grinned at her. "Right before we left, when you were in the barn preparing the last of the mares for travel, Mr. Carson came to talk to me. He said he's never met anyone, other than Miles, who shares the same passion for the Cleveland Bay breed that he does. He knows he's getting old, and he doesn't know how much longer he'll do what he does. He confided that he wants to make sure the breed continues going strong."

"There are a lot of Cleveland Bay horses in Canada," Susan protested.

"But not in America," Harold informed her. "He wants the breed to expand through all of North America, and he believes you're the person who can make it happen in the US, Susan." His eyes glowed with pride.

Susan's eyes flooded with tears. "What an honor," she whispered. She stared again at the horses waiting for transport. "I won't disappoint him," she vowed. She had already agreed to write Mr. Carson on a regular basis to give him updates; now she would make sure she provided more than just facts and figures. He had entrusted his most valuable possessions to her in the hopes she would continue to build on his legacy. It was not something she would take lightly. "Let's go home."

Chapter Seventeen

Carrie shifted her satchel to her other hand and craned her neck to see over the crowd. "Where is Janie?" she asked worriedly.

"She'll be here," Abby said calmly. "She warned us she might be cutting it close to departure time."

"The train leaves in twenty minutes," Carrie muttered.

"Which means she still has time."

Carrie stared at her and then laughed. "You are always so calm. Doesn't it get terribly exhausting?"

Abby chuckled. "Not nearly as exhausting as your needless worry."

"That's what I keep telling her," Frances chimed in.

Carrie grimaced at her daughter, glad she was able to join her on this trip. "Young lady, you are hardly the paragon of patience."

Frances shrugged. "Like mother, like daughter."

Carrie felt a thrill jolt through her at the words. She had adopted Frances only a year earlier. To hear her speak those words made Carrie's heart fill with joy. She locked eyes with Abby, knowing her mother knew just how she felt. Carrie might not be Abby's biological offspring, but she was her daughter in every sense of the word.

"I'm so glad to be going back home for ten days. I've been back in Philadelphia only three weeks, but when Dr. Wild decided to close his clinic for a much-needed break, there was no way I would miss the opportunity, especially since Anthony was called back to Richmond on business."

Abby smiled. "I'm happy I was able to stop here for a few days on my way home, but I'm glad to get back to the plantation. I have a lot to do there, and I'm so glad my daughter and granddaughter are coming, too."

"I can hardly wait to see Peaches," Frances said excitedly. "I'm glad I didn't have to stay here for this trip. Now that Lillian isn't there to ride her, Peaches needs me."

Carrie understood how much Frances missed her beautiful palomino mare. "She will be so happy to have you home."

Frances craned up on her toes. "There's Janie!"

Carrie spun around, happy to see Janie rapidly weaving her way along the crowded platform.

"I made it!"

"It's about time," Carrie retorted.

Janie's blue eyes danced with amusement. "I told you I wouldn't miss the train." She shifted Robert on her hip. Her eighteen-month-old son's bright blue eyes were wide with discovery as he peered around at the train and the throngs of people. "Matthew left for Richmond last night."

Carrie opened her mouth to ask what Matthew was doing in Richmond, but Robert held his arms out to her. Helpless to resist his wide grin, she swung him into her arms and held him up so she could kiss both pudgy cheeks. "You get more adorable every day," she cooed.

"You just saw him two days ago," Frances reminded her, "when they came for dinner."

"And he's gotten even more adorable in the last two days," Carrie said, grinning when Robert chortled with delight. "See? He agrees."

Abby was watching Janie. "What is Matthew doing in Richmond? He didn't mention going down there when you were at the house for dinner."

Janie's expression grew serious. "He got a telegram from his editor yesterday morning. He asked him to go down to cover tomorrow's trial to determine who will finally be mayor. Evidently, it's going to be quite controversial, no matter what's decided."

"That's why Anthony is there, as well," Carrie said, pulling Robert around to sit on her hip.

"Thomas is coming in from the plantation for the trial," Abby informed them. "I received a telegram just before we left the house. He believes the trial is going to be very important to the future of Richmond. He doesn't want to miss it."

Carrie pushed away a sudden sense of foreboding. "At least we'll all be able to have dinner together tonight before we head out to the plantation in the morning." She cared what the results of the trial would be, but she was more eager to get home. Granite was waiting for her, and she knew how excited Frances was to be with Peaches again. "Whatever the outcome is, we don't need to be there for the news. We'll find out as soon as Father gets home."

Abby hesitated. "I believe I'll stay in Richmond and come home with Thomas."

Carrie couldn't miss the sudden flare of anxiety in Abby's eyes. "Do you know something I don't?"

"No," Abby insisted, "I just want to come home with your father. I haven't seen him for ten days."

Carrie knew that was plenty of reason for Abby to stay in town, but she couldn't push away a nagging worry. Of course, she was good at worrying for no reason, so it was probably nothing.

"Mama, I want to stay in Richmond for one day to be with Daddy."

Carrie looked at her with surprise. "He just left two days ago, honey, and he's coming out to the plantation when the trial is over."

Frances met her eyes unflinchingly. "I know."

"Then why do you want to stay in Richmond?"

Frances shrugged. "I don't know, I just want to."

"All right..." Carrie said slowly, recognizing the stubborn set to her daughter's mouth. "We'll stay one day, but then we're going home."

Frances smiled happily. "All right, Mama."

Carrie locked eyes with Janie. She wished she could ask her friend if she was feeling the same uneasiness, but she didn't want to create worry if there was no reason.

The whistle of the approaching train signaled the end to any more conversation.

*****

Freshly bathed and rested, Carrie joined the others around the dining room table. Little Robert was sleeping peacefully upstairs. She gazed around for a few moments, a smile playing on her lips.

"Why the smile?" Abby asked quietly.

"I love having some of my favorite people all together," Carrie answered. Her father, Matthew and Anthony were already at the table when she came down. Janie and Abby were seated next to their husbands as Carrie slipped into the chair next to Anthony.

"You're all right with staying in town another day?" Abby asked. "I know you're eager to get home."

Carrie watched Frances talking happily to Anthony, her conversation interspersed with giggles. "Frances is so thrilled to be here. One more day in town will be fine."

Conversation stopped when May entered the dining room carrying a massive country ham, surrounded by tiny white potatoes dug from the garden just that afternoon. Micah followed her, holding platters of carrots glazed with honey, and a heap of fresh salad.

Baskets of hot bread were already sending their heavenly aroma into the room.

"This looks wonderful," Thomas said. "Thank you."

"You're welcome, Mr. Thomas," May replied. "It's good to have this home full again. A house this big needs to have people in it."

Matthew leaned over to sniff the country ham. "You keep cooking like this, May, and we'll always come back."

"When ain't I ever cooked like this?" May demanded indignantly.

"Exactly," Matthew said with a grin. "It's why we keep coming back."

Thomas turned to Carrie when the laughter died down. "How are Lillian and Ben doing in Philadelphia?"

"They're doing well," Carrie answered. "Lillian has already found a teaching job that she enjoys."

"She's teaching at *my* school," Frances said excitedly. "I told them she was the best teacher in the world. Next to Rose, of course," she added with a smile. "Everybody loves her! And," she added, "it's amazing that she comes home every night to live with us!"

Carrie smiled. "It's true that everyone loves her," she agreed, knowing Frances' progressive Quaker school was one of the few in the city that would have accepted Lillian's breeches and short hair so open-heartedly. "She's settling into the city and seems to like it."

"Of course, she likes it," Frances said indignantly. "Philadelphia is a wonderful city."

"One that you're anxious to leave," Anthony reminded her with a smile.

"Well, yes, but that's to be expected," Frances replied impishly. "I'm a child who needs to be on the plantation with her horse."

"And not one of us will disagree with that," Thomas assured her with a laugh before he turned to Carrie again. "And Ben?"

"Jeremy gave Ben a job at the factory," Carrie reported. "He's thrilled to have work already. More importantly, he's happy to be working in a place with both black and white employees. He had a hard time believing Jeremy is half black, and Rose's twin, but once he saw Sarah Rose, he knew it had to be true. He also can't believe Marcus and Sarah Rose are twins."

May chuckled. "It's right hard to believe that little red-haired boy is the twin to that tiny brown-skinned beauty." She turned serious. "Are my children safe up there in Philadelphia?"

Anthony nodded. "They are," he assured her, but then hesitated.

"What ain't you telling me, Mr. Anthony? Don't you be hiding anything from me."

Anthony met her eyes. "They're fine," he insisted, "but I know it will get harder as the twins grow older. Right now, they don't have to be around a lot of people. The people who come to the house know about the twins' heritage and love them equally."

"But mulattoes ain't very welcome in the North either," May said bluntly. "That's what you don't want to tell me about?"

Anthony sighed. "Prejudice and ignorance are everywhere, May. They're certainly safer in the North, but that doesn't mean Sarah Rose won't have challenges growing up."

Carrie hated that his statement was true. "Jeremy and Marietta are making sure the twins have the best opportunities possible. They're around blacks and whites on a regular basis."

May looked doubtful. "How are they getting those children around black folks?"

Carrie grinned. "Jeremy is playing baseball."

Her statement was met by silence as May and Micah stared at her. "Come again?" Micah muttered.

Anthony laughed. "Jeremy has joined a baseball team in Philadelphia. He's loved the game for a long time and has wanted to play. He's having a great time."

"What kind of baseball team is Jeremy playing for?" May asked once she had found her voice again.

"A black team," Anthony answered.

May eyed him thoughtfully. "Why ain't Mr. Jeremy playing for a white team? He looks as white as all you do."

"That's true," Matthew answered, "but if he chooses to pass as white, he would never be able to bring the twins to any of the games. One look at Sarah Rose, and everyone would know the truth. He would most likely be kicked off the team immediately."

"That's not the main reason, though," Janie added. "Both he and Marietta want the twins to have black friends, and to be part of the black community. What they do in the future with their heritage will be their choice, but while they're young, he wants them to know they have nothing to be ashamed of."

Micah nodded. "That's the right thing to do," he agreed. "I still think it's crazy that those two could have a child that looks black. Blond-haired Jeremy and red-headed Marietta... Who would have thought?"

"Jeremy always knew it was a possibility," Carrie replied. "There are a lot of studies being done about inherited traits within families. Jeremy came out looking like his great-grandfather, but Rose carries more of Sarah's dark genes. He was afraid Marietta wouldn't want to marry him once she knew there was a possibility they would have a child that looks black, but we all know how that turned out."

"They're a fine couple," May said fondly. "I just wish them and the twins didn't have to leave Richmond and Virginia. I sure do miss my children."

Carrie knew how much May loved the twins. Even though she understood, it had broken her heart when Jeremy and Marietta took them to Philadelphia.

"And I wish Sarah had been alive long enough to meet her son and see the birth of her wonderful grandchildren," Carrie murmured. It was something she thought about every time she was with Jeremy, Marietta and the twins. "I know the joy she would have felt."

Thomas changed the topic. "Tell me more about the baseball team."

Carrie understood his need to talk about something else. Despite all her father had done to redeem his earlier actions as a slaveholder, he would always regret selling Jeremy when he was a few days old so that no one would discover Thomas' father had raped Sarah.

The two half-brothers were extremely close, but nothing could undo the past.

Anthony, oblivious to the reason for the change of topic, grinned. "Jeremy is quite good," he told them. "He plays for the Pythians."

"We've gone to see some of the games," Frances cried. "Jeremy plays first base. He even hit a home run in the last game!"

"Ben is learning how to play as well, but it will be some time before he's good enough to play for the team. In the meantime, he's happy to have been connected with Octavius Catto," Anthony continued.

"Octavius Catto?" Thomas asked.

"Octavius is an extraordinary man," Matthew answered. "We've spent quite a bit of time together. He formed the team because white teams didn't want black players, but he's long been an advocate for abolition and equal rights. He helped organize black volunteer troops from Philadelphia to fight for the Union, and he was at the forefront of desegregating the trolley systems."

"He's tried to get black baseball teams to be recognized by Pennsylvania's association of amateur baseball clubs, but they refuse to consider admission to any team that has even one black member," Anthony said disdainfully.

Thomas scowled his disapproval. "What else does this young man do?"

"Octavius is the president of the Institute for Colored Youth," Anthony answered. "He also founded the Banneker Literary Institute back in fifty-four to improve literary life for Philadelphia's black population."

"Impressive," Thomas murmured.

"That's not all he's done," Matthew added. "In sixty-four, he and some other black leaders established the National Equal Rights League. Their whole focus is on removing racial barriers."

"He and Jeremy have become close friends," Carrie told her father. "Jeremy works with him on many equality issues. Ben has also joined the effort now."

"Octavius must be quite excited for blacks to finally have the vote," Abby remarked.

Anthony hesitated. "He is..." he said, "but he also knows they have a long way to go."

"Because of the property requirement," Abby said angrily. When Anthony looked surprised, she added, "It's an issue in New York, as well. I talked about it in-depth with the Stratfords. Blacks have the right to vote, but they're being blocked because of the two hundred and fifty dollar property requirement."

"That's *one* of the requirements," Matthew replied. "The United States passed the Fifteenth Amendment so blacks could vote, but the Supreme Court also left the responsibility of protecting most of the basic rights of their citizens to the individual state governments. The result is that many of them are passing laws that make it almost impossible for black men to exercise their new right."

"What other requirements?" Abby demanded.

Matthew shook his head. "Some states are passing poll taxes. Since most former slaves are poor, they can't pay the tax, which means they can't vote. Other states are working on literacy tests to prove someone can read or write before they vote."

Micah shook his head. "White folks sure don't want us to have a say."

"Not all of us," Thomas replied, "but far too many."

Carrie decided to change the subject. "What do you think will happen with the trial tomorrow, Father?" If they were going to stay in town for it, she wanted to know the most recent news.

Thomas tightened his lips. "The whole situation is a mess," he said. "For almost six weeks, Richmond has had two governments. Neither man will back down. General Canby supports Mayor Chahoon. Walker, our newly elected governor, backs Ellyson." He shook his head with disbelief. "Both parties sought the support of the courts. The case eventually ended up in the hands of Chief Justice Salmon Chase in Washington, but ultimately it was decided by both parties that the case should be heard by the Virginia Supreme Court of Appeals."

"At least they agreed on something," Matthew said sarcastically. "When did the case start?"

"Fourteen days ago, on April twelfth. There have been endless testimonies and opinions, but it's over. The court will hand down the decision tomorrow, and the city will finally learn who is to be crowned mayor of Richmond."

"Do you feel good about either man?" Matthew probed, every bit the journalist in search of the truth.

Thomas shrugged. "In my opinion, neither of them has dealt with this admirably, but I don't know that it was possible to do so. They were both put into an untenable position. The violence and bloodshed have been inexcusable, but I understand the frustration on both sides."

Matthew nodded. "I hear Governor Wise was at one of the hearings."

"He was," Thomas agreed. "He served as Virginia's governor from 1855 to 1859 before serving on the Secession Convention in sixty-one. He was a general during the war, but I don't believe his heart was ever truly in it once he realized the cost to the South. When the war ended, he resumed his law practice here in Richmond and has worked hard to rebuild our state."

"He argued for Ellyson?" Matthew asked.

Thomas shook his head. "Chahoon."

Matthew's face revealed his surprise. "He argued for Mayor Chahoon?"

Thomas smiled wryly. "When the war ended, Governor Wise was tired of conflict. He tried to reclaim his plantation, Rolleston, outside of Norfolk, but he was told that he'd abandoned that residence when he moved his family to another plantation at Rocky Mount for safety during the war. Rolleston, along with other plantations, had already been appropriated by the government for the Freedmen's Bureau to establish schools for the freed slaves. He learned that two hundred freed men were taking classes at his plantation. He gave up the effort to get it back."

"He wasn't bitter?" Matthew asked with astonishment.

"No. He became a Republican and a strong supporter of President Grant. Governor Wise is quite an extraordinary man. He never emphasizes his Confederate service, and he's never sought a pardon.

He just wants to help rebuild the city and state that he loves."

"What was his argument for Chahoon staying in office?"

"He believes that even though Virginia has approved a new constitution, it hasn't been officially approved and confirmed. Until that happens, Virginia is technically under the rule of Congress. Mayor Chahoon was made mayor of the city under federal guidelines, and he doesn't believe Governor Walker has the ability to overturn that."

"What do you think, Father?" Carrie asked.

Thomas shrugged. "It hardly matters what I think because the final decision will be made tomorrow, but for what it's worth, I believe Mayor Chahoon should stay in office. It's just a matter of time, though, before the Democrats regain control of the state."

Anthony frowned. "Do you honestly believe that?"

"Unfortunately, yes," Thomas replied. "I try every day to feel differently about it, but there's too much evidence to the contrary. It's taken Virginia far too long to go through the process of constitutional revision in order to be readmitted to the Union. The economy is stagnant and very little new investment is coming from the North or from England."

"But they've just been readmitted to the Union," Matthew argued.

"Yes," Thomas agreed, "but at what cost? The same men who ran Virginia before the war—the men who led us into war—are now going to run the state again. The people of Virginia are still worshipping the same heroes who created the mess we're in, and Southern goals are still the same. I can't see that anything has really changed," he said heavily. "Too many people want life to go back to normal, without federal interference, but they don't truly understand what that means."

Carrie stared at him, stunned by the resigned certainty in his voice. "So the war was for nothing?"

Thomas shook his head. "I didn't say that. Tremendous change came from the war. Much of it was good change, but the feelings it left behind will haunt us for generations, I'm afraid. We may have lost the war, but the men who controlled Virginia before the war are about to take control again. I don't know what it all means, but I certainly don't feel good about it." He sighed. "In the meantime, we have to see what happens tomorrow."

"You believe they'll keep Ellyson in office," Matthew said bluntly.

"I do," Thomas replied. "The Democrats are determined to take back control of Virginia, and I believe the courts will support them."

"Because it's right, or because it's what they want?" Anthony asked.

Thomas' voice was suddenly tired. "Does it matter? At the end of the day, all we can do is deal with the results.

*****

Carrie was staring out the window when Anthony entered the room.

"Can't sleep?" Anthony asked.

Carrie had excused herself after dinner, gone for a walk with Frances around the neighborhood to attempt to clear her mind, and had then retired to their bedroom. "No," she said quietly.

Anthony came up behind her and wrapped his arms around her. "Do you want to tell me what's bothering you?"

"I would," Carrie said, "if I knew what it was. I just have a feeling..."

Anthony waited a few moments. "A feeling?" he prompted.

Carrie shook her head. "I don't know what it is," she admitted. Again, her voice trailed off as she struggled to put words to what was rampaging in her mind.

Anthony turned Carrie to him so he could look into her eyes. "What is it, Carrie?"

Carrie sighed. "I really don't know, dear. What I do know is that every time I've had this feeling in the past...something bad has happened." She shook her head again. "I don't know what else to tell you. I've tried to tell myself my feelings are ridiculous, but I can't shake them."

"I see," Anthony murmured. He opened his mouth to respond and then closed it. With a tender look on his face, he wrapped her tightly in his arms and held her close.

Carrie melted into him, the strength of his arms giving her comfort. She was relieved Anthony didn't attempt to talk her out of her feelings. She just wished they would go away on their own.

Chapter Eighteen

Carrie had lost none of her uneasiness over breakfast the next morning. She smiled and chatted as May brought out thick stacks of pancakes, sausages, and containers of warm Canadian maple syrup that Susan had left behind on her way back to the plantation with the Cleveland Bay mares. She could hardly wait to see the new horses Susan had bought, but she would have to be patient for one more day.

"Don't you like that syrup?" May demanded, a worried look on her face.

Carrie looked down and realized she'd only had a few bites of her breakfast. "It's wonderful," she said quickly. "I suppose I'm just not hungry." She fought to keep her voice light. The frustrating thing about feelings was that you often couldn't identify a source. "Dinner last night was so delicious that I'm afraid I ate far more than I needed."

May gave her a piercing look that said she didn't believe her, but finally turned away.

"Are you feeling all right?" Anthony asked. "Would you rather I stay home this morning?"

Carrie wanted to tell him yes. She wanted to insist that everyone around the table stay in the house that day, but she knew it wouldn't make sense to them. Truth be told, it didn't make sense to her. Besides, if trouble was truly coming, hiding in the house wouldn't protect them. She wished Rose was with them; she knew her best friend would also be sensing whatever was causing her to feel so anxious.

"Carrie?"

Carrie belatedly realized she hadn't answered Anthony's question. "No, you should go," she said hastily. "That's why you're in town."

Anthony hesitated. "You're sure you're all right?"

Carrie forced a bright smile to her face. "I'm fine. I'm going to spend time with Abby, Janie and Frances while y'all are at the court. We'll be waiting to hear the result."

Anthony nodded, but his searching eyes didn't leave her face.

"Quit looking at me like that," Carrie commanded. "Go!"

*****

When the women had seen the men off in the carriage, waving to them from the shaded porch, Abby turned to Carrie. "What's wrong?"

Frances frowned. "Is something wrong, Mama?"

Carrie searched for the right words to express her feelings, but she came up empty. She shrugged helplessly. "I don't know," she admitted. She thought about the conversation on the station platform before they'd left Philadelphia. "You didn't want to leave for the plantation this morning, Abby. Why?"

Abby took a deep breath but didn't look away from her probing eyes. "I don't know," she admitted. "It was just a feeling... one that said I should stay."

Carrie considered her response. "You think something bad is going to happen?" When Abby hesitated, Carrie had her answer. Abby did, indeed, think trouble was coming. "What is it?"

"I don't know, Carrie. There was something in me that said I needed to stay in the city. That's all I can tell you." Abby looked as confused as she felt.

"That's what I was feeling, too," Frances announced. "We need to be in Richmond."

Carrie stared at her sensitive daughter and then looked at Janie expectantly.

"I'm sorry to be the only one who doesn't seem to be feeling anything," Janie replied, "but I don't. Other than a desire to go shopping on Broad Street."

Carrie managed a chuckle. She knew that no matter what she was feeling, only time would reveal if trouble was on the way.

"Richmond is a powder keg right now," Abby said quietly. "We all know this trial could end in violence, no matter what the verdict is."

Carrie knew she was right. "Broad Street is probably not the safest place to be if trouble is going to break out, Janie. I'm not sure I want to take Frances down there."

"Mama!" Frances cried. "You promised we could go shopping when we came to Richmond."

Carrie gazed at her daughter. "You're right," she admitted, "but I don't want to put you in any danger. We can shop at the end of the trip, before we return to Philadelphia."

"I thought you told me that we shouldn't borrow trouble until it comes," Frances said persuasively.

Carrie managed a smile. "I didn't know you listened to me."

"I do when I need it for ammunition," Frances replied with a grin.

All the women laughed, but Carrie quickly sobered. She was proud of her independent, strong-willed daughter, but wanted to keep her safe.

"What would you have done when you were my age?" Frances asked.

Carrie knew she had lost the battle. "Gone shopping," she admitted with a small laugh. "Father would have tried to talk me out of it, and I would have convinced him."

"Like mother, like daughter," Frances teased.

Carrie shook her head, giving up the futile fight. "Go get ready," she commanded. "We'll leave in a few minutes."

Spencer appeared on the porch. "You ladies need a ride somewhere this morning?"

Carrie smiled up at her old friend. "We'd like to go to Broad Street, please. I've promised Frances a shopping trip."

"I'll be happy to take you. I figure y'all will want to avoid the chaos around the Capitol, but is it all right if I wait there for the results after I drop you off?

"Of course," Carrie said quickly, determined to push her uneasiness aside. She could ruin the morning, or she could listen to the words Frances had echoed back to her. She wouldn't borrow trouble before it came.

Ten minutes later, all the women were in the carriage, hats pulled down over their heads to protect them from an unusually warm sun. May had insisted she was happy to take care of little Robert, so Janie was a free woman.

"Wait a minute!" May called from the porch. She dashed inside and then came back out a few minutes later, something dangling from both hands.

Carrie stared at her with surprise as she approached the wagon. "Our medical bags? Why do we need them to go shopping?"

May shrugged. "I have no idea, Miss Carrie. I just reckon you ought to take 'em."

Janie reached for her bag calmly. "Thank you, May. It's always best to be prepared."

Carrie took her bag, but once again, her thoughts were spinning.

What was going to happen?

*****

Anthony and Matthew joined the throng of men moving to the top floor of the Capitol. Thomas, as a former member of the Virginia government, was seated on the bottom floor, several rows away from the judge's bench.

"This place is a madhouse," Anthony muttered.

Matthew nodded his head in agreement. "The city of Richmond has been waiting for a resolution to this case for weeks. Major court cases are always seen as a form of entertainment, but this case has created even more drama than normal. It certainly meets all the media's criteria for scandal and controversy in high political office," he said ruefully.

Anthony gazed around. "I wonder how many people this place will hold?"

"I suppose it depends on how closely packed the spectators are willing to be."

Matthew wove his way to two seats. He sat down quickly and motioned for Anthony to join him. As they sat and watched, more and more men streamed through the doors. The lower level had filled quickly. Now, the upper level was becoming just as full, with men standing against the wall when there were no more seats to be found.

Despite the seriousness of the occasion, the conversation was easygoing. After weeks of tension and hard feelings, resulting in countless numbers of fights around the city, the decision was going to be made. It seemed to have already been accepted that some would go away happy that day, while others would gnash their teeth over the decision. Regardless, Richmond would have a mayor. Everyone could return to rebuilding their city.

Matthew gazed around. "I had no idea the Capitol courtroom could hold this many people."

A man sitting behind them overheard his comment and leaned forward to answer. "It didn't used to. My father was one of the men who helped remodel the building back in the twenties."

"What did they do?" Matthew asked.

"They added the floor where we're sitting right now," the man responded proudly. "The original Capitol building was finished in 1792, but by the twenties, it was obvious it was too small. When they were trying to decide what they should do, they realized the forty-foot ceiling above them gave them enough room to add another floor, as well as the balcony we're sitting in. The courtroom is up here, but it also holds a conference room and offices. Essentially, they added two floors."

"That was smart," Matthew replied.

Anthony was watching the man closely as he talked. "You seem uneasy about something, or am I just imagining it?"

The man shrugged, looked away, and then looked back. "I'm an architect," he explained. "I've been telling people for several years that work needs to be done on this floor."

"What kind of work?" Matthew asked.

"When the third floor was added, they chose not to embed the ends of the floor beams into the walls. They decided to use an already existing offset in the wall that created a four-inch or so ledge. The ends of the beams are rested in small notches that were cut into the offset to hold them." He took a deep breath. "When it was first built, they added support pillars on the floor of the House chamber, adding one midway along the length of each floor beam."

"When it was *first* built?" Matthew asked sharply.

"Yes. Some of the members of the House of Delegates complained because they thought they were unsightly."

"Unsightly?" Anthony asked incredulously. "So they took them *out*?"

"They did. Architects warned them it would be dangerous then, but the delegates ignored them, insisting the floors were supported by the walls of the Capitol. They demanded that their chamber look like a dignified seat of government, not some industrial building with ugly pillars running down the middle of it," he said ruefully. "They got their way."

Matthew stared at him and then looked down at the floor beneath his feet. "What's holding the beams in place?"

The man met his eyes. "Gravity." His lips tightened. "There have been reports of the floor sagging for more than thirty-five years."

Anthony felt a twinge of alarm, but quickly pushed it down. "You obviously believe it's safe or you wouldn't be sitting up here."

"It's held for almost forty years," the man answered, "although I believe it needs reinforcing for the long-term. But yes, I believe we're safe." Another man asked a question that took his attention. "Excuse me," he murmured as he turned away.

Anthony leaned close enough for Matthew to hear him. "Did you mind being sent down here to cover the trial?"

Matthew shrugged. "I don't really care for reporting anymore, but even I believe this is important. I'm covering the story, but I'll admit I'm as curious as anyone else to know what's going to happen. Besides, I'm happy to spend a few days on the plantation as my reward. It's been too long since I've been there."

"You were there at Christmas," Anthony said with amusement.

"Four months is a long time," Matthew countered. "I suppose Cromwell Plantation will always feel like home."

"I understand the feeling," Anthony replied. He looked down at the crowded floor and then glanced at his watch. "It's almost eleven o'clock. The judges should be coming out any minute. There must be close to four hundred men jammed in here. I wonder if they'll have to pontificate for a long time, or if they'll just render their decision and put everyone out of their misery."

"Only some of the men here will be put out of their misery," Matthew observed dryly.

Anthony knew that was true. Suddenly he leaned forward. "The door to the chambers is opening," he reported.

The crowded courtroom suddenly went quiet as two of the judges approached the bench. The court reporters quickly took their positions. Moments later, the back door opened again for the other judges to enter.

CRACK!

Anthony looked around, wondering what activity in the courtroom had caused the loud noise. Suddenly, he felt movement beneath his feet.

CRACK!

Anthony thought of Carrie as the floor collapsed beneath him. He was vaguely aware of clouds of dust, piercing screams, and the tangle of falling, flailing bodies.

Then...nothing.

*****

Carrie, leading the way with her arms full of packages, walked rapidly toward the Capitol building. All of them had decided they wanted to be waiting outside when the men exited with news of the verdict. The shopping had been fun, but every conversation that buzzed around them was focused on the outcome of the trial. She had pushed aside any worry about rioting after the verdict. It felt important to be there.

Up ahead, she saw Spencer leaning against their carriage, just a hundred feet from the Capitol. "Spencer!" she called, hoping to be heard over the throngs of people that had obviously had the same idea.

He looked up and smiled broadly, motioning them to join him. "You can sit in the carriage," he shouted. "It's crazy around here!"

Carrie beckoned to the others and began to cross Grace Street, taking a moment to admire the stately building surrounded by flowering dogwoods that would soon drop their glowing white blooms. Even with the grounds completely full of people, the Capitol maintained its elegance.

CRACK!

Carrie froze in her tracks, gazing around to identify the source of the noise.

"Mama, what was that?" Frances cried.

Before Carrie could attempt an answer, another sharp, splintering crash ripped through the air, drowning out the noise of all the people. A series of sharp noises that sounded like gunfire followed.

Moments later, the towering windows of the House Chamber blew out in a sparkling shower of broken glass, the jagged shards catching the rays of the sun before they rained down on the unsuspecting people below. Carrie barely registered the screams before thick, billowing clouds burst from the windows as an explosive sound ripped from the building.

Carrie stared at the Capitol, her shock making it impossible to figure out what was going on. She was vaguely aware of Frances gripping her hand and screaming, but she was incapable of movement. Only one thought exploded in her mind as loudly as the explosive sounds coming from the building. *So I'm going to lose Anthony, too.*

As she stood, trapped in disbelief, a massive gray cloud rolled through the windows, completely obscuring the Capitol dome. "No," she whispered. "No…"

While the smoke was still pouring from the building, clanging bells announced the approach of the fire departments.

"Daddy!" Frances screamed. "Grandpa! Matthew!"

"Thomas!" Abby cried. "Anthony! Matthew!"

"No!" Janie shouted. "No! No! No!"

Cries and shouts of confusion rolled over them as the cloud enveloped them, making it almost impossible to see.

"Miss Carrie!"

Carrie stared into the billowing smoke, still unable to register what she was seeing. Her heart and mind had shut down ahead of the grief that she knew would soon follow.

"Miss Carrie!"

Carrie slowly became aware of Spencer shaking her by the shoulders. She focused enough to see his wide eyes staring at her, and then looked over his shoulder to watch the destruction of her life.

"Miss Carrie!"

"What?" she finally mumbled, the utterance of the word clearing a portion of the fog from her mind. "What happened?"

"The floor has fallen!" The shout came from a man standing on the columned porch. "The courtroom floor has collapsed!"

Carrie tried to make sense of what she was hearing. Her mind struggled to recreate the handful of times she'd been inside the Capitol to visit her father. She could envision the House Chamber, with its third-floor balcony that looked over the courtroom.

"The floor has collapsed!" Another man burst from the building, his face and body barely recognizable through the grime covering him. "We need help in here!"

In the moment of shocked silence that followed his horrifying announcement, the sound of screams and cries erupted through the windows, floating out over the crowd that was still trying to make sense of what was happening.

Moments later, the first firetruck clanged up to the building.

Carrie turned slowly, wondering what they could do. Surely everyone inside had died. Anthony was dead. Her father was dead. Matthew was dead.

"People in here need help!"

Fighting to conquer the fear paralyzing her, Carrie struggled to focus on the words. Slowly, they filtered through. *People in here need help.* She caught her breath. If people needed help, not everyone was dead.

Not everyone was dead.

That thought exploded through her as forcefully as the glass had blasted from the windows.

Not everyone was dead.

There was hope. The men they loved might have survived the terrible tragedy unfolding around them.

Carrie spun around. Abby and Janie were both staring at the building, shaking their heads as tears poured down their faces. Suddenly, she became aware that Frances was clinging to her leg, sobbing uncontrollably.

"Daddy! Daddy!"

Carrie knelt down to take her daughter's face in her hands. "Frances," she said firmly. "Your Daddy might still be alive. I have to go help." Frances continued to sob, her breath coming in frantic gasps. Carrie looked up to find Spencer. He was standing right in front of her, his huge hand gripping her medical bag.

"I'll take care of Frances," he promised. "I won't leave her. If we're not here when this is all over, it's because I took her home."

Carrie nodded, hoping she would remember what she was hearing. She grabbed Janie's hand. "Matthew might not be dead," she yelled, the noise increasing as the horses pulling the firetrucks came pounding up. "We have to help!"

Spencer pressed the handle of her medical bag into her hand. Carrie gripped it tightly, knowing she might be holding the difference between life and death for the men they loved.

Finally, she turned to Abby. The act of holding her medical bag had calmed her. She had lived through the war. She knew how to handle disasters and massive casualties. Her stepmother, protected by her life in

Philadelphia, had never experienced anything like what she was witnessing.

Abby stared at her wildly as her head shook in denial, her gray eyes glazed with shock. Her mouth opened and closed, but nothing came forth.

Carrie stepped forward and wrapped her arms around her mother. "We don't know anything yet," she soothed. "We don't *know*. They could all be alive."

Abby continued to stare, more tears pouring forth as she looked at the building. "They can't possibly be alive," she groaned.

Carrie watched over Abby's shoulder as another man burst from the Capitol. "We need help in here! Men are trapped. Men are alive!"

"Men are *alive*," Carrie repeated, pulling Abby close. "You have to hold onto hope, Abby. Father needs you to hope."

Her words had the desired effect. The panic subsided from Abby's eyes as she took a shuddering breath. "*Hope...*" Slowly, she nodded. "I will hope."

Carrie squeezed her hands and then led her to the carriage. "Sit down for a few minutes," she urged. "Janie and I are going to see what we can do." She turned to find her friend again.

Janie, a determined expression on her face, was waiting, her medical bag firmly in hand. "We have work to do," she yelled.

The expression that passed between the two of them told Carrie they were both remembering all the horrific battles from the war that had delivered wagon after wagon of wounded soldiers desperately in need of care.

Carrie grabbed her bag, took Janie's arm, and began to thread her way through the crowd to the front of the Capitol. Her mind steadied, even as her heart and soul cried out for the men she loved.

*****

Matthew came to slowly, wondering why there were so many screams and cries threating to swallow him. He blinked his eyes but saw nothing except darkness. Gradually, he became aware of a crushing weight on his chest, followed quickly by a searing pain in both legs. He couldn't stop the groan that ripped from his mouth as consciousness stole the oblivion that had protected him.

As he struggled to make sense of what was happening, memories began to filter in. *They were in the Capitol courthouse... They were there to hear the results of a trial.* He couldn't remember what trial at the moment, but he was fairly certain about where he was. He struggled to remember more, the pain in his legs growing sharper. He fought the blackness that threatened to engulf him.

The judges had entered the Chamber... He had leaned forward with Anthony to watch... A cracking noise... The floor had collapsed.

Matthew groaned again as he tried to stretch out his arm. *Anthony.* What had happened to Anthony when the floor collapsed? The cries of agony surrounding him revealed men had survived. He was still alive. *Was Anthony?*

Something else niggled at his mind. He strained to figure out what it was, his breath coming in gasps as the pain exploded through his body. *Thomas...* Matthew's eyes opened wide as he put the final piece into place. The groan that ripped from him this time was because he knew Thomas had been directly below the floor when it had collapsed. He couldn't possibly have lived through it. "No..." he groaned. "No..."

His final thought before the blackness swallowed him again was of his wife and son. *He had to live. He had to love Janie. He had to raise Robert.*

*****

Thomas stared in disbelief at the chaotic scene surrounding him. Beseeched by a Richmond attorney to give up his seat, Thomas had reluctantly moved over to stand against the wall just moments before the judges had exited their chambers and taken the bench. He had watched with horror as the floor collapsed, tossing bodies amid the debris as it came crashing down.

He had heard the explosion of glass and watched the smoke swallow everything. He struggled to clear his thinking. He couldn't see any flames, so the clouds billowing around him couldn't be smoke.

Dust!

It had to be dust from the collapsing floor. He coughed as the dust coated his throat and clogged his nostrils. He reached blindly into his coat pocket, pulled out the handkerchief that Abby had placed there so carefully, and wiped frantically to clear his air passages. Once he could breathe again, he held the cloth over his nose to keep it clear.

Cries and moans of pain exploded around him. Thomas knew he was unharmed, but carefully moved his arms and legs to be certain. When his movement caused no pain, he took a deep breath, lowered the handkerchief and plunged into the chaos, searching for survivors.

"Matthew!" Thomas yelled. "Anthony!"

Neither man answered, but he heard another voice just a few feet away. "Help! Help me! I'm under here!"

Thomas saw other men, uninjured from the collapse, moving around the room like sooty ghosts, pulling men from the rubble. He leaned down and began to pull frantically at the wooden wreckage at his feet. He had to save whomever he could.

*****

Carrie was standing at the foot of the stairs when the first man was carried out. A quick glance told her it wasn't anyone she hoped to see, although she would be grateful for every survivor that came from the building.

"We need help!" The two carrying the wounded man yelled and looked around.

Carrie stepped forward. "Bring him to me. I'm a doctor."

The men looked skeptical, but their desperation overcame their skepticism. "Thank you, ma'am," one of them gasped.

"I'll take care of him," Carrie assured them. "Go back and keep helping." She was certain the two frightened men didn't want to go back into the building, but she needed everyone looking for Anthony, her father and Matthew. As she bent to check the injured man's condition, another survivor was carried out, just as more men from the grounds ran into the building to help.

Janie hurried forward. "I'll take care of him. I'm a doctor."

Within minutes, they were treating ten men. Five minutes later, more doctors arrived on the scene, called forth by the clanging bells and the explosive sound that had jolted the entire city.

Carrie, calling on her years of battle experience, blocked everything out of her mind and leaned down to examine the first survivor who had been carried out. His eyes were glazed with pain and his breathing was shallow. Gentle probing revealed a badly broken leg and a shattered lower left arm. She had no supplies to set his broken limbs; the best she could do was alleviate some of his pain before he could be transported to the hospital. She knew the ambulances would have a hard time getting through the crush of people and firetrucks, but she hoped they would arrive quickly. She reached into her medical bag, pulled out a bottle of arnica, and placed it under the man's tongue. It wouldn't stop his pain, but it would help. She had quit giving morphine to patients after seeing the horrible effects of addiction. "Help is coming soon," she said soothingly. "You have some broken limbs that will have to be treated at the hospital. Lie there quietly until someone comes for you."

The man's eyes bored into her. "What...happened?" he gasped.

"The floor fell in the courtroom," Carrie explained, certain his confusion was as bad as his pain at that moment. "You're lucky to be alive." A sudden thought kept her from moving on to the next man. "Were you in the balcony?"

"Yes," the man said weakly. "I didn't know what was happening. The whole world just seemed to fall away from under us."

Carrie knew it wasn't likely, but she had to ask. "Do you know anything about Anthony Wallington?"

The man shook his head silently, sympathy radiating through the raw pain.

Carrie forced a smile. "You're going to be fine," she told him. "Someone will be here soon."

"Water?" he asked weakly.

Carrie looked around. Of course, these men needed water after all the dust they had inhaled. She was relieved when she saw Abby at the head of a small army of women walking rapidly across the Capitol grounds, all of them armed with water pitchers and glasses that must have been provided by area restaurants. "It's coming," she assured him. She motioned to Abby to give her patient water and moved on to the next man. She would come back to try and set his limbs once everyone had received emergency care if the ambulances had not arrived. Casting would have to happen at the hospital, but she could start the procedure and give him a modicum of relief.

One look at her next patient told her the slender man with a narrow face wouldn't make it. His head had been almost cleaved by what must have been a falling beam, or perhaps a desk. His face was ashen, and his breathing was so shallow she had to lean close to detect anything at all. When she heard the death rattle gurgling from his mouth, she knelt down to take his hand so he wouldn't be alone when he died. When his final sigh confirmed he was gone, she gently closed his eyelids, pulled his handkerchief from his pocket, laid it gently over his face to signal his death, and then moved on to the next patient.

Ten wounded men had already grown to thirty-five bodies laid out on the ground beneath the towering Capitol. Carrie knew the number would go much higher. As she walked down the growing line to find the next patient who needed help, she watched a fire company lay ladders against the outside wall of the building. She was grateful Richmond now had a salaried fire department and a telegraphic alarm system.

A weak cry pulled her attention back. "Hello," Carrie said gently as she knelt down next to a portly man with a nasty gash on his head. Additional blood on his clothes indicated he had received more injuries. She reached into her bag for a thick cloth and pressed it tightly to his head to stop the bleeding enough so that she could stitch it closed. "I'm Dr. Wallington. Let's see what we can do to help you."

*****

When Thomas was finally able to pull away enough wreckage to uncover the trapped man, he was astonished to discover it was a business colleague. "Ethan Buckley," he exclaimed, trying to keep the dismay from his voice. The man's body was covered with wet blood that poured from a gaping gash on his head, and his left leg was twisted oddly. Clearly, he'd been beneath the floor when it fell.

"I know I look bad," Ethan whispered, his jaw clenched from the pain wracking his body. "Can you get me out of here?"

As Thomas turned to yell for help to lift his friend, two men appeared from the dust cloud. "We've got him," they said. From the looks of their relatively clean clothing, Thomas knew they must have come to help from outside. "Thank you," he said, and then turned away to continue his search.

"Hey, mister," one of the men said, grabbing his arm to stop him. "Were you in here when the building collapsed?"

Thomas nodded, not wanting to waste energy on words.

"You should let us take you out. Help is here."

Thomas merely shook his head and turned away. By a complete fluke, he was not trapped under the rubble, and he had also not tumbled from the top floor. He wouldn't leave until he'd helped everyone he could. A sudden thought made him turn back. "My wife and daughter are outside," he said urgently. Wherever they had been when the disaster happened, he was confident they were outside now. "My daughter is Dr. Carrie Wallington. I'm sure she's treating men as you take them out. Will you find her and tell her that her father is uninjured?"

"We'll do our best," the youngest man replied. "Is there anything else you want us to tell her?"

Thomas yearned to tell her Anthony and Matthew were all right as well, but he wouldn't lie. "No," he said unsteadily. "That will be all." He turned away again and began to look for someone else he could help.

"Help!"

Thomas looked around but couldn't identify the location of the clear cry.

"Help!"

Thomas looked up, his eyes widening with amazement when he identified six men through the haze of dust, all of them clinging desperately to window frames that were thirty feet above the wreckage. There was no possible way to reach them. "Hang on!" he hollered. "Hang on!" His mind spun through possibilities, but he couldn't conceive of a way to save the men before their grip failed, and they all plummeted to the floor.

As he watched, his heart in his throat, he saw men's faces appear where windows had once been. *Firemen!*

"We've got you," one of the firemen called. "Don't let go."

Thomas held his breath as one man was pulled to safety. Another ladder. More faces. Another survivor lifted out. He silently prayed all of them would be able to hold on until they could be rescued.

"Help!" Thomas tore his gaze away from the drama unfolding above him as a weak cry arose from the rubble a few feet away.

There were people who needed his help.

Chapter Nineteen

"Are you Dr. Wallington?"

Carrie looked up from tending to a man who had escaped relatively unscathed. "I am. What can I do for you?"

The young man smiled at her, his teeth startlingly white against his grimy skin and clothes. "I have a message from your father."

Carrie gasped. "My father? He's alive?"

"He's most definitely alive," the man assured her. "He's inside helping to rescue victims. He refused to leave but asked if we would get a message to you." He looked away, taking in the growing number of bodies being laid out on the lawn. "Thank you for what you're doing."

Carrie smiled warmly, her heart exploding with happiness that her father had lived through the collapse. Then she sobered. "Do you know anything about Anthony Wallington? Or Matthew Justin?"

"I'm sorry, but no," the young man said. "But there are still a lot of men to rescue."

When he looked away uncomfortably, Carrie finished what he wasn't saying. "And a lot of bodies to bring outside," she whispered.

The man met her eyes, nodded, and then turned to re-enter the Capitol.

Carrie looked around until she located Abby, pouring water for a survivor. Her next patient would have to wait. "Abby!" she called loudly. "Abby!"

Abby looked up, her eyes growing wide when she saw the smile on Carrie's face. She stood quickly and began to walk toward her.

Carrie met her halfway and grabbed her hands. "Father is alive!"

Abby held a hand to her mouth. "Thomas is alive?"

Carrie nodded. "He sent a rescuer out to find me. He knew we would come here once we knew what had happened."

"He's all right?" Abby whispered. "Really?"

"He's enough all right that he's inside helping to rescue victims," Carrie assured her.

Abby's eyes filled with tears of relief. "Thank God." Then she peered into Carrie's face. "Anthony? Matthew?"

"We don't know anything yet," Carrie admitted, her heart squeezing with the knowledge. She knew all the wounded men would be brought out first; bodies would be brought out later. There were already at least one hundred men laid out on the lawn, being tended to by citizens eager to help. No one was alone. "I'm holding onto hope," she said, knowing her voice reflected far more confidence than she felt.

"Of course," Abby murmured, her eyes radiating sympathy and love.

Carrie turned away, knowing she couldn't afford to be distracted by her own pain. "I have victims to care for," she said quietly. "Will you let Janie know Father is safe?"

"I will," Abby replied, and then hesitated. "Carrie, how do you do it?"

Carrie raised a brow, impatient to keep working. "How do I do what?"

"Push aside your own worry to tend to all these wounded men."

"The same way you did," Carrie said gently. "Unfortunately, I had a lot of experience during the war. You learn to shut down your feelings so that you can do what's needed."

Abby reached out to take her hand. "I'm sorry you learned that so well, my dear."

Carrie shrugged. Now wasn't the time to consider pain and fear. If she let the feelings past her shield, she knew she would crumple beneath the unbearable agony. "I have to go."

"Of course," Abby said quickly. "I'll go find Janie."

*****

Matthew regained consciousness slowly, regretting the awareness of pain slicing through him. He vaguely registered that breathing was becoming more difficult. Wherever he was, the air supply was diminishing. He thought of Janie and Robert, but when the darkness came to swallow him again, he welcomed it to escape the agony he was feeling.

"Call out if you can hear me!"

Matthew's eyes fluttered open reluctantly just before unconsciousness claimed him.

"Call out if you can hear me!"

Matthew thought longingly of the pain-free dark, but followed the ringing authority in the voice making the demand. "Here..." He suspected his voice was too weak to be heard. "Here..." he croaked, in what he hoped was a louder voice. "I'm here..." He closed his eyes as the effort cost him what little strength he had.

"There's one beneath this pile!" he heard a voice yell.

Moments later, a wisp of air floated through the darkness. Matthew sucked it in eagerly, but the movement caused a sharp pain in his chest to join the pain slicing through his legs.

Next, he saw a sliver of dim light crack through the black darkness. He forced himself to stay awake, forced himself to endure the pain of consciousness.

"There's a beam across his legs!" a voice called out. "I need some help over here to lift it off!"

After what seemed an eternity but was probably no more than a minute, Matthew felt the crushing weight lift off his legs, but the pain didn't diminish.

"There's another board across his chest," the man muttered. "Hang on, mister. We're getting you out of here."

Matthew had no more energy to utter a sound. He was soon able to breathe better, so they must have removed the board. He fought to stay conscious, though he wasn't certain why.

"It's going to hurt to move you," one of the men said, his voice full of thick sympathy. "We've got to get you out of here."

Matthew gazed up at him, just managing to give a slight nod. He groaned when a man lifted him by the shoulders. When he felt his legs shifted, the pain was more than he could bear. He welcomed the darkness that claimed him once again.

*****

Thomas was pulling aside more of the wreckage when a flash of red hair passing by him grabbed his attention. "Wait!" he called urgently. He hurried over, holding back his cry of despair when he saw who was on the makeshift stretcher. "Is he..." He swallowed and forced the words around the block in his throat. "Is he alive?" One look at Matthew's broken body made it almost impossible to believe.

"He's alive," the rescuer assured him. "Do you know him?"

"It's Matthew Justin. He came down from Philadelphia to cover the story for his newspaper. His wife is a doctor. I'm sure she's outside working on the wounded."

The young man who had helped him earlier spotted him and came over. "I found your daughter. I let Dr. Wallington know you're alive."

One of the rescuers looked confused. "This man is your son-in-law?"

"No," Thomas answered. "Both my daughter and his wife, Dr. Justin, are physicians." He looked at the young man. "Will you...?"

"Mr. Cromwell, it's time for you to leave the building," the man said firmly. "Go out with Mr. Justin and find his wife. You're not hurt, but you've inhaled enough of the dust. We've got plenty of men here to find any remaining survivors and carry out the bodies."

Thomas flinched, but acknowledged he was right. It was becoming more and more difficult to breathe, and the flurry of activity told him men were coming in from all corners of the city to assist in the rescue operation.

"Anthony Wallington..." He looked at the men. "He's my son-in-law. If you find him..." His voice trailed away. He didn't want to think of the possibilities.

"Come on, Mr. Cromwell," one of the men carrying Matthew urged. "We have to get Mr. Justin some help."

"Of course." Thomas cast a final look behind him as they exited the building.

*****

"Dr. Justin!"

Janie's head jerked up when she heard her name being called loudly enough to conquer the bedlam of activity. She stood quickly, her heart racing when she saw four men walking toward her with a stretcher between them. Suddenly, a man broke from behind them and approached her. "Thomas!"

Thomas reached her first and pulled her into a warm embrace. He held her back gently. "We've got Matthew," he said hoarsely. "He's badly hurt."

Janie felt her heart stop for a moment, and then it began to race so hard she could scarcely breathe. "Matthew..." she whispered.

Moments later, Carrie appeared at her side and took control. "Lay him right here," she said crisply, indicating an empty area that had been vacated by a man carried to the hospital in one of the ambulances. They were transporting patients as quickly as they could, but it would take time to get to them all.

The rescuers lowered Matthew. "I hope he makes it," one of them said gruffly. Then the four men turned and disappeared back into the building.

Carrie bit back her groan when she looked down at Matthew's battered, unconscious body. She could tell at a glance that both legs were broken. His shirt was stained with blood that must be coming from his chest and a jagged wound that crisscrossed his forehead.

"Matthew!" Janie cried, panic making her voice high and shrill.

Abby materialized a moment later. She gave Thomas a warm kiss and then took Janie into her arms.

Carrie interpreted the look that her mother directed at her. "He's alive," she mouthed.

Abby leaned back to look into Janie's face. "He's alive," she said softly, and then her voice grew firmer. "Janie, look at me."

Janie tore her eyes away from Matthew's face, tortured fear twisting her features.

"He's alive," Abby repeated. "Do you hear me?"

A glimmer of hope appeared in Janie's eyes. "He's alive?" she whispered. "He's *alive*?"

"And I'm going to keep him that way," Carrie promised, praying she could uphold her word. Matthew's wounds were massive. His broken legs wouldn't kill him, but she had no way of knowing if internal organs had been damaged by whatever had landed on his chest. Was he unconscious from a concussion, or was he bleeding internally?

She pushed aside thoughts of Anthony for the moment, knelt beside Matthew, and gently began to cut away his jacket and shirt.

"Would you like some help?"

Carrie looked up, unable to believe her ears. "Michael?" Surely the man standing above her was a hallucination, not the doctor she was doing her surgical internship with in Philadelphia.

Dr. Michael Wild knelt beside her, his features grim. "I was at the train station, waiting to catch a connector train to visit my family. I arrived in Richmond after the collapse, but I pieced enough together to realize what had happened. What can I do to help?"

Carrie gulped back a sob of relief. "Matthew is badly hurt."

Dr. Wild's eyes narrowed. "Matthew Justin? I didn't recognize him through all the dust and grime."

"Yes," Carrie answered. "Both legs are badly broken. I'm fairly certain he has a concussion, but..."

"Let me look for internal injuries," Dr. Wild finished for her. "Do you mind?"

Carrie shook her head, knowing she was much too close to Matthew to be the best one to treat him. "Please," she murmured. She moved over so Dr. Wild could examine him.

Dr. Wild probed gently, watching Matthew's breathing and the pallor of his skin.

Carrie carefully washed his face, clearing his nostrils of the dust that threatened to suffocate him, and then slipped arnica tablets under his tongue. She could feel Janie hovering over her, but her friend remained silent, letting them work on her husband.

Michael finally settled back on his heels. "I don't detect any internal injuries," he announced. "I suspect his body has simply shut down to escape the pain from his legs and the concussion."

Carrie stared down at his badly broken legs. If they had seen injuries like this during the war, they would have had no choice but to amputate both limbs. She knew Janie was aware of the same thing, but couldn't bring herself to voice the question.

Dr. Wild read her thoughts. "We'll do our best to save his legs, Janie."

Janie gazed at him as she struggled for control. "More importantly, can you save his life?"

"He's going to live," Dr. Wild said firmly. "There is nothing life-threatening that I can find." He looked around. "How long before an ambulance can take him to the hospital?"

"Grandpa! Grandpa!"

They all looked up as Frances barreled across the lawn and launched herself into Thomas' arms.

"You're alive! You're alive!"

Thomas held his granddaughter tightly, his face buried in her hair for a long moment, and then held her away. "I'm very much alive, and very happy to see you, Frances." He pulled her close again.

Spencer arrived a moment later. "I couldn't stop her," he apologized. "She saw her grandpa across the grounds and took off running."

"It's fine," Carrie replied. "I would have done the same thing."

Frances suddenly gave a cry of disbelief and wrenched away from her grandfather. Her eyes were wild. "Matthew? Is that *Matthew*?"

Carrie took a deep breath and leaned down to hug her close. "It is, Frances," she said softly. "He's badly hurt, but he's very much *alive*."

Frances gulped and gazed up at her. "Can you help him, Mama?"

"Yes," she said confidently, as she realized immediately what needed to be done. She turned to Spencer. "Can you get to River City Carriages and come back with a wagon? We've got to get Matthew home."

"Yes, ma'am," Spencer said quickly. "It might take me a few minutes to get it down the roads through all this mess, but I'll get a wagon here." He turned and sprinted off.

Carrie turned to Dr. Wild. "Will you go to the hospital and get the supplies we need? The hospitals are adequate, but they're going to be far past capacity. Matthew will receive much better care at the house."

"I agree," Dr. Wild said quickly. "I'm still well-known there, so I'll have no trouble getting the supplies we need."

"Take our carriage," Thomas urged.

Carrie shook her head. "It's too congested." Her mind was racing. "Michael, River City Carriages is two blocks over, on Broad Street. Go there and tell them you need a horse. You'll make much better time if you're on horseback." She hesitated. "Will you be able to carry everything?" She thought of all the casting material they would need for Matthew's legs.

Dr. Wild nodded. "I'm sure they'll have saddlebags. I'll make it work." He turned and took Janie by her arms. "Matthew is going to be all right," he said firmly. "Believe that."

Janie nodded, fighting the tears that threatened to conquer her. She turned to Carrie. "I'll ride with Matthew in the wagon to the house. You need to stay here."

She didn't voice what all of them were thinking. *Carrie needed to stay until she knew what had happened to Anthony.*

Carrie turned to her father next. "Will you please stay here with Frances?" When he nodded, she knelt down in front of her daughter. "I want you to stay here with Grandpa. I know you're scared, but the best thing you and I can do right now is to believe your daddy is still alive." She brushed her daughter's tumbled hair away from her face tenderly. "Can you do that for me?"

"Yes, Mama," Frances said bravely, only her eyes revealing her fear.

"Good girl," Carrie replied as she kissed her cheek. "I'm proud of you."

When Carrie turned away she struggled to fight the terror that once more threatened to strangle her. In the time since Matthew had been saved, close to forty more men had been laid out on the lawn. Bracing herself, she set out to discover if any of the new victims was her husband.

She'd gotten no more than a few feet before she felt Abby's arm encircle her waist. She smiled up at her weakly, grateful beyond words for her support. She tried to focus on the fact that her father had survived. Matthew, although he was badly wounded, had also survived. Anthony could too.

Please be alive, her mind screamed. *Please be alive.*

Anthony was not among the new survivors. As the hours ticked by, she knew the chances of finding him alive were growing slimmer, but she stubbornly refused to give up hope, even while her heart quaked with terror.

All she could do was try to help all the survivors she could. It was the only thing enabling her to hold onto her sanity. Many of the men had been triaged and transported to the city hospitals. With hospitals filled to overflowing, some had been taken directly to doctors' offices, and others, who were not severely wounded, were being housed by nearby residents.

As far as she could tell, only a handful of men had walked away relatively unscathed. If she was right, close to two hundred men had been pulled from the rubble. They were leaving the dead behind...pulling them out last so the living would have the best chance of survival.

Carrie took deep breaths to steady her trembling hands and knelt down to examine a new patient.

*****

"We've got one over here!" a fireman yelled. "He's breathing, but just barely!"

Four men scrambled over the heaps of wreckage, their eyes growing wide when they saw the man trapped under four feet of wood, desks and chairs. The fireman who had called them had been pulling away rubble, not really believing anyone could still be alive after this long, but they'd made a commitment to search until everybody had been located, setting aside the dead until they were certain there were no remaining survivors.

"How in the world is he still alive?" one of the men muttered, looking at the heaps of wood and debris that had been pulled aside. "You're sure he's still breathing?"

The fireman knelt again to put his ear close to the man's mouth. "He's breathing!" he said triumphantly. "Who has a clean cloth?" When one was pressed into his hand, he gently probed the inside of the man's mouth, pulling out clods of dirt and grime. Immediately, the breathing became a little stronger.

"That's better.   Not anything to celebrate, but he's getting more air." He wiped the man's face to get a closer look at his features.

"Hey!" one of the men said sharply, pushing forward to get a better look. "That's Anthony Wallington!"

"You're sure?" the fireman asked sharply. "His wife has been outside treating the wounded. She asks me about him every time we take another man out."

"I'm sure," the man said. "I work for him at River City Carriages."

*****

"Dr. Wallington!"

Carrie lifted her head wearily. She was used to her name being hollered out to request assistance. Every bone in her body ached, her heart most of all, but she was here to help. "Yes?" she called, standing to see what was needed.

"We found him, Dr. Wallington!"

Carrie struggled to register the words as the kind fireman she had spoken so much to since the collapse appeared in front of her. "What?"

"We found your husband, ma'am. We found Anthony." He reached out a hand to steady her.

Carrie gasped and held her hand to her mouth. "Is he...?" She couldn't bring herself to ask the question.

"He's alive," the fireman assured her, "but he needs help."

Abby, obviously alerted by the expression on her face, appeared at her side. "Carrie?"

"They found him," she cried.

Carrie grabbed her medical bag, praying frantically, and hurried after the fireman, Abby close behind her. As soon as she saw Anthony lying on the ground, sheltered by the limbs of an oak tree, she broke into a run. She knelt beside his unconscious body, her eyes devouring his face. She was astonished to realize there was no blood and no obvious lacerations. Gentle probing revealed there were no broken bones, but she knew the force of the impact from falling to the chamber floor could have caused internal injuries. More probing revealed no swelling of organs. She motioned for two of the firemen to raise his shoulders. Finally, she found what she was looking for when her fingers encountered a massive lump on the back of his head.

"Water, please," she said quietly. When Abby pressed a glass into her hands, she gently tipped a small amount into Anthony's mouth. He remained unconscious, but his throat constricted reflexively to swallow the water. Carrie refrained from cheering. It was too soon to celebrate, but his acceptance of the water was a good thing. She carefully placed six arnica tablets under his tongue. They would dissolve quickly and help with the swelling in his brain.

"What are you giving him?" the fireman asked.

"Arnica."

The fireman shook his head. "What's that? I got a concussion last year while I was working a fire. The doctor told me there wasn't anything they could give me. They just told me to rest and take it easy until I felt better. I've never heard of arnica."

"No, I'm sure you haven't," Carrie replied, her eyes never leaving Anthony's face. She might be imagining it, but she thought his breathing was a little better and he wasn't quite as ashen.

"Why not?" the fireman muttered.

Carrie didn't really feel like discussing the controversy between traditional medicine and homeopathy, but the fireman had been kind enough to find her as soon as they discovered Anthony. "I'm a homeopathic physician," she explained. "Arnica has long been known to be a very effective treatment for concussions—not only what Anthony is suffering now, but also the long-term consequences of head trauma. Traditional medicine has decided they have trouble with homeopathic remedies, so they ignore the treatments that can help their patients."

"But why?" the fireman demanded.

Carrie shrugged. "There's no good reason," she said bluntly. "If you ask a regular doctor, they'll spout something about homeopathic medicine defying their limited pharmacological conception of what constitutes a viable medical therapy." She spoke the words sarcastically, too fatigued to worry about graciousness. "While they're busy telling us it doesn't work, we're treating patients successfully."

"That's not right!" the fireman said angrily.

Carrie looked up just long enough to meet his eyes. "The next time you get hurt, go visit Dr. Hobson here in town. He's a homeopathic physician."

"Daddy!"

Carrie heard Frances' tortured cry. Obviously, she had figured out who Carrie's new patient was. She turned to catch her in her arms as she barreled toward Anthony. After losing her biological father a few years earlier, she knew her daughter was terrified to lose Anthony as well.

"What's wrong with him?" Frances whimpered, twisting away to stare down at her father. "Is he alive?"

"He's alive, but he's got a bad concussion," Carrie replied, confident Frances had learned enough in the clinic to understand. "He's unconscious right now, but he's going to be alright."

Frances stared at her. "Are you telling me the truth?" she demanded desperately.

"I promise," Carrie said tenderly. "You stay with me. We'll take care of Daddy together."

She was vaguely aware of Thomas striding up to join them.

Quickly, she turned back to Anthony, giving him another sip of water. When Abby placed a larger bowl of water next to her, along with a clean cloth, she began to wash Anthony's face, taking special care to wipe his nostrils free of dust and grime. She lifted his eyelids and poured in a gentle stream of water to clear them. After hours lying trapped under the wreckage, his whole body was encased in the remnants of the collapse.

"Wake up, Anthony," Carrie said softly. "It's over. You're safe. You can wake up now."

She stroked his face and hands, and continued to talk to him, calling him back from the darkness that engulfed him.

*****

Anthony felt the first flutterings of awareness.

The dark veil that had fallen over him seemed to grow thinner, allowing a faint glimmer of light to pierce the blackness.

A soft voice whispered through the veil, causing it to flutter like leaves in the wind.

Anthony strained to identify the sound. He was certain it was somehow familiar, but he couldn't pinpoint how he knew it. He wasn't certain he *did* know it. The effort suddenly caused a pain to explode in his head. He moaned softly and then surrendered to the agony, relishing the darkness as it engulfed him again.

*****

"He moaned!" Carrie exclaimed, her heart leaping with joy.

"That's good?" Abby asked cautiously.

Carrie nodded. "His brain is registering pain." She knew head trauma could be so severe that patients never emerged from it; they never made a sound, and they remained completely unaware of their surroundings. "It's a good sign," she said. "He's in bad shape, but he's in there."

Thomas knelt beside her. "How long will he remain unconscious?"

Carrie shook her head. "I don't know," she admitted. "It's impossible to know the extent of the swelling in his brain."

"Miss Carrie!"

Carrie looked up to see Spencer looming over her, his eyes devouring Anthony's face.

"They found him!" His voice grew more cautious. "Is Mr. Anthony all right?"

"He will be," Carrie said calmly, choosing hope over despair. Against all odds, Anthony had survived hours under a mountain of wreckage. Surely, he would come back to her. She looked over Spencer's shoulder. "Did you get Matthew to the house?"

"Yes, ma'am. Dr. Wild and Janie are working on him right now. May is taking care of little Robert."

"Did you bring the wagon back?"

"I did," he assured her. "We put all new blankets and pillows in it in case they were needed."

Carrie smiled with relief and then turned to the men who had pulled Anthony out. "Will you please carry my husband to our wagon? I'm taking him home."

Chapter Twenty

Carrie finished positioning Anthony in their bed, tucking the covers in securely. He had not regained consciousness, but he was still occasionally making moaning sounds that indicated he was trying to fight his way back. She had taken him out of his filthy, ripped clothing, washed him carefully, and dressed him in clean nightclothes. She gave him another dose of arnica to further alleviate the swelling in his head.

There was nothing to do now but wait.

She walked over to the window and gazed out at the magnolia tree that was just beginning to burst into bloom, its milky white flowers nestled in deep green leaves. A purple lilac bush sent up a sweet aroma, while a soft breeze rustled the limbs of the oak tree positioned at the end of the house. She gazed east toward the plantation, but her gratitude that Anthony, her father and Matthew were still alive far outweighed her sorrow that she wouldn't make it home.

A soft tap at the door pulled her attention away from the window. "Come in," she called. She wasn't worried about being quiet. Anything that would bring Anthony out of the darkness was a good thing.

Spencer appeared at the door. "How is he?" His worried eyes rested on Anthony's face.

"The same," Carrie replied, "but he just needs a little time."

Spencer looked away from Anthony and bored his eyes into hers. "Are you sure?"

"I am," Carrie replied quietly.

"How can you be so sure?" Spencer demanded.

Carrie was wondering the same thing. "I can't really answer that question," she said honestly. "I'm just certain." In truth, she was.

Spencer hesitated. "You really ain't worried, are you?"

Carrie turned to gaze at Anthony's face, somehow miraculously unscathed. "No, I'm not," she said softly. "His brain needs time to heal. He'll wake up when he's ready." Spencer nodded, but she didn't miss the worry in his eyes. "What is it, Spencer?" When he started to shake his head, she held up her hand to stop him. "Don't say it's nothing because I can see it on your face."

Spencer managed a chuckle. "You've known me a mite too long, Miss Carrie."

"I'd say I've known you just the right amount of time," Carrie retorted, and then stared at him, waiting for him to answer.

Spencer looked uncomfortable, but he met her eyes evenly. "Back when I was still a slave, one of my friends got beat real bad. They whipped him with the lash first, and then my owner's son went after him with a board."

Carrie gave a soft cry. "Why?"

Spencer shrugged. "He tried to run away. The overseer went after him with the dogs and brought him back." His lips thinned. "They were teaching him a lesson."

"What happened to him?" Carrie asked, not sure she wanted to know the answer.

"He didn't come to for a long time," Spencer admitted. "When he finally woke up again, he weren't the same man he'd been before," he said slowly. "His head weren't ever right again. He couldn't talk the same..." He shook his head. "He'd been real smart before they beat him so bad..." His voice trailed away again as he swung his eyes back to Anthony's ashen face. "How do you know Mr. Anthony ain't gonna be like my friend?"

Carrie had already considered all the possibilities. "Spencer, I love my husband. We'll cross whatever bridge we come to, but only when we come to it. Right now, I'm confident he's going to wake up. That's enough for me."

Spencer looked at her, his eyes glowing with admiration. "You ain't the same wild, reckless woman you used to be, Miss Carrie."

Carrie managed a small laugh. "Let's hope not, Spencer." She thought about all the trouble she had caused him by her reckless decisions during the war. "I suppose we all have to grow up at some point."

Their conversation was interrupted when Janie appeared at the door. "Matthew is waking up," she said urgently.

"You go," Spencer said. "I'll stay here with Mr. Anthony. If he wakes up, I'll come get you."

Carrie, despite her desire to be there when Anthony regained consciousness, also wanted to be there for Matthew and Janie. She suspected Anthony wasn't going to wake up for many more hours. She gave Spencer a grateful look and hurried from the room.

*****

Matthew was vaguely aware of movement around him. He could hear soft voices that seemed to be moving toward him from behind a thick curtain. They were muffled, as if he were hearing them from a great depth. He struggled to identify where he was. For a moment, he thought he was back in the bowels of the earth, imprisoned in Rat Dungeon within Libby Prison.

Fear gripped him until he realized light was also filtering through the dark curtain. There had been no light in Rat Dungeon. And, wasn't the war over? He couldn't still be in prison.

His brain reached for understanding through the shrouded fog encompassing him. Somehow, he knew that if he pushed aside the curtain, unimaginable pain waited for him. The fog and darkness were comforting. Perhaps he would stay there.

"Matthew..."

A voice that he knew penetrated the darkness. He knew the voice, but he couldn't identify *how* he knew it. Confusion swirled through him.

"Matthew. Wake up, my love..."

Matthew stilled. He knew *the voice*. He could hear the tenderness and the love in the soft words.

"Wake up, Matthew."

The voice was more insistent now. It wanted something from him.

"Open your eyes, Matthew. Come back to me."

Matthew considered the request. Was he brave enough to face what waited on the other side of the foggy darkness?

"I love you, Matthew. Please come back to me..."

Slowly, the pain in *the voice* penetrated his own pain and fear. *The voice* loved him. *The voice* wanted him to come back. Where had he gone? What had happened?

Still afraid to push aside the curtain, Matthew strained to make sense of things. He tried to find the pieces of the puzzle that would create a picture he could comprehend.

"It's all right, Matthew. You're safe now."

Matthew listened carefully. He must have not been safe before. Where had he been?

The voice seemed to understand his silent questions.

"You were at the Capitol for the trial, Matthew. The floor collapsed. You were badly hurt, but you're going to be all right, my love. I'm here for you. I'll always be here." There was a brief pause. "So will Robert."

Robert? Somehow, even in the shrouded mist, he knew Robert was dead. His best friend was dead. Could *the voice* not be trusted?

"Wake up, Matthew." *The voice* was insistent again. "Your son and I are waiting for you to come back to us."

Your son? Like a crack of lightning splitting the night sky, the words *your son* split the thick curtain of darkness. Janie... Robert... His wife. His son. *The voice* was Janie. His wife.

Along with the clarity came the return of the searing pain he had escaped from before. He looked up to see the dark curtain closing around him but willed it to remain open. Janie. Robert. His wife and son wanted him to come back. He loved them.

He had to choose pain over the darkness in order to return to them.

Matthew reached deep into his soul and forced his eyes to open, blinking against the light and the searing pain that accompanied his return to consciousness.

"Matthew!"

He could feel kisses rain down on his face, the love easing the worst of his pain.

"Janie..." Matthew was shocked at the weak gravelly sound coming from his mouth. Waves of pain made him want to choose the darkness. Love made him choose the light. "Janie..."

"Welcome back, my love," Janie said tenderly.

Matthew blinked again, willing her face to come into focus. Gradually, the blur became a pair of soft blue eyes. Light brown tendrils surrounded a face creased with worry and streaked with tears of relief. "Janie," he whispered. "What happened?"

"You were in the Capitol building for the trial, Matthew. The floor you were on collapsed. They found you under wreckage from the collapse. You were rescued, and then we brought you home."

Matthew stared at her. Wasn't home Philadelphia? How had he gotten back home? He struggled to make sense of what she was saying. "Home?"

"You're at Thomas and Abby's house in Richmond, dear."

Matthew relaxed. Yes, he was home. Images and memories began to filter in, bringing in new waves of pain. "Thomas? Anthony?" It took every bit of his strength and courage to ask the questions, but he had to know.

"Thomas is fine," Janie soothed, not looking away from his eyes. "He wasn't hurt."

Matthew stared at her hard, willing her to tell him what else he needed to know.

"Anthony was hurt, but he's recovering."

Matthew absorbed the news. "What happened?" he whispered again, unable to form more words than that. He willed her to understand what he was asking.

"You were badly hurt," Janie said quietly. "When you fell, a beam from the ceiling landed on you, along with other boards from the flooring. They didn't find you for a long time." She took a deep breath, tears coursing down her cheeks.

Matthew steeled himself, sure that whatever she had to tell him wasn't good. He had been hurt before, but he'd never felt anything quite like what he was feeling now.

"Both your legs were broken," Janie said steadily. "Dr. Wild and I have casted both of them. You have a concussion, but arnica is helping with that already. That's why you've woken up so quickly. You also received a nasty gash on your head, but we've taken care of it."

Matthew blinked, trying to take it in. At least the news explained why his head ached so badly, and why pain was radiating from his lower body. He grabbed onto one word. "Casted?" he ground out. He had seen too much of what happened on battlefields with badly broken limbs.

"Yes," Janie said. "You have both your legs, Matthew. You're going to keep them." She forced a lighter tone to her voice. "You're going to be miserable for a while, but you'll fully recover."

Matthew stared up at her. He knew Janie wouldn't lie to him. He would fully recover.

"You need to rest, my love."

Matthew blinked again. "Tired..." he murmured.

"Yes, you're tired. Go to sleep. I'll be here when you wake up." Janie reached for his hand and held it gently.

Matthew gazed at her for a moment, imprinting her face, and then closed his eyes. This time, the blackness didn't swallow him, it merely welcomed him to sleep.

*****

Carrie looked up when the door to her bedroom opened again.

Abby appeared with a wooden tray loaded with food. "May sent this up." She placed it on the nightstand and looked down at Anthony. "Any change?"

"No," Carrie replied, glancing out at the stars beginning to twinkle above the treetops.

"I'm sorry," Abby murmured.

"He's going to be fine," Carrie said quickly, her voice harsher than she meant it to be. "He's going to be fine," she repeated in a softer tone. "He just needs time." She pushed aside thoughts of Robert lying unconscious for months during the second year of the war, but one look at Abby's face told her that her mother was already thinking it. "I don't care how long it takes," she whispered. "I'll be here when he wakes up."

"You're exhausted," Abby said gently. "You've got to get some rest, too."

"I'm going to," Carrie agreed, knowing Abby was right. The long day of caring for patients, combined with the emotional toll, had taken everything from her. "How is Matthew?"

"Sleeping," Abby told her. "He actually ate a little bit of May's soup, but then went right to sleep."

"It's exactly what he needs," Carrie said. "He knows the truth about what is ahead. Now he just needs to let his body heal." She frowned. "His head will heal quickly, but his legs will take months."

Abby nodded. "Dr. Wild said to expect three to four months, perhaps longer because the breaks were so severe."

"That sounds about right. It's going to be a long road for him."

"Janie already sent a telegram to the medical college, telling them she's withdrawing from this term. She's staying here to care for him."

"I'm glad," Carrie murmured. "We won't open our medical clinic next January because Janie won't have her degree, but everything will happen when it's meant to."

Abby opened her mouth, but then closed it quickly.

"Go ahead," Carrie encouraged her.

Abby met her eyes, her own shining with bright compassion. "I want to know how you are, Carrie."

Carrie raised a brow. "How I am?"

"Yes," Abby said. "You lost Robert. You were afraid for hours today that you'd lost Anthony. He's lying here unconscious, and you really don't know what condition he'll be in when he wakes up." She reached over to take her hand. "You haven't shed a single tear all day, and you're exhausted."

Carrie thought about it, but already knew the truth. "I can't feel anything."

"Can't? Or won't?"

Carrie considered the question, and then shrugged. "Does it matter?"

"Yes," Abby said softly. "Carrie, I've seen you like this before. When your emotions get too much to handle, you simply shut them down."

"Sometimes it's the only way to get through a difficult time," Carrie argued. "The only thing that's important to me right now is to be here for Anthony."

"I understand that," Abby said gently, "but you are important to *us*. We're deeply concerned about Anthony, but we're also concerned about you."

Carrie shook her head with frustration. "What do you want me to do? Dissolve into a puddle of tears? How is that going to help?" The questions ignited something inside her. "I know there's nothing wrong with crying—you've taught me that—but I really don't see how crying is going to help this situation, Abby. It won't change anything." Her breath caught. "It won't change the fact that Anthony is stuck in unconsciousness because of a swelling brain. It won't change the fact that..." She bit back her words and turned away.

"It won't change what fact, Carrie?" Abby pressed. "What were you going to say?"

Anger sparked through the fatigue and forced hopefulness. "It won't change the fact that Anthony may never again be the man I married! It won't change the fact that, even if Anthony lives, I'll still be alone!" Her breath came in gasps as the fear and anger she had buried all day forced its way to the surface. Her earlier confidence hung in shreds around her.

The next words were ripped from her. "Am I cursed, Abby? Will I always lose everyone I love? Is this simply my destiny?" Her heart seemed to stop, locking her in a dark room for which she had no key. She searched frantically for a way to escape the darkness but could find no way forward. Sobs, suppressed during the long day, threatened to choke her as she fought to hold them back.

"Carrie," Abby murmured as she stepped closer to pull her into her arms. "Let it go, Carrie. Let it go..."

Carrie tensed and pulled back. "I can't!" The cry was wrenched from deep in her soul. "I can't let go because I'm afraid I'll never find my way back!" Robert's laughing face crowded into her thoughts...images of Bridget...and now Anthony. A quick glance at the bed told her what she already knew. He was the same.

"I'm here," Abby said soothingly, refusing to let Carrie go as her arms tightened around her. "You're not alone. You're not cursed."

"How do you know?" Carrie gasped, hanging on for dear life to her final remnants of self-control. "How do you know?" The words were wrenched from her.

Abby held her back so she could look into her face. "Because Anthony is alive. Anthony is *alive*, Carrie. He should have died under that rubble. He should have been crushed by the weight of the wreckage trapping him. He should have come out fractured, shattered and covered with blood."

Carrie flinched at the brutal rawness of Abby's words, but the truth penetrated.

"He didn't," Abby continued. "It's true that he hasn't woken up yet, but I believe it's a blessing. You don't know how long he laid there, certain he was going to die. You don't know how long he fought to live before he could no longer fight. You don't know how he longed to see you one last time. To see Frances." She shook Carrie slightly. "Do you know any of these things?"

Carrie was shocked into silence. "No," she whispered.

"Isn't it possible that Anthony just needs to sleep? That somewhere, deep in his soul, he knows he's safe with you, and now he just wants to sleep?" Her voice sharpened. "Isn't it possible, Carrie?"

"Yes," Carrie whispered, her eyes caught by the loving intensity shining from her mother's eyes.

"What will he want to come back to?" Abby continued. "A woman who has shut down her feelings, or a woman who is brave enough to feel them?"

Carrie wanted to scream her denial that it took bravery to feel fear, but she couldn't force the words to her lips. She couldn't force the words, because she knew Abby was right. "I'm afraid," she groaned. "I'm afraid..."

Abby's voice gentled. "Of course you are. Anyone would be, my dear. I'm afraid for Anthony. For you. It's all right to be afraid. You can tremble with fear, but still hold onto hope," she said softly. "You can cry tears and still choose to be strong. You don't have to choose one or the other. They can all exist at the same time."

Carrie felt the fear welling up inside her again. This time, instead of trying to stuff it deep inside, she examined it. She embraced it. The man she loved with all her heart was lying on the bed unconscious. The man she loved with all her heart had almost been killed today. The man she loved with all her heart may never come back to her the same man he had been before the accident. Spencer's words about his friend had haunted her all afternoon, robbing her of the fragile peace she had struggled to hold onto.

A sob tore from Carrie's throat as her shoulders heaved with grief. Wild cries erupted as whimpers as she clung to Abby. No longer able to control what she was feeling, she let it come pouring out like gushing water from a pump. Her whole body trembled as tears poured down her face.

Abby remained silent, holding her tightly while she stroked her back and hair.

Carrie didn't know how long she cried before she hiccupped and fell silent. She still clung to Abby, desperately needing her strength, but she could once again feel glimmers of hope. "I'm tired," she whispered.

"I know," Abby whispered back. Gently, she led Carrie to her dressing table, unbuttoned her dress, slipped it off her, and then pulled a soft nightgown over her head. Leading her to the bed, she pulled back the covers and helped her lie down. "You'll be here when Anthony wakes up," she said softly. "In the meantime, he'll have your warmth to remind him of your love."

Carrie blinked up at her. "Thank you."

Curling into Anthony's warm body, she was soon asleep, her arm resting on his chest.

*****

Anthony felt the pressure in his head lessening. The tight vise that had squeezed him until he had no choice but to escape was suddenly looser, more bearable. He was confused, though, by the weight across his chest. It wasn't heavy, and it was somehow comforting, but he couldn't identify the source. With no energy to open his eyes, he took refuge in the unexplained comfort and sank back into a restful sleep.

He dreamed of falling...crashing sounds...screams of agony...cries of fear...searing pain...blank nothingness.

Anthony jerked awake, his eyes opening slowly to darkness. Confusion fogged his brain. Where was he? What dark place had entombed him? He fought for his breath, until he realized it was coming easily, with none of the choking dust that had haunted his dream.

He blinked, his eyes adjusting to the dark. He blinked again, things slowly coming into focus. He wasn't trapped. He was in his room. The confusion swirled anew. Had his dream really only been a dream? Had nothing happened? He struggled to make sense out of everything.

If nothing had happened, why was his head hurting? Why were flashes pounding behind his eyes? Why did his body ache?

Slowly, he once again became aware of the warm weight across his chest. Reaching up his free hand tentatively, he encountered soft flesh. Carrie! The feel of her warmth brought the memories rushing back like an avalanche. He had been in the Capitol. The floor had collapsed. As he remembered the horrific event, the questions pressed in. The pressure of not knowing increased the pounding in his head.

*****

Carrie woke to the sound of Anthony's moan. Instinctively, she tightened her arm across his chest. "It's all right," she said tenderly, hoping her voice could reach beyond his darkness. She didn't know how long she'd been asleep, but the room was still shrouded with night.

"Carrie..."

Carrie gasped and sat up. "Anthony? Are you awake?" Joy exploded through her at the sound of her name. Her husband was awake and still knew who she was.

"Yes," Anthony murmured. "My head..." His voice was twisted with pain.

"I'm sure it hurts," Carrie said softly. She reached over to the nightstand for the bottle of arnica. Shaking out six tablets, she turned back to him. "Open your mouth," she said gently. When Anthony responded willingly, she placed the tablets under his tongue. "This will help with the pain."

"What...?"

"You have a concussion, my love," Carrie told him. "Your head is going to hurt for a little while longer, but you're going to be fine." She hesitated. "Do you remember what happened?"

"Yes." Anthony moaned again. "Thirsty...."

Carrie pushed back the covers, hastily lit the lantern hanging on the wall, and poured a glass of cool water. "Don't try to sit up," she commanded. "Just let me lift your shoulders enough to give you some water."

Anthony lay quietly, his eyes fixed on her face. "Whatever you say."

Carrie chuckled, relieved beyond words to see the glimmer of amusement in his eyes. "So, all I need to do is knock you out with a concussion in order to make you compliant?"

"Evidently," Anthony muttered thickly. "What happened?"

"What do you remember?" Carrie asked again. His answer would help her ascertain more of his mental state.

"Floor collapsed," Anthony said weakly. "Your father? Matthew?"

Carrie grinned. "Father is fine. He wasn't hurt at all. Matthew is going to take longer to recover, but he's going to be fine. He's in his and Janie's room down the hall."

Anthony watched her face as he thought about her words. "Longer?" he finally asked.

"Matthew broke both legs."

Anthony grimaced and then looked at her with an unspoken question.

"You didn't break anything," Carrie told him. "Miraculously, you don't even have a cut. What you do have is a massive bump on the back of your head that gave you a concussion. You've been asleep for a long time."

"How long?"

"The floor of the building collapsed at eleven o'clock yesterday morning." Carrie glanced at the clock just visible in the dim lantern light. "It's four o'clock in the morning now. You should be feeling well rested," she teased.

Anthony grimaced again. "Not a...rest."

Carrie sobered. "No, it wasn't. You scared me to death, Anthony. I would appreciate it if you would stay away from collapsing floors in the future."

Anthony managed a brief smile before he pressed his hand to his head.

"All you need to do is sleep," Carrie said. "Now that you've come out of the unconsciousness, your sleep will be healing." She pressed the glass to his lips again. "Take a few sips and then go back to sleep. When you wake again, I'll get you something to eat."

Anthony stared up at her. "Love you..."

Tears welled in Carrie's eyes. "I love you too, Anthony." She pressed a gentle kiss to his forehead. "Go back to sleep."

"Stay..." Anthony whispered.

Carrie crawled into the bed next to him, pressing her body against his. "I'm right here," she promised. "Sleep."

Moments later, Anthony's body went slack.

Carrie stroked his arm until sleep claimed her again as well.

Chapter Twenty-One

Thomas, unhurt from the previous day's tragedy, but deeply fatigued, leaned his head back against the chair in the parlor. He had woken early, too disturbed by the tragedy to be able to sleep.

"Thomas?"

He managed a smile. "Hello, my dear. I couldn't sleep. I'm sorry I disturbed you."

"You didn't disturb me," Abby replied, and then hesitated. "Would you prefer to be alone?"

"No." Thomas waved his hand toward the chair on the other side of the cold fireplace. "Please join me."

Abby sat down but remained silent. Thomas, grateful for her presence, took deep breaths as a wind blew in through the window, carrying the aroma of lilac and the first English roses of the year. It astonished him that such beauty could still exist in a world that could also produce the horror of the Capitol collapse.

Dawn slowly began to claim the morning, casting a rosy haze on the parlor floor as the sun rose above the horizon and glistened in through the window panes.

"It was horrible," he said softly. It was the first time he'd been willing to give words to what he had experienced.

Abby reached over to take his hand, but still didn't speak.

Thomas knew she was giving him time to process what he was feeling and thinking. "So many were killed yesterday, Abby. I've known most of them for many years. They were my friends." Now that the agony of waiting to discover if Anthony and Matthew were still alive was over, the reality of the day was sinking in, encasing him in its weight.

"Do you know how many were killed?" Abby asked, her voice warm with sympathy.

Thomas sighed and held up a piece of paper. "This was on the porch when I got up. Yesterday, I asked a friend to keep me updated if he could."

Abby eyed the paper. "It's bad."

"It's bad," Thomas said somberly, his heart catching at just how horrible the news was. "So far, there are sixty-two dead, but that number will rise."

Abby gasped. "Sixty-two?"

Thomas nodded grimly. "Over two hundred were wounded, many of them severely."

Abby absorbed the news with wide eyes. "How many did you know?"

Thomas closed his eyes briefly as the pain squeezed his heart. "Too many," he muttered. "I saw some of them crushed by the falling beams. Abby, it wasn't just the balcony that fell. There were at least three hundred and fifty men up there. When it fell, the weight of it crushed the courtroom floor, making the entire thing crash into the house chamber on the bottom floor. Many of those who fell plummeted forty feet." He closed his eyes as he thought about the gaping cavern that had opened, hundreds of bodies scattered, covered with lime dust and blood.

"I saw Patrick Henry Aylett and Nat Howard crushed under a falling beam," he choked. "I've known them since I was a boy. Five other attorneys I've done business with were killed. Judge Meredith, another friend of many years, is still alive but not expected to live. He was terribly crushed. He has broken ribs and internal injuries they don't believe he can survive."

Thomas shook his head. "This list of people isn't complete, but it holds the names of forty more men that I knew. Good men who cared about this city and this state. They have wives and children..." His voice trailed off again as he tried to understand the scope of what had happened. "Many of them served during the war.

They survived four years of hell, only to be killed by a collapsing balcony." He made no attempt to disguise the anger in his voice. "It's all so senseless."

"What about the judges who were to render their decision?"

Thomas shook his head. "Unbelievably, none of them were injured. They had only just opened the door to the courtroom when the balcony collapsed. Thirty more seconds, and they would have been buried beneath the rubble."

Abby shuddered. "As you would have been," she said softly, her voice thick with unshed tears.

Thomas closed his eyes again. "I know." He opened them to gaze at her. "My dear friends are dead, and I came through without a scratch. How can that be? I am hardly more important than they are."

"No," Abby agreed. "Not one of those men deserved to die or be wounded."

Thomas peered at her. "You're not going to tell me I lived for a purpose?" he asked, aware his voice was sharper than he intended.

Abby met his eyes. "Thomas, over 600,000 men were just killed in a war. More than that were wounded. Hundreds of thousands of innocent people have died from cholera, influenza and Yellow Fever. All of them had people who loved them, people who are grieving their loss. Are you more special than any of them?" She smiled slightly. "You certainly are to me. You certainly are to Carrie. You certainly are to all the people who love you." She paused. "Do I believe you were saved for a special purpose? I don't know. I do know, however, that if you're still alive, there's a purpose for it.

However," she added firmly, "before any thoughts of purpose, you need to grieve the people you lost."

Thomas nodded, taking comfort from her words. "The whole city is grieving. Thousands of people have been directly impacted, but the whole city will feel the loss of the men who died yesterday." His brow creased. "The whole court has had to be adjourned. The Clerks office, with all the city records, was completely destroyed. More than half the lawyers have been killed or wounded." He shook his head with disbelief. "And we don't even have someone to lead the city through this terrible loss. Mayor Chahoon? Ellyson? We still don't know."

"What happened to them?" Abby asked. "Surely they were in the building?"

"They were both injured," Thomas said wearily, holding up the letter again. "Neither were hurt badly, but I don't know how long their recoveries will take. In the meantime, we still don't know what the court's decision was going to be, and it can't be announced without reconvening the court."

Thomas clenched his jaw. "I would say it hardly matters, but the city is going to need a leader who can help us recover from what has happened. Instead, we're left with the uncertainty of who our mayor actually is. The entire political landscape of our city has been changed in one disastrous action that will take years to recover from."

*****

Carrie assured herself that Anthony was sleeping peacefully before she eased out of bed, slipped on a robe and went downstairs.   Her stomach growled the entire way down the stairway. She could hear May bustling around the kitchen, but she followed the sound of soft voices coming from the parlor.

"Carrie!" Abby welcomed her with a broad smile. "Good morning!"

"It is a wonderful morning!" Carrie responded with a brilliant smile.

Abby gasped and stood. "Anthony is awake?"

"He's awake," Carrie confirmed happily, "and fully aware of everything."

Abby rushed forward to wrap her in a warm embrace. "I'm so happy!"

Thomas' arms wrapped around her a moment later. "That's the best news you could have given me, my dear!"

Carrie nodded. "He has to take it easy for several weeks to allow the concussion to fully heal, but he's going to be completely fine."

"Can we go see him?" Abby asked eagerly.

Carrie shook her head. "He's sleeping again. When he wakes up, I know he'll be happy for company." She glanced at the stairway. "Has Janie been down?"

"Not yet. I hope she's sleeping," Abby answered.

"Dr. Wild?"

"Present and accounted for!"

Carrie spun around when a cheerful voice sounded behind her. "Michael!" When she wasn't in the office or in a professional setting, it was natural to call him by his first name. Their years of working together during the war, combined with their recent months doing surgery, had given them an easy friendship.

"What's it take to get food around here?" Michael asked, his green eyes sparkling. "I'm starving!" He moved forward to give Carrie a hug. "I overheard the news. I'm so glad Anthony is doing better."

"Thank you. Did you check on Matthew?"

Michael nodded. "He's sleeping. He woke a few times during the night, but Janie gave him arnica and he fell back asleep quickly. Yesterday was brutal for him, but now that his legs are cast, the pain will be manageable. In a couple of days, the pain will become negligible while his bones heal," he explained to Thomas and Abby. "He'll be in those casts for three to four months. I suspect it will be closer to four."

Carrie told them the rest of what her parents needed to know. "Which means he'll have to learn how to walk again and build the strength in his legs when the casts come off."

"Yes," Michael agreed. "It's going to be a long haul for him, but he's strong and healthy, and he has Janie to support him."

"Along with the rest of us," Thomas said firmly.

Spencer walked into the room. "May sent me to get all of you. She's putting breakfast on the table now."

"Those are the words a starving man needs to hear!" Michael answered.

"You ain't starving!" May's indignant voice floated to where they were standing. "You ate enough last night for two men, Dr. Wild."

"A mere snack," Michael called back teasingly. "I'm ready for a real meal now."

Laughing and chatting, they moved into the dining room.

Michael stopped when he saw the dining room table loaded with food. A broad smile on his face, he closed his eyes, folded his hands in prayer and looked to the ceiling. "Ah, Heavenly Father, I thank you for a woman who knows how to cook. This truly be a sight for me sore eyes."

Thomas chuckled. "So your red hair and green eyes don't make you look Irish for nothing."

Michael grinned. "I was ten when my parents came over from Dublin. My father always told me to never choose a woman who couldn't cook as well as my mother."

"Does that explain why you're still single?" May retorted.

Michael shrugged, his eyes dancing. "Spencer is much larger than me. I think I would lose if I fought him for your hand, May."

May laughed. "You be talking nonsense, Dr. Wild." Then she waved a hand over the table. "Y'all sit down and eat while it's hot. I got work to do."

Frances appeared in the door of the dining room. Yawning widely, she stopped abruptly when she saw Carrie. "Mama! You're down here." Her eyes widened with fright. "Is Daddy...?

Carrie knew how frightened her daughter had been. After losing both her biological parents, Frances had reason to feel terrified. She moved forward to wrap her daughter's slender body in her arms. "Daddy is fine," she said firmly. "He woke up early this morning. We talked, I gave him water, and he went back to sleep."

Frances peered up at her. "Really, Mama? He's going to be all right?" Her voice demanded to know the truth.

"I promise," Carrie answered. She held Frances back from her and gazed down into her brown eyes. "Have I ever lied to you?"

"No," Frances whispered. Slowly, the fear left her eyes. "When can I see him?"

"When he wakes up again," Carrie replied. "He's eager to see you, too."

Frances nodded and glanced at the table. "I'm hungry!"

As everyone erupted in laughter, a faint cry filtered down from the floor above them.

Frances grinned. "That's Robert. I'll go get him and bring him down."

Carrie watched her run lightly up the steps. "She's growing up," she murmured.

"That girl was a godsend yesterday," May declared. "She seemed to be everywhere at once. She was taking care of Robert, but then she was helping me carry supplies in and out to Dr. Wild and Janic. She knew what was needed before they even asked her sometimes!"

Carrie smiled. "She helps me at the clinic a lot. She claims she wants to be a doctor, though she might change her mind in the future. In the meantime, I'm giving her as much experience as I can. There are many days that I don't know what I would do without her."

Moments later, they were all seated at the table, filling their plates eagerly.

Michael, his face bright with anticipation, sliced open two fluffy biscuits, topped them with thick slices of country ham and fried eggs, and then carefully spooned redeye gravy over everything. A smile broke across his face and his eyes closed as he leaned in close to inhale the aroma, before he carefully cut a portion and took a bite. "Ah..." he moaned.

Carrie laughed. "You would think you never eat," she taunted him.

"When was the last time you had a meal like this in Philadelphia?" Michael shot back, his delight not diminishing as he took another bite.

"Point taken," Carrie agreed. "Now, leave me alone so I can eat."

*****

A knock at the door startled all of them.

"Are we expecting someone?" Abby asked Thomas.

"Not that I know of, but with everything going on in the city, it doesn't surprise me to have visitors today."

Spencer entered the dining room. "I reckon it's gonna be Harold."

"Harold?" Carrie asked. "What is he doing here? He and Susan went back to the plantation when they brought the horses back."

"I figured *I* would want to know if my twin brother was almost crushed to death under a falling building," Spencer replied. "I sent Eddie out to the plantation to tell him—he was happy to go. I had a feeling Harold would come."

Carrie glanced at the clock. "He must have left at the crack of dawn," she said with astonishment.

"Probably in the middle of the night," Spencer said.

Micah moved past them to open the door. "Mr. Harold! Good morning." A moment later, his voice sounded again. "Rose! Moses! Come inside right now. Y'all be here just in time for breakfast. That is, if that Dr. Wild don't eat every bite before you get to the table."

May grinned happily. "I got more biscuits cooking in the oven. Won't take but a few minutes to fill those platters back up. Ever'body gonna be real hungry!"

Carrie was already rushing toward the door. "Good morning! I'm so happy to see you, but what are y'all doing here?" She rushed into Rose's arms and held her tightly. "It's barely ten o'clock. What time did you leave to get here?"

Moses yawned. "Six o'clock. Are you planning on making a habit of this, Carrie?"

"A habit?" Carrie asked.

"The last time you were coming to the plantation, you ended up taking care of patients from the riot. Now it's the Capitol collapse," Harold said wryly. "We could do with a little less drama, if you don't mind."

Carrie laughed, and then hugged Moses and Harold. "May is putting more food on the table. I'm sure you're hungry."

"Starving," Harold agreed.

"Oh, please," Rose retorted. "You've been eating Annie's ham biscuits since we pulled out of the plantation."

Harold shrugged. "Driving a carriage is hard work. And besides, when is hunger a prerequisite for enjoying May's cooking?" Then he turned serious. "Matthew? How is he?" His eyes flickered with anxious fear.

"He's going to be miserable for a while," Carrie answered, "but he'll heal." Quickly, she gave them an update.

Rose moved closer to slide her arm around Carrie's waist. "Anthony?" she asked softly.

Spencer spoke from behind them. "When I sent Eddie out to the plantation, they still hadn't found him."

"Well," Carrie said calmly, "I would hardly be downstairs eating breakfast if Anthony wasn't all right."

"I'm telling myself that," Rose agreed, "but I still want the story."

Frances arrived, holding little Robert close. "Rose! Moses! Harold!"

Robert babbled happily and waved his pudgy arms. May scooped him up so Frances could fling herself into the newcomers' arms.

Everyone laughed and claimed seats at the table as Micah pulled in more chairs. May bustled back and forth from the kitchen, her face glowing with satisfaction as she loaded the table with more food.

When everyone's stomach was full, they turned back to serious conversation.

"What is Matthew going to do?" Harold asked.

"It will be quite some time before he can travel," Carrie answered. "He won't be able to return to Philadelphia for a while. Janie has withdrawn from this term and will care for him here in Richmond. He'll have to take it easy, just as Anthony will, to heal from the concussion, but his legs are going to be very difficult for him. He'll be confined to a wheelchair for months."

Harold looked at her with disbelief. "My brother in a wheelchair? I'm not sure who I feel sorrier for, him or Janie."

Carrie was sure he was right. "He's been wanting undistracted time for his new book. At least he can be sure his editor can't send him on any more assignments."

"That's one way of looking at it," Harold said ruefully. "I'll let you be the one to share that positive little note with him."

Carrie chuckled, but then grew serious. "He came very close to dying," she said softly. "If they hadn't found him when they did...'"

Harold met her eyes. "I know. Eddie told me. That's why I'm here." He looked grim. "Eddie told me they'd found him, but he hadn't regained consciousness... I had to see him," he finished.

"And we had to know what was happening," Rose said quietly. "After..." She shook her head and didn't finish what she was saying.

Carrie knew how she would have finished that sentence. *After Robert died.*

"It was terrifying," Carrie admitted. "The whole day was like a never-ending nightmare." She sobered. "So many men died. So many will never be the same again." Every time she closed her eyes, she thought about the broken bodies she'd treated. "We are so very lucky," she whispered.

"Don't you mean blessed?" May demanded, walking in with a fresh pot of coffee.

Carrie hesitated. "Are we? What about all the men who died? Had they done something wrong to not deserve to live? To not be blessed?"

"What you talking about?" May asked, her eyes flashing. "Don't you recognize a blessing of God when you see it, Miss Carrie?"

Carrie met her eyes. "I recognize that something very extraordinary happened yesterday. Something I am extremely grateful for..."

"Blessed," May said firmly.

"Perhaps," Carrie murmured, trying to give words to what she had spent so much time thinking about recently. "It's just that I hear people say they're blessed, instead of fortunate or lucky, so often. It's like they're wanting to add emphasis to the idea that God had something to do with their circumstances."

"You saying God didn't save Mr. Thomas, Mr. Anthony and Mr. Matthew?" May asked incredulously. "What have they done to you up in Philadelphia?"

Carrie thought about dropping the whole conversation, but suddenly it was important to not pursue. "I'm not saying that, May, but if I use the word *blessed*, doesn't that mean God has focused on our wellbeing more than others because of...what?" She shook her head. "Because we're so much better than everyone else? Because we're special?"

May stared at her. "Everyone in this house *is* special," she said.

"They certainly are to me," Carrie agreed, "but don't you have to reach the conclusion that in order for someone to be special, there must be people who are *not special*?"

The room remained silent while Carrie and May carried on their debate.

"Doesn't that mean that if I say I'm blessed, I must consider my life to be better than others?" Carrie continued. "Or Father's life? Or Anthony's? Or Matthew's?"

May opened her mouth to fire back a response, and then closed it slowly. "I reckon I never thought about it that way, Miss Carrie."

Carrie continued to think furiously. "I guess I believe that when I say I'm blessed, I'm saying I'm better than all the wives and families suffering right now because their loved one died, or will never be the same because of their wounds," she said. "When I say I'm *lucky*, it implies that my circumstances can happen to anyone. It doesn't make anyone feel bad—or at least not as bad as basically being told that God didn't love them enough to give them a better outcome." She paused. "I suppose I want to focus on how grateful I am without putting words to it that might make someone feel worse than they already do."

"You've thought about this a great deal," Abby said.

"I have. I see suffering all the time. I see some people live and some people die. I see loved ones suffer. Robert died; Anthony didn't. Was I not blessed enough for Robert to live? Not blessed enough for Bridget to live? Yet, suddenly I'm blessed enough for Anthony to live?" She took a deep breath. "I've decided the only way I can live with that dichotomy is to simply choose gratitude for the good things that happen."

May cocked her head and finally nodded. "I see what you're saying, Miss Carrie," she said slowly. "I sure don't want to make no one feel bad. I guess we get so used to using a word, that we don't think about what it might mean to someone else."

Spencer had walked into the room at the beginning of the conversation. Now, he was looking at Carrie with a broad smile on his face. "Yep, you done grown up for sure, Miss Carrie."

*****

Matthew opened his eyes, relieved to find the blinding pain had dulled to a steady ache. His head still hurt, but there were no longer flashing lights exploding through his brain. Relieved, he tried to swing his legs out of bed and stand. He sucked in his breath sharply and groaned as pain claimed him again, along with confusion. Why wouldn't his legs move?

Janie appeared at his side immediately. "Good morning, my love. I'm glad to see you're awake."

Matthew stared at her, blinking back the fresh bout of pain. "My legs..." He remembered Janie telling him about the Capitol collapse, but what had she said about his legs?

"Both your legs were broken in the collapse," Janie said gently, her eyes radiating warm sympathy.

Matthew shook his head, the truth of her words pushing aside the remaining fog. "Both my legs are broken?" He thought for a moment. "You told me that last night, didn't you?"

"I did, but you were still in a tremendous amount of pain, dear." She took his right hand. "I'm so sorry."

"Can I see them?" Matthew asked. Some part of him needed to convince himself they were still there.

Janie helped him slide up in the bed until he was sitting against a mountain of pillows. Then she pulled his covers back.

Matthew couldn't stop the gasp that escaped his mouth. Hearing her say the words, and actually seeing the casts, were different creatures. He stared at the thick casts stretched out in front of him for a long time, pondering what it meant. "Will I walk again?"

"Yes," Janie said without hesitation. "The breaks were clean. Dr. Wild was able to reset them and cast them. When they're healed, you'll be able to walk again."

Matthew registered her response with gratitude but continued to gaze at his bandaged legs. "How long?"

"Three to four months," Janie said apologetically, squeezing his hand as she relayed the facts.

Matthew's eyes widened as he tried to absorb what that meant. "Will I have to stay in bed?" he finally asked. He needed all the facts he could get in order to process this new development in his life.

"For about a week," Janie answered. "Although, not because of your legs. Dr. Wild doesn't want you to move around until we're sure the concussion is completely healed. Once the week is over, you can get out of bed, but you'll still have to take it easy while your brain is healing."

Matthew reached down to touch one of the rock-hard casts. "How will I get out of bed?" He heard Janie take a deep breath.

"In a wheelchair," she answered steadily.

Matthew clenched his teeth. "How am I supposed to get back to Philadelphia? A wheelchair is one thing, but trying to travel with my legs out in front of me is something completely different."

"You're right," Janie agreed. "We're staying here in Richmond until you're well. When you're able, we'll move out to the plantation."

Matthew swung his head to stare at her. "We can't stay here," he protested. "You've got school! You're finishing your medical degree this year."

Janie looked at him calmly. "*Next* year, Matthew. I telegrammed the school to let them know I'm withdrawing from this term. They understand completely. They already sent a return telegram saying it was fine for me to finish next year."

Matthew ground his teeth, frustration welling up inside him. "I'm sorry," he muttered as his hands tightened into fists.

Janie took one of them and gently released his fingers. "Sorry for what? For living? You would rather have left me a widow? Left your son without a father?" She lowered herself to sit on the bed so she could gaze into his eyes. "Matthew, you are the most important thing in the world to me, and to Robert. Medical school means nothing to me without you in my life." She stroked his hand. "Wouldn't you do the same for me if I was the one hurt?"

Matthew knew she was right but hated that he was keeping her from her dream. "What about the clinic you and Carrie are starting here in Richmond?"

"We'll start it next spring after I graduate," she said casually. Her voice grew firmer. "Matthew, all I care about is that you're well. All I care about is that you didn't die beneath that rubble. Sixty-two men *died,* Matthew. You lived."

Matthew stared at her in horror. "Sixty-two men *died?*" He tried to conceive the depth of the tragedy. "How many were hurt?"

"Over two hundred," Janie replied. "Many will never fully recover." She forced his chin up so she could gaze into his eyes. "You *will,* Matthew. You will fully recover."

Matthew looked into her eyes and saw a wellspring of love that warmed him to the core. He knew he would face moments of frustration and anger in the months ahead, but he also knew he wouldn't have to face anything on his own. "Thank you," he whispered.

Janie leaned over and kissed him warmly. "You're welcome. Would you like to see your son now?"

There was nothing Matthew wanted more.

Chapter Twenty-Two

Rose smiled up at Jeremy as their carriage worked its way through Philadelphia's crowded streets. "We're really going to a baseball game?" The late May day was warm and balmy. A gentle breeze blowing in from the harbor carried a faint aroma of brine. Glorious blooms exploded from flowerboxes and the sidewalks were thronged with children playing hoops and hopscotch. Mothers hung laundry on narrow balconies or lounged on porch steps, gossiping with their neighbors.

"We are," Jeremy assured her. "Marietta said there was no way you were coming to visit Philadelphia without coming to a game. She'll be there with the twins when we arrive. Abby, Carrie and Frances will be there too." He paused. "Are you sure you don't want to go by the house first? You must be tired after your long train ride." He eyed her with concern.

"I'm fine," Rose assured him. "It's my first time off the plantation in a while. I'm thrilled to be here, and I don't want to miss a thing."

"A baseball game it is, then!"

Rose gazed at her twin's wide smile. "You really do love baseball, don't you?"

"Are you surprised?"

"Nothing you do *surprises* me," she teased. "I just never knew you were interested in sports."

"Neither did I," Jeremy replied. "There really wasn't much opportunity during the war, and since then, most of my time's been spent working to get all the factories going. Until I met Octavius Catto, I wouldn't have said I even cared about baseball at all. Now, it seems to have become a passion."

"Because of the game or because of the political aspect?" Rose asked, thinking about Marietta's recent letters to her.

"Both," Jeremy responded instantly. "I love the game itself, but it also helps that Octavius is so committed to racial equality and is using baseball as a platform."

"How is he doing that?" Rose asked, curious how a game could be a political pawn.

"Baseball is becoming quite the national sport," Jeremy answered. "In the beginning, it was largely restricted to the Northeast and the Midwest, but the war changed all that. Both Confederate and Union soldiers played baseball at their camps. It seems like every soldier was exposed to it. Even prisoners of war used the game to pass time. Now baseball is played all over the country, with hundreds of leagues in competition."

Jeremy pulled the carriage to a stop to avoid a child darting out in front of them after a rolling hoop. "Be careful!" he called, and then returned to what he'd been saying. "When teams with black players were barred from the National Association of Baseball Players, Octavius decided to start his own team. They play against other black teams, but last year they did something never done before."

Rose listened avidly, caught by the passion in Jeremy's voice.

"Octavius negotiated a game between the Pythians and the Philadelphia Olympics team. The Olympics are an all-white club. The Pythians lost the game, but they played well and gained a lot of respect. It was the first time ever that a black team had played a white team. It forced the white players and the spectators to rethink equality issues, and Octavius has developed a friendship with some of the white players."

"Is that the only time it's happened?" Rose asked. "The only time a black team has played a white team?"

"No. Once the barrier was broken, there have been a few more games played, though it certainly isn't common. We're hoping that will change in time."

"It's ridiculous that white teams won't allow black players," Rose stated. It was one more example of segregation issues that were springing up all over the country.

"Well, at least not if they *claim* to be black," Jeremy said wryly.

"What do you mean?"

"There are more than a few blacks playing on major league teams," Jeremy explained, "but they don't identify as black. They say they're Indians, or that they're from South or Central America. Mulattos that can pass as white, do. There are even more blacks playing for minor leagues and amateur teams. As long as they conceal the truth of their race, they're welcome on the teams."

Rose gazed at Jeremy's blond hair and blue eyes. "Do you regret not playing for a white team?"

"Not a bit," Jeremy replied immediately. "As much as I love the game, I began playing as a way to create a community here in Philadelphia that would accept *both* the twins, not just Marcus. Sarah Rose has become the unofficial darling and mascot of the team. I love that her life has as many black people in it as white people."

"And Marcus?" Rose asked. "How do they feel about a white baby? Prejudice is not just limited to white people, you know."

"I do know that," Jeremy assured her. "He's a baby. They love him. And, since Sarah Rose adores him, that seems to have resolved everything. All the players would do anything for her. I'm hoping the fact that Marcus will grow up around the team will protect him from being looked down on. In the meantime, I have many white friends, as well. I'm doing to best I can to keep things in balance."

"And the players? How do they feel about *you* playing?"

"They adore Sarah Rose, but it took them a little longer to trust me," Jeremy admitted. "They've been treated badly by white people all their lives. As much as they loathe segregation, they also like the safety of an all-black team. They were suspicious about me being there in the beginning. They also had a difficult time believing I'm mulatto," he added drily, as he rolled his blue eyes.

Rose grinned, suddenly understanding the true purpose of her attending the game. "So, you're eager for me to experience baseball, but you're more eager for them to meet your very black twin."

"That could be true," Jeremy agreed with a smile. "I moved to Philadelphia to find acceptance and an easier life for my children. I'm not below doing anything that will help to accomplish that. I didn't think you would mind."

Rose sobered. "I miss having y'all in Richmond so much, but I realize you felt you had to come to

Philadelphia to keep your family safe. I'll do whatever you need to make things easier for my niece and nephew."

"Just be your charming self," Jeremy said with a smile. "That's all it will take to win them over."

Rose wasn't sure it would be that easy, but she was excited to see everyone. She hadn't seen Marietta and the twins since Christmas.

"We're here," Jeremy announced, turning the carriage under a spreading arch. "Welcome to Fairmount Park. This is where we play."

Rose gazed around in delight as the curving drive led them beneath lush trees creating a blanket of shade. "This is absolutely beautiful! I had no idea Philadelphia had a park like this." She gasped when they rounded a curve. "What river is that?" The swiftly flowing waters danced like sparkling diamonds in the sunshine.

"That's the Schuylkill River," Jeremy explained. "Back in 1812, the city purchased this land to protect Philadelphia's water supply and preserve some natural area because they realized the city was going to become very industrialized. In the beginning, all this land was owned by wealthy Philadelphians who built their estates out here."

"I'm so glad Philadelphia did this," Rose said enthusiastically. "I appreciate people who have the vision to see into the future."

"The original size has grown considerably," Jeremy continued. "They've bought more and more land in order to expand it. Now it stretches five miles on either side of the river. It's definitely a Philadelphia treasure. All the baseball teams play here."

"No wonder you love the game so much," Rose observed. "I would play myself if I were able to play in such a beautiful park." As they wound down the graveled roads, she spotted arbors and arches, a beautiful, domed band house perched above a dam that created a waterfall in the river, and another nestled in a grove of trees. She could imagine sitting outside on warm evenings, listening to concerts. "Watch out," she said over the sound of the rushing water. "Someday, women will play baseball, too. Once we get the right to vote, of course!"

*****

Marietta waved enthusiastically when she spotted them approaching the ball field. "Rose!"

Laughing, Rose rushed forward to hug her sister-in-law and then scooped the twins up to kiss their plump cheeks. "I can't believe how much they've grown in just five and a half months!" she exclaimed.

Jeremy waved to everyone and went to join the team.

Sarah Rose reached up her hand and patted Rose's cheek. "Auntie Rose!"

Rose laughed with delight. "She couldn't say that at Christmas."

Marietta rolled her eyes. "They're still limited to two or three-word sentences, but they talk all the time now, even if I still can't understand most of it. They're best friends, but they also compete for the most attention. The only time the house is quiet is when they finally collapse into sleep."

Marcus leaned over to stare into her face. As if to prove his mother right, he was demanding equal attention. "Auntie Rose!" he cried.

"Hello, Marcus," Rose said solemnly as she kissed his cheek again. "You are so handsome."

While Marcus beamed, she turned back to his sister. "Hello, Sarah Rose," she said softly, seeing so much of herself staring back at her. She suspected this adorable baby was the spitting image of her namesake when she was a child. Rose wished with all her heart that Sarah had lived long enough to know her grandchildren. "You are a beautiful little girl."

Sarah Rose smiled and clapped her hands. "Boo'ful!"

Marcus squirmed to be let down. "Dada baseball," he said insistently.

Rose laughingly obeyed.

Marietta patted the empty space next to her on the wooden bench. "Sit down. Abby, Carrie and Frances went to talk to someone. They'll be back soon."

Rose stared out at the green field where nine men stood. "Are you going to explain this game to me? I've seen some of the men playing it around the plantation, but I've never paid any attention."

Marietta nodded. "It's a rather fascinating game that has, from what I'm told, changed a lot in recent years. The overall purpose of the game is to score the most runs. The players hit the ball with what they call *the ash*. The ash is a bat made from ash wood. They try to advance to different bases without getting out. Runs are scored when a hitter makes it all the way to home plate."

Rose eyed the men standing out on the field. "How do they get the batters out?"

"Until last year, it happened in one of two ways. They threw the ball to the base where the runner is trying to get to, before he gets there, or they threw the ball at the runner and hit him."

Rose swung around to stare at her. "They throw the ball at the runner? Doesn't that hurt?"

"My feelings exactly!" Marietta responded. "Baseballs are much more painful than the big balls used in dodgeball. Evidently, the Association finally agreed it wasn't the way to treat their players if they didn't want them to get hurt, so they changed the rules to make that illegal."

A lady sitting nearby leaned over to offer more information. "They changed the rule about hitting the batter, too."

"Hitting the batter?" Rose echoed. "What do you mean?"

Marietta quickly made introductions. "Rose, this is Gail Williams. Her husband, Derrick, is the pitcher for the Pythians. Gail, this is my sister-in-law, Rose."

When Gail eyed her appraisingly, Rose knew the real reason for the offered information was an excuse to meet her. "Hello, Gail," she said warmly. "It's a pleasure to meet you." She flashed what she hoped was her most charming smile.

"It's a pleasure to meet you, too," Gail said courteously, but continued to appraise her. "Are you really Jeremy's twin?" she finally asked.

Rose nodded. "I am." She was sure Gail had heard the story but decided repeating it would only add believability to Jeremy's story. "Jeremy was sold when he was a few days old. I grew up on the plantation with my mama, who was a slave. I didn't know Jeremy existed until we found records just before the war started. I met him when the war ended."

"How did Jeremy end up looking so white?" Gail asked suspiciously. "Most mulattos look at least a little black."

"That's true," Rose agreed. "They're still trying to scientifically understand how inherited traits are passed down. For us to look so different is rare, but it certainly happens." She nodded her head to indicate Marcus and Sarah Rose. "My niece and nephew are perfect examples. Sarah Rose isn't as dark as I am, but she certainly doesn't look like Marcus' twin."

Gail nodded thoughtfully. "I suppose you're right," she acknowledged and then shook her head. "I just don't understand why Jeremy would make his life more difficult by joining a black team."

Rose knew Marietta should be the one to answer that question.

"Jeremy may not look black," Marietta said, "but he has a twin that struggles with all the same things you do, Gail. He couldn't live with himself if he didn't do everything he could to change that. Equally important, we left the South because we want to make life easier for our twins."

"It's not exactly easy up here for mulattos," Gail said skeptically. "Blacks either for that matter."

"Have you spent much time in the South?" Rose asked.

"No," Gail admitted. "My parents were never slaves. I grew up in Philadelphia. It's not that I don't know plenty of blacks who are from the South, and who were slaves, but I've never experienced it." She paused. "I was lucky."

"You were," Rose agreed. "It's far harder in the South to be mulatto. The KKK and other vigilante groups seem to have a special vendetta against what they call half-breeds. It's as if a mulatto is viewed with extra hatred because they're proof you can't easily separate the races. They're afraid mixed-race children will dilute their white superiority."

"The twins would have been in far greater danger in Richmond," Marietta added. "Jeremy would have been in more danger as well, if he'd taken the children out in public. Life is hard enough without giving the twins that extra burden."

Gail nodded slowly. "I see your point." Then she flashed a warm smile. "Welcome to Philadelphia, Rose. Your brother is becoming quite the baseball player. My husband says he's a wonderful shortstop."

"I'm glad," Rose answered. She had no idea what a shortstop was, but her mind was focused on something Gail had said earlier. "Will you tell me what you meant about hitting the batter? It can't possibly be a good thing."

Gail grinned. "There's a new rule in place for this season. Until this year, it was perfectly legitimate for the pitcher to hit the batter with a pitch, or for the batter to attempt to hit the pitcher with a pitched ball by hitting it back at him. Because the pitcher is so close to home plate, some players are very good at smacking it back at them."

Rose stared at her as she absorbed the statement. "Why? I thought baseball was a sport. It sounds like something quite barbaric."

Gail laughed. "I agree with you. Derrick has come home with more than a few bruises from being whalloped with a ball that was hit right back at him. He's also been hit by a pitcher more than his fair share."

"But the rule has changed?" Marietta prompted. "We don't want Rose to hate baseball before she even sees a game."

"It's changed," Gail assured them. "At least some." She hastened to explain. "Up until now, hitting the batter or hitting the pitcher with a hit ball has been part of the game strategy, as a means of intimidation."

Rose fought to control the look of distaste on her face. Gail's husband was the pitcher, after all. Jeremy had asked her to be charming, not combative. She wasn't going to start this new relationship by saying she thought the strategy was stupid.

Gail pulled out a pamphlet, opened it to find what she was looking for and began to read. *"All balls delivered by the pitcher which are not within the fair reach of the striker, such as balls pitched over the striker's head, or on the ground in front of home base, or pitched over the head of the batsman, or pitched to the side opposite to that which the batsman strikes from, or which hit the striker while he is standing in his proper position, shall be considered unfair balls, and must be called when delivered."*

"Interpretation, please?" Marietta implored. "Pretend we know hardly anything."

"Which should be easy to do since it's true," Rose quipped.

Gail smiled. "Basically, it means that if a pitcher throws a pitch that meets any of those criteria, they will be penalized by having a *ball* called on them. If they throw three unfair balls, including hitting the batter, the batter immediately goes to first base."

"Batter up!"

Gail turned toward the field as cheers and calls erupted from the spectators. "Jeremy is the first batter. It's time to watch the game."

"Is my brother a good hitter?" Rose asked, caught up in the excited atmosphere despite her lack of knowledge.

"He's very good!" Marietta said proudly. "Octavius says he's a natural ball player. He even told Jeremy he could probably play professionally."

"For a living?" Rose asked in amazement.

Marietta laughed. "Don't worry. As much as Jeremy loves baseball, he also loves building the factories. He's not going to stop doing that."

Relieved, Rose turned to watch the game. She admired the uniforms both teams wore, the white fabric glistening impressively in the sunlight. The Pythians had black letters on their uniforms; the Excelsiors, which she had learned from Jeremy was the first black baseball team in Philadelphia, had red letters sewn on.

Her relief was short-lived. Jeremy stepped up to the plate, his blond hair glimmering in the sunshine, standing in stark contrast to all the black curls of every other man on the field. The opposing pitcher wound up and threw the ball. Jeremy stepped back quickly, but not quickly enough to avoid the ball hitting his shoulder. "Hey!" she yelled, as she saw him grimace. "You can't do that!"

Jeremy glanced her way, but simply flashed her a smile and got ready for the next pitch.

Rose waited for the umpire to call a ball, but he remained silent. She turned to Gail. "Why isn't he calling a ball? That man hit my brother!"

Marietta was the one to answer. "The first pitch doesn't count, Rose."

Rose stared at her. "Doesn't count? What do you mean?"

"They don't count the first pitch as anything," Marietta explained. "It's only the rest of the pitches that will either be balls or strikes."

Rose shook her head with disbelief. "So, the pitcher can decide to hit any batter he wants with the first pitch, and there will be no penalty?"

"Yes," Marietta said reluctantly. "I don't like it either, but there's nothing to be done. It's how the game is played."

Rose whipped her head around when she heard the crack of wood against the ball. Jeremy dropped the bat and sprinted toward first base. She saw the ball flying over the heads of the players.

"Go, Jeremy!" Marietta yelled.

"Great hit, Jeremy!" Gail cheered.

Rose smiled as a chorus of cheers rose up around her and the bench erupted into calls for her brother. She watched him round first base, amazed he could run so fast. "Go, Jeremy!" she screamed, clapping loudly. "Great hit!"

Jeremy continued running, until he finally came to a stop on a white square.

"He hit a triple!" Marietta cried with delight, and then laughed when she saw the confusion on Rose's face. "That means he got to third base."

Her excited eyes told Rose that Jeremy had done well, as well as revealing that the white squares were called bases. "Way to go!" she yelled again.

"I see you've become a baseball fan."

Rose laughed when she heard Carrie's voice over her shoulder. "Jeremy hit a triple," she said proudly.

"I see that," Carrie replied. "It was a wonderful hit! Jeremy is quite good." She chuckled when Rose lifted a brow. "I come to every game I can," she admitted. "Frances doesn't want to miss even one."

Frances ran up, her long braids bouncing against her back. "Did you see Jeremy hit that ball, Rose?" she demanded. "That was an excellent lead-off hit for the beginning of the game. He's in a good scoring position. I bet the next batter will bring him in."

Rose hugged her closely and then held her back. "I'm not sure I understand a thing you just said, but obviously you're a fan."

Frances nodded eagerly. "Oh, yes. I'm trying to talk Daddy into taking me to see the game between the Cincinnati Red Stockings and the Brooklyn Atlantics in a few weeks. They're playing at the Capitoline Grounds in Brooklyn, New York!"

Rose stared at her with amusement. "You sound as passionate as my brother. Is there something in

Philadelphia's water supply that makes one a baseball fanatic?

Frances laughed and turned back to the field when they heard the sound of another bat cracking a ball. "Go, Derrick!" she screamed. "Run! Run!" She jumped up and down, clapping her hands wildly. "Jeremy scored a run! Great job, Jeremy!" She turned back to Rose. "I have to go now, Rose. Some friends are waiting for me." She spun around to run off, but then looked back. "I'll see you at the house for dinner!"

Carrie laughed helplessly. "I do believe she loves the game of baseball more than any of the men out on the field. She talks about it at home and reads all the papers so that she knows what's going on with the games."

"Hence, her desire to go to Brooklyn?"

Carrie nodded. "Anthony has promised her a trip to New York City this summer. She doesn't know yet that he's taking her to the game. If he told her now, she probably wouldn't sleep a wink until they leave."

"I promise to keep the secret," Rose vowed and then turned back to the field. "Explain more of this game to me."

"You're over the fact that the pitcher can hit the batter with the ball with the first pitch?" Marietta teased.

Rose smiled serenely. "As long as I know the batter has the freedom to hit the pitcher. It seems only fair."

All the women laughed loudly as the next batter stepped up to home plate.

Rose looked around after the next player struck out. "Where is Abby?"

"She ran into a group of women who work at the factory where she fired the manager. They started clapping when they saw her and told her she had restored their hope for the future. When I left to come find you, she was busy listening to all their stories," Carrie replied.

"Giving them advice, I suppose?" Rose wasn't surprised.

"When I left, she was promising to meet with all of them at the factory before she goes back to Richmond," Carrie answered fondly. "She wants to find out what they want to accomplish with their lives."

Rose smiled. "She told me about her experience in New York City. When we get back home from this trip, we're going to start a Bregdan Women meeting at the schoolhouse. We already have a list of women who want to come. They're quite excited."

"That's wonderful!" A glint appeared in Carrie's eyes. "You're going to love the woman coming to the first one here in Philadelphia..." Her voice trailed off.

Rose waited, but no more information was forthcoming. "Who is it?"

Carrie shook her head. "You're going to have to wait to find out," she teased. "I'm not telling you." She paused. "You're going to be incredibly happy, though."

Rose knew by the bright light in Carrie's eyes that she was probably right. She also knew her best friend wouldn't reveal a secret until she was ready. She turned back to the game. "Doesn't it hurt to catch that ball with bare hands?"

"I suppose," Carrie replied. "It doesn't seem to bother them too much. Of course, I've treated a few broken fingers since Jeremy started playing. He sends all the injured players to me."

"Other than striking out, how do players get out?" Rose's desire for knowledge about baseball was growing.

"They can be thrown out by someone getting the ball to the base before they reach it," Gail explained. "They're also out if they hit the ball and someone catches it, either in the air or on the first bounce."

Rose continued asking questions, already in love with the game of baseball. She hoped there would be another game before she returned to Virginia.

*****

Rose hugged Anthony when she arrived at their house later for dinner. Jeremy and Marietta decided to stay home because the twins were worn out after their long afternoon at the ball field. Rose was tired, but didn't want to miss one thing during her visit. "You certainly don't look like a man who almost died from a balcony collapse." She eyed him carefully.

"I'm as good as new," Anthony responded. "Did you see Matthew before you caught the train here? The letters from him and Janie sound positive, but I need to know from you that they're truthful."

"They're truthful," she assured him. "Of course, he's going crazy with those leg casts on, but he's choosing to make the best of it, and May is spoiling him like crazy."

"Now I understand," Anthony said sagely. "Janie is an amazing woman, but she's not much better at cooking than Carrie is."

"I heard that!"

Anthony laughed as Carrie's voice floated in from the dining room. "I love you, dear."

"And I love that you hired us a wonderful cook," Carrie called back. "I don't know what we would do without Deirdre."

Anthony winked at Rose. "It's true. Carrie would be treating all her family members for symptoms of starvation if Deirdre didn't feed us."

"I can still hear you!"

Rose laughed, tucked her hand into the crook of Anthony's elbow and headed for the dining room. "What's for dinner?"

Deirdre appeared at the kitchen door, her pink cheeks flushed from the heat. "You must be Rose. I've heard so many wonderful things about you."

Rose walked over to take her hand. "And you as well, Deirdre. I'm so glad to meet you. Frances has told me so much about Minnie, too. Is she here?"

"The two of them are upstairs playing," Deirdre confirmed. "When I'm working late, she's here with me. Her brothers and sisters are older, so they're fine on their own until I get home, but she always wants to be with Frances."

Frances raced into the dining room in time to hear Deirdre's statement. "That's because Minnie is my best friend," she announced to Rose. She slid to a stop in front of Deirdre. "May I please have some cookies to take upstairs?"

"You may not," Deirdre said firmly. "You know we're about to have dinner. You'll do nothing but spoil your appetite, young lady. You and Minnie need to stop playing and get cleaned up." She waved her hand toward the stairs. "Now."

Frances peered up at Rose. "I do nothing except get ordered around," she said morosely, her eyes dancing with laughter.

"That's the way it's supposed to be," Rose answered lightly. "When you're old, you can do your share of ordering around. Until then, one of the benefits of getting older is being able to do the bossing."

Frances rolled her eyes, giggled, and dashed back up the stairs. "We'll be right down," she called over her shoulder.

"I love that little girl," Deirdre said fervently. "I still can't believe Carrie plucked her out of an orphanage. She is truly something special."

"That she is," Rose agreed. She lifted her nose and sniffed. "What is that amazing smell? I'm famished."

Deirdre stared at her and then laughed. "*Famished?* You sure enough do sound like a teacher." Her Irish brogue rolled off her tongue. "I suppose that's a fancy word that means you're starving to death."

Rose laughed. "It does, but you're still not telling me what we're having for dinner. I'm hungry... Starving... About to faint... I need to be put out of my misery."

"I fixed a big pot of Irish stew," Deirdre told her. "Lots of beef and lots of potatoes. Course, before we had to leave the Old Country, there was no beef to be had, and the potatoes were almost gone as well." Sadness filled her eyes. "I like America fine, but I'll always miss the emerald beauty of Ireland," she confessed. "Of course, if we hadn't been forced to leave, I wouldn't be here cooking, and my children wouldn't be going to school. I suppose it all worked out for the best." She paused thoughtfully, her bright blue eyes looking off into the distance, as if she could span the ocean. "I'm learning that sometimes the worst situations can produce the best results. You just have to survive the process."

Rose knew just how right she was.

"Is Rose here?"

Rose laughed when she heard Lillian's voice ring through the house. "I'm right here!" She grabbed Lillian in a hug as soon as she entered the dining room. "It's wonderful to see you. How are you?" From the look of peaceful happiness on Lillian's face, she already had her answer.

"Leaving Virginia was the right decision for me," Lillian answered. "I love Philadelphia and I love my new job teaching at the Quaker School."

Rose hugged her again. "I'm very happy for you, Lillian."

"And I'm happy for *me*," Frances announced as she and Minnie entered the room. "I love having Lillian here."

"Except for the fact that Lillian always corrects your language like Rose used to," Minnie reminded her slyly.

Rose laughed. "You must be Minnie. It's a pleasure to meet you."

Minnie gazed up at her with large blue eyes that were the perfect complement to her red hair and freckled face. "'Tis a pleasure to be meeting you too, Miss Rose," she said sweetly.

Frances rolled her eyes. "She really lays on the Irish brogue when she wants to impress someone," she explained. "I don't know why, though. The Irish don't get treated so good here in Philadelphia."

"Well," Rose said automatically.

Frances sighed dramatically. "Two teachers in one house. It's not fair." She corrected her statement. "The Irish don't get treated very *well* in Philadelphia."

Rose leaned down to gaze into Minnie's elfin face. "I'm sorry if you ever get treated badly." She knew the story of how Carrie had taken care of the little girl after her scalp had almost been torn from her head by one of the factory machines. Deirdre's job as Carrie's cook had freed her children from slave labor in the factory.

Minnie shrugged. "You get used to it," she replied. "Besides, I don't care how badly people treat me as long as I don't have to work in that factory anymore. I can hardly believe I'm in school."

Lillian laid a hand on Minnie's shoulder. "She's my star pupil," she said proudly.

Minnie's eyes shone with happiness. "I learn at school, and then Lillian comes home to make sure I do my schoolwork right when I'm here. Frances helps me, too."

"That's wonderful," Rose said softly, just as she heard the front door close again.

Minnie grinned. "That's Ben. He's my friend!" She turned and ran from the room.

Rose smiled when Ben's voice rang through the house.

"There's my girl! How are you today, Minnie?"

"Great! I'm glad you're home! How was work today?"

"I can't complain," Ben said good-naturedly. "Is Rose here?"

"In the dining room," Minnie replied. "She sure is pretty, Ben. Too bad she has a husband. You need someone like her!"

"Have you ever seen Rose's husband, Minnie?"

"No," Minnie admitted.

"He makes me look like a child," Ben told her. "I wouldn't mess with any other man's wife, but I certainly wouldn't mess with Moses' wife. Moses is the biggest man I've ever seen. You can keep looking for a wife for me, but make sure they don't have a husband."

"All right," Minnie replied. "I believe you deserve a good wife, but right now we have to eat. Mama is almost done with dinner."

"Then lead me to it," Ben answered. His eyes were laughing when he entered the dining room, Minnie's hand tucked firmly in his. "It's wonderful to see you, Rose. Make sure you tell Moses I turned down Minnie's suggestion that I should be your husband."

"I'll do that," Rose said with a laugh as she marveled at the diversity of people living together in one home. It gave her hope for the rest of America.

Chapter Twenty-Three

Carrie shivered with excitement. After months of dreaming about a Bregdan Women meeting, the first one was about to happen. Following in the example of the Sorosis Club in New York City, she'd made luncheon arrangements at James W. Parkinson's Café on Chestnut Street, a Philadelphia treasure. The restaurant, housed in a three-story, elegant brick building was the perfect location for their meeting.

Abby clapped her hands when they arrived at the entrance. "This really is an excellent place to begin Bregdan Women. I ate here many times when I lived in Philadelphia. The food is wonderful and the atmosphere is superb."

"Did you know that Parkinson won a cook-off with New York's Delmonico Restaurant in 1851?" Carrie asked, pleased to have dug up a bit of trivia.

"I didn't," Abby answered with surprise.

Carrie nodded. "They faced off on a seventeen-course dinner that took twelve hours. Parkinson was given a standing ovation when it was over. The papers later called it the *Thousand Dollar Dinner*."

Abby stared at her. "It cost one thousand dollars to produce the meal?" she asked with disbelief.

"That's what I'm told," Carrie replied. "Parkinson's was just an ice cream shop until the challenge. It quickly grew into the restaurant we're eating at now after he won the cook-off."

"I never knew that history," Abby murmured, looking at the building with fresh appreciation. "What a brave thing to do."

"No braver than you taking over your deceased husband's clothing factories," Carrie responded. "You've taught me so much about being willing to take risks to achieve what you want in life."

Abby squeezed her hand. "You already knew how to do that, my dear."

"Perhaps I had it in me, but it was you that believed in me and gave me the courage to take many of the steps," Carrie argued. "Thank you."

Abby squeezed her hand more firmly. "And now we're going to start a new adventure together. Are you ready?"

*****

Carrie stood at the front of the banquet room, looking out over the twenty women she'd invited to the first Bregdan Women meeting. Abby, Rose, Marietta and Lillian all gave her warm smiles. Elizabeth Gilbert and Florence Robinson, two of her housemates when she'd first started medical school, were deep in conversation. They were both physicians now. Faith Jacobs, the elderly woman who had been Biddy Flannagan's best friend and housekeeper for thirty years, and who now ran the foundation that distributed Biddy's wealth, was watching her with glowing pride.

It was the new women she had invited, however, that made her so excited. She was eager to hear all their stories, but she was waiting on one woman who had telegraphed to say she would be a little late but was most certainly coming. A sound in the hallway alerted Carrie that the wait was almost over.

When she saw a slim, well-dressed black woman slip through the back door, she raised her hand to get everyone's attention. "Welcome to the first meeting of Bregdan Women," Carrie began. She smiled warmly at Faith. "We owe the name of our group to a very special woman named Biddy Flannagan. She is no longer with us, but her legacy will live on forever. When I first met Biddy, she introduced me to the Bregdan Principle." Carrie lifted up the sheet of paper she was holding. "I'd like to begin today by reading it to you."

The Bregdan Principle

*Every life that has been lived until today is
a part of the woven braid of life.*

*It takes every person's story
to create history.*

*Your life will help determine
the course of history.*

*You may think you don't have
much of an impact.
You do.*

*Every action you take will reflect
in someone else's life.*

Someone else's decisions.

Someone else's future.

Both good and bad.

Carrie paused and let the words sink into the minds of every woman there. Reading the words out loud made the first meeting even more poignant. She could feel Biddy's presence and could almost see her beautiful, glowing blue eyes smiling at her.

"The idea for this meeting came from a group of women on the bank of the James River this past New

Year's morning as we watched the sun rise. We realize the power of women joining together for the purpose of making a difference. We vowed to share the Bregdan Principle with as many women as we can, and we came up with the idea of starting a group where women could meet other women who are living out the Bregdan Principle." She smiled. "Today is the first meeting of Bregdan Women!"

Applause broke out across the room and smiles lit every face.

Carrie nodded her appreciation. "Every woman here is an example of what being a Bregdan Woman is all about, but there is one in particular I want all of you to hear. Her name is Fannie Jackson. I could give her a glowing introduction, but she assured me she would rather tell her own story." Carrie beckoned Fannie forward, loving the look of awed shock on Rose's face.

Fannie Jackson moved gracefully to the front of the room. "Thank you so much for having me today," Fannie began. "It is truly a wonder to look around the room and see so many great women all in one place. Society may try to limit what we can do, but as long as we all stick together for support and encouragement, there is nothing that can stop us."

Murmurs of agreement rippled throughout the room.

"I was born a slave in Washington, DC on October fifteenth, 1837," Fannie began. "I lived as a slave until my aunt, Sarah Orr Clark, was able to purchase my freedom when I was twelve years old. She worked for six dollars a month and yet somehow, she saved one hundred and twenty-five dollars to buy my freedom. Even though I was still a child, I knew I wanted to do important things with my life. I just didn't know how to do it. My days of being a slave were over, but all I knew how to do was serve. I worked as a servant for the author George Henry Calvert for ten years. Because of his love for literary works, he gave me access to his library, and I attended as much school as I could. His wife was especially wonderful to me, and gave me many opportunities that I'm sure other girls in my situation never received. We're still close."

Fannie smiled. "When I was almost twenty-three, I had earned enough money and gained enough knowledge to enroll as a student at Oberlin College in Ohio. You might not know that Oberlin College was the very first school in America to accept both black and female students. I was thrilled to be there, but I wanted more than what they offered women students at the time," she continued. "The faculty didn't forbid a woman to take the gentleman's course, but they certainly didn't advise it. I don't think they believed we were capable," she said in a stage whisper.

Carrie laughed with everyone else, enthralled with the story Fannie was telling.

"I chose the gentleman's course of study. There was plenty of Latin and Greek, and as much mathematics as one could shoulder." She smiled brightly. "I loved every minute of it. All was going smoothly until..." She paused dramatically. "Until I was called before the faculty in my junior year. I discovered it was custom that forty students from the junior and senior classes were employed to teach the preparatory classes. The faculty informed me that I was to have a class, but they warned me that if the students rebelled, they wouldn't force them to keep me as their teacher. It had nothing to do with my being a woman; they simply weren't sure the students would want to be taught by a *black* woman. In the history of the college, no preparatory class had ever been taught by a black woman. It wasn't because they were discriminatory, rather, it was that teaching was reserved for those who did the gentleman's course of study. I was rocking the boat by being both female *and* black."

Women all over the room shook their heads, leaning forward in their seats so they wouldn't miss a word.

"They didn't rebel," Fannie said. "In fact, I realized teaching was my passion. My class grew so much they had to divide it. I loved every minute of teaching those preparatory classes. At the same time I was teaching those classes, freed slaves started arriving from the South. They were hungry to learn, so I taught an evening course in reading and writing for them as well. I loved every minute of it because they were so passionate."

Carrie thought about Rose's secret school hidden deep in the woods of Cromwell Plantation. She could hardly wait for these two women to meet and talk.

"I graduated with my Bachelor's degree five years ago, in 1865," Fannie told them. "That same year, I took a position as the principal of the Ladies' Department at the Philadelphia Institute for Colored Youth. A year earlier, the Institute had contacted Oberlin College looking for a black woman who could teach Greek, Latin and mathematics. They answered that they had just the right person, but that the Institute would have to wait a year for me because I had to graduate. They agreed and sent me a surprise gift of money to make my last year much easier. When I arrived at the Institute, I taught Greek, Latin and mathematics—all the subjects it was at first doubted I could even learn," she said, laughter lighting up her eyes.

Chuckles rang out around the room.

"I'm happy to say I was appointed principal of the Institute just last year," Fannie continued. "I am the first black woman to become a school principal anywhere in the country."

She smiled when the room exploded with applause, but quickly held up her hand for silence. "I'm telling you this, not to boast, but to let you know that a woman can do anything she wants to do if she wants it badly enough, and if she's willing to work hard enough for it." She paused. "You also have to be willing to be in an uncomfortable position," she said firmly.

Carrie watched her closely, wanting to understand exactly what she was saying. Though Fannie was only thirty-three years old, she had earned the right to be heard by what she'd accomplished.

"No one thought a woman could succeed in a man's course of study. I had to show them they were wrong, and I had to be willing to be the only woman in my class. Some of the men were encouraging, but many of them fully anticipated I would fail, so they ignored me. That was all right with me, ladies. I was there to learn, not to become part of some male club."

Fannie gazed around the room. "All of you are here because you don't want to be a typical woman who goes along with the flow of societal expectations. I applaud each one of you. It takes courage, and it takes determination. There are countries in the world where women don't have to fight quite so hard to prove they're equal, but we don't happen to live in one of them. So be it. You can use that as an excuse to accomplish less than what you're capable of, or you can use it as a challenge to be an example for every female who is watching you."

She paused to take a drink of water, and then finished what she'd come to say. "Every day, I look out at the faces of young people who are the future of the United States. I see children who will never have to worry about being slaves. I see children who have the freedom to get a good education. I challenge them every day to use these privileges to make a difference for each generation that will follow. I'm happy to say that I'm teaching them in accordance with the Bregdan Principle. Thank you for having me today."

Warm applause followed Fannie as she walked back to her seat.

Carrie waited for quiet and then addressed the group again. "You now have the opportunity to talk amongst yourselves about what you've heard. If you're seated next to someone you already know, I would encourage you to move around to meet new women. I don't know about you, but I already know I'm going to leave here with an even greater determination to know that my life matters. To know that the legacy I leave behind will reverberate throughout generations to come."

*****

Rose wove her way through the tables and claimed a seat next to Fannie Jackson. "Thank you so much for coming, Miss Jackson. I've heard about you before today and am thrilled to have the chance to meet you. My name is Rose Samuels."

Fannie smiled. "I've heard about you as well, Mrs. Samuels."

Rose gasped. "How?"

"I'm close friends with Sojourner Truth. She's told me how remarkable you are. Carrie assured me you would be here today."

Rose opened her mouth to dispute what Fannie had said, and then stopped. "I suppose every woman in this room is remarkable," she said thoughtfully.

Fannie nodded firmly. "I completely agree. I had a close woman friend who told me that false humility is imprinted on women since birth. She convinced me there's nothing wrong with being extraordinary, and that there's nothing wrong with *knowing* you're extraordinary. The key for me is to not be prideful about what I've accomplished, but to be grateful for the chance to show what I *can* accomplish." She paused. "I can't convince other women they can be great if I don't embrace my own greatness."

Rose cocked her head. "Thank you," she said quietly. "That's a wonderful way to communicate that."

"Where are you teaching now, Mrs. Samuels?"

"Please, call me Rose."

"I'll be happy to, as long as you call me Fannie."

"Agreed," Rose said happily, still amazed she was chatting with a woman she'd admired from the moment she heard about her. She glanced up, caught Carrie watching her, and gave her a blinding smile of gratitude before turning back to Fannie. "I'm teaching at the school I began on Cromwell Plantation," Rose said. "My husband Moses is part owner, along with Thomas Cromwell. We're teaching both black and white children, as well as holding classes for adults in the area."

Fannie nodded. "How do you feel about what Virginia is doing since the ratification of their new state constitution that mandates segregated schools?"

Rose frowned. She had learned more about the new developments in the two days she'd been in Richmond before coming to Philadelphia. "I think it's another way for whites to deal with the black problem," she said bluntly. "Once the war ended, the Freedmen's Bureau created a statewide system for black children, but not for whites. It wasn't right that white children weren't being educated. Education should be available for all, but they're doing it in the wrong way."

Fannie listened intently. "What has your experience been with integrated teaching?"

"Wonderful," Rose replied. "There were certainly issues in the beginning, but now the students are all friends and they're learning from each other. The white parents have become ardent supporters and have developed friendships with black families. The whole experience has given me hope for racial healing in the South." She shook her head. "The new state constitution takes all that away because they're going to force segregation between white and black students. I applaud Virginia's commitment to free public education for all, but separating the races is going to create even more division at a time when we desperately need to find ways to build unity." She paused. "I already know that black students will pay the biggest price because they'll be provided with a lesser education."

"I fear you're right." Fannie gazed at Rose. "What do you believe is the answer?"

"I wish I knew," Rose said honestly. "I'm going to continue running my school the way I always have. I doubt the white students will be forced to leave, at least not right away. I suppose the time will come when that happens, but I also suspect our area will be one of the last to get a public school with state-paid teachers for white children." She shook her head. "I'll do all I can to build solid relationships between my students while I have the chance."

"You're worried," Fannie said perceptively.

"I am," Rose admitted. "I had such hopes when slavery ended that the South would truly change, but I see it steadily returning to its old ways. Slavery has ended, but the hatred and disdain for blacks has not. Everything possible is being done to return the control of the South to the people who took us into the war in the first place." She paused. "I believe it will get worse before it gets better," she said honestly.

"You would be welcome at any school in the North. Why don't you leave?" Fannie asked.

"We did," Rose admitted. "I dreamed of being a school administrator just like you. I wanted to teach in the North and run my own school someday."

"What happened?"

Rose shrugged. "I can't ignore the need in the South for good teachers. If I leave, how are things ever supposed to change? If every black teacher wants to teach in the North, how are we supposed to help all the children in the South?"

"Is the danger for teachers as bad as they say it is?"

Rose thought about the school burnings, the vigilante attacks and Robert's murder. "It's dangerous," she said soberly, "but there's hope." Briefly, she explained what Carrie had accomplished by treating the veterans at her clinic. "There's been no violence since January." She pushed aside the warning they had received that there would come a time when outsiders would end the uneasy truce.

Fannie turned to gaze at Carrie admiringly. "She's basically blackmailed the veterans into compliance."

Rose chuckled. "Let's say they have good reason to make sure they keep violence from happening. None of them want to go back to the relentless pain they suffered before Carrie started treating them." She turned the conversation back to Fannie. "What's it like for you being the first black woman principal?"

"I won't pretend it's been easy, but it's deeply satisfying. Coming to Philadelphia after so many years in Oberlin was quite shocking, however."

Rose understood. Oberlin was the perfect example of what society could be if everyone lived as equals, but it was nothing more than an oasis in a vast desert of reality. Oberlin College was meant to be a waystation to prepare students to go out into the world, but the transition was usually shocking. "What happened?"

Fannie shrugged. "I was in Oberlin for so long that I quite forgot about my color. I was sharply reminded when, in the middle of a nasty rainstorm, I was refused a ride on a streetcar that was only for whites. I'll never forget that long wait for a 'colored' streetcar."

Rose grimaced. "I well remember my first winter in Philadelphia after Moses and I escaped Virginia through the Underground Railroad. I lost count of the number of times passing streetcars threw slush on me as I walked down snow-covered sidewalks and sloppy roads. The streetcars were not an option."

Fannie nodded. "I'm told I should be grateful that the streetcars are available at all, instead of being outraged that they're still segregated. I prefer outrage. It's the only way things change," she said bluntly.

Rose nodded. "My brother is close friends with Octavius Catto. I know the freedom we have to ride the streetcars now is because of actions he and his friends took."

"Who is your brother?" Fannie asked.

Rose suppressed her smile. "Jeremy Anthony. He owns the Cromwell factories here in Philadelphia."

Fannie was unable to hide the surprised curiosity on her face. "Jeremy Anthony? But..."

"I know," Rose said with a smile. "He looks white. Actually, he's my twin."

"Your *twin*?"

"It's quite the story," Rose replied. Briefly, she explained the events that had led to the discovery of her twin brother. "He's playing for the Pythians as a way to make life easier for his children, but he fights for equal rights as a way to honor me and my family."

Fannie shook her head in amazement. "What a story!" she exclaimed, and then grew thoughtful. "Perhaps the reason I'm most passionate about teaching is because such prejudice is almost impossible to eradicate if it has not been loosened or fertilized by education. Ignorance makes prejudice a weed that grows without hope of being ripped out."

Rose nodded. "The longer I watch what's happening in our country, the more I realize there is nothing more frightening than ignorance in action. I've seen the difference education can make through the plantation school, but it's nothing more than a drop in a very massive ocean of prejudice."

"Perhaps the drop is larger than you will ever realize," Fannie replied. "You never know who is sitting in your classroom. Every day when I look out at my students, I wonder if I'm looking at the next Frederick Douglass...or the next Sojourner Truth..."

"Or the next Fannie Jackson," Rose said softly. "I look at my children and I wonder what they will become. I wonder what kind of country they'll live in."

"How is Felicia doing at Oberlin?" Fannie asked suddenly.

Rose stared at her. "How do you know about Felicia?"

Fannie chuckled. "Your daughter is making as big of a stir at Oberlin as you did. Besides the fact that she's brilliant, several professors have commented on how passionate she is about pursuing equal rights for blacks and women."

"For good reason," Rose said quietly. "I'm proud of her beyond words, but I also wonder if she is positioning herself for the same future as her parents."

Fannie raised her brows quizzically. "Another story?"

Rose told her how Moses had rescued Felicia after the little girl had watched both of her parents be brutally murdered in the Memphis riot four years earlier. "There's not a black child in this country who hasn't had to grow up faster than they should, but Felicia's experience was particularly horrible. She has already declared herself a Bregdan Woman."

Fannie watched her closely. "You're frightened for her."

"How could I not be?" Rose asked. "I know she's safe in Oberlin, but just like you did, she will leave and be confronted with the realities of prejudice. Despite the country's attempt at creating equality through Reconstruction, I don't believe the commitment is strong enough to carry the belief into reality."

Fannie leaned forward. "Do you really mean that?"

Rose sighed. "This is the first time I've put my belief into words," she admitted. "Unfortunately, I do mean it. The war has been over for five years, but the men who pushed us into war in the first place are already reclaiming positions of power in the South. They can't undo the Fourteenth and Fifteenth Amendments, but the acts of violence and intimidation to frighten blacks and white Republicans into a place of compliance are increasing. What is that going to mean? What will it lead to?" As much as she hated what she was saying, it was freeing to verbalize it with someone like Fannie Jackson.

"I realize life is very different in the South," Fannie said slowly. "I suppose I'm shielded by my life in Philadelphia." She eyed Rose keenly. "Can you see a time when you would leave the South?"

Rose shrugged. "I think about it often," she confessed. "Might the time come when I would decide to leave in order to protect my children? Perhaps. Moses and I aren't there yet. I pray the time will never come when we're forced to make that decision, because there are so many things we love about our life there, but..."

"You can't make a difference if you're not alive."

Rose was stunned by the directness of the statement, but she knew it was true. The two women exchanged a long look, knowing there was no need for further words.

*****

"Well, I'd say the first Bregdan Women meeting was a complete success," Carrie said happily as the carriage pulled away from Parkinson's Café with Carrie, Abby, Rose, Marietta and Lillian.

"I'd say you're absolutely correct," Abby replied. "I met so many fascinating women, and it was thrilling to hear the conversations going on among the attendees. It meant so much to all of them to connect with other strong women who want to make a difference. It was wonderful to watch the beginning of so many close friendships that will last for years to come."

Rose reached over to take Carrie's hand. "I can never thank you enough for inviting Fannie Jackson to attend the meeting. I have dreamed of meeting her ever since I heard about her at Oberlin."

Carrie grinned. "Watching your face when she walked to the front of the room made all the planning and secrecy worth it." She leaned back against the carriage seat. "The entire meeting, I kept thinking about when all of us were together on the bank of the James

River six months ago. You never know when a moment in your life will change things completely."

Rose gazed at her. "Do you believe the meeting today has changed your life completely?"

Carrie sobered and looked thoughtful. "Not just this meeting," she said slowly. "I realized when I watched all the interactions today how much this is needed. I understand the power of the Bregdan Principle, but I don't think I realized until today how badly women need to connect with other women." She paused and looked away.

"Which means?" Rose prompted.

Carrie swung her eyes back to meet Rose. "I'm not sure," she admitted. "I suppose I realized that today's meeting wasn't simply a culmination of our time together on New Year's Day. It felt more like..."

Abby finished the thought for her. "It felt more like a beginning."

Carrie nodded. "Yes, that's it exactly. It felt more like a beginning. It's just that I don't know where it's supposed to go from here."

"I do," Abby said.

"Women all over the country need what we experienced today," Marietta said. "Abby, you told me about the Sorosis Club in New York City. They're starting new chapters. Do you think there is a need for a different group?"

"Absolutely," Abby said. "There's room for every group that wants to empower women to be more than our society believes they can be. There's room for every group that will connect women who often feel they're alone."

"That's it," Carrie said excitedly. "All of the women I talked to today said they felt so alone in what they're doing. Going against the flow is hard and lonely, because you're also going against the norm of how other women choose to live their lives. Being able to share your experience with other women gives you the strength to keep going." She smiled at the women in the carriage. "Each one of you has played a role in helping me become a doctor. More importantly, each of you is playing a role in helping me to make choices that most other women don't make."

Rose nodded. "I know just what you mean." She looked at Abby. "You said you know where Bregdan Women is supposed to go from here. Would you care to share what you mean?"

"It's still coming together in my mind, but I think that what I began to realize in New York City is only a small part of the picture." She paused. "I'm eager to start a Bregdan Women group on the plantation with you, Rose, but..."

Carrie finished for her this time. "But you're also going to start groups in other cities."

A smile spread across Abby's face. "Yes." She shook her head. "I don't exactly know what that means yet, but I know the idea has ignited a passion in me that running the factories never did. Oh, I loved growing the factory business, but it was more because it was a challenge to prove to men I could do it. This is different because it ignites a true passion that seems to touch the very core of who I am."

"So much for retirement," Marietta said wryly.

"Well, she has retired from the factories," Rose said quickly. "Perhaps her retirement was simply meant to free her to pursue a new adventure."

"Exactly," Abby said with a broad smile. "I'll still spend most of my time on the plantation with Thomas, but that won't keep me from traveling. We've talked about wanting to visit other cities together while we still can. I think it will be tremendous fun to do it together."

Carrie smiled. "You make it sound very appealing. Perhaps I'll retire, too."

Abby laughed. "Retirement is not an option for you, my dear. At least not yet. Think of how many people are waiting for you to bring all your new surgical skills back to Virginia." Her eyes swung to Rose. "And you still have so many children and people to educate. Don't even *think* about retirement."

Rose knew Abby was teasing, but she hadn't been able to stop thinking about her conversation with Fannie. "What if the time comes when I'm supposed to retire from the South?" she asked.

Silence fell over the carriage.

Carrie was the first to break it. "What do you mean, Rose?"

Rose struggled to put her thoughts into words. "What if the time comes when the South is simply too dangerous for my family to stay? All of you know that Reconstruction isn't achieving what it was meant to achieve. How bad will it get with Klan and vigilante violence? How long will it be before the plantation is attacked again? What happens if they target Moses? And Thomas? And Anthony? It's happening all over the South." She fell silent as emotions churned in her gut.

"I know you're afraid," Abby said gently.

Rose shook her head. "That's the thing. I'm not feeling afraid, at least not right this moment. It's simply a reality that I'm beginning to accept. Fannie and I talked about it."

"What did she say?" Carrie asked.

"She told me I couldn't make a difference if I was dead."

Carrie took a deep breath. "I see," she said, reaching out to take Rose's hand. "I certainly can't disagree with that, but I still have hope that Reconstruction will change things in the South. Anthony told me yesterday that President Grant has just passed an Enforcement Act that was created to stop Klan activity."

"It doesn't mean much," Marietta said. "I appreciate the intent that it's meant to protect the constitutional rights of citizens, but it's weak. Jeremy brought it home for me to read yesterday. The biggest problem is that it doesn't include a clause that will allow perpetrators to be punished under federal law."

Rose frowned. "Which means punishment is still up to the courts in each state. All that means is that very few people will be punished, because the courts are mostly controlled by conservatives that are too often part of the Klan themselves."

"Unfortunately, that's true," Marietta agreed. She reached out for Rose's other hand. "You know Jeremy and I will support whatever you and Moses believe is the right thing to do. It was so hard for me and Jeremy to leave Richmond, but the more I read about what is happening in the South, the more I know we made the right decision."

Rose met her eyes but didn't respond. The idea of the life she and Moses had worked so hard to build being ripped away by continued Klan violence was infuriating. She couldn't rid her mind, however, of the words Fannie had spoken.

You can't make a difference if you're dead.

Chapter Twenty-Four

Moses swung down from Champ wearily. He had been riding the fields since early that morning. The sun beginning to dip below the treetops revealed it had been a long day. He felt deep satisfaction from how well the tobacco crop was doing, but he was tired. He glanced at the house, looking forward to the meal he knew his mama would have waiting for him. Rose would be home in two days. He was glad she'd had the opportunity to go to Philadelphia, but he'd missed her.

Miles emerged from the barn and reached for Champ's reins. "I'll take care of him, Moses. You go on inside and let your mama feed you."

Moses nodded gratefully. He usually took care of Champ himself, but he was happy to relinquish that responsibility tonight. "Thank you, Miles."

The sound of hoof beats drew his attention. He watched as two riders approached. The first he recognized instantly. Franklin was the plantation manager, but also a close friend. The second man, also black, was someone he had never seen before. It was the expression on Franklin's face, though, that told him it wasn't going to be a quick conversation. He had seldom seen his friend look more serious.

Miles recognized it as well. "You go and talk to those two. I'll take care of Champ and then bring you out some food."

"Thank you." Moses took a deep breath, preparing himself mentally to face whatever was coming. His gut told him it was as serious as Franklin looked.

Franklin dismounted, beckoning the thin, narrow-faced man who was with him to do the same.

Moses watched the man's haunted eyes dart around with suspicion. "You're safe here," he said quietly.

The man swung his eyes to meet Moses'. "That's what I thought down in North Carolina," he replied, his voice a mixture of fear and anger. "I don't reckon there be any place safe in this country right now."

Moses beckoned the two men to join him on a bench under the large oak tree near the barn. Whatever the man had to say, Moses suspected he wouldn't want to share it on the house porch. "My name is Moses Samuels."

"I'm Daniel Blue," the man replied.

"Does the name mean anything to you?" Franklin asked.

Moses shook his head. "Should it?"

"Probably not," Franklin responded. "It didn't mean anything to me either until today. There's far too much going on in this country right now to keep track of things down in North Carolina." He met Moses' eyes. "You need to hear this, Moses."

"I'm listening."

Daniel took a long breath and launched into his story. "It all started back in January. I done saw some of the Klan beat a black man real bad. When I got asked to testify about it in court, I decided to do it. Some friends told me it was a real bad idea, but there be times when a man just got to do what's right."

"I agree," Moses said encouragingly, although he knew the ending of the story was going to be bad.

Daniel took another long breath and turned to stare out over the pastures. Finally, he looked back at Moses. "It was a real cold night a few weeks later that the Klan came. It was pretty late, about eleven o'clock, when they beat down my door. We was all sleeping. I woke first and went to find out what was happening. One of those hooded Klansmen shot me as soon as I walked out." He shook his head. "I wish they'd killed me," he muttered.

Moses waited, letting Daniel tell his own story.

After a long silence, Daniel continued. "My wife was pregnant. We had five other children."

Moses stiffened when Daniel said the word *had*.

"The Klan killed my wife," Daniel whispered, "then they shot three of my children." His voice caught as his eyes filled with tears. "They found my other baby hiding in the corner," he choked. "Instead of shooting him, one of the men walked up and kicked him real hard in the head." Daniel shook his head and swallowed hard.

Moses stared at Daniel, unable to comprehend what he was hearing. "They killed your entire family?" he demanded. He made no attempt to hide the tears in his eyes.

Daniel shook his head. "My oldest girl sleeps like the dead. She never heard a thing. Since she didn't run out, they didn't know she was there. They figured I was dead, too. I reckon I almost was, but they didn't quite kill me." His voice thickened with fury. "They was laughing when they walked out of my house. They boasted that what they did to my family would teach a lesson to anyone else who figured they oughta testify against the Klan." He paused. "Right before the last one walked out, he lit a pine torch and tossed it into my home. It started burning the cabin real quick. Somehow, I managed to crawl into the back room and wake up my daughter. We climbed out the back window and got away before the cabin burned plum to the ground."

Moses closed his eyes, forcing out the image of the same thing happening to his family. "How did you get here?"

"I done got real sick after they shot me," Daniel revealed. "Me and Angel, that's my daughter, snuck through the woods to a friend's house. They were real scared to take us in, but they did. The woman nursed me until I was well again. She took real good care of Angel, too. Nobody came looking for us 'cause they figured we were all dead." His eyes hardened. "When I was finally well enough to walk a fair distance again, me and Angel left. I figure we been walking about a month to get here."

"Why here?" Moses asked, astonished by what he'd heard.

"Word gets around," Daniel said. "I heard there was a place up in Virginia that treated black people right. They told me this place was owned by both a white man *and* a black man, but I don't reckon that be true."

"It's true," Moses told him. "Thomas Cromwell and I both own the plantation. I used to be a slave here."

Daniel's eyes widened.

"It's a long story," Moses said. "I can tell you another time."

Daniel looked at him hopefully. "Another time?"

Moses didn't have need for another worker, but there was no way he would turn Daniel and Angel away. "I assume you're here for work?"

"You got any?" Daniel asked hopefully.

Moses met Franklin's eyes, saw what he expected to see, and then looked back at Daniel. "I do," he said.

"Daniel and Angel can stay with Chooli and me until we get a cabin ready for them," Franklin offered.

Moses nodded. It would be best for the tiny family not to be alone. He could only imagine the nightmares and pain they lived with on a daily basis. He suspected the only reason Daniel was still alive was because he was determined to care for his only remaining child. "You'll be safe here, Daniel."

Daniel shrugged. "For now," he said. "The Klan ain't gonna stop until they've killed all of us they can. Killed us or whipped us," he said bitterly. "I reckon I know about thirty other people done been whipped by the Klan real bad. They ain't all black, neither. Some of them be white. Their crime is not hating black folks like us. The South might have lost the war, but they ain't done killing."

Moses hoped his next words were true. "Not every place is the same, Daniel. My wife teaches at the school she started here. We have both black and white students. White parents are friends with black parents. We've had bad things happen in the past, but I think those times are behind us."

Daniel stared at him with an inscrutable expression. "I hope you right, Mr. Samuels," he finally muttered. "I hope you right." Then he managed a tight smile. "I thank you for the job. I'll work real hard for you."

Moses returned the smile. "I'm counting on that," he said evenly. He hoped he wasn't making a mistake by hiring Daniel. He had seen terrible things make men so bitter that they couldn't think straight anymore. The bitterness and rage became a disease that ate them from the inside out.

He met Franklin's eyes again, knowing his unspoken message had been received when Franklin nodded slightly. His manager would keep a close eye on Daniel. If anyone could help the grieving man, it would be Chooli. Driven from her Navajo homeland and everyone she loved, she'd somehow managed to find peace and happiness in her new life.

Only time would tell if the same miracle could happen for Daniel.

*****

Matthew reached for the bar that Moses had rigged above his bed, hauled himself upward, and swung himself into his wheelchair. He had become quite adept at it in the two months since the Capitol collapse, but on this particular day, he was having a hard time fathoming two more months of limitation. They'd finally been able to move him out to the plantation the week before, cushioning his place in the wagon with mountains of blankets. He was glad to be out of the city, but he still felt like a trapped bird who'd had its wings clipped.

He was writing every day and had just sent a completed manuscript to his publisher, but he was still chafing under the restrictions. Janie was being an absolute angel, but he hated that he was keeping her from finishing her medical degree. She claimed she was grateful for the uninterrupted time they were spending as a family, but he was having a hard time believing it.

He gazed at the magnolia tree stationed just outside his window, taking a deep breath of the perfume wafting in on the breeze. White blossoms were tucked away on almost every branch. The tree always calmed him. He and Janie were staying in a room at the back of the house on the ground level so that stairs didn't have to be considered.

"Good morning," Janie said cheerfully as she walked into the room with Robert balanced on her hip.

"Daddy!" Robert cried, his round face bright with a smile.

Matthew forgot his frustration and angst as he reached for his son. "Hello, little man. How's my boy?"

Robert grinned up at him. "Ride!" he demanded.

Matthew chuckled. His son loved the wheelchair as much as he hated it. To Robert, it was nothing but a big toy that included sitting on daddy's lap. "Where to?" Matthew asked indulgently.

"Cookies!"

Matthew knew Annie must be baking again. As soon as he opened the door to his room, he could smell the tantalizing aroma of Irish oatmeal cookies. He shook his head. "If I don't get out of this chair soon, I'm going to be fat. I fear I'm well on my way. First May's cooking, and now Annie's."

"More pull-ups should take care of your new eating habits," Janie teased. "Your arm muscles have become quite impressive."

Matthew playfully flexed his arm. He was using the bar Moses had installed to do pull-ups several times a day, but there was nothing to be done about the legs he could almost feel withering away in the casts. He tried not to think about what they would look like when the heavy plaster was finally removed in late August. Dr.

Wild and Carrie had assured him he would walk again, but he wouldn't know for certain until he was standing on his own two legs.

"You have company coming in a little while," Janie announced.

Matthew raised a brow. "Company?" People on the plantation were always in and out of the house. He was certainly never lonely, but it sounded like Janie meant someone different.

"Peter Wilcher is coming," Janie informed him. "We received a telegram earlier this morning. A special courier came in from Richmond."

"Peter Wilcher!" Matthew was thrilled. He hadn't seen his friend in close to two years. "How did he know I was here?"

"He received notice from your editor at the paper. Evidently, he was trying to track you down in Philadelphia. When he got to Richmond, Micah told him you were on the plantation. Evidently, he stayed there last night and is on his way out," Janie replied. "Annie almost has breakfast finished. You've got time to eat and get ready before he arrives."

"We're having Irish Oatmeal cookies for breakfast?"

"No," Janie chuckled, "but as soon as Annie heard Peter was coming, she started baking his favorite cookies."

"Cookies!" Robert chortled, his tiny hands reaching down to push the wheels on Matthew's chair.

"You'll need some help with that," Matthew said with a laugh. "Let's go for a ride."

*****

Matthew was seated in the parlor when a knock came at the front door.

"Hello, Janie. You keep getting more beautiful, and I still don't see how in the world Matthew won your heart."

Matthew smiled at the familiar sound of his friend's voice and navigated his wheelchair around the corner into the entrance hall. "You're still dumb, and I see you haven't lost any of that New York accent," he teased.

Peter stood in front of the door, still tall and muscular, his dark brown hair almost matching his eyes. "And I see you still have a flair for the dramatic," he returned, his face full of a concern he was being careful not to voice.

Matthew waved a hand in the air. "I believe my publisher made sure I was seated where I was in the balcony of the Capitol. He thought he wouldn't get my newest book until the end of the summer. He's going to be quite pleased to receive the telegram today saying it's in the mail. I've decided to blame my broken legs on him. He does, indeed, have a flair for the dramatic."

Matthew turned his chair to move back into the parlor. "Come on in and make yourself comfortable."

Peter followed and took a seat close to him, his eyes serious. "How are you, Matthew? I was devastated to hear about your injuries, but I'm glad you weren't hurt worse."

"Or killed," Matthew said, speaking the words he knew Peter was thinking. So many good men had died in the Capitol collapse. He knew Peter had been colleagues with many of them. "After surviving riots and the explosion of the *Sultana*, did you really think a collapsing balcony was going to rid the world of me? I fear it will have to be something far more dramatic than that."

"I prefer no more drama at all," Janie stated as she followed them into the parlor. "I'm so glad you're here, but what has brought you all the way to the plantation?"

Matthew tensed when Peter looked uncomfortable. He hadn't imagined that Peter would search him out if it wasn't important, but there was something in his eyes he'd never seen before.

"I came to see for myself if Matthew is really unable to travel," Peter said lightly.

"I can assure you that's true," Janie said steadily, her eyes instantly protective. "I don't care what's going on in this country – Matthew isn't going anywhere."

"I can see that," Peter said easily. "Why don't you two tell me what's going on in Richmond? I came a long way to get news I believe I can trust."

"That's not what you're here for," Matthew said bluntly.

"Perhaps not," Peter agreed smoothly, "but I still want to know. We'll have plenty of time to talk about everything."

Annie appeared at the door to the parlor. "Does that mean you're gonna be here for a while, Mr. Peter?"

"I hope to stay for a couple of days, if it's not too much of an imposition."

"Of course not," Janie said immediately. "Everyone will be thrilled when they discover you're here. It's been far too long since we've seen you."

Peter smiled. "Wonderful! We've got a lot to catch up on."

Matthew eyed him. "Where is your baggage?"

"It's still in the carriage. I didn't want to appear too presumptuous by showing up with it at the front door."

Matthew snorted. "No one would think you traveled all the way out here without planning on staying. And since when have you ever hesitated to be presumptuous? You're a newspaper reporter."

"I suppose there could be truth to that," Peter said good-naturedly. "However, I'm learning to conceal the presumptuousness until I'm ready to go in for the kill."

Matthew chuckled. "Glad to know you're finally getting older and wiser."

"Every day, my friend. Every day."

Matthew saw the flicker in Peter's eyes and heard the heaviness in his voice. Peter was doing a good job of hiding whatever he was there to talk about, but they'd been friends for far too long for him to be able to conceal it entirely. He looked at Annie. "Would you please bring us some tea and cookies?"

"Of course, Mr. Matthew. I'll have it ready in a few minutes."

Peter lifted his nose and sniffed. "Do I smell Irish oatmeal cookies?" he asked with a hopeful smile.

Annie nodded. "I been baking ever since we got the word you were comin', Mr. Peter. I ain't forgot how much you love these cookies."

Peter held a hand to his heart. "You do know how to make a man feel welcome, Annie. Thank you."

Annie smiled and hurried back into the kitchen.

"Robert and I are going out for a walk on this beautiful morning," Janie said. "I'm going to leave you two to solve whatever problems of the world you need to solve."

Matthew's heart swelled with gratitude. Janie had said nothing earlier about going for a walk. She knew as well as he did, that Peter needed to talk about something. She was giving them the privacy for a real conversation.

Janie leaned down to kiss him softly. "See you two later."

Matthew turned to Peter as soon as the room was quiet. "Why are you here? I can tell something is bothering you."

"I'll tell you," Peter promised, "but first, I really would like to know what's going on in Richmond. I've been too preoccupied with other things to pay much attention."

Matthew knew his preoccupation must have to do with what was bothering him, but he also knew Peter wouldn't talk about it until he was ready. "Things are as crazy as they were before the Capitol collapse," he said with disgust.

"Richmond still doesn't have a mayor?"

"Well, they do if you want to call it that," Matthew responded. "I think of it as more of a forced servitude."

"Details, please."

Matthew sighed. "Two days after the collapse, the court convened in a temporary location to announce that Ellyson would be mayor, but they also announced that a popular election would be held at the beginning of June to defuse the tension in the city."

Peter cocked his head. "What were the results?"

Matthew shook his head. "We'll probably never know the *true* results. Chahoon appears to have won, but the men carrying the completed ballots from Jackson Ward—"

"Down in the Black Quarters?" Peter asked keenly.

"Yes. The black voters down there cast the largest vote for Chahoon. Anyway, the men bringing the ballots back were attacked in broad daylight and robbed of the votes."

Peter scowled. "That should have made the entire election invalid."

Matthew scowled along with him. "You would have thought so, but the Election Committee is dominated by Conservative Democrats—probably the same men who arranged the robbery. They decided to recognize only the votes that could be accounted for. Without the stolen ballots to prove Chahoon had won, they proclaimed Ellyson as our new mayor."

"So *Ellyson* is Richmond's new mayor," Peter said heavily.

"Yes, and no." Matthew smiled at the look of confusion on Peter's face. "Don't worry. Anyone in Richmond with a brain is confused as well. Once Ellyson found out about the stolen ballots, he refused to serve since he hadn't been elected honorably."

Peter stared at him. "I can only imagine what the Democrats thought after all they did to make sure he was elected. What now?"

"There will be another election," Matthew said ruefully. "Only, it won't happen until next year. Ellyson will serve as mayor until there can be another election eleven months from now. Hence, the forced servitude. I think he would love to walk away, but feels he can't leave the city without a mayor. In the meantime, things remain in chaos because no one is truly operating as the leader of the city."

"Will the new election be between Ellyson and Chahoon again?"

"No. Ellyson is truly done with politics. He'll serve for one year, but he's not interested in being in public service any longer. I believe he's seen a little too much of reality. The election will be between Chahoon and whomever the Conservatives want in office."

Peter's eyes filled with disgust. "The Conservative Democrats will stop at nothing to claim control of the South again, you know."

Matthew heard the bitter resignation in Peter's voice. "What do you mean?" he asked quietly. "What have you been doing, Peter? Where have you been?" It was time to find out what he was really doing on Cromwell Plantation.

"North Carolina," Peter replied, evidently ready to talk. "I fear, though, that what I'm experiencing there is being played out all over the South." He frowned and stared out the window.

Matthew waited, giving him time to reveal why he'd made the long trip.

"It's a mess down there," he finally muttered.

"It's a mess everywhere," Matthew responded. "It's impossible to keep up with everything that's going on in this country. Too much of it is bad."

Peter sighed. "I know." He shifted in his wingback chair and looked back at Matthew. "I'm afraid though, that what's happening in North Carolina is a harbinger of things to come all over the South. The *bad* is quickly becoming the *worst*."

"I'm listening." Matthew wondered if Peter was there for help, or simply because he needed to vent his frustration.

"Have you ever heard of Wyatt Outlaw?" Peter asked. When Matthew shook his head, Peter continued. "There's no real reason you should have. Outlaw was born a slave, but was mulatto, the son of the plantation owner and one of his slaves. Unwilling to acknowledge what he'd done, the plantation owner sold him to a tobacco farmer."

Mathew listened quietly, thinking of Rose and Jeremy. It was a story that had been played out time after time in the South.

"Outlaw escaped slavery in 1864, served in the Union Army, and then returned to Alamance County in North Carolina. He found the whole area impoverished and devastated, but he was determined to create a life there."

Peter took a breath before he continued. "Before the war, most white men in Alamance County had never owned slaves. They were subsistence farmers that just wanted to live their lives. They voted against secession, despised the Confederate government, and were drafted into the army against their will. When they came home from the war, those that did, their lives and livelihoods had been destroyed and there was no one to help them rebuild."

Matthew suspected how some of this story was going to go, because he'd heard versions of it many times.

"They resented the blacks who were getting help from the Freedmen's Bureau."

"Yes," Peter acknowledged. "The blacks were worse off than them, but at least they were getting help. In their minds, they were being punished for doing what the Confederate government ordered them to do. After the war ended, the punishment continued from the Federal government. I can't blame them for being angry and resentful, but their actions have made things worse." Peter stopped and shook his head. "Things got bad down there very quickly. Crime rates have soared."

"What about the U.S. Army?" Matthew asked. "It's their job to control that during Reconstruction."

"That's the idea," Peter said ruefully, "but there aren't enough of them, and soldiers are just humans. The whole situation is very complicated. Many of the soldiers are openly hostile to white Southerners because they believe they deserve to suffer for causing the horrible war they endured. Most of the freed blacks just want to be left alone, but there are certainly some that are lashing out with anger and violence. The soldiers tend to remain uninvolved when the whites bring their complaints to them, but most of the violence is being done by the white men, which means the soldiers are even less likely to intervene when something happens."

"You mean they're ignoring the black complaints, too?" Matthew asked. "If they believe the veterans are to blame for the war, why aren't they cracking down on them? That doesn't make sense."

"You're right," Peter admitted. "None of it makes sense. I think the whole mess is more than the soldiers bargained for, and more than they want to try to control. Even when they do step in, the courts let the white criminals go. As a result, too often they choose to remain uninvolved. There are certainly those that care, but there's simply too much violence for them to control."

"That means everyone suffers," Matthew said angrily, knowing the situation was indeed very complicated.

Peter nodded. "When things are chaotic, people start looking for a scapegoat to blame for their problems. Whites blame all their problems on blacks and Republicans. The blacks blame all their problems on Southern whites," he said. "As long as there are scapegoats, no one spends time and energy looking for a solution. They look for ways to express their anger and resentment."

Matthew watched disgust fill his friend's face again. "What happened to Outlaw?"

Peter sighed. "He was a good man. He wanted to help Alamance County rebuild. He started a chapter of the Union League and began recruiting blacks to vote and become involved politically. The Ku Klux Klan was less than pleased. Outlaw was doing a good thing, but there are freed slaves in the area that believe the only way to fight back against the KKK is to meet violence with violence. Wyatt fought against retaliation, mandating that they needed to operate within the bounds of the law. He became a County Commissioner and was known as a powerful leader."

"He was a friend of yours?"

"Yes," Peter acknowledged. "I met him when I was covering the activities of the KKK for my paper. We had many long conversations." He shook his head. "No one really cared about the good he was doing. When Wyatt started the Union League, the KKK strengthened their numbers to combat it. As far as I can tell, there are over eight hundred Klansmen in the county. They've targeted both blacks and whites for nightly *visitations*," he said angrily. "However, the violence is certainly not limited just to Alamance County—it's happening all over North Carolina."

Matthew grimaced. He'd heard the stories.

"Their nightly visitations result in beatings and whippings," Peter continued, his eyes reflecting his pain. "There are white victims, but most of them are black. By the end of last year, the KKK effectively controlled the county. Anyone who doesn't support them lives in fear for their life," he said bitterly.

Matthew tensed, certain of what was coming.

"Back in February, around seventy masked Klansmen came after Wyatt. He was sleeping when they arrived. They bashed down the door with axes, beat his seventy-three-year-old mother who confronted them, and then went for Wyatt, tossing aside his six-year-old son who tried to help his father. Then they hauled him out of the house."

Matthew closed his eyes briefly against the horror of the picture Peter was painting with his story.

"The next morning, when I was headed to his house to talk to him, I saw his body hanging from a tree near the courthouse. A crowd was gathered around him." Peter's voice caught, but he forged on. "There was a sign attached to Wyatt's chest that read, *'Beware! Ye guilty parties, both black and white.'"* Peter shook his head. "Wyatt was a good man. He was murdered for trying to give blacks a political voice in the state. He could have made life better for everyone. Instead, they killed him."

Matthew reached out and laid his hand on Peter's arm. There were no words that could make sense of senseless violence. Peter was right. As long as people needed a scapegoat for their problems, things like this would continue to happen. "I'm sorry," he said softly.

Peter took a deep breath, obviously needing to say what he'd come to say. "The Klan activity has continued. Governor Holden has been fairly successful in tamping down the violence in most of North Carolina, but he's had no success in Alamance County or Caswell County. Meanwhile, the Klan has become more arrogant because they're getting away with everything." He met Matthew's eyes. "On May twenty-first, the Klan killed a state senator in the Caswell County Courthouse."

"What?" Matthew asked in disbelief. "In the courthouse? Two months ago?" How had he missed all this? He knew he'd been focused on his book, but this was vitally important to the efforts to rebuild America.

Peter nodded, his eyes grim. "John Stephens was elected a state senator just two years ago. He was wildly popular with blacks because he served as an agent with the Freedmen's Bureau and was also an active member of the Union League and the Republican Party. The Klan hated him because they saw him as a racial and political renegade who had completely betrayed his people. They made so many threats against his life that he fortified his house, took out a life insurance policy, and carried a knife and three pistols with him everywhere he went."

"Yet they still killed him," Matthew muttered.

"Yes." Peter clinched his fists. "The reality of the situation, however, is that Stephens was actually quite moderate. He stopped a lot of potential black retaliation. I'm not sure if we'll ever know what really happened, but Stephens was somehow lured down to the basement of the courthouse when he was there observing a Democratic convention for Governor Holden."

"For Governor Holden?"

Peter nodded. "I learned during one of my conversations with Senator Stephens that the Democrats had made it almost impossible for him to live and support his family. The fact that he was a senator should have put him in a position of power, but the vast majority of his support came from blacks and poor whites—the people he fought to help. The Conservative Democrats have most of the wealth, so they successfully blocked any economic opportunity for Senator Stephens and ended his access to credit. He'd lost almost everything, except his determination to fight for equality. He refused to quit speaking the truth." Peter shook his head. "Governor Holden hired him to be part of the team of detectives that provided information about the Klan in Alamance and Caswell counties. It was the only way he could support his family."

Peter stopped talking as he turned to stare out the window. After several long moments, he turned back. "Somehow they lured him down to the basement. His body was discovered on top of a woodpile the next morning by his two brothers who had come searching for him when he didn't come home the night before. He'd been stabbed several times and there was still a rope around his neck."

"My God," Matthew breathed. "They haven't caught whomever did this?"

"Everyone knows it's the Klan, but so far there's no conclusive proof of who actually stabbed him. And even if there were..."

"Let me guess," Matthew replied, horrified by what he'd heard. "Community leaders and the courts are either in the Klan, or sympathetic to it. They aren't trying to stop anything; they're fueling the violence." He didn't need Peter to confirm his assessment. It was happening all over the country. "What is Governor Holden doing about it?"

"He's declared martial law," Peter said grimly. "The governor cares about North Carolina. He also cares about black suffrage. Needless to say, the Conservative Democrats hate him. I've talked with the governor. He believes his duty is to uphold the law of North Carolina without respect to color or party. He's fought to stop the Klan's terror tactics for quite a while. His efforts to change things have been effective in many counties, but they've failed entirely in Alamance and Caswell counties. The Federal government has refused to step in to help."

"Can he declare martial law? Is it legal?" Matthew asked keenly.

"That probably remains to be seen, since I'm sure his actions will be decided by a court. I do know, however, that he has President Grant's support."

"President Grant?" Matthew was surprised.

Peter nodded. "He consulted the president after Stephens was killed to make sure he had the power to declare martial law. Grant's reply was to ask him why he'd not led troops in himself by now."

Matthew whistled.

"Grant assured Holden that North Carolina law gave him the authority to put disorder down, and that if federal troops were needed, he would send them. In addition, the president directed the war department to provide Holden with any gear and equipment he needed."

Matthew wasn't surprised.

"What is it?" Peter demanded as he leaned forward to stare into his face. "What are you thinking?"

Matthew shrugged. "President Grant is a military man. I'm not surprised he endorses military action to quell the violence in North Carolina, but I'm not as certain as he is that Holden has the legal right to declare martial law, no matter how much I agree it's needed." He shook his head. "Our president is a passionate man, and I believe his heart is in the right place, but I'm not confident of his political and legal acumen. I'm also not sure he'll support Governor Holden if the courts disagree with him."

"I'm afraid you might be right, but in the meantime, Alamance and Caswell counties are under martial law."

"Which means?" Matthew probed. He sensed they were getting to the real reason behind Peter's visit.

"Holden enlisted George Kirk to restore and maintain order."

"George Kirk?" Matthew tried to place the name. "Wasn't he a Union cavalry officer during the war?"

"He was," Peter agreed. "He has quite a reputation throughout North Carolina for terrorizing western mountain communities during the war. He's earned the undying enmity of anyone who supported the Confederacy, but he did the job he was given to do. I suspect he'll wage a very effective campaign against the Klan," he said with satisfaction. "He began by enlisting hundreds of men for his militia. He fought with many of them in the war."

"Has he taken action yet?" Matthew probed.

Peter hesitated. "He will soon."

"Which is what you're here to tell me about." When the front door opened, Matthew cocked his head to listen.

"Matthew, are you here?"

"In here, Harold," Matthew called back, certain the solution to what Peter wanted had just walked in the door. He turned to watch Peter's face, wanting to see his reaction when Harold rounded the corner. He wasn't disappointed.

"You have a twin?" Peter asked, his eyes wide with surprise. "I knew you had a brother, but I didn't know he was your twin." He looked back and forth between them. "The two of you are mirror images."

"We weren't close for many years, and didn't keep in touch," Harold explained. "Then I grew up, got smarter and realized I was being a fool. My brother was a big enough man to forgive me." He strode forward with a smile and pumped Peter's hand. "Janie told me you were here. It's good to finally meet you. I've heard stories about you."

"Don't believe everything you hear," Peter said good-naturedly. "Of course, most of it is probably true."

Matthew waved Harold to a seat. "Peter has a job offer for you."

"I do?" Peter asked.

"That's what you're here for isn't it?" Matthew asked calmly. "You came to ask me if I would come to North Carolina with you to cover what happens when Kirk goes after the Klansmen."

"You figured that out?"

Matthew shrugged. "Evidently, I'm not as dumb as I look."

Peter laughed. "All right. You got me." He turned to look at Harold appraisingly.

"Harold is also a newspaper reporter," Matthew stated. "Like me, he has stepped away from most of it. He and I are working together on the books we're publishing, but I think once he hears what's going on in North Carolina, he'll want to be involved."

Harold looked intrigued. "North Carolina?"

"Tell him what you told me, Peter."

Peter complied, not missing a single detail. "I need help covering what's going on down there, Harold. My editor offered my pick of our reporters to help me, but I need someone I can trust to cover this thoroughly and accurately. I don't know you, but you're Matthew's twin. If he tells me I can trust you, well..." He shrugged. "I trust you."

Suddenly, his face tightened. "There is one other story I forgot to tell you. It's important to hear before you make your decision."

Harold nodded. "I'm listening."

Matthew heard the back door to the kitchen open, and then a soft murmur of voices. Moments later, Moses' voice boomed through the house.

"Peter Wilcher is here?"

Peter laughed and stood just as Moses pushed through the kitchen door. "Hello, Moses!"

Moses wrapped him in a bear hug. "It's good to see you, Peter. What are you doing here?"

Matthew didn't want Peter to have to report the entire situation in North Carolina for a third time. "If I promise to make sure you have all the details at dinner tonight, can Peter go on with the story he was getting ready to tell Harold about North Carolina?"

Moses stiffened, the laughter dying on his face. "North Carolina? Yes, I'll listen."

Matthew wondered at the sudden ferocity in Moses' eyes, but beckoned for Peter to continue.

Peter took a deep breath. "Moses, I was getting ready to tell Matthew and Harold about something that happened in North Carolina several months ago. Without going into a lot of detail until later, I can tell you this all revolves around the activities of the Ku Klux Klan."

Moses nodded. "Go on."

"Back in January, there was a black man who was called to testify about Klan violence. Against advice, he chose to do what he believed was the right thing. He testified. In retaliation, the KKK broke into his home, killed him, his pregnant wife and all his children. Before they left, they burnt his cabin to the ground with all the bodies still inside."

Matthew gasped. "My God," he muttered. "What kind of animals could do that?" He'd heard terrible stories about Klan violence, but this was the worst. "They killed the entire family?"

"They did," Peter said angrily.

"Actually," Moses said, "they did not."

The three other men stared at him.

"What do you mean?" Peter asked.

"You're talking about Daniel Blue?"

Peter's mouth dropped open. "Yes. How do you know that?"

"I know that because I hired Daniel Blue to work here on the plantation two days ago. He arrived from North Carolina with his oldest daughter, Angel."

Peter's mouth gaped open wider. "Daniel Blue isn't dead? And one of his children is alive?"

"Yes," Moses answered, "though it's best if no one else knows that."

"Of course. I'm just thrilled he wasn't killed. How did he get away?"

Moses filled them in on the story. "He's been on the run since that night," he finished. "He's staying with Franklin and Chooli until we can erect a new cabin for him. When Rose returns from Philadelphia, we'll get Angel started in school. It will help her to be with other children. She's been horribly traumatized by what happened." He would never forget the broken-hearted haunted look on the little girl's face, her eyes almost dead.

"Rose is in Philadelphia?" Peter asked.

"She'll be home later today," Moses replied. He briefly explained about the first Bregdan Women meeting. "According to the letter I received, they had a wonderful time." He was looking forward to hearing all the details.

Chapter Twenty-Five

Abby and Rose had arrived in time for dinner, and now silence engulfed the table as Peter talked about what was happening in North Carolina.

Thomas had listened to only part of the story before he stopped Annie from returning to the kitchen with an empty platter. "I'd like you and Miles to join us," he said solemnly.

"I'll sit down with y'all once I'm done with everything, Mr. Thomas."

"I'd appreciate it if you would join us now, Annie," Thomas replied. "You and Miles both. What we're hearing is very serious. I believe we should hear it all together as a family."

Annie nodded reluctantly but her eyes shone with appreciation. "All right, then. Miles just came in from the stables. He was keeping me company in the kitchen, but I'll bring him in."

"Go on," Thomas urged Peter when Annie and Miles took a place at the table.

Peter finished the story he had told Matthew, Harold and Moses earlier. Matthew interjected at several points. Horrified expressions were on every face as the situation unfolded before them.

Rose listened carefully, having to force herself to breathe several times. Listening to Peter was like having her worst nightmare play out right before her. She clasped her hands under the table, willing them to stop trembling, but failing.

"You came here to ask Matthew to join you in North Carolina," Thomas said when Peter was done with his recitation.

"I did," Peter acknowledged. "I had hopes that the news of his injuries was more exaggerated than the reality, but obviously that's not the case."

Susan turned to Harold. "So you're going instead."

Harold gazed at her with surprise. "I was going to talk to you about it later."

Susan smiled softly. "Of course you're going. You could never live with yourself if you didn't help Peter cover this story." She paused. "What's happening in North Carolina could completely destroy the hope of Reconstruction in America," she said soberly. "If the Democrats, in conjunction with the KKK, are able to mandate what happens in the South through violence and intimidation, there's no hope that equality can ever be achieved. The fact that the federal government is turning its back is inexcusable."

Annie shook her head. "You heard Mr. Peter say that President Grant told that Governor Holden he can use force to make things right."

"Yes," Susan agreed, "but I also heard Matthew say that Governor Holden's actions might not be legal, and that if the issue is pressed, President Grant might pull his support. The federal government should step in to stop the violence. They already fought one war, but there's very clearly another one going on right now. If Governor Holden can't stop the violence, or if he loses support from the president, it's nothing but a prediction of what could happen all over the South. If the Klan and the Democrats know they can get away with unspeakable atrocities, what is ever going to stop them?"

Peter looked around the table. "Unfortunately, Susan is completely right. The situation in North Carolina is horrible for everyone in the state, but the repercussions are far bigger than just one state. I know every other Klan and the rest of the Conservative Democratic Party are watching what's happening. If they're able to escape consequences for what they're doing, then it's going to embolden them everywhere."

*****

Rose snuggled into Moses as soon as they crawled into bed. More than anything in the world, she needed his solid strength. She had managed to conceal her terror from John and Hope, singing to them as they drifted off to sleep, but the long day of travel, combined with the horror of Peter's story, had crumbled her defenses.

"Talk to me," Moses said softly.

Rose struggled to find words to express what she was feeling. In the end, she only had one short question. "What if the same thing happens to our family?" Uttering the words made the horror even more real. "What if the same thing happens to *our* family, Moses?" she cried as she began to tremble again.

"I'm not going to insult you by pretending it couldn't happen," Moses said gravely.

Rose was grateful for his honesty, while also wishing he could have convinced her it wasn't possible. She knew she wouldn't have believed him, but at least the effort would have been made. "What do we do?" she whispered. She thought about Fannie's comment that she couldn't make a difference if she wasn't alive. She couldn't even consider the possibility of Moses, John and Hope being killed all at the same time. For the first time, she was sincerely glad Felicia was far away from them. "You know we're targets. The Klan and every other white supremacy group hates us for what we're doing here."

"I know," Moses admitted. He pushed himself up higher in bed but continued to hold her close. "I've been thinking about it ever since Daniel arrived."

Rose somehow drew comfort from the fact that Moses felt the same way, even though the knowledge also terrified her.

They sat in silence for several long minutes. The wind picked up, rustling oak tree limbs against the house. Owls hooted in the distance, while a coyote's mournful howl seemed to rise as a warning of danger. An answering call came, and then a chorus that seemed to swirl in the air. Rose shivered again and pressed closer, wishing she could disappear into her husband's strength.

Moses finally broke the silence. "We knew when we decided to leave Oberlin and return to the plantation that we were taking a risk. We decided it was worth it," he said slowly. "We felt we needed to be here, and we wanted John and Hope to grow up on the plantation."

"I know," Rose admitted in a whisper, "but the things that are happening are more horrific than ever, and they seem to be happening more what will?"

"I don't know," Moses replied. "It's better here on the plantation, though. Carrie taking care of the veterans has stopped the violence."

"For now," Rose said somberly, aware he was trying to locate hope.

"For now," Moses agreed. "I don't know what to do either, Rose. I've been haunted by Daniel Blue's story ever since I heard it. I've heard a lot of stories from my men, and we've lived through Robert's murder and the attacks on the plantation, but none of it hit me quite as hard as this. The raw brutality shows just how heartless people can be, but the reality that nothing is being done to stop the violence is perhaps the hardest for me to deal with. I wonder where it will stop, or if blacks will finally be driven out of this country."

"Governor Holden is trying," Rose said quietly, trying to gather some comfort from that thought. Moses' next words made it short-lived.

"The fact that he's having to battle so many forces to attempt to stop the violence is horrifying," Moses said, anger seeping into his voice. "After close to two hundred years of slavery, are our people supposed to sit and wait until the Klan shows up at their home, too?"

Rose could feel his massive muscles tense. "We could leave." Saying the words made her insides clench, but the idea of living with daily fear was almost more than she could bear. The idea of her children being murdered was inconceivable.

"And go where?" Moses demanded. "From what Jeremy tells me, the North is better, but not by much. I've thought about heading out West, but then I feel furious at the thought of giving anyone the power to mandate how we live our lives. I thought that ended with the abolition of slavery, but daily events show me how wrong I am."

Rose ached at the pain she heard vibrating in his voice. After all he'd suffered as a slave, and after all he'd done to make Cromwell Plantation more successful than any plantation in the area, it wasn't right that they had to consider leaving in an attempt to stay alive. "I wish they'd finished what they started," she said bitterly.

"What do you mean?"

"The war was fought over many things, but slavery was a big issue. President Lincoln set us free with the Emancipation Proclamation, but that was just the first step. I know he was assassinated, but it's now the responsibility of the Republican Party to undo all the harm that centuries of slavery did to our people. Most black people are working hard to create a new life of freedom, but they live with fear at every turn. What's going on in North Carolina shows they're willing to abdicate responsibility for our people while they focus on things they obviously believe are more important." She shook her head. "There are too many of us to simply ignore. Don't they realize answers have to be found for four million freed slaves if there is ever going to be peace in our country?"

Rose felt her words releasing a passion she hadn't fully recognized in herself until now. "I think about the Bregdan Principle often. There's a growing number of us that are determined to launch positive things that will reverberate throughout history, but what about all the negative things happening now? The decisions being made that give the Klan more power are going to have a lasting impact as well. Decisions being made by Congress are empowering them to keep taking action. How many generations will the hatred last? How many generations will believe violence and intimidation are the way to deal with problems? How many children will carry forward the hatred?" She stopped, breathless, as the emotion swamped her.

Moses pulled her closer but didn't respond.

Rose knew he didn't have answers to the questions either.

Unable to sleep, they lay together, listening to the night sounds drifting in through the windows.

"I guess I hope we'll know," Moses finally muttered.

"Know what?" Rose asked.

"Know when it's the time to leave," Moses said flatly.

*****

Abby and Rose were at the schoolhouse when they heard a wagon approaching. The Bregdan Women meeting wasn't scheduled to start for two more hours, but they'd come to finalize the room preparation. Curious, they both went outside to see who their visitor was.

Rose had never seen the white woman approaching the schoolhouse, but it wasn't unusual to have parents show up to meet her. "Hello!" she called cheerfully.

The woman smiled and raised her hand.

As she pulled the wagon to a stop in front of the schoolhouse, Rose could see the fatigued blue eyes and the weary droop in the woman's shoulders. "Good afternoon," she said warmly. "I'm Rose Samuels. This is Abby Cromwell."

The slender woman, with black hair carefully coifed into a bun, managed a smile. "Hello. My name is Helena Garrison."

"It's a pleasure to meet you," Rose responded, waiting to discover the reason for Helena's visit.

"It's nice to meet you, Helena," Abby said.

Helena nodded to Abby, then turned to look at Rose. "I came to talk to you, Mrs. Samuels."

The schoolhouse was still hot from the summer sun beating down upon it. "Let's sit on the bench beneath the tree. It's cooler than inside," Rose responded.

Helena set the brake on her wagon and stepped down. "Thank you for a few minutes of your time, Mrs. Samuels."

Rose couldn't miss the cultured sound of Helena's voice. She also couldn't miss how it contrasted sharply with the worn dress the woman somehow managed to wear with elegance.

Jeb appeared from behind the schoolhouse. "I'll take care of your horse, ma'am. There's water out back, and I can give him some shade."

Helena looked startled but smiled. "Thank you."

After the three women settled down on the bench, Rose turned to their visitor. "What can I do for you, Helena?"

"I've recently moved back to the area," Helena replied. "I have two children who need a school to attend."

"We'll be happy to have them," Rose replied. "The school days are short in the summer because the schoolhouse gets so hot. We start at eight o'clock and send the children home at noon."

"The children are in school during the summer? I heard they were, but I had to find out for myself."

"Not all of them can attend," Rose answered, "because they're needed by their families to work in the fields, but we teach the ones who can come. At night, many of the women come to continue their education."

"Both black and white women?" Helena's expression was openly inquisitive.

"Yes." Rose decided a simple answer was best until she could determine all the reasons for Helena's visit.

"Even though the new constitution mandates separate education for blacks and whites?"

Rose stiffened. Had Helena been sent by the Department of Education? She fought to keep her voice calm. "Yes. Our white children wouldn't have a school if I didn't teach them. That may change in the future, but right now we have both black and white students."

Helena peered at her closely and then nodded. "Good."

Rose relaxed, seeing nothing but acceptance in Helena's eyes. "Tell me about your children."

Helena smiled. "Paul, my son, is eleven years old. His sister, Katherine, is ten."

"You said you're new to the area. Where did you come from?"

Helena hesitated. "That's a long story."

"We're happy to listen," Abby assured her.

Rose was certain that Helena had a fascinating story. She hoped she would be comfortable enough to tell it.

Helena gazed at them for a moment and then sighed. "I don't suppose it's really much of a story. It's happening to women all over the South." She took a long breath. "I grew up on Garrison Plantation just a few miles from here. My family owned it before the war. When I married, my husband moved out to the plantation to help run it. The plan was that Wyatt would take it over when my father wanted to quit working so hard. Neither of them received their wish, I'm afraid."

Rose knew about Garrison Plantation. She had often sent Carrie off to parties there. "You know Carrie Cromwell, then."

"Yes," Helena replied. "She was at my house often for parties and dancing when we were children, but I can't say we were extremely close. Carrie was never fond of the idea of being a Southern lady," she said ruefully. "She would much rather have been on her horse, roaming the plantation."

Rose chuckled. "She hasn't changed much."

"So I've heard," Helena replied without rancor. "I've also been told she's a doctor now?"

"She is," Rose answered. "She's in Philadelphia right now, completing an internship in surgery." The realization that Helena knew Carrie meant that she also knew her father. "Abby is married to Thomas Cromwell." She decided not to reveal that she was Thomas' half-sister.

"I'd heard that, as well. Carrie's mother was a wonderful woman, but I don't believe she would have endured the war any better than my own mother. I'm glad Mr. Cromwell has someone to share his life." She smiled at Abby and then launched back into her story. "My husband died at the first battle in Cold Harbor, and my family lost everything during the war," she said matter-of-factly. "Both my brothers were killed in battle. My father put the entirety of his money into the Confederate cause, losing it all. Two months after Lee's surrender, he committed suicide. My mother died of a heart attack a few months later."

Rose put a hand to her mouth. "I'm so sorry."

Helena nodded. "Thank you."

Rose recognized the numb look in her eyes. This was a woman who'd had her whole life ripped out from beneath her and was struggling to survive. "Are you back at Garrison Plantation, Helena?"

Helena's laugh was a mixture of harshness and amusement. "Certainly not. My family's plantation was purchased by a Northern carpetbagger two years ago. I suppose I should be grateful it sold, but of course, it went for a pittance of its worth. It paid the remainder of my father's debts and left me just enough to buy a small house about a mile from here. I've been working in Richmond as a nanny for the last several years, but I find the city has too many reminders of all that's gone." She met Rose's eyes. "My children and I came out here to start a new life."

Rose refrained from asking Helena how she was going to make a living. It wasn't any of her business. "Have your children been going to school?"

"How?" Helena asked. "I had no money. Free education was only available to the slaves until very recently."

"*Emancipated* slaves," Rose corrected her. "There are no longer slaves in America." She had learned the importance of clarifying things when white parents first arrived at the school.

"Yes, of course," Helena said dismissively, and then shook her head. "I'm sorry for the way that sounded," she apologized. "Life has been very difficult."

"I'm sure it has," Rose said softly. "I'm sorry too."

Helena met her eyes. "Do you have any idea how hard it's been?" she asked bluntly. "Really?"

Rose opened her mouth to tell her she did, because blacks all over the South were dealing with far worse, and then closed it. She sensed she needed to listen. "Please tell me. I'd like to know."

Helena stared at her for a long moment and then glanced at Abby, almost as if for permission.

"Please tell us," Abby urged. "We want to know. Neither of us have faced what you've been dealing with."

Helena continued to look at them for a long moment and then sighed. "I know slavery was wrong," she began. "Of course, I didn't know that as a child. It was simply the life I'd always known. We always had slaves, and I was told it was the way things were meant to be. My father and mother were raised the same way. We treated our slaves well, but I realize now that all they wanted was to be free. They all escaped the plantation as soon as we retreated to Richmond for safety during the first year of the war. I've never heard from any of them, but I sincerely hope they're doing well."

Helena watched a blue jay flit through the tree before she continued. "I didn't pay much attention to what was going on in the country until I saw my husband and brothers heading to war. Not one of them wanted to go, despite the fact they were told they were fighting to uphold the glorious honor of the South," she said bitterly. "They upheld the *glorious honor* until they were buried in a shallow grave somewhere on a battlefield. I never saw any of their bodies to tell them good-bye. While I was still grieving them, the war ended. The South gave the very best of who we were, but it wasn't enough. We lost."

Rose watched Helena carefully, aching at the lost look in her eyes.

"I suppose I thought when we lost, and it was all finally over, that we could begin to rebuild our lives. My father, however, couldn't live with the reality that the world he had always known was gone. I was downstairs in our Richmond house when I heard the gunshot. A few minutes later, I heard my mother scream when she found my father's body." Her voice caught. "Mama was never the same. She could have lived without the plantation, but she couldn't live without my father. They say she died of a heart attack, but I know it was nothing more than a broken heart." Helena's eyes filled with tears that she brushed away impatiently.

"I was caught between grief and the reality that somehow, I had to survive for my children. I chose to survive, but there is never a day that goes by that I'm not aware of all I lost." She shook her head. "I see it all around me," she said, and then hesitated, obviously uncertain whether she should continue.

Rose was struck by the intense light that shone for an instant in her eyes. "Please continue," she urged. "I want to hear what you have to say." She wasn't sure that she actually did, but something inside was telling her it was important.

Helena remained silent for another long moment, but finally looked up to meet Rose's eyes. "The South is a mess right now. I never understood the war—it was just suddenly there. Most of the men forced to fight never understood it either. Yes, my family owned slaves, but most of the soldiers never owned another person. They were forced to fight for a right that a few men wanted to keep. While they were fighting, everything they knew was being destroyed. Their homes were destroyed. Their livelihoods were destroyed. Women lost their husbands and their sons. They lost their homes. *They lost everything...*" Her voice faltered and then strengthened.

"When the war was over, all they wanted to do was go home and start living their lives again, but what lives?" Helena demanded. "They had nothing to go back to and nobody has helped them. The blacks were the only ones getting help through the Freedmen's Bureau."

Rose knew that wasn't true and knew that many white families had received assistance, but she remained silent. Helena's perspective deserved to be heard.

"Southern men are desperate," she said. "The war ended with the South in shambles. It would have been bad enough if only the soldiers had returned home to try and find work, but suddenly there were millions of freed slaves competing for the few jobs available. It's not that I'm not aware they've suffered too, but *everyone* has suffered horribly. It's created a desperation that has led to terrible things. I don't like the Ku Klux Klan, nor any of the groups that have formed, but I suppose I understand *why* they have formed." Helena met Rose's eyes evenly. "I imagine you think the KKK exists only because these men hate black people. I realize there is a modicum of truth to that, but that's not the only reason. The true reason it exists is because these men are desperate. What they don't know is that they're just being used again."

Rose was startled. "What do you mean?"

Helena shrugged. "They're being used as pawns again. They were used as pawns during the war to fight something they never wanted. Now they're being used as pawns by the same men who got us into the war in the first place. The Conservative Democrats are using Klan violence to achieve their goal of reclaiming political control of the South."

"You see this very clearly," Abby observed. "I hope you won't be offended if I say that I've not met many former plantation daughters with your level of understanding and knowledge."

Helena shrugged again. "I was a nanny in the house of a Virginia Democratic legislator. He had no qualms about discussing politics around me, and I had free access to his library and all the newspapers delivered to his home. What he didn't realize is that I quite despise what he and his kind have done to the South."

"You're a Republican?" Abby asked with surprise.

"I'm a Southern woman who has lost everything," Helena said angrily. "I'm disgusted with anything political because I believe it's all a ploy for greedy men to get what they want. They don't care about the poor whites who have joined the KKK out of desperation. They don't care that white men and women are desperate for survival," she said. "The South certainly isn't helping them. The federal government is helping the freed slaves, but they seem intent on only punishing Southern whites for what they were forced to do during the war. The end result is that they have nothing."

"The KKK and other groups are doing terrible things," Rose said, thinking of Daniel Blue and his family. She was listening, but she couldn't remain silent.

"Some of them are," Helena agreed, "but most of the members of the Klan and other groups are simply looking for an affiliation that will help them make sense of what has happened to their lives," she said firmly. "These families need help just as much as the blacks who were freed from slavery. Desperate men do desperate things."

"Blacks aren't to blame for their situation," Rose argued.

"Of course they're not," Helena said quickly, "but the KKK members believe they are."

"Please explain more of what you mean," Abby urged.

"They're *pawns*," Helena said again. "As long as the politicians can convince poor white men that the blacks are their enemy and the cause of all their problems, they'll have the force they need to terrorize blacks and keep them from voting." She shook her head. "I know it's true because I've heard it being talked about." Her voice grew angrier. "The Democrats know the white men are desperate, but they'd rather feed the desperation because it serves their purpose. *Everyone* in the South needs help. It makes me sick that they're promoting chaos in order to achieve what they want."

"That's a strong indictment," Abby said gently.

"Yes," Helena replied. "It also happens to be the truth. Do you disagree with me?"

"No," Rose and Abby said in unison.

Helena's eyes ignited with a renewed determination. "I came back out here to the country because I heard about your school, Mrs. Samuels."

Rose didn't understand. "The new constitution mandates public education for all white children, Mrs.

Garrison. Paul and Katherine could receive an education in Richmond."

"That's true," Helena said, "but the South is only going to get better for my children if change happens. If I put them in an all-white school in Richmond, they're going to be taught that all blacks are their enemies and someone to look down on. That's not what I want for them. Whether white people want it to or not, the South is changing. I want to be *part* of the change, not spend all my time and energy trying to stop the inevitable."

Rose gazed at her, astonished at the depth of her perception. "You realize that at some point, they'll make me stop teaching white children."

Helena nodded. "I know. That makes it more important that I start my children in your school now. I'm hoping what they learn will stick."

Rose hesitated to make her next statement, but she felt compelled to be sure that Helena understood what she was doing. "We have had white parents come under attack for allowing their children to attend my school."

Helena tightened her lips. "I know. I thought about the risk I'd be taking, but decided the benefit to my children would be far greater than the risk."

Abby reached out to take her hand. "You're an extraordinary woman, Mrs. Garrison."

"I don't see it that way, but thank you. From what I'm told, Cromwell Plantation is full of extraordinary women."

Rose exchanged a quick look with Abby to confirm they were thinking the same thing. "We're heading to the plantation for some dinner, and then tonight is the first meeting of Bregdan Women here at the schoolhouse. We'd love for you to join us for both."

"Bregdan Women?"

Rose smiled. "We'll explain it on the way. Will you join us for dinner?"

"I would love to, Mrs. Samuels."

"My name is Rose. This is Abby. We don't stand on formality very much around here."

"Then I'm Helena, she said graciously."

When Rose stood, Jeb appeared again. "I've unhooked Mrs. Garrison's horse and tied him in the back next to the water trough. I also gave him some hay. He'll be fine until we all get back."

"Thank you," Helena said. When they were all seated in the carriage, with Jeb on the driver's seat, she looked at them quizzically. "Does he accompany you everywhere?"

Rose nodded. "Jeb is a good friend, and yes, he does. We've had our share of trouble with vigilantes and Klan members. Even though things have been peaceful for the last seven months, my husband refuses to let his guard down." She hesitated. "I'm very grateful he's so cautious. You never know when something might happen." She pushed away thoughts of Daniel Blue's family again.

The three women laughed and chatted all the way back to the plantation.

Chapter Twenty-Six

Abby was delighted when she looked out over the schoolhouse full of women. She'd hoped for a good turnout, but never expected fifty women for the first Bregdan Women's meeting. All of them had been greeted and treated to platters heaped with Annie's cookies.

Annie was seated in the corner, beaming as the compliments flowed for the Irish oatmeal cookies she'd been baking all day.

Abby was equally thrilled that the room was evenly represented by white and black women, most of them chatting easily among themselves. The last two years had worked miracles. Standing at the front of the room, she enjoyed watching Helena's wide-eyed disbelief as she took in the scene.

"Welcome, everyone," Abby called. Within moments, the room was silent with all eyes turned to her expectantly. "I'd like to start this meeting by reading something to you."

She pulled out the parchment Carrie had given her on New Year's Day.

The Bregdan Principle

Every life that has been lived until today is a part of the woven braid of life.

It takes every person's story to create history.

Your life will help determine the course of history.

You may think you don't have much of an impact.
You do.

Every action you take will reflect in someone else's life.

Someone else's decisions.

Someone else's future.

Both good and bad.

She told them the story of Biddy Flannagan, and she told them about her experience in New York City. "Most of you know that I've retired from running my factories in Philadelphia and Richmond. I thought I would be content to live out my life here on the plantation in ease, but I've discovered that's not true. I have more to give," she said, overjoyed to know that was true.

She smiled at the faces looking back at her. "All of you are women living in a very difficult time. It really doesn't matter if you're white or black in the South right now."

The earlier conversation with Helena had driven that home in a way nothing else could have. The Klan was a horrible thing, but it had been formed as a response to blatant disregard for the men who had fought for the South. Their anger and bitterness had demanded an outlet. The easiest target for the Klan were the black people who had started after the war with even less than them, but had at least gained recognition from the government.

"The only way all of you can improve your life, and the life of your family, is to join together as women. The only way you can make the world better for you and your family is to acknowledge that every single act you take is going to cast ripples throughout all of history."

"It takes all I got just to keep food on the table," one woman called. "How am I supposed to do more?"

Heads nodded all over the room.

"I like that thing you read about our life making a difference throughout history, but right now, it seems to be all I can do to just survive!" another woman called in agreement.

"I know," Abby said gently. She had anticipated just such a reaction. "But whether you know it or not, every action you take and every word you speak, is being observed by someone or heard by someone who will carry that with them for the rest of their life." She held up a hand when the woman opened her mouth to protest again. "I realize that can be a heavy burden to carry. I also know that most of the time, each of you in this room feels alone. You feel like no one understands your struggle, and you feel that the responsibility of every single person in your family rests on your shoulders. It can be exhausting."

"That's true," several murmured as their heads nodded in agreement.

"I do what I can to help my neighbors, but I'm only one person," another woman said.

"You're right," Abby acknowledged. Her initial thought when she'd been in New York City had been that she could teach classes about business. That was still a good idea, but it was several steps down the road. First, she had to give these women a road to walk on. Most of them were widows, simply doing their best to raise their children, put food on the table, keep everyone clothed, and make sure their children were educated. The cycle of poverty would keep all of them in desperation if something couldn't be done to break it.

"How many of you quilt?" Abby asked.

"How many of us *quilt*?" one woman asked in astonishment. "You know that would be all of us. How else are we going to provide warmth for our families?"

Abby looked around. "Is that true?"

Every head nodded.

"Why you asking a question like that, Miss Abby?" Annie demanded.

Abby smiled. She'd known she could trust Annie to open the door for what she wanted to say next. "Because I think the thing all of you need most is money," she replied. "You can't even imagine a better life for you and your family if you don't have some kind of way to make it happen."

"What do quilts have to do with it?" a petite woman with tired eyes asked.

Abby held up the letter she'd received from Nancy Stratford two days earlier. "Women in New York City don't have time to quilt. They do, however, have money to *buy* well-made quilts." She paused, letting the first part of her statement sink in. "Making quilts will solve two problems," Abby continued. "One, it will give you a way to make extra money. Two, you will be with other women, so you won't feel so alone. I have a friend in New York City who already has women eager to buy your quilts."

"Women in the North want to buy our quilts?" a woman asked in amazement. "Why don't they make their own?"

"Not every woman is good with her hands, Cindy. And, there are women who either don't have the time, or it's not how they want to spend their time. Especially in New York City, where many of the women have professions."

"What kind of quilts?" someone called.

"High quality quilts," Abby said firmly. "If you want to make quilts to help change your life and the life of your children, you have to make *excellent* quilts. I'll be inspecting every one of them before I send them on. If you want to be paid for your work, you have to do it well."

There was a short silence as the women absorbed her words.

"Now I see how you were able to run a factory full of people," one woman muttered. "Are you always so bossy?"

Abby laughed. "Always." Then she sobered. "Ladies, this is a chance for all of you to change things in your life. I told you about the young lady I saw again at the luncheon in New York who is now a doctor. She started with nothing. She had to work hard at something she hated in order to have a chance to do what she really wanted. If you're willing to work hard, then someday, either you or your children will have different choices."

"Where are we supposed to get the money to buy material for the quilts?" a woman called in a sharp voice.

"That's an excellent question," Abby responded, pleased the woman was thinking ahead. "I'm prepared to buy all the material you'll need for the first two or three quilts you make. When the quilts are sold, I'll be repaid for my investment, and you'll get the rest. I'll teach you how to make sure you always have enough money to purchase the materials to make the next quilt.

Buying material in bulk will make sure you get the lowest price for what you need."

The women looked at each other in astonishment, hope beginning to flicker in their eyes.

"How are we supposed to make quilts for rich people when we already work all the time?" a woman called out.

Abby wanted to respond sympathetically, but now wasn't the time. "By working harder than you've ever worked," Abby said firmly. "I agree that the government should step up to help the widows of deceased veterans, or to help all of you who are fighting to regain what you lost during the war, but they're not. You can be bitter about that..." She let her voice trail off deliberately, waiting until every eye in the room was focused on her. "Or you can do whatever it takes to make your life different. There are too many people in the South who are choosing to be bitter and resentful. They have that right, but I certainly don't see how it's making their life better."

"That's right!" one woman called. "Mrs. Cromwell, did you ever think of becoming a preacher? You're better than any man I ever heard."

Abby laughed. "Not even for a second. But if I can help all of you live a better life, there's nothing I would like better."

"Why?" a woman in the back demanded. "Why do you care about us?"

"Because all of you are now my neighbors," Abby replied. "We're *neighbors*," she repeated, and then decided to tell them more of her story. Right now, they saw her as a rich white woman married to a wealthy plantation owner. They had no idea what she'd been forced to overcome. "When I first took over my husband's factories after he died, I was scared to death because I didn't know how to do it. I'd always talked to Charles *about* business, but I'd certainly never run one. No one thought I could do it, and there were a lot of men who were determined to stop me. I was threatened and almost assaulted a few times."

"Why?" a woman called indignantly.

"Because I was crazy enough to think I could do what only men had done up to that point," Abby said bluntly. "My life was very lonely for a long time, but I was determined to succeed. I worked harder than any man dreamed of working, and I did without a lot of things I needed, because I knew I had to keep pouring my profits into the business." She took a long breath. "I was willing to do whatever it took."

"Which is why you're telling us that's what we all got to do," Annie said loudly. She stood and looked around at all the women in the room. "You all think Mrs. Cromwell ain't nothing but some rich woman coming down here to tell us what to do. You are all more wrong than you can know. She ain't got to be doing this. Neither does Rose. They both be doing this because they care." She paused. "It's more than that, though," she stated, her dark eyes scanning the room. "They believe every single one of you can do more than you're doing. I reckon I've lost count of the times these two women have made me believe I could do something I was darn sure I couldn't do. They believed it so hard, they made me believe it too." Annie, unused to speaking in public, sat down abruptly.

Abby smiled through the tears swimming in her eyes. "Thank you, Annie."

"What if you don't know how to quilt?"

Every head turned to stare at Helena who had stood to ask her question.

Helena smiled. "I don't know how to quilt, but I'm willing to do whatever it takes to learn. I want my life and my children's lives to be better than they are now. Mrs. Cromwell is offering us an incredible opportunity." She looked around the room. "Will someone teach me?"

Abby held her breath. She knew Helena's cultured voice made her stand out as being someone very different from the rest of these women. She hoped her courage would appeal to even the most suspicious.

Polly, seated near the back of the room, stood. "I'll teach you," she offered. "It takes time and patience, but anyone can learn."

Helena smiled gratefully. "Thank you."

Abby refrained from cheering. It was like watching a miracle occur to see a former plantation owner's daughter accepting the offer of a former slave to teach her how to quilt. Poverty could either divide people or unite them in an effort to change it. Abby would do everything she could to make sure that it would unite the women in this room.

Abby didn't need to say anything else that night. The time would come when she could teach them business skills. Right now, they just needed to believe it was possible to change their lives. The women needed to talk among themselves about the plans they had for their future. They needed to encourage each other and tighten the bonds of friendship.

*****

Harold had been in North Carolina for more than six weeks. He missed Susan more than he thought possible, but every day he remained revealed how important it was for Peter and him to tell the truth of what was happening in the beleaguered state. The Democratic newspapers in the state either downplayed the truth or simply lied, creating a chaos of confusion that was impossible for the average citizen to interpret or understand.

A knock at his door caused him to look up from his work. "Come in," he invited.

Peter entered, his dark eyes lined with fatigue. "Are you done with the article for the *Philadelphia Inquirer*? I received a telegram this morning assuring me it would be distributed to every major newspaper in the North."

Harold handed him the article he'd labored over all night, only succumbing to sleep for a couple of hours when a glow on the horizon had revealed dawn was coming.

Peter reached for it eagerly and began to read.

Is it possible to watch the demise of democracy in six short weeks? My experience in North Carolina tells me it is so. I have watched as a good man has fought to protect the citizens of his state, only to be thwarted at every turn by the very governmental bodies sworn to support him. I've watched as politics have destroyed the rights of people who now live in fear for their lives.

Six weeks ago, under order of Governor Holden of North Carolina, who declared martial law in both Alamance and Caswell counties, George Kirk raised a militia and took action against the violence and intimidation perpetrated by the Ku Klux Klan. Responding to the pleas of thousands that have been beaten, brutalized and whipped, along with the voices of the dead rising from the graves, one hundred men were arrested for these abhorrent crimes.

These men are well known to be leaders in the Ku Klux Klan, and there is ample evidence of their crimes against the citizens of North Carolina. Oh, but that is not enough in a state determined to turn its back on justice.

When the federal government should be stepping up to provide protection for its citizens, as well as for Governor Holden, a brave man willing to stand against the woeful wrong, they have turned their backs. While these prisoners, who were sure to be exonerated by corrupt courts, should be tried in federal court, the political situation has mandated they be tried in the local jurisdictions that have already proved themselves to be complicit in the actions of the Ku Klux Klan.

Governor Holden has fought hard to hold accountable these men who have been responsible for many murders, including the brutal murder of State Senator Stephens, whose only "crime" was speaking out for the rights of black voters and white Republicans in the state.

Though the courts have sought to dismiss and hide the atrocities of the Ku Klux Klan, most certainly because too many lawyers and judges are themselves members of the KKK, the truth is coming to light.

A man, whose only crime was to testify to a beating he saw, was shot and killed along with his pregnant wife and five children.

An Alamance County Commissioner was hanged for daring to believe in black rights.

Hundreds have been beaten or whipped.

Countless homes have been burned.

Thousands have fled the state in fear for their lives.

I ask you, is this why this great country fought a war that claimed almost one million lives, and left others maimed for the rest of their existence? I must raise my voice and say, No!

Our very own President Grant, who assured Governor Holden of his support, has now turned his back to leave this brave man on his own. Oh, the folly of politics when they are used against the very citizens they were created to support and protect. What use are the Fourteenth and Fifteenth Amendments if they are not upheld by the government that created them?

While Governor Holden may have indeed overextended his authority when he suspended habeas corpus, he rightly believed that it was the only way to bring Klansmen to justice, since local and state courts have proven completely ineffective in convicting violent members of the Ku Klux Klan. Governor Holden considered his course of action as his only option to stop the violence, confident that federal officials would support him and not allow Klansmen to get away with such a mockery of justice.

To the great dismay of this reporter, the federal government has indeed allowed such a mockery of *justice that every American should be frightened for the future of our country.*

Fifty of the Klansmen were released with no trial at all. Another fifty were indicted but remanded to local courts. Not one of those tried was convicted of a crime. Governor Holden's assertion that the civil government is powerless against the Ku Klux Klan has been confirmed in a most terrifying way.

Whether through intimidation, collusion or outright perjury, Klansmen have ensured their brethren will not be punished for their crimes.

While it remains to be seen what the repercussions will be for Governor Holden, a good man being attacked relentlessly by the Democratic press determined to take back control of the South, it is obvious to this reporter that every state in the country has been watching this debacle. Every Klansmen has been watching, receiving assurance they will not be tried and convicted for the crimes they are increasingly guilty of.

Such blatant disregard for justice has merely emboldened the violence ripping at the shreds of the democracy we fought so hard to protect and sustain. Surely, just as the arrogance of the Ku Klux Klan has reached new heights in North Carolina, the ripple of injustice will embolden watching Klansmen and other vigilante groups across our great country.

I ask you again, is this why this great country fought a war that claimed close to a million lives, and left others maimed for the rest of their existence? I must raise my voice and say, No!

Peter finished reading, gave a long whistle and shook Harold's hand. "Well done. You have written outstanding articles in the weeks we've been here, but I daresay this is your most powerful."

"Thank you," Harold said wearily, "but I fear it will do no good. The damage has been done. We both have sent dozens of articles detailing the atrocities and the complete denial of justice, but still, all the Klansmen are free."

"True," Peter said solemnly, "but it's also true that the KKK activity has ceased entirely in Alamance and Caswell Counties."

"For now," Harold said bluntly. The last weeks had filled him with disillusionment and skepticism. He had kept hoping for a moment of justice that would vindicate the price so many had paid to fight the battle, but it had never come. "Governor Holden may have perhaps won this battle, but I fear he will lose the war."

"Perhaps," Peter said heavily. "Our work here is done. Let's go home."

Chapter Twenty-Seven

Matthew was sitting on the porch in his wheelchair, soaking up the afternoon sun, when he heard the sound of a carriage approaching. He grinned when he realized it was Harold. "It's about time you came home!" he called.

"My sentiments exactly," Harold said as the carriage rolled to a stop. "Where is my beautiful wife?"

Susan emerged from the barn and gave a cry of joy. "Harold!"

Harold leapt down from the carriage, met her halfway between the barn and the house and grabbed her in his arms. "Hello, my love."

Susan was laughing as she kissed him. "I thought you would never come home."

"It felt like that to me at times, too."

Matthew narrowed his eyes, hearing the pain in his brother's voice.

Susan heard it too. She leaned back in Harold's arms and peered into his face. "It was terrible."

Harold hesitated. "Pointless might be a better description," he said wearily. "Only for Governors Holden and Kirk, however, along with all the citizens of North Carolina who hoped for a reprieve. The Klan achieved exactly what they hoped for."

Annie appeared on the porch, carrying a tray. "Welcome home, Mr. Harold. Can I interest you in some cookies and lemonade?"

Harold grinned. "I can't think of anything that sounds better. Thank you, Annie."

Annie laid the tray down on a table and stared down at him from her higher vantage point, her fists bunched on her hips. "You look like a man that's a mite tired of life, Mr. Harold. Things must have been real bad down there in North Carolina."

Harold took Susan's hand and together they climbed the stairs. "Nothing some of your cookies and lemonade won't fix, Annie."

Annie sniffed. "I reckon it's gonna take more than that, but I also know you done come to the right place. Home is the best thing for you."

"I couldn't agree more," Harold replied.

Amber ran from the barn to unhook his horse from the carriage. "I'll take real good care of this mare, Harold."

"Thank you, Amber." Harold waved his hand and took a long drink of his lemonade. He squinted at Matthew. "I thought you would have those casts off, brother."

"Today," Matthew assured him with a smile. "Carrie, Anthony and Frances arrived last night for a visit. She's going to remove the casts when she's done at the clinic later." He was counting the minutes, hoping he wouldn't be devastated by the appearance of his legs. Carrie had told him over and over last night that he would walk again, but he was having a hard time fully believing it. He knew it would take time, but the first glimpse of his legs in almost four months was the important first step.

A brief silence fell on the porch while they drank their lemonade and ate their cookies.

Matthew knew Susan was giving Harold a moment to acclimate to being back on the plantation.

"How bad was it?" Susan finally asked.

Harold stared down into his empty glass for a long moment. "I turned in my last article yesterday morning. Then Peter and I left. We did all we could, but I fear it had zero impact or influence."

"We haven't received that article, of course," Matthew replied, "but we've read all the other ones. You and Peter did an excellent job of reporting on the state of affairs in North Carolina."

Harold shrugged. "Our excellent reporting did absolutely nothing to sway the outcome," he said flatly. "Not one single Klansman was convicted of a crime, and unless I'm very mistaken, Governor Holden's career has ended. He's not up for re-election this year, but I've already heard rumors of impeachment proceedings that will probably start after the August elections."

Matthew tightened his lips. "The Republicans could still hold onto power," he argued. "Governor Holden might be able to retain his position despite all that has happened."

Harold shook his head. "You know as well as I do that this whole debacle has shifted the popular support in North Carolina to the Democrats. Most of the good citizens of that state aren't interested in the truth. They believe the outright lies being told by the Democratic newspapers that dominate the press throughout the state. They either don't believe what the other papers are saying about Klan activities or they just don't care. Unfortunately, many North Carolinians are members of the Klan. Most of the remainder of the white population supports what they're doing, convinced it's the only way to try to rebuild their state."

Matthew sat silently, considering what he'd heard. He was disappointed, but certainly not surprised. He was all too aware of what the Democratic Party would do to regain control.

"Is Janie here?" Harold asked.

"No, she went to the clinic with Carrie today. One of the plantation workers was badly injured by a falling tree. He'll be all right, but it's going to take some time for him to recover. They're setting a broken arm."

"Perhaps you can share all your tips for how to survive confinement," Harold said dryly.

"I doubt I could be encouraging," Matthew replied. "Why did you ask about Janie?"

Harold hesitated. "There's something I think she should know about."

Matthew tensed at the uncomfortable look in his brother's eyes. "What is it?"

"You know that Kirk arrested one hundred men during his sweep of Alamance and Caswell counties." Harold didn't wait for a response. "One of the men he arrested was Clifford Saunders."

Matthew took a deep breath. "Are you sure it's the same Clifford Saunders?"

"The piece of scum that abused Janie when they were married? The man who came after her, only to have Robert persuade him with his fists that he should never show his face again. Yes, I'm sure. Peter and I both went to the jail ourselves to confirm it. Although Peter had met him at the end of the war, Clifford didn't recognize him. You should have seen the look on his face when he saw me, though."

"He thought you were me," Matthew said slowly.

"He did. He looked like he'd seen a ghost. He also looked less than happy. It did my heart good." Harold smiled. "I chose not to say anything, letting him believe it was you seeing him trapped like the dog he is. I just stared at him for a long time and then walked back out."

"How long was he in jail?" Matthew asked sharply.

"The whole month," Harold replied.

"It's a shame they couldn't lock him up and throw away the key," Susan said angrily. "That man was horrible to Janie!"

"What's going to happen to the men who were arrested?" Matthew asked, wondering how Janie would react to the news. "Are they free to go back to their lives?"

"Technically, yes, but some of them will face other consequences for their involvement. Once Holden and Kirk cracked down on the KKK, there were members that decided their involvement wasn't worth the price they might have to pay. They've renounced involvement and are turning on some of the members."

"You think that will happen to Clifford?" Matthew pressed, knowing he would take great satisfaction if the man was made to suffer some kind of ramification. Matthew would have much preferred for him to languish in jail, but at least for the moment, that wasn't going to happen.

"I think many of the former clients who made him wealthy are going to want to distance themselves from him," Harold replied. "Anyway, I thought Janie should know."

Matthew wasn't sure there was any reason for Janie to know her ex-husband had been in jail. She didn't need any more evidence to realize what a cruel scoundrel he was. Would the news just open old wounds for her?

Harold read his thoughts. "Sometimes, you need to know the bad guy doesn't always win, Matthew. Clifford was horrible to Janie, and then he just went right on rising through the political ranks in North Carolina while he built a flourishing law practice. Despite all he did to your wife, people exalted him as a lawyer and looked to him as a leader. Now, he's paying the price for his hatred and violence. There are those that will still applaud him, but not everyone feels that way. The most important thing is that he can't hide from what he's done anymore."

Matthew considered his words, wondering if he was right.

"Closure can help with healing old wounds," Harold said quietly. "I believe that knowing Clifford is facing at least some of the consequences of his actions will help her, but it's certainly up to you what you want to do with this information."

Matthew knew that wasn't true. He respected Janie too much to keep information like this from her once he'd discovered it. They had promised to not keep secrets from each other. He knew he would tell Janie the truth about Clifford. He just hoped it wouldn't hurt her more than it helped.

*****

Matthew eyed the crutches Carrie brought into the room with distaste. He knew he wasn't just going to stand up and walk again, but the idea of continued immobilization was maddening. Janie had explained the whole process to him numerous times, but now that his casts were actually about to be removed, he found himself surprisingly nervous.

Carrie eyed him keenly. "What you're feeling is absolutely normal."

"How do you know what I'm feeling?"

"Everyone who has been in extensive casting for a long time feels it," Carrie said calmly. "You've hated every moment of the casts, but now you're afraid of what you're going to see when the casts are removed, and you wonder if you're going to walk again. Sometimes, the not knowing is somehow more bearable than the reality you're faced with when the casts are removed."

Matthew looked away uncomfortably. "I suppose there's some truth to that," he muttered. He hated the vulnerable feeling that threatened to swallow him.

Janie smiled and smoothed back the hair on his forehead. Her touch made his feelings more bearable. He had been reminded every day since the collapse how much he needed and relied on her. The knowledge filled him with gratitude.

Moses and Anthony entered the room with big buckets of hot water. Matthew watched as they filled the tub in the corner. He'd been warned that his legs would be covered with dry skin that had not been able to slough off while the casts were on. Once Carrie and Janie removed the casts, Janie would take over, brushing the dry patches from his legs before he would soak in a warm oatmeal bath to soothe his irritated skin.

"I'm sure I don't have to remind you, but you're not supposed to try and walk tonight," Carrie said in a no-nonsense tone.

"Yes, General," Matthew replied, only half-kidding. "The South would have probably won the war if you'd been in charge of the troops."

"If *I'd* been in charge of the troops, there would never have been a battle," Carrie retorted. "All I care about is that you rehabilitate your legs exactly the way I tell you."

"Between you and Janie, I don't think I stand a chance of not obeying orders," Matthew replied, trying to smile. "Can we just get this done?"

Carrie returned his smile. "Yes." Then she hesitated. "It's scary for me too," she admitted. "Michael and I know we've done exactly what you need, but we don't know for certain what the true results will be until we remove the casts."

"You're not exactly building my confidence," Matthew complained.

Carrie laughed. "Ignore me. Let's set you free from these ridiculous things. It's going to take us a while, but at least it won't be painful." She beckoned to Moses and Anthony and then walked over to pour a quart of apple cider vinegar into the tub. The solution would help to soften the rock-hard plaster.

Moses and Anthony lifted Matthew and placed him in the tub. It was just long enough for his casted legs to stretch out in front of him. After months of making sure the casts would stay dry, it was now time to soften them with water so they could be removed.

"We'll let them soak for about twenty minutes." Carrie smiled at Moses and Anthony. "We won't need the two of you again until we're done. Janie or I will call you when he's ready to be transferred back to his wheelchair or bed."

Matthew leaned against the back of the metal tub, willing his legs to not have complications. When Dr. Wild had applied the casts four months earlier, he had explained that the breaks could have also caused damaged muscles, nerves or blood vessels that could lead to loss of movement or feeling. They couldn't possibly know the extent of the damage until the bones had healed and the casts had come off. Matthew supposed he should be grateful that the bones hadn't perforated the skin, increasing the risk of bone infection. Each of the four breaks had stayed beneath the surface of his legs.

Carrie and Janie chatted with him while occasionally testing the strength of the plaster that was slowly beginning to soften and dissolve.

"You know, I could have made this faster by using the old-time method of a sharp knife," Carrie told him teasingly. "It's good for you that doctors finally decided those knives were equally hazardous for doctor and patient."

"I'm glad enough doctors were cut to convince them it wasn't the most effective method," Matthew said dryly. "I would hate to be nothing more than another statistic."

Janie chuckled. "I've used plaster shears at school. They work, but they're exhausting to use. The idea of doing two long leg casts with shears is beyond my comprehension. I'm sure I don't have the arm strength."

"Even for your husband?" Matthew teased.

"Be grateful you don't have to find out," Janie countered. She gave one final push against the plaster beneath the water and turned to Carrie. "I think it's ready."

"You're right," Carrie responded. "Let's get these off."

Slowly and carefully, leaving the casts submerged, they pulled back the plaster casing and began to unroll the layers beneath the surface. The work was slow and tedious, as they were only able to advance as the vinegar water continued to soften the cast. Bright with the late afternoon sun when they began the process, the room was now glowing from the remnants of the setting sun when they finally pulled away the last strips.

"We're done," Janie said joyfully.

Matthew had kept his eyes fixed on the ceiling, his head supported by a pillow Janie had positioned for him. He didn't move, suddenly more afraid than ever of what he would see. "Have the breaks healed?"

He could feel Carrie gently probing his legs. "Can you feel this?"

Matthew was thrilled that he could answer yes with every request. At least he knew that he hadn't lost feeling.

Carrie continued to push and probe. "The bones have completely healed, Matthew. They're as good as new!"

Matthew's heart soared, but he was still afraid to look.

"Let's check the movement," Carrie said calmly. She lifted each leg carefully, bending it at the knee gently.

Matthew felt a twinge of pain, but she'd already told him to expect that because all his muscles would be cramped.

"Matthew, your legs are perfect," Carrie said with confidence. "I'm going to leave the two of you now."

Matthew heard the door close when she left.

Janie's face appeared in his line of vision. "Did you hear that, Matthew? Your legs are perfect!"

Matthew knew they were far from perfect, and that it would take weeks, possibly months, of exercise to restore them to the strength he'd had before the accident. He held his wife's eyes. "How do they look?"

"Like you were afraid they would," she said honestly. "They're much smaller than they used to be, but that's to be expected. Also," she said lovingly, "they're the best-looking legs I've ever seen."

Matthew laughed, suddenly released from the fear that had gripped him most of the day. Janie was here. She loved him. His legs had healed perfectly. So what if they looked funny? Now that the casts had been removed, he could once again wear long pants. Only he and Janie would know what was beneath them. In time, they would be strong again.

Leaning forward, he stared at his legs. Even though he was prepared, the sight of them made him suck in his breath. Gone were the strong, muscular legs he'd always had, even during his prison confinement during the war. Thin, shriveled legs lay beneath the water in the tub, taunting him with their weakness.

Janie leaned down to stare into his face again. "It's temporary, Matthew. They'll get stronger every day, and you'll be able to use them more and more. You and Robert and I will take walks on the plantation, going a little farther every day. It will be good for all of us." Her voice softened. "You're alive, Matthew. That is absolutely all I care about. You're *alive*."

Matthew's fear and distaste dissolved in the warmth of her love. "You're right," he whispered. "Thank you."

Janie kissed him soundly. "I'm going to pour oatmeal into the bath water and then brush the skin off your legs. You'll soak in the oatmeal bath daily for a while to help your skin heal. It will also just feel good and keep you from itching. Once you're back in bed, I'm going to use some milk compresses to help your skin heal even faster."

Matthew suddenly realized how tired he was. The stress of the day had sapped all of his energy. He rested his head back on the pillow, enjoying the feel of the warm water against his legs as Janie washed and massaged them.

*****

Later that night, Janie snuggled against his chest as Matthew pulled her tightly to him. "I have something to talk to you about."

"I know," Janie said quietly. "What is it? I know you were scared about removing the casts, but I could tell something else was bothering you when I got home from the clinic."

Matthew didn't bother to ask how she knew that. His wife knew him almost as well as he knew himself, perhaps better. While Janie listened, he told her everything Harold had shared with him.

Janie tensed, pulled away and sat up in bed to stare at him. "Clifford was one of the men arrested?"

"Yes." Matthew watched the avalanche of emotions on her face.

"What's going to happen to him?"

"He's been released, but Harold was able to determine that his law practice has been negatively affected because of his involvement with the Klan. He's lost several important clients since he was arrested."

"But everyone is going to know who he really is?" Janie pressed. "Even though he's been released?"

"Will they know that Clifford is a violent Klansman?" Matthew asked. "Yes. At least those who read the newspapers. North Carolina is dominated by Democratic press coverage, but the articles Harold and Peter wrote are being distributed through the more liberal papers in Virginia, as well as all the Northern papers. Harold made sure to include Clifford's name every time he wrote about the men who were arrested." He hesitated. "Not everyone is going to care, Janie," he reminded her. "Too many Southerners see the Klan as their saviors and heroes."

"I know," Janie acknowledged, "but Clifford always liked to operate below the surface. He thought he could have more power that way, and he liked the protection it offered him because he's basically a coward. He will hate being brought out into the light."

Matthew saw the pleasure the idea gave her. Harold had been right that Janie should know. "Does it bother you that he was in jail?" he asked carefully.

Janie looked at him and laughed. "*Bother* me? I think it's rather wonderful!" She sobered quickly. "Does that make me a bad person? I mean, at one time, I cared enough about him to marry him!"

"And he lost all rights to your loyalty and caring when he abused you," Matthew said firmly. "You're perfectly justified in feeling glad that he's finally being held accountable for some of his actions. I know I am."

Janie gazed into his eyes as a broad smile spread across her face. "I'm glad he was arrested," she said staunchly. "It's not just what he did to me, even though I suppose that would be enough. It's the harm he's brought to so many people in North Carolina, especially the blacks who are trying to rebuild their lives. Unfortunately, the only language the KKK understands is violence, but they do everything they can to hide their identity. If they realize there will be grave consequences for their actions, perhaps the cost will become too high for them to continue."

"That's the hope," Matthew agreed. He pulled Janie back down to his side and kissed her soundly. "You're an amazing woman. I can be nothing but thrilled that the man who abused you is finally being brought to some justice."

Chapter Twenty-Eight

September 1870

Carrie felt the first twinge of fall, but she knew an Indian summer would soon eliminate the touch of crispness in the air, holding it at bay until October. A crescent moon seemed to dance over the treetops as a brisk wind scuttled the clouds surrounding it. Dry leaves rustled and crackled, seeming to send a message she couldn't quite interpret, and didn't really care to.

She took deep breaths, drawing the beauty into her soul before she had to return to Philadelphia the following day. Two weeks on the plantation had restored her energy and passion. She was ready to travel north for the last three months of her internship, comforted by the fact that when she returned for Christmas, she would be coming home for good.

"I'm going to miss you," Rose said softly as she slipped an arm around her waist.

"I'm going to miss you too," Carrie murmured. "Are you sure you're going to be all right?" The best friends had spent many hours talking through Rose's fears of what was happening in the South.

Rose looked up at the moon, letting the wind blow against her face. "*All right* is such a relative term," she mused. "Can any of us really know whether we'll be all right from one moment to the next? I know that I'm all right tonight..." Her voice trailed off.

Carrie was ready to finalize the last stage of her education, but she was also fighting her fears. She was afraid something would happen to the people she loved. The veterans she was treating assured her they would stop any violence, but she wondered what actual power they had. The stories of what was happening all over the South haunted her. All she could do was hope.

Granite seemed to be fine, but would he be waiting for her when she returned home? Again, all she could do was hope. There were times she felt peace, but too often she feared she was drowning in the chaos of her emotions. She was glad she at least felt peace at that moment.

"The last few weeks have given me hope," Rose said. "Tonight, I have even more."

"Tonight will be a special night," Carrie agreed. "Everyone will be arriving soon. The schoolhouse looks beautiful."

"It does," Rose replied. "The women and children have worked hard to make it beautiful."

The schoolhouse had been cleared of all desks. Chairs were placed around the perimeter of the whole building. Candles burned brightly in every window. The children had gathered huge bouquets of purple, yellow and white asters, creating charming arrangements that were scattered around the building. The oil lanterns glowed brightly, turning the schoolhouse into a beacon of light for all those who were coming. The Harvest Festival was coming in just a month, but the Bregdan Women group had insisted on having a dance now to celebrate all that had been accomplished.

"The first batch of quilts went out yesterday," Rose said with deep satisfaction. "The women are so proud of what they've done."

"As they should be," Carrie answered. "I saw the quilts as Abby was packing them to send to New York. They're stunningly beautiful."

"I quite agree. I believe the women were rather amazed at what they could create once they had something besides worn-out clothing to make the quilts. Abby brought dazzling material back from Richmond. They've told me over and over what a joy it's been to work with. I believe it's what got them through the long nights of quilting while their children slept." Rose's eyes glowed with happiness. "Each of those women earned more from making a quilt than they've earned in months. The ones with husbands say the extra money is helping their families more than they could have imagined."

"Helena told me she actually believes she can support her family out here," Carrie said. She was still amazed that her spoiled childhood friend had turned into such a thoughtful, educated woman. They'd had many long conversations about how they had transformed into the women they were now. Helena had truly become a friend.

"Now that they've actually finished a quilt and made money, they're asking Abby about how to expand what they're doing. They want to know how to make more money."

Carrie laughed. "Abby is absolutely in her element. I believe she's the happiest I've ever seen her."

Abby emerged from the dark shadows with Janie at her side. "How could I not be? I worked all those years just to make money. I know I did a lot of good, but the stress seemed to always outweigh the good. Now, I'm simply working to make a difference. You're right that I've never been happier. Working with these women is such a source of joy for me, and Nancy is going to be thrilled when she sees the quilts they've made. I predict the demand will outstrip their ability to make them. That's always a good problem."

The four women stood side by side, letting the night wrap its magic around them.

Janie, Matthew and Robert were returning to Philadelphia with Carrie, Anthony and Frances the next day.

"It's hard to leave after so many months on the plantation," Janie stated. "I hate what happened to Matthew at the Capitol, but our time down here has been so wonderful. I'm not looking forward to returning to Philadelphia."

Carrie empathized with her completely. She wrapped an arm around Janie's waist. "I'm glad Matthew is doing so much better."

"He walked an entire mile today," Janie reported. "His legs are getting stronger every day. I wish we could stay longer because it's so much easier to walk on the plantation, but he is insistent that I start school again next week."

"He knows how much you've given up for him," Abby said gently. "He also doesn't want to extend your time in Philadelphia any longer than necessary."

Janie looked at her with surprise. "He told you that?"

"He did. He's eager for you and Carrie to start your new practice so he can be closer to the plantation. He knows that can't happen until you're done with school."

"He told me the same thing," Janie confessed, "but I thought he was just saying it to make me feel better."

All four women laughed and then settled back into a comfortable silence.

"Two months ago, I was so terrified that I couldn't imagine staying in the South," Rose murmured after a few minutes.

"And now?" Abby asked.

Rose was silent for a long moment before she answered. "I've been through too much to ever be naïve again. I know terrible things can happen. I know the time may come when Moses and I decide that the only way we can keep our family safe is to leave, but…"

"But?" Carrie prompted after another long silence.

"But that time is not now," Rose said with determination.

They fell silent again, watching the moon battle the clouds fighting to obscure it. Just when the clouds seemed to have won the war, a strong burst of wind cleared a hole that allowed the moon to glimmer through.

Carrie felt a deep knowing in her heart. "Our country is once again fighting dark clouds that threaten to swallow it, but we have to hold onto the hope that we can shine through them." Speaking the words filled her with resolve. "It doesn't matter what's happening elsewhere in the country. We've created a harmony here that other people can't believe exists. We'll continue creating it, letting our actions prove to others that things can be different."

Rose nodded. "Shining through the dark clouds… I love that image. Thank you."

The sound of wagon wheels, loud laughter and talking drifted to them on the breeze.

"I believe a dance is about to start," Abby said happily. "Thomas, Anthony, Moses and Matthew are at the head of that line of wagons. I say we focus on nothing but dancing and fun tonight."

Carrie laughed. "There is nothing I love more than dancing. Let the fun begin!"

To Be Continued...

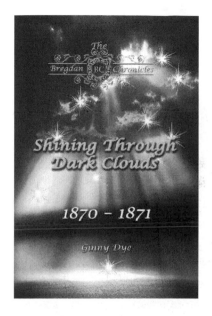

Coming Spring 2019

Would you be so kind as to leave a Review on Amazon?

Go to www.Amazon.com

Put Misty Shadows of Hope, Ginny Dye into the Search Box.

Leave a Review.

I love hearing from my readers!

Thank you!

The Bregdan Principle

Every life that has been lived until today
is a part of the woven
braid of life.

It takes every person's story to create
history.

Your life will help determine the course of
history.

You may think you don't have much of an
impact.

You do.

Every action you take will reflect in
someone else's life.

Someone else's decisions.

Someone else's future.

Both good and bad.

<u>The Bregdan Chronicles</u>

Storm Clouds Rolling In
1860 – 1861

On To Richmond
1861 – 1862

Spring Will Come
1862 – 1863

Dark Chaos
1863 – 1864

The Long Last Night
1864 – 1865

Carried Forward By Hope
April – December 1865

Glimmers of Change
December – August 1866

Shifted By The Winds
August – December 1866

Always Forward
January – October 1867

Walking Into The Unknown
October 1867 – October 1868

Looking To The Future
October 1868 – June 1869

Horizons Unfolding
November 1869 – March 1870

Many more coming... Go to DiscoverTheBregdanChronicles.com to see how many are available now!

Other Books by Ginny Dye

Pepper Crest High Series - Teen Fiction

Time For A Second Change
It's Really A Matter of Trust
A Lost & Found Friend
Time For A Change of Heart

Fly To Your Dreams Series – Allegorical Fantasy

Dream Dragon
Born To Fly
Little Heart
The Miracle of Chinese Bamboo

All titles by Ginny Dye
www.BregdanPublishing.com

Author Biography

Who am I? Just a normal person who happens to love to write. If I could do it all anonymously, I would. In fact, I did the first go 'round. I wrote under a pen name. On the off chance I would ever become famous - I didn't want to be! I don't like the limelight. I don't like living in a fishbowl. I especially don't like thinking I have to look good everywhere I go, just in case someone recognizes me! I finally decided none of that matters. If you don't like me in overalls and a baseball cap, too bad. If you don't like my haircut or think I should do something different than what I'm doing, too bad. I'll write books that you will hopefully like, and we'll both let that be enough! :) Fair?

But let's see what you might want to know. I spent many years as a Wanderer. My dream when I graduated from college was to experience the United States. I grew up in the South. There are many things I love about it but I wanted to live in other places. So I did. I moved 42 times, traveled extensively in 49 of the 50 states, and had more experiences than I will ever be able to recount. The only state I haven't been in is Alaska, simply because I refuse to visit such a vast, fabulous place until I have at least a month. Along the way I had glorious adventures. I've canoed through the Everglade Swamps, snorkeled in the Florida Keys and windsurfed in the Gulf of Mexico. I've white-water rafted down the New River and Bungee jumped in the Wisconsin Dells. I've visited every National Park (in the off-season when there is more freedom!) and many of the State Parks. I've hiked thousands of miles of mountain trails and biked through Arizona deserts. I've canoed and biked through Upstate New York and Vermont, and polished off as much lobster as possible on the Maine Coast.

I had a glorious time and never thought I would find a place that would hold me until I came to the Pacific Northwest. I'd been here less than 2 weeks, and I knew I would never leave. My heart is so at home here with the towering firs, sparkling waters, soaring mountains and rocky beaches. I love the eagles & whales. In 5 minutes I can be hiking on 150 miles of trails in the mountains around my home, or gliding across the lake in my rowing shell. I love it!

Have you figured out I'm kind of an outdoors gal? If it can be done outdoors, I love it! Hiking, biking, windsurfing, rock-climbing, roller-blading, snow-shoeing, skiing, rowing, canoeing, softball, tennis... the list could go on and on. I love to have fun and I love to stretch my body. This should give you a pretty good idea of what I do in my free time.

When I'm not writing or playing, I'm building Millions For Positive Change - a fabulous organization I founded in 2001 - along with 60 amazing people who poured their lives into creating resources to empower people to make a difference with their lives.

What else? I love to read, cook, sit for hours in solitude on my mountain, and also hang out with friends. I love barbeques and block parties. Basically - I just love LIFE!

I'm so glad you're part of my world!

Ginny

Join my Email List so you can:

- Receive notice of all new books
- Be a part of my Launch Celebrations. I give away lots of Free gifts!
- Read my weekly BLOG while you're waiting for a new book.
- Be part of The Bregdan Chronicles Family!
- Learn about all the other books I write.

Just go to www.BregdanChronicles.net and fill out the form.

DISCARD

48991327R00289

Made in the USA
Columbia, SC
14 January 2019